Pelican Books
History's Mistress

Paula Weideger trained as an experimental psychologist before becoming a writer. She has taught and lectured at universities in the United States and is the author of the pioneering *Menstruation and Menopause* (published in Great Britain under the title *Female Cycles*), which has become a classic, as well as of essays, short stories and the film *Middle Age*.

History's Mistress

A new interpretation
of a nineteenth-century
ethnographic classic

Paula Weideger

Penguin Books

Penguin Books Ltd, Harmondsworth, Middlesex, England
Viking Penguin Inc., 40 West 23rd Street, New York, New York 10010, U.S.A.
Penguin Books Australia Ltd, Ringwood, Victoria, Australia
Penguin Books Canada Limited, 2801 John Street, Markham, Ontario, Canada L3R 1B4
Penguin Books (N.Z.) Ltd, 182–190 Wairau Road, Auckland 10, New Zealand

This selection from Ploss and Bartels's *Das Weib (Woman)*
first published 1985

Introduction and selection copyright © Paula Weideger, 1986
All rights reserved

Printed and bound in Great Britain by
Cox & Wyman Ltd, Reading
Typeset in 9/11 Monophoto Photina

Title-page: Carved wooden female figure from New Britain
illustrating the concept of menstruation as the work of supernatural
or external deities, here represented in the form of a totem-bird
dragging an object out of the figure's genitals (Mus. f. Völkerk., Berlin)

This book is dedicated to
Hermann Heinrich Ploss (1819–85)
in the centenary year of his death

Contents

Acknowledgements

John Hawker of the New York Public Library and Thessy Schoenholzer have been most helpful in decoding archaic German, for which I thank them both. In Aachen, Heike Schwarzbauer, though her subject of specialization is modern American and British literature, put both her skill as a researcher and her belief in feminism to use on my behalf, tracking down the early publishing history of *Das Weib* insofar as it could be found. Until I am able in some way to offer help in kind I here offer my thanks for all she's done.

Thanks are also due to Artelia Court for her inspired help in coming up with the title of this book, and to Tom and Susan Dichter and Myra Jehlen, who gave me their impressions of my essay as it progressed. Louise Newman took time away from finishing a manuscript of her own to give a most detailed and spirited criticism of the work which has been of great use and I thank her, too.

Friendly aloofness can itself be helpful in getting a manuscript done and so I thank Henry Lessore for his. In a similar vein, albeit in a very different sphere, I thank Walter Zervas, administrator of the Frederick Lewis Allen Room of the New York Public Library, and here join those writers who have expressed in print their gratitude for the privilege of working in the Allen Room, which, despite its foul air, is a superb resource and a refuge as well. I also wish to thank Dr Vera Rubin, who graciously offered me the use of the library at the Research Center for the Study of Man, and to convey my appreciation to Frank Parkin and Terry Eagleton at Oxford and G. J. Barker-Benfeild at S.U.N.Y., Albany, for their most supportive and encouraging letters.

Kristin Masters was not only diligent and precise in her typing of what was a most difficult manuscript but thoughtful and well organized, too. I've been lucky in having Barbara Baran copy-edit the manuscript in London. She's proved to be brainy, strong-minded and thorough, and I am most appreciative indeed.

Lastly, and firstly too, I might say, I want to thank Neil Middleton, because his knowledge and his editorial enthusiasm have been instrumental in turning *History's Mistress* from a manuscript into a book.

INTRODUCTION

A Double Portrait

Woman: An Historical, Gynaecological and Anthropological Compendium first appeared in English in 1935. *The Times Literary Supplement* marked the début of this immense three-volume translation with the comment that *Das Weib* had been a 'standard work for half a century'. And among the scholars before and since who have used this work as a reference when writing books of their own have been Franz Boas, Germaine Greer and Mircea Eliade.

In fact different scholars have profited from different editions of the work because each of the men who shepherded *Das Weib* into print had his own idea of what – or who – his subject ought to be. Four men saw the book through its eleven German editions, and each, like Eric Dingwall, the English translator, did quite a bit of fiddling with the text, too.

Hermann H. Ploss, the book's author, had set out in the 1880s to describe what he called 'the characteristic life and personality of woman'. To accomplish this he felt certain limits would have to be imposed, and he therefore restricted himself to 'facts taken from natural and cultural history' – that is, anthropology and ethnography. His editors tampered with, slashed, reshuffled and tacked on, using material of much the same kind.

The result was a massive account of the legends, myths, rituals and beliefs that shaped women's lives. In this sense the work is very much like Frazer's *Golden Bough* – though meant to be only about women. And about women *Das Weib* surely is. But the distance between its day and our own is such that today the reader can observe that the book is by no means 'her' history only. Now, as if in shimmering superimposition, one can also see the men who set her story down. It is because of this that *History's Mistress* gives a view into that amazing and distorted history which men and women share.

The mythologies and medical reports, rumours and tales about women are easy enough to make out in the text of *Das Weib*. But when it comes to the portraits of the men who selected them and set them down, they hover between what might have been written and what was. It is for this reason that, as someone who has been poring over the book's pages, I offer myself as a guide.

First I want to talk about the book's own history because that in itself has a bearing on the shape *History's Mistress* took. Then I will talk about the material the men involved used, both because anthropology and ethnography were revolutionized during the period in which *Das Weib* was produced and because they were at once put to scientific and political use. It is here that reference to such contemporaries of Ploss as Darwin, Marx and Elizabeth Cady Stanton comes in.

By the time this discussion has taken place the reader may well have noticed a sometimes rather porcine expression on the faces of the men who wrote *Das Weib*. And so I will go on to speak about bigotry as well, for simply to discredit these men for their biases is both too dismissive of their accomplishment and too flattering to ourselves.

Finally I want to say something about an image of history that does *not* appear in *History's Mistress* but is evoked by it nevertheless.

In looking at the men who made the images of woman found in the pages of *Das Weib* and at the images themselves, I have become more and more aware of the history that is absent from the book – perhaps in the way that amputees are said to feel the phantom presence of their missing limbs. But however much this record of women's history has been hacked away at, women's history itself is not an amputee at all, of course. It waits more or less intact, if also in the shadows, to be rediscovered and brought forth. Full of anthropological treasure as *Das Weib* already is, there is treasure more to be salvaged from its pages, treasure that can be used to create a much larger view of women and of those with whom they've lived. Indeed, I hope to show in what now follows that *History's Mistress*, in addition to its quirks and kinks, can be enjoyed as a valuable contribution to the excavation of women's history that is now going on.

His contemporaries described Ploss as a man who needed little sleep. Whether this came to him naturally or as a result of training is not important, but it certainly helps explain how he was able to accomplish all he did. A lifelong bachelor, he liked going about in society, but he was also a practising gynaecologist who wrote many scientific papers and a book about children (in relation to the society of adults) before publishing his study of women in serial form. Ploss was also Leipzig's representative in the German Medical Association, served as an elected member of the city council between 1875 and 1881, established the first midwifery clinic in Leipzig, and became chairman of the Leipzig midwifery association.

One of his editors described Ploss as 'having founded a new branch of science called anthropological and ethnographical gynaecology'. Perhaps. But perhaps it is enough simply to say that, besides all his other activities, Ploss was able to find the time to keep up with the then very rapid progress being made in anthropology and give it application in his work. The subtitle he gave *Das Weib* when preparing for its publication as a book was, in fact, *The Natural History of Woman*, and here is the way the author set forth his intentions in his preface to the work. His group of readers were not, he hoped, only to be specialists like himself. 'Not only . . . anthropologists and doctors . . . Every better-educated man will find pieces of information in my book that will broaden his horizons with respect to the field of physiology of the female sex, ethnography and cultural history,' Ploss wrote. (As well 'every better-educated woman', to bring the sentiment up to date.) Indeed, the response to the published instalments of Ploss's research about women was so favourable that in October 1885 he had the pleasure of seeing the work take on the author:ty of being printed in book form. He did not, however, have the additional pleasure of seeing how many people were to read it: by the time the first anniversary of *Das Weib*'s publication came round, all 1,500 copies had been sold – but in December 1885, only two months after the book's publication, the sixty-six-year-old Ploss had had a stroke and died.

The Leipzig Anthropological Society then approached Dr Maximilian Bartels, a gynaecologist colleague of Herr Ploss's, and asked if he would oversee republication of *Das Weib*. Bartels agreed.

Bartels then discovered that thousands of jotted-on scraps had survived the author–doctor's death. Notes in 'astonishing number', Bartels called them. Many more notes about women than Ploss had put into his book, and notes for books he had planned on the subjects of tobacco and prostitution as well. Much of the material on prostitution Bartels in fact made part of the woman book. In general, however, despite his reference to the original as a 'striking success', and even though he had been charged with the task of keeping *Das Weib* true to the Ploss original, Bartels was neither awed nor restrained when he set to work.

He did not approve of Ploss's prose style, it turned out. The language was too technical, the form too much a series of essays, the paragraphs too long. Editing was Bartels's springboard for rewriting, because evidently there were also problems for him in the content of what H. H. Ploss had produced. And Bartels was in a position to do more than just cluck and criticize. Not only did he include a great deal more about his speciality, gynaecology, than Ploss had done, but he also wrote about woman from birth to death, rather than from puberty to childbirth alone. In fact he wished to go further than that, aiming to show woman even from the other side of the grave. Female spirits and ghosts therefore made their way into Bartels's version of the book. And new version, not merely a reprint, is what the second edition of *Das Weib* became.

In fiddling with the text of *Das Weib*, Max Bartels began what was to become a half-century-long tradition. The next editor was his own son Paul, an anatomist–anthropologist who added many illustrations to the work; and he was followed by Ferdinand von Reitzenstein, an anthropologist who was eager to share his opinions about everything from sexology to feminism, and did.

The book's translator was a self-styled collaborator, too. Eric John Dingwall, who called himself a sexual anthropologist, wrote in *Woman*, his 1935 edition of the work: 'In certain cases I have ventured here and there, even at the risk of being accused of tampering with the text, to change or to modify some of the statements and theories of my predecessors . . .'

Dingwall excused his meddling by saying that the image of woman found in *Das Weib* had not always been based on sufficiently sound scientific material, and he attempted to increase the book's scientific stature by adding new facts or arguing against old ones, either in parenthetical entries or in footnotes to the earlier text.

Obviously these men were competing with one another, each believing his perception of woman to be the most true-to-life and complete. But they were also collaborators in a way – even if in fact each worked by himself – because they were united in the belief that their subject was rather more alluring and exotic, but also rather less important, than they were themselves. How do I come to such conclusions? In part they are the result of the images of these men which have appeared between me and the pages of their woman book, images such as these:

Gathered near the fire after a delicious if rather heavy meal, the makers of *Das Weib* relax. With goose fat still wet on the hairs of their moustaches the men gossip about this woman they are so keen to find out more about.

'Breasts!' one of them exclaims.

'Yes, breasts!' another agrees at once and then, setting down their glasses of schnapps, two more clap their hands in accord. Dingwall, as he finishes his port, can be heard to clear his throat and whisper, 'Hear, hear.'

Eventually there would be black breasts and tan ones, yellow breasts and white ones as a result of editorial decisions the men in fact did make. Breasts of maidens and the wizened, too. Thirty-two large photographs of breasts alone are to be found in the version of *Das Weib* published as *Woman* in 1935.

When I say 'breasts alone', what I mean is this: there are other drawings and photographs in *Das Weib* in which the naked breast is evident. But in those the breast appears because a topic like scarification is being discussed and because the woman whose scars are illustrated happens to be wearing no clothes from the waist up. However, in the thirty-two photographs of breasts which carry with them the superimposed male group portrait described above, there is no other reason for breasts being shown except that they give a peek at what the Oceanic or African woman looks like when she is bare to the waist.

Ploss does not appear in this group portrait, by the way, because there were no photographs in the first edition of *Das Weib*. It was only after 1891, when Max Bartels responded to his publisher's suggestion, that hundreds of illustrations of women, artefacts and art objects, dwellings and customs began to appear in *Das Weib*. Many increased the merit of what Ploss had begun. There are, for instance, drawings and photographs of menstrual huts which are not to be found anywhere else, and a rare series of photographs of a female circumcision ceremony. Images like those of the thirty-two bare-breasted ladies, however, are among those that diminish the stature of Ploss's *Das Weib*.

Reviewing the 1905 edition, Richard Andree wrote: 'Now the eighth edition is out, a success which a similar work has rarely had, a great deal of which is admittedly based on the scholarly value of the work. Another part of the success, however, is certainly due to the partly erotic contents and the frequent pictures of naked women which have found their audience.' (That there was an audience for this material even in the 1960s was made clear when an American publisher brought out a book, *Feminina Libido Sexualis*, consisting of just these 'partly erotic contents'.) A Viennese review of the same edition added that 'an incredible amount of facts has been collected, many authors are quoted and the quantity of illustrations leaves nothing to be desired. Unfortunately, however, the quality! . . . Every study on "animal life" that has come out in recent years contains artistically more precious illustrations than this woman's life.'

In Andree's opinion, greed was the reason so many illustrations of an erotic kind had been added to *Das Weib*, the commercial value of such illustrations being as well established then as now. And greed may be the explanation for their inclusion, or part of the explanation at least. But when I looked again at those photographs of naked ladies, and again a group portrait of the editors and translator floated between their book and myself, I did not see expressions of money lust on the fellows' faces; I saw expressions that were boyishly lewd instead. And very, very familiar.

Ploss's amenders, though surely of higher mind and more advanced age, look very much like the lads with whom I went to fifth grade. Whenever we had a library period, those classmates of mine always made straight for the low metal shelves on which copies of the *National Geographic* were stacked. Back then, the yellow-framed covers of the magazine had a pattern of black tracery too, and on the shiny pages inside there were always a few photographs of bare-breasted 'savages' to be found – in Africa or Oceania. The aisle in front of the *National Geographics* was packed with fervent ten-year-old boys – and with girls who were curious about grown-up breasts and growing-up boys as well.

This vision of my classmates has remained fixed in my mind the way childhood memories do. But of course the image of *Das Weib*'s editors does not. As I read their book I sometimes saw these men as if they were boyish breast-oglers grown up. And among these superimposed portraits of them, one has dominated all the rest. Boldly drawn, rather like a cartoon (and cartoonish in its message as well), it shows the author, editors and translator of *Das Weib* as those familiar husbands of stereotype: bald or bearded, paunchy or fit, they are resigned veterans of many domestic campaigns. The men look both comforted and stupefied by marital routine. Some are world-weary, others naïve, but each, on closer examination, is not resigned altogether, for each betrays a restive twitch.

Half dozing, the 'husbands' hear a strange creature sashaying somewhere outside the house. Between snores they pick up her scent. The men become so excited, sniffing these foreign pheromones, that they are lifted off the horsehair chairs in which they're sunk and find themselves rolling towards the door before they've quite had time enough to open both eyes, let alone give the matter thought.

They do not pass through that door. They freeze and consider. 'Hold on!', 'Careful!', 'Watch yourself!', one can almost hear them caution themselves. Besotted as the husbands are by the sexy smell in the air, they are not so besotted that they forget how much they like the cosy familiarness of the place in which they work and live.

It is of course as scholars that these particular 'husbands' will make their pursuit. Spectacles, note-pads, pencil stubs, files – these are the implements with which they outfit themselves for the chase. The anthropological society, the library, the physician's office are the terrain through which they dart, cut a path or plod . . .

But more than this needs to be said about that terrain, both because it has quite a lot to do with the sort of fauna Ploss and his collaborators thought they would find, and also because its difference from our own leads today's reader to think they came up with something else instead.

'Both historians and anthropologists are dependent upon that which occurs in the natural course of human life for their materials, every facet of which becomes precious,' wrote Margaret Mead. It is an observation that can be applied as well to the choices anthropologists and historians make when they decide what is and what is not material and also to the way in which that material is then given shape.

Certainly Ploss and his editors were dependent on the natural course of female life for the material that is in the book they made. But when one considers what it was they actually went out looking for in the first place and how they selected from what they found; when it comes to how they gave these measurements, observations, rumours, notes and visions a form; then the 'natural course of human life' on which they were dependent was not exclusively that of women but was their own as well, part of that shared experience which is called the character of the time in which they worked.

What of this character, then? Well, as one student of it has observed: 'This period must be reckoned as one of the great epochs in the enlargement of Western man's comprehension of his place in nature.' Indeed, so much was going on in Europe during the period between the middle and the end of the nineteenth century that a book at least as long as the *Das Weib* compendium would be needed to survey it sensibly. Here I will talk only of what was then taking place in anthropology, ethnography, biology and the 'woman question' – the purview of the book.

Given what concerns us here, perhaps the outstanding feature of the time in which Ploss and his editors worked was the pitch of its scientific curiosity. There was a fever to know more about birds and plants and rocks and trees and furry beasts and *Homo sapiens*. The distinguished periodical the *Westminster Review* divided the books being written by these avid studiers into the following categories: Theology; Philosophy; Science; History and Biography; Belles Lettres; and, finally, Politics, Sociology, Voyages and Travels. (At the time, anthropology referred only to the physical history of the different races and was considered part of the sciences, whereas ethnography referred to the largely anecdotal description of the cultural differences between the races and belonged more to the category of Voyages and Travels.)

These categories were not only separate one from the other but were also treated quite often as though they were completely unrelated. Not by Ploss and his editors, however, and in this Darwin's influence is to be seen. While *Das Weib* does not argue for or against the theory of evolution by means of natural selection, it reflects the increased discourse between areas of study which Darwin demonstrated could reveal more about man's present and his past.

'The great event in the biological world, and the one which was to revolutionize all the sciences, was the voyage of the *Beagle* in the years 1831 to 1836,' writes T. E. Penniman. 'Like the voyage of Columbus it opened a new world.'

Anthropology, which was then a very young enterprise carried out by devoted amateurs, was indeed revolutionized by Darwin's theory. After *The Origin of Species* was published in 1859, people began to take the findings of anthropologists more seriously, recognizing that anthropology had a contribution to make to that revolution in the perception of the world and the place of people in it which Darwin had begun.

For example, in 1856, when human-like bones were dug up in Germany's Neander valley, most scientists rejected the idea that these were remains of fossil man. And when, soon after, Cro-Magnon man was found by workers building a railway in France, French scientists thought the claim that this was a fossil man so idiotic they didn't even feel it worth their while to take a look at the bones for themselves. A man *before* history, before the Creation? Obviously impossible. 'For the most part,' Penniman writes, 'the learned world before 1858 was content to laugh at a theory which made bones and objects older than the world itself.'

English scientists, on the other hand, having heard Darwin's reports before the *Origin* was printed, rushed to France to look at the remains, and concluded that the Cro-Magnon bones did indeed represent a fossil man. A conclusion quite similar, in fact, to the one Rudolf Virchow had come to in Germany with respect to the Neanderthal bones.

Virchow, whose stature has been likened to that of Pasteur, Darwin and Mendel, was probably the most eminent German scientist of his time. The credit for changing medicine from an art into a science has been given to him. It was Virchow who worked out cell theory, likening the body to a 'cell state' in which every cell is a citizen. This hypothesis made possible the scientific study of diseases and of their cure, and dramatically accelerated the understanding of both. Describing Virchow's approach, Ashley-Montague and Brace write: 'His contributions to medical and anthropological research are of permanent value, and the value of his insistence upon accumulating documented proofs before accepting likely theories far outweighs the slight inhibiting effect such an attitude has . . .'

The second edition of *Das Weib* was dedicated to Virchow on the occasion of the seventieth anniversary of his birth. When Ploss writes, 'One has to be extremely careful . . . when interpreting enigmatic phenomena concerning the lives of different people; this is not the job for a quick imagination,' one hears echoed the teachings of Virchow.

Ethnography also was given new stature by Darwin's theories. If bits of bone could yield information about European man's physical history, stories about the lives of older societies might illuminate European man's cultural past.

Ethnography was far, far older than anthropology, of course. Herodotus, writing in the fifth century BC, was not only the 'father of history' but also the first ethnographer. And Marco Polo, telling his tales of the East at the end of the thirteenth century, was probably the first ethnographer to have mass appeal and international celebrity.

Merchants, missionaries and religious pilgrims were sometimes ethnographers, too, as were the great voyagers of the fifteenth and sixteenth centuries. Columbus, after all, discovered not only America but also the Americans when he went sailing in 1492. (This latter discovery provoked a terrible fuss in Europe, as Ashley-Montague with quite some relish points out. People were so bothered, it seems, that the Pope felt he had to settle the arguments they were having about just what kind of beast it was Columbus had found. In 1512 the Pope let it be known that Amerindians were also descendants of Adam and Eve. Grudgingly this was accepted, though many chose to believe that Red Indians were on a very, very distant branch of the family tree indeed.) By the end of the seventeenth century, the young sons of rich men had taken to travelling in numbers so great that 'the "grand tour",' writes E. S. Bates, 'became a subject for hack writers'. And hack writers, too, like the rich young men, were to be counted among the ranks of amateur ethnographers, as were colonizers and colonials.

It was from the mammoth amount of material amassed by all these voyagers that Ploss and his editors had to choose. But this was not all: there were also the accounts of their own contemporaries, of whom there was an abundance going about. In fact, by the time Ploss set to work on *Das Weib*, so many Europeans were out travelling in pursuit of everything from exotic plants to sunsets made freshly stirring by the fresh prospects in which they were framed that the term 'globe-trotter' was coined as a handy way of referring to them, and for them Baedeker began writing his guides. Ploss himself travelled Europe, eager to keep up with the accounts these explorers were bringing home, and sent out letters of inquiry to those still far away in other lands.

The revolution in anthropology had pushed back estimations of how long people had inhabited the earth, and the discovery of human fossil remains supported Darwin's assertion that people had an ape-like ancestry. Ethnography, too, was drawn into this revolution. It was no longer only a collection of anecdotes, adventure stories and reports of scouting parties, but was beginning to look like an actual source of cultural history.

'By 1860,' writes anthropologist Marvin H. Harris, 'the speculation that Europeans must formerly have been savages had already been confirmed by unimpeachable evidence brought out of the earth. Without keeping this triumphant vindication in mind, we cannot appreciate the strength of the conviction among evolutionists of the period 1860–1890 that contemporary primitives could provide valid information about the ancient condition of humanity.'

Even if not everyone thought the evidence 'unimpeachable', and even if not everyone thought it either 'triumphant' or a 'vindication', the fact is that the revolution in anthropology had pushed ethnography further into Darwin's territory. Although Darwin himself did not address *human* evolution in the *Origin*, people soon began to look on primitives who were their contemporaries as if they were fossils come to life.

Ploss and his editors, like those at the time out busily collecting insect specimens in distant lands, had no way of telling whether one fact or a thousand would be revelatory, so they collected from what was then being made available in ethnography and anthropology in sometimes awesome – and sometimes almost comical – bulk and breadth.

Thus not only do the readers of *Das Weib* learn about the sacro-pelvic angles found in female gorillas, chimps and orang-utans, as well as in yellow, white and black human beings, but also about the anatomical underpinnings of dimples on the female rump. They also discover that the European physicians of Ploss's era were busy measuring the relative distribution, density and colour of pubic hair in their female patients, rather in the way other anthropologists were measuring and weighing different human skulls. Or perhaps not that way at all. In any event such tabulations are given their place in *Das Weib*.

Ethnographical information, while certainly no less abundant or various, seems less often comical or kinky when it appears in the pages of *Das Weib*. Indeed, discussions about the ways in which different races greet the birth of a baby girl, for instance, or the ways in which different people approach courtship – whether the source of the information is a missionary, a colonizer, or a traveller in search of bedazzlement – have an interest that may be felt even more keenly by today's reader than it was in Ploss's time. This has more than a little to do with the political changes that have occurred since Ploss and his colleagues first set to work.

'I believe we have seen that a knowledge of anthropology may guide us in many of our policies,' wrote Franz Boas in 1932. And what a guide it had sometimes been!

The first conference devoted to the question of European partitioning of Africa (a result of European arguments about who was to get what of the Congo) took place in Berlin in 1884. And, as J. D. Faye points out, 'colonial expansion could be morally justified only if Europeans chose to believe that they and they alone knew what was best for Africa, not only in their own interest, but in that of the Africans, also'. It was here that ethnography could and did play its part in policy-making. (Policy-making played its part in ethnography, too, of course, because the need for material with which to rationalize and/or advance policy meant that expeditions were financed that might otherwise never have been able to get under way.)

Ploss did not like to think of his work being used to make, rationalize or justify policy where the 'woman question' was concerned. In his introduction to *Das Weib* he wrote: 'Perhaps my book will not gain full satisfaction with readers who approach the reading of it with unjustified expectations. But it would be wrong to demand of such a work the attempt to "solve" the "woman question".' With a women's movement just getting under way, however, inevitably people would do exactly that.

The first women's rights convention ever to be held took place in the United States in 1848 when Elizabeth Cady Stanton and a handful of other women sent out a call. It brought so many women, men and children to the New York State village of Seneca Falls that, in order to hear what was being argued in the packed chapel as the declaration of women's rights was ratified, people literally dangled from the trees outside.

The movement grew rapidly in the U.S. and quickly spread to Europe. The first organized German support for the woman question took place in Ploss's own city of Leipzig when, in October 1865, *Der Allgemeine Deutsche Frauen-Verein* was formed. In 1870 John Stuart Mill's *The Subjection of Women* was translated into German.

Accounts from the period state that the women's movement in Germany was both smaller and slower-growing than in other Western European countries or in the U.S.A. Yet its impact was great enough to produce that stinging condemnation which a century later would be called a backlash. Consider, for instance, the following passage from Nietzsche's *Beyond Good and Evil* (published in 1886): 'The weaker sex has in no previous age been treated with as much respect by men as at present ... What wonder is it that abuse should immediately be made of this respect?' Nietzsche complains that woman 'wants more, learns to make claims, in the end finds the tribute of respect well-nigh offensive; she would prefer rivalry for rights, indeed actual strife itself; in a word, woman is losing modesty'.

Indeed woman was. As many of Nietzsche's contemporaries were telling him, strife was preferable when the alternative was the respect of men demonstrated in such ways as denying women university degrees, rights of inheritance and access to the ballot box.

While the women's movement in the United States existed as a branch of the movement to grant Negroes full rights of citizenship as well as a movement in its own right, in Germany the women's movement existed both in and of itself and as part of the Social Democratic Party which was founded there in 1875.

'It is the common lot of woman and worker to be oppressed,' read the opening lines of *Women Under Socialism*, written in 1883 by August Bebel, one of the party's founders. Women and men workers alike were the victims of patriarchal capitalism, and the end of patriarchal capitalism would be the beginning of freedom for both – or rather the return to the earlier freedom of both.

In *The Origin of the Family*, published in 1884, Engels relies on the American ethnographer Lewis H. Morgan's study of Indian tribes to support Marx's assertion that, before patriarchy, society had a communistic, non-aggressive, non-competitive structure. Society had then been more respectful towards its female members (and more particularly to those who laboured on its behalf). After the revolution, Marx and Engels claimed, so it would be again.

Ploss, of course, had no idea that this sort of argument might be advanced or countered by anything in his book, since *The Origin of the Family* was published the year after his death. But when earlier I said it was more or less inevitable that *Das Weib* would be put to political uses, I had in mind not only the uses to which readers would put the information in *Das Weib* but also the uses its editors would make of their opportunity to work on the book.

In the last German edition of *Das Weib*, the editor, von Reitzenstein, surveys the work of such ethnographical theorists as Johann Jakob Bachofen (whose *Mother Right* (1861) is an enormous tome arguing for the early existence of gynocracies) and concludes: 'The probability is not to be denied that so long as settled marital relationships had not developed, and even beyond that time, maternal government was in advance of paternal government over a wide area. Among many living tribes now, the former remains unchanged in power.'

Dingwall, when translating these words, added a footnote in which he said: 'The following section illustrates the views of those who do not hold generally accepted ideas relative to primitive monogamy, matriarchy, etc.' But even forty years later people were still arguing about whether or not early matriarchies had in fact existed, and for some members of the women's liberation movement of the 1970s and 1980s Bachofen's work was a kind of bible. The fact that *Das Weib* is a cumulative record of so many different truths, some controversial, others contradictory, is one reason why it continues to have a life as an invaluable reference book.

Our scholar–hunters were very lucky men when they went out a-hunting after women, it would seem. They were, for instance, much luckier than those of their friends who might have set out for hot and dusty lands in search of tiger, antelope or elephant. After all, what Ploss and his editors might hope to capture would not simply sit mounted on the library wall, a mute testimonial to blood and majesty – what Ploss and his editors hoped to capture might speak to man's desire to know more about his past in such a way that his conception of his present would be profoundly changed.

It cannot be claimed for Ploss or his editors that they were instigators of the changes taking place in ethnography, anthropology or political theory. But they must have believed that what they were compiling about women would contribute to man's ideas about himself and his relation to the world. And their belief was not misplaced. Indeed, their work can be said to have grown with time because, as *History's Mistress*, it contributes also to woman's ideas about herself and her relation to the world, i.e., the world of men and women both.

But what about the book's bigotry? Doesn't it rather cancel out this contribution? Not at all, since history is hardly confined to those subjects which one approves of or those subjects which are rendered in an agreeable-seeming way. The people who have written histories have not been prejudice-free, though certainly some among them have claimed that they were. But it would be negligent of me if I closed the discussion of *Das Weib*'s bigotry having said only this much.

Not only is there racial and sexual prejudice in the pages of the compilation first made by Hermann H. Ploss and added to for some fifty years: one editor even threw in the occasional anti-Christian diatribe (related to his passion for sexual liberation and what he saw as the Church's attempt to crush that cause). There are also those prejudices which look more like theoretical orientations, such as the statements for or against gynocracy that have already been mentioned, or the trotting out of Freud's view that sexual repression causes neurosis by an editor wanting to justify his opinion that prostitution is not only inevitable but also healthy. Such prejudices are in *Das Weib* and in *Woman* and, therefore, though I have not passed them on wholesale, they are in *History's Mistress* too.

It is not enough to say that, because readers are, so to speak, consenting adults, they are armed well enough once they've been made aware that, along with its treasures, *Das Weib* contains its bigotries, too. One wants to feel sure that by being passive witness to such prejudices one is not somehow perpetuating them as well.

But better to wade into the text with all its bigotry than to call its creators pigs (or some current equivalent) and slam the door on them, I say, for that would also mean shutting the door on women's history, the history of the relations of women and men. Best to put on galoshes first, however. A further, more detailed look at the background of the double portrait may provide this protection, I suggest, a look at attitudes that, however we judge them today, were once thought intellectually estimable, the opinions to which a well-informed gentleman was certainly entitled.

In 1863, James Hunt delivered an address on 'The Negro's Place in Nature' in which he said: 'In time the truth will come out, and then the public will have their eyes opened and will see in its true dimension that gigantic imposture known by the name of "Negro Emancipation".' James Hunt was not braying from a box in Hyde Park's Speaker's Corner when he spoke these words. He was addressing the Anthropological Society of London in his capacity as its president.

Charles Darwin was on the whole far more discreet in his employment of specific statements about the relative merits of the races – until he neared the end of *The Descent of Man*. Then, having applied the theories of evolution he had made public in his earlier *Origin* to the evolution of human beings, Darwin seems to have been overtaken by the fear that readers might feel so repelled by the idea of having apes for ancestors that they would reject his theory rather than accept the company it put them in.

'For my part,' Darwin cajoles, 'I would as soon be descended from that heroic little monkey, who braves his dreaded enemy in order to save the life of his keeper, or from that old baboon, who descending from the mountain, carried away in triumph his young comrade from a crowd of astonished dogs – as from a savage who delights to torture his enemies, offers up blood sacrifices, practises infanticide without remorse, treats his wives like slaves, knows no decency, and is haunted by the grossest superstition.'

It was only the teeniest, tiniest step from this statement to the thought: Better a monkey than an indecent, wild brown man. Darwin led the other civilized chaps to take this step as if he held each one of them by the hand. The reader, somehow soothed by this journey, would come to feel that really Darwin's theory of evolution wasn't all that bad.

Darwin was by no means the only important figure of the period to prey on the racial prejudices of his audience as a way of making his own cause look more palatable. Nor was this a tactic used only by ambitious men.

Elizabeth Cady Stanton, a lifelong radical and leader of the woman's cause from its beginnings at Seneca Falls in 1848, used just this approach when she felt support for woman's suffrage was in jeopardy after America's Civil War.

.Constitutional amendments had been proposed which, if ratified, would give former Negro slaves – the men among them, that is – full rights of citizenship, including the vote. Cady Stanton's anxiety was that, once they had it, the majority of Negro men would act like the majority of white men and themselves oppose giving the vote to women. She was even more worried that those abolitionists who all along had been fighting for the vote for women as well as for Negro men might now relax their campaign, feeling that their number-one goal had finally been achieved.

At the first meeting of the all-woman National Woman's Suffrage Convention held in Washington on 22 January 1869, Elizabeth Cady Stanton gave an address in which she tried to bring abolitionists round: 'If American women find it hard to bear the oppressions of their own Saxon fathers, the best orders of manhood,' she began, 'what may they not be called to endure when all the lower orders of foreigners now crowding our shores legislate for them and their daughters? Think of Patrick and Sambo and Hans and Yunt Tung, who do not know the differences between a monarchy and a republic, who cannot read the Declaration of Independence or Webster's spelling book, making law for Lucretia Mott, Ernestine Rose, and Anna E. Dickinson!'

Cady Stanton trusted that even the abolitionists in her audience would agree that while it was a fine thing to give 'Sambo' the vote it was not at all acceptable to be ruled by 'Sambo' using it.

Ethnographers, anthropologists, theoreticians and politicians all shared such racial prejudices; each thought his (or her) race by far the superior. This cannot be said of sexual prejudice, however, for that was shared by men and women alike, with the exception of the suffragists, of course – though not always even then.

In *The Philosophy of Right*, published in 1821, Hegel states: 'Women are capable of education but they have not been made for activities which demand a universal faculty such as the more advanced sciences, philosophy, and certain forms of artistic production. Women may have happy ideas, taste and elegance, but they cannot attain the ideal.'

In the United States, when the movement for greater civil rights began to include the rights of women as well as of Negroes, the Council of Congregational Ministers of Massachusetts sent out a pastoral letter which declared, 'The power of woman is in her dependence, flowing from the consciousness of that weakness which God has given for her protection.'

Herbert Spencer meant to give these views the status of scientific fact when he wrote *The Physiology of the Sexes*, published in 1873. He said: 'That men and women are alike mentally, is as untrue as that they are alike bodily ... The first set of differences is that which results from somewhat earlier arrest of individual evolution in women than in men, necessitated by the reservation of vital power to meet the cost of reproduction.' Spencer also said that women who learned to be passive and deferential to men had the greatest chance for survival because those were precisely the attributes prized by the most successful men.

Certainly not every person who held such beliefs was male. In the last of the German editions of *Das Weib*, von Reitzenstein, a rabid anti-feminist, delighted in presenting the 'opinion of a lady ... at the women's celebration of the centenary of Heinrich Pestalozzi's birth'. (Pestalozzi was an educational reformer.) The lady, Ida Klug, speaking in 1846, had observed: 'Women, unless we can regard as the rule one exception in thousands, are just as little capable of reaching a development of the intellectual powers as high as that of the male mind, as men are of attaining the same degree of self-sacrificing, self-denying love as women ... woman cannot penetrate into the realms of science and art with the acuteness and assurance of the male mind. She attains only a certain height where she encounters the impassable snow-line, while man is able to ascend the giant peaks of cold, inflexible inquiry. Therefore,' La Klug concluded, 'if we demand a deeper, more intellectual education of women, this must take place only with respect to their real vocation, and there they can, of course, be allowed to have a say in the matter.'

As for Rudolf Virchow, who had so brilliantly formulated cell theory and so boldly judged the Neanderthal bones to be relics of fossil man, this is what he had to say, *circa* 1863, about the female sex: 'Woman is woman in virtue of her reproductive glands ... In a word, *all* that we admire and venerate as womanly in the true woman, is dependent on the ovary.'

To say 'all that we admire and venerate as manly in the true man, is dependent on the testicles' is the sort of illuminating acid turnabout that not even the most radical of nineteenth-century feminists would have put into words. No, in the nineteenth century what would have been an impossibly *outré* thought to have about men was taken as natural fact about women – and by both sexes, too. In fact, the majority of people, intelligent or otherwise, male or female, believed men to be the superior sex, just as the majority of Darwin's readers shared the 'knowledge' that Europeans were the superior race. Feminists, like abolitionists, were mavericks rebelling against commonly held beliefs (though not perhaps as radically as some contemporary readers might wish).

Referring to the bigotry of the nineteenth-century ethnographers, Marvin Harris writes: 'We condemn them not because they expressed value judgements, but because their judgements were based on false facts and theories. Their arrogance with respect to contemporary primitives and preliterate societies is intolerable first, because they assume that, had they themselves been brought up among London's poor or among the Hottentots, they would nonetheless have behaved like Victorian gentlemen; and second, because in expressing shock over cannibalism, infanticide, and head-hunting, they naively assumed that comparable practices had already been, or were shortly about to be, extirpated from the repertories of their own civilized communities.'

Many of the nineteenth-century ethnographers do seem awfully smug. Their certainties, being Victorian rather than, say, existential, were a lot more wholeheartedly expressed and, perhaps, more wholeheartedly felt. Their arrogance, lack of candour and downright blindness is certainly unappetizing. After all, when Darwin talked of savages who treated their wives like slaves (and were therefore inferior to baboons and such), he was addressing a race of men who had profited enormously from the shipping of slaves from Africa to Britain and the United States. Nevertheless, Darwin and these profiteers in human flesh felt sure they were these savages' superiors.

But to conclude on that account that the work and character of these nineteenth-century ethnographers is intolerable ... No, that is a bit too flattering to ourselves, I think. Harris, for example, writing in 1968 when the second great American civil rights movement was at its peak, was attacking the racial bigotry in earlier ethnographers, bigotry to which this movement was making many people sensitive for the first time in their lives. But about sexual prejudice? It would be a few years before the women's liberation movement had a similarly widespread impact. When it did, maybe Harris had his blinkers removed. I don't know. What I do know is that in 1968 he surely had them on: there is not one single word about sexual prejudice in ethnography in his book. So for us to feel superior to the Victorians in the matter of bigotry may not be so very different from the Victorians feeling themselves superior to the Hottentots.

It is Lévi-Strauss who, in *Tristes Tropiques*, first published in 1955, makes an observation that is rather more eye-opening. Writing about the ethnographers of the sixteenth century, he says: 'The men of that time had no feeling for the style of the universe – just as, today ... an uninstructed person ... would be unable to distinguish a faked Botticelli from a real one ... Sirens and sheep trees [as they referred to sea-cows and cotton plants] are something different from, and more than failings of objectivity; on the intellectual level they should rather be called faults of taste; they illustrate the falling short of minds which, despite elements of genius and a rare refinement in other domains, left much to be desired where observation was concerned. Not that I mean this by way of censure: rather we should revere those men the more for the results which they achieved in spite of their shortcomings.'

And, indeed, in spite of their shortcomings, I did come to revere H. H. Ploss and some of his editors as I worked on *History's Mistress*. I got to be fond of them; grateful to them for having made their effort; appreciative (if also overwhelmed by) their thoroughgoingness. On certain days even their lust and greediness seemed endearingly human to me instead of coarse or lewd.

But affection, fondness, gratitude and appreciation are not the only feelings I have had about Ploss and his editors, I am sorry to say. Sorry, because I would have preferred Lévi-Strauss's generosity of spirit to my spiritual ups and downs. Still, Lévi-Strauss could count among his privileges the fact that he was *not* of the race those ethnographers of the sixteenth century showed such lapses of taste about. I lack the big-heartedness such privilege provides; I am of the sex Ploss and his editors sometimes so tastelessly portrayed. I am therefore touchy as well as grateful; thorny as well as appreciative; disdainful as well as enthusiastic.

I applaud the men who made *Das Weib* for their pages devoted to customs having to do with marriage, childbirth, abortion, divorce and so on. I am fascinated by the accounts of the ways in which women decorate (and/or mutilate) their bodies in order to make themselves attractive to a mate, and sobered by the understanding I found in these pages that a woman would no more choose to give up scarification of her body in those cultures where men think it attractive than a woman among my contemporaries would agree, say, to give up washing her face and hair. In both cases a female would become an outcast; to those who might otherwise have desired her she would have become of no account at all.

But – and this I say in a tone that is not admiring or even neutral – why in the text of *Das Weib*, a text which is thousands of pages long and which devotes hundreds of these to pregnancy and childbirth, are there only four pages about women mothering the children they bear? And why is there practically no evidence at all that women work; no account of women weaving, say, or making pottery, tending animals, building their dwellings, farming the land? Yes, there *are* three photographs of women grinding corn, but these illustrate a discussion of pelvic flexibility, if you please. And yes, there *is* one photograph of a woman at a loom, but that is part of a series illustrating the social life of women to which such other activities as paying calls and preparing tea also belong. One learns of sorceresses, fortune-tellers and witches as they make or break spells; but about how women learn to find the tubers and roots with which to feed their families, about how they know the poisonous from the nourishing, there is not one word. Even in the area of what Ploss and company found attractive a particular narrowness is evident, too. They appear to have been exclusively fixed on the rudiments of the primary and secondary sexual characteristics. One learns about infibulation, say, but nothing of the subtlety and range of eye movement in peoples among whom women are veiled.

How does one explain such omissions? Well, one might say that the reason why those qualities that the women of *Das Weib* had in common with the women who kept its compilers' kitchens steamy, their children dressed and their beds made are not to be found in the pages of the book is because such women's work for them was familiar to the point of invisibility.

One might also say that such work as women did was thought too insignificant to pay much attention to – except when something like consideration of the division of labour made it seem significant because of its proximity to or juxtaposition with the work of men. This is most apparent in the case of childbirth. By giving a disproportionately large amount of space to delivery and lying-in, our gynaecologist editors enhanced in parallel the apparent importance of their own profession.

This brings into clear focus the fact that *Das Weib* is not the natural history of females at all but the history of a 'sex object', if you will. The book is the product of a hunt for titillations as well as a hunt for facts about man's past and, evidently, there was no titillation to be had in the neighbourhood of women working – unless the women were employed in the oldest profession, that is. Girls, woman, *Das Weib*, really it was all pretty much the same to them, at least where the more exotic aspects of female life were concerned. Ploss, in the first sentence of his preface to the book, speaks of his subject as 'beautiful' and 'attractive', if also complex. One needn't refer to Simone de Beauvoir to observe that for its compilers Woman surely was the *subject* sex.

The gap between women and *Das Weib*'s compilers was not so much a chasm, say, as it was a hierarchy. As a result of the distance the men put between themselves and their subject, women were assumed to be their inferiors and were found sexier on that account.

Now, if I were secure in my belief that women and men co-exist as equals or at least soon will, I would ignore all this or laugh it off, calling the fellows cranky, dim, old-fashioned and so on. But to have the real McCoy where such a feeling of security is concerned, one has to live in a world that confirms it, and, like the world in which Ploss worked, my world does not.

In the eighteenth century, David Hume, setting down the facts about the merits of different races, wrote: 'There never was a civilized nation of any other complexion than white, nor even any individual eminent either in action or speculation. No ingenious manufacturer among them, no arts or sciences . . . Such a uniform and constant difference could not happen, in so many countries and ages, if nature had not made an original distinction betwixt these races of man.'

Such views, as we know, were common throughout the nineteenth century too, and also in the first half of the twentieth century. (Even in that splendid book *Out of Africa*, for instance, one finds that Isak Dinesen, who, unlike most Europeans in Kenya at the time, perceived Blacks as individuals rather than as living fossils, wrote about the black people she knew in much the same spirit that white American Southerners have written about their black mammies – with a special intimacy and love, certainly, but also with an assumption of her own superiority.) In fact, it is only since the Second World War that many will have had the intelligence, imagination and good taste to read Hume's statement and find it rubbish. Those who would not would be cast out of the civilized life of this day, would they not? But now consider Hume's statement written like this:

'There never was a civilized person of any other sex than male, nor even any individual eminent either in action or speculation. No ingenious manufacturer among them, no arts or sciences ... Such a uniform and constant difference could not happen, in so many countries and ages, if nature had not made an original distinction betwixt these sexes of man.'

The intelligence, imagination and good taste to read the second version of Hume's statement and find it rubbish are not often enough part of the civilized life of today. (And as I think on this perception so readily available to me because of my sex, I reckon that were I black I might not be so quick to say that racial prejudice has declined so very much since 1945.)

I have called my interpretation of Ploss's work *History's Mistress* because I hope to catch the reader's attention at the beginning, and to keep reminding the reader throughout that this text is *not* a compendium in which the natural history of woman is to be found but rather one in which will be found only that part of woman's history that was attractive to the men who sought it out.

I, too, became part of the book's history as I extended the tamperer's tradition to span a full century. And while I am of the book in that sense and cannot therefore see all the ways in which I may have altered its meanings, I can at least let the reader know what alterations I intended to make when I set about my cutting and pasting, for obviously, in reducing the size of *Woman* from its almost 2,000 original pages to the present 250 odd, a colossal number of cuts had to be made.

What drew me to *Das Weib* was its mass of legends, myths, rites, poems, rituals. Certainly not everything in it would meet current ethnographical standards for validity, but then that can also be said of that grand and garbled work of Sir James Frazer, *The Golden Bough*, a work which continues to be very much alive – as, indeed, does *Das Weib*.

The variety of actions, attitudes and roles women have played, and the accounts of how their bodies function and are made to function which are set down in the pages of this book are education as well as stimulation for thought and for dreams. That is one reason why I have concentrated as much as I have in *History's Mistress* on the historical and ethnographical material in *Das Weib*.

There is a second reason for this choice. The gynaecological and, to a lesser degree, the anthropological material that was in the original work is, most of it, now thoroughly out of date. Physiological or medical knowledge once superseded really has very little use other than for the specialist historian in these fields. For the rest of us it is on the whole so much dead weight. This has particular bearing on the shape of *Das Weib* and the shape of *History's Mistress*, for in the earlier editions so much space was given to the female as she who conceives and delivers a child that the gynaecological material alone would have made for a rather large-sized book.

As for the form I have chosen for *History's Mistress*, of course I have followed Ploss and his editors to some extent. As is already obvious, I could not have had a section on woman's work, for example, and just as obviously to bow to some notion of feminist purity and leave out a section on beauty would have been foolish, given the quantity of marvellous – if also disturbing – material in *Das Weib* on the subject of what women do or have done to themselves in order to be found alluring.

For the rest, the book is divided according to the stages of female life and the conventional roles women play or have played, though there is also a chapter on those women who are somehow out of the ordinary: Amazons, witches, prophetesses and so on. Interspersed with these are chapters on each of the great biological divides – or rather two of the three of them, for while there was a large amount of material on the subject of menstruation and, as I have said, on pregnancy, there was hardly anything at all about the menopause. This is not surprising, since the average age of menopause and the average female life expectancy were both about forty-eight years at the turn of the twentieth century. For women as well as for ethnographers, the menopause usually did not signify.

Some of the book's previous editors appear not even to have read through the text once they had fiddled with it. There were a vast number of repetitions, and material about, say, courtship was often flung hundreds of pages headlong into a subject like menstruation. I have therefore done a good deal of tidying as well as pruning of the original, but always I have tried to retain its geographical variety and cultural diversity. And of course some bits have been included only because they appealed to me. For the first time ever an index appears at the end of the text. There is another first: apart from this introductory essay I am the only editor not to add material of my own to the book. This should not be taken as evidence of female modesty or deference – it is not.

The men who added photographs of naked ladies to the pages of *Das Weib* or who wrote anti-female diatribes, the editor who instructed 'Gretchen' to stop being such a prude and learn from the 'better class' of prostitutes about the merits of fancy underclothes so that her husband might more often stay at home, and the men who favoured or attacked theories about prehistorical gynocracy were honouring their vision of woman's history in this fashion. I honour my vision in mine.

History's Mistress is *Das Weib* cut and trimmed and with the image of the men who made it clear to see. One learns from looking at them not only that they were scholar–hunters who tracked down and recorded many wonderful and curious facts; not only that they felt themselves to be far more important than she whom they hunted and also terribly attracted to her: in gazing at this double portrait one comes to have an ever stronger sense that when it comes to the writing of women's history a very great deal has been left out.

Ploss's work is not the encyclopaedia that size alone might suggest it to be. Neither is it the natural history he claimed it was. But *Das Weib* is a very rich work indeed, if also a distorted one, a superb and a blighted archive in which part of women's history is stored. It is entertaining as well as aggravating, a treat for the imagination and, in its bigotry, an assault on one's sensibilities as well.

In preserving *Das Weib*'s rich content, by making visible its double subject – woman and the men who sought her out – *History's Mistress*, this offspring of anti-woman prejudice, surely also becomes an aid to bringing that prejudice to its end. And if *History's Mistress* makes us ache with the pain of all that has been left out of woman's history and man's, in its images and also in its shadows it suggests the shape of that history which has yet to be more fully revealed.

PAULA WEIDEGER
London / New York, 1985

PART ONE
La Différence

CHAPTER I

Status

We shall not detail the countless theoretical attempts that have been made to degrade and deprecate the special anthropological characteristics of Woman as compared with those of Man. Suffice it to say that there have been the most arrant misreadings of natural fact – according to the particular cultural climate and institutions in which these speculations took place. In the sixteenth century, for example, which abounded in bizarre metaphysical controversies and word-spinning, there was the thesis, anonymous but attributed to Acidalius, entitled 'Women are not human beings' ('*Mulieres homines non esse*'), a hypothesis already debated at the Synod of Macon in 585. Another example is the address by Paul Albrecht, delivered at an Anthropological Congress at Breslau in 1884, in which he maintained that the anatomy of the human female showed more pronounced animal traits than that of the male. Among the nine proofs of this given by Albrecht were the greater frequency of hairiness in women and the corresponding infrequency of baldness.

Nevertheless, there *are* two great differences in the organic life of women and men. Women are primarily much more concerned with and specialized for reproduction. They have to deal with menstruation, pregnancy, childbirth, suckling and the care of children. Beyond this complex reproductive function, their whole nervous sytem is differently keyed. Their emotions predominate and their mental and cerebral activity is lower. This difference shows in all movement and action. What follows is an introduction to the ways in which this is made manifest. Many of the points made will be elaborated later in the book.

i. A Grand Tour

Already in the tombs which belong to the relatives and the highest officials of the ancient kingdoms of Egypt, who had pyramids set up to themselves as memorials, we see the wife called the mistress of the house and the children named not only after the father, but also after the mother. Indeed, in some cases, only the mother's name is mentioned. Already among the pyramid-builders, princesses might become heads of state, either regents or queens-regnant, and receive the full divine honours accorded to the male sovereigns. The Egyptian women appear to have followed the example of the queen and to have taken full part in public ceremonies and social life.

In Ancient Israel, the women were generally secluded from public life and had little share in the studies of men and but little social life. Respect and a certain consideration were shown them, but their chief part was to bear numerous children and care for the household. They were expected to perform all the household work themselves, unless they had brought slave-girls as part of their dowry.

There is substance and justice in the reproach often addressed to the people of Ancient Greece that they gave an inadequate status to their women, at least in the ages of their greatest political and intellectual achievement. As Decker has pointed out, in earlier, for instance Homeric, ages, women, although very low in position, were respected for more than personal beauty. Wisdom and skill in female occupations were appreciated as qualities for which wives were loved and honoured. For example, in the *Iliad* Achilles speaks these words:

> Every man whose heart beats truly and with good will
> Honours his wife and tends her carefully.

In Athens, however, things were different. The young maidens were secluded in the women's part of the house. They sat at their mothers' feet and spun and wove. The wife was a mere child when she entered her husband's home. She bore children but had not even a free hand in household management, nor any educative role where her sons were concerned. She might not leave the house without express permission except to take part in the great public religious festivals. It is not surprising that a being so undeveloped failed to inspire either human interest or passion. Imagination and desire were thus sharply separated from the family and the home, with disastrous results.

The other Greek states seem to have shown an improvement on Attica in this respect. The Aeolians and Dorians, for example, gave their women considerable freedom of movement, a large share in public ritual and education – especially physical culture – and a voice in public affairs. The Aeolian women had an especially active role in poetry and philosophy (cf. the poetess Sappho). In Sparta these tendencies were crystallized in the Code of Lycurgus. Elsewhere, both on the islands and in the Greek colonies throughout the Mediterranean, the results were more favourable, both intellectually and aesthetically.

When Greek trading enterprise brought material wealth to the towns and acquainted the Greeks of the mainland with the habits of Asia, it was the subordinate position and inadequate personalities of the Greek wives that brought about the favoured status of the hetaera and the ordinary prostitute. The rich citizens of the Greek towns summoned slave-girls, skilled in music, song and dance, to their symposia, and there grew an active and persistent demand for wit and grace and skill in conversation and interpretative art, as well as for beauty of body in these women. (See also 'The Prostitute', Chapter IX.)

Roman women enjoyed better status than those of Greece. They were permitted to walk abroad in public, and a special festival, the Matronalia, was celebrated in their honour. Romulus decreed that they should be exempt from all household toil excepting spinning and weaving and the making of garments and household furnishings. Injuries done to matrons and maidens through word or deed were punished – in the gravest cases by death. If a wife was divorced for any lesser cause than adultery or poisoning, the husband was compelled to give her half his property.

Under the Empire, women obtained the right to hold property absolutely and independently of their husbands. Very wealthy women had their own land agents or *procuratores* who were responsible to them only. Some women were highly educated, with various interests, which included an acquaintance with the Greek language and with music. Ovid remarks that even ignorant girls wished to appear clever, and Greek was used occasionally in society.

In later times women's interests outside the house were almost unlimited, for circus, theatre and amphitheatre stood open to them. The result was the disruption of family life, and divorces, which were easily obtained, became the order of the day. Prostitution flourished and the decline of female virtue became everywhere apparent.

It seems to be clear that in the general view of life held by the northern Teutons women held a peculiar and ideal position. From this, as Dahn has pointed out, arises the fact that the Teuton woman, even in the somewhat crude civilization in which she moved, occupied a more honourable position than that in Greece and Rome. Much has stated that the Teuton women accompanied their men to battle and cheered them on, encouraging them to fresh efforts by baring their breasts as a reminder of hours of love and as an indication of what fate would await them were they seized in battle. In religion women also played a prominent part, and the goddesses Frigg,

Freyja, Nanna, Gerdhr, etc. are only idealized women. It may be that the heavy punishments which were inflicted by the early Teutons for rape and assault were due to this high regard for women.

It is interesting to follow the results which the mingling of Teutonic customs with Gothic and Roman elements in the Middle Ages had on the position of women. After the kingdom of the Franks had been founded, new customs arose which were not without influence.

The position of girls in the ruling classes of the early Middle Ages was distinctly subordinate. The daughter of the house was trained rigidly to household duties and hospitality. She welcomed the guests, brought water for washing, loosened their armour, fed and watered their horses and conducted the guests to their rooms. The instruction of these girls appears to have been somewhat less rudimentary than that of their brothers. They learnt foreign tongues, and above all the romance languages.

By the thirteenth century, in the German territories at least, the unmarried woman had gained the right to hold and dispose of private property. But the wife was still in an inferior position to her husband – this being an essential part of German law.

In the age of chivalry women were dedicated to a kind of fanciful service, and it was from this time that their position began to change. The woman of the period had received a certain degree of information and a considerable proficiency in music, writing and reading during her secluded girlhood. She made her own clothing and her husband's and executed marvellous embroideries. In the art of healing she was also instructed, and a tender female hand knew well how to care for the wounded knight. She presided at the tourney and crowned the victors in the lists, and she rode out hunting and hawking beside her husband and kinsfolk. The most honourable and intimate form of greeting was a kiss, always a jealously guarded distinction reserved for near relatives, guests and specially favoured suitors.

The peoples of Arabia treat their women as definitely inferior, and certain Arab theologians have denied women any place in Paradise. Under traditional Islam, no provision is made for either the religious or the intellectual education of women. Instead of definite religious belief we find the grossest and most puerile superstition. Even before the time and teaching of Mohammed, Arab women were treated as chattels. The nomads of Asyr, for example, sold their maiden daughters to the highest bidder in the public market place, and a wife could be lent for a night to her husband's guest.

The veiling of women from all but their husbands and nearest male relatives is also characteristic, and naturally tends to exclude women from any wider social or mental life. There is no doubt that, although he wished to counteract the indiscriminate licence of Arabia in his time, the Prophet's deepest motive was an intense jealousy and temperamental suspicion. The absolute command to veil women became compulsory through a later interpretation and has left its mark on the whole emotional life of Islam. (Incidentally, the custom of the veil and the seclusion of women was originally not Arabic, but Persian and pre-Islamic, like the castration of male slaves, which was practised in the Byzantine Empire as in classical antiquity.)

The Koran emphasized women's weakness, but we must also, in justice, remember that Islamic law has also defended certain important rights of women and improved their position as compared with the state of things obtaining previously in Arabia. Nevertheless, we must admit that Islam is, and remains, the extreme representative of a patriarchal civilization and a wholly male outlook, and regards this world and the next from an androcentric point of view.

Virchow found poor health among the Egyptian women. Anaemia and consumptive tendencies were common, due, probably, to their rigid seclusion and to the very restricted choice of diet. He found these conditions, with few exceptions, throughout Egypt and Nubia, and the Egyptian Christians, the Copts, actually secluded their women even more rigorously than the Moslems. Virchow visited Coptic ladies who were not allowed to leave their rooms to join their menfolk at mealtimes or to cross the street and take the air in a magnificent public park at their very doors, however well attended.

Narbeshuber, who studied the life of Islam among the Tunisians of the desert as a doctor, and whose wife learnt the language and became friends with various wives and daughters of well-to-do Arab townsmen, was of the opinion that they had become adapted to their environment. But he admitted that the Bedouin women of the nomad desert tribes had a very hard and restricted life of toil and but little consideration. Often they were beaten, and always treated by their lords as servants. The accounts of other travellers and authorities concur in this.

There is a curious custom among the Shammar Bedouins (who live east of Arabia in the valley between the Tigris and Euphrates) which may be a legacy from other more archaic conditions. Certain tribes choose their most valuable camel and place a highly decorated litter on its back for the comeliest of their maidens. The litter is termed *dulla* or *merkab*, and girl and mount are the palladium of the tribe in battle. The girl sings war songs and fires the men of her tribe to deeds of prowess and courage. If she is captured in battle, it is, according to Geyer, considered a terrible disgrace to her tribe, which loses all further right to a human palladium.

Among the Tuareg of the Sahara, who profess allegiance to Islam but are habitually monogamous, the women occupy a rather high social position.

They are taught to read and write and become as proficient in these arts as the men. They have as much freedom of movement as women in contemporary Europe; the wife administers the household and the joint property, and her rank is inherited by her children.

The Tuareg women are considered very handsome, and are dignified and reserved in their treatment of foreign men. They are true Amazons, showing prowess in horsemanship and the chase, and take part in forays and tribal warfare.

The Afghans were still very primitive before Western civilization was known among them. Elphinstone relates that their girls are rated at a definite tariff which, in his time, was 60 rupees a head. They are also used for the direct payment of debts and fines in kind. Twelve maidens are paid over for a case of manslaughter, six for the loss or mutilation of a hand or a facial mutilation, and three for the loss of a tooth.

The status of woman in India changed in the course of the ages, in consonance with the cultural conditions of that country. Knowledge is lacking for the pre-Vedic ages, but in the Vedic era she was the man's comrade. She may have stood side by side with him in battle, and sacrificed with him. During the religious and social changes inaugurated by the Brahmins, the Hindu woman was permitted only to be the mother of her children, and under all subsequent transcendental speculations she was the more deeply enslaved to a religious ritual. In the days before Buddhism the status of women was certainly not a high one. Daughters were not desired and wives were not the equals of their husbands. Horner is of the opinion that a change became apparent during the Buddhist epoch, when what she calls the 'exclusive supremacy of man' began to give way. According to this authority, woman under Buddhism was an individual in command of her own life. She had become an integral part of society.

Among the vast majority of Hindus today, the home is the centre of existence, but especially among the higher castes it is guarded jealously, and the father exercises therein an almost unlimited authority. Hindu wives, many of whom fulfil the traditional ideal of devoted self-abnegation, humility and chastity, are not supposed to leave their houses or even enter the outer apartments which custom relegates to the men of the family without the permission of their husband or father. It is considered unseemly for them to eat in the presence of men, so they wait till the men have had their meals. There is also the traditional tyranny of the older women of the household, especially the mothers-in-law, over the younger, who must remain veiled and silent before them unless specially addressed. Very few women can read, but many solace themselves with telling or hearing tales of an extravagantly fantastic kind, or they embroider very skilfully, or play games. The thoughts of the girls are deliberately directed towards marriage from their tenderest years, and they pray for tender and loving husbands.

The Ladakhi women are extremely free and fortunate compared with those of the Indian plains. They go about unveiled and, according to Ganzenmüller, do their share of the fieldwork side by side with the men. Marshall gives a similarly favourable account of the position of women among the Todas of southern India. They have considerable freedom of movement, and are treated with consideration by the men.

In the traditional civilization of China, Confucius dealt with certain rules for domestic ethics and manners, ordaining that man and woman should inhabit different parts of the house and keep to a strict division of labour – the husband should never discuss domestic, nor the wife public, matters. (Such suggestions regarding separate quarters and occupations could only have been carried out by the wealthy. The poorer classes must have shared each other's burdens and anxieties from time immemorial.) When husband and wife converse together, they each bow as they answer each other.

H. A. Giles gives a detailed account of the life of women in traditional Chinese homes and in modern times. He emphasizes the social life of the women among themselves, their skill in household arts and the fact that most of the girls in the more prosperous and leisured households are taught to read.

Gray emphasizes the feeling of dependence which surrounds the girl's childhood, the loneliness and oppression of the young wife, whose mother-in-law has almost unlimited authority over her.

Cooper states that Chinese women cannot bear witness before the law and that fathers are permitted to sell their girl-children for household slavery or prostitution and often do so in the poorer classes. Husbands may also sell their wives, according to Cooper, though this is very seldom done and is considered dishonourable. Concubines share the roof with the official wife and their sons inherit, as a rule equally.

In Japan, the women have a greater share in social and aesthetic life than in China (cf. Bacon), although among the nobility and wealthy classes they are still somewhat strictly secluded.

In the ancient kingdom of Korea, on the other hand, women are considered either as labour material or as mere instruments of pleasure. They have no equality in any respect and, as a French missionary has aptly said, their individuality is not morally recognized. This denial of personality goes so far that the Korean woman has no name of her own. As a child, she has a nickname or pet-name in her home circle, but for those outside she is just so-and-so's daughter or sister. After marriage, even this is obliterated and she is generally known by the name of her birthplace or native district. The women of the lower ranks do all the fieldwork and toil incessantly. The high-born and wealthy man's wife is a prisoner in her husband's house, for she may not even look down on the street without asking and receiving his permission to do so. If a Korean man has to mend the roof of his house, he is under an honourable obligation to warn his neighbours, who hasten to shroud their women's windows and double-bar their doors. Jealousy is common, and it often leads to murder and suicide.

When travellers pass along the roads, they hardly ever see a peasant woman; if they meet one she turns her back to hide her face. Near the towns, according to Petermann, the slave-girls showed their faces, but their heads and shoulders were draped in heavy cloaks. There is, however, an elaborate code of politeness towards women, and men make way for them in public, while the private apartments of the wife and mother are sacred and may not even be invaded by officers of the law.

The Li-si people of the island of Hainan in the Gulf of Tonkin, between China and Annam, give their women 'supremacy', according to Wolter. They look after agriculture or rather tillage while the men hunt animal food.

Wangemann has described the subordinate position of the Bavenda and Batlaka women, and tells how, while he was on a visit to the chief of the former tribe, which lives in northern Transvaal, the principal wife entered the hut on her knees with gestures of homage and placed food prepared by her before the chief and his guest. In the Batlaka territory, a passing group of women threw themselves on their knees before Wangemann and his companions and made gestures of homage, then crawled past them on their knees.

Merensky, in his account of the Transvaal Basuto, emphasizes that the women have quite clearly defined duties, but that the death of, or injury to, a woman is fined as heavily as in the case of a man, and that the corn and produce grown by each woman in her own garden may not be touched without her consent by anyone, even her husband.

The Dinka woman has a particularly inferior position. She is simply property, and has no right of inheritance, passing with other goods and chattels to her husband's next-of-kin if he dies first.

The Manganya (Anyasa), on the other hand, treat their women better than the neighbouring peoples, and this comparative enlightenment is ascribed by some to their agricultural livelihood. They practise formal purchase of the wife by the husband, but it is a mere symbolical formula, for the price handed over to the girl's parents is a hen. Women may even attain the office of chieftainship of their tribe.

The peculiar status of women is evident in cases where it is reported they are fed like cattle for the slaughter, killed and devoured. Such cases have occurred on some of the islands of the Pacific, and the belief in the possible appropriation or reincarnation of *mana*, or the soul, is certainly one contributory factor to this practice.

One of the most detailed and well-authenticated cases led to the dispatch of a punitive expedition to the island of Nissan, where the practice had occurred. Thurnwald, who was a member of the expedition, gives a full account of it. The victim was a woman from Buka Island, married to a man of Nissan who had died ten months before she was killed, for, as Thurnwald states:

> The women chosen by preference for these cannibal feasts are those with few or no near relatives. Widows are especially liable and are also considered and treated as common property of the whole village.
>
> The woman in question . . . had lived with two chieftains since her husband's death. Salín of Malés had been her mate for five months and she was pregnant by him at the time of her death. Salín at first objected to handing her over to his creditor, Somsom of Banjalu, near Siar, a well-known cannibal to whom he had promised her. But, finally, on the appearance of the killer, Mógan of Torohabau – who had received as prepayment a pig, two bundles of arrows, each containing sixteen shafts, five bracelets and a knife – Salín gave way and held the wretched woman, who had her hands and feet tied, while she was slashed and shot to death with arrows by Mógan and two of Somsom's men, Sinai and Nataweng.
>
> The body was dragged to the beach, rowed over to Somsom's island and stored overnight in his house. Next day she was roasted, and then there was an elaborate *kilué*, or cutting up and division of the roasted flesh, among the thirteen men of Siar and the neighbourhood.

As a final characteristic fact we may record that there is a firm conviction among these people that to devour the roasted flesh of a woman stimulates and increases genital potency.

The status of Javanese women is thus summarized by Captain Schulze:

> They are not allowed to enter the mosques unless they have studied for the priesthood, which is seldom the case, so the women of the upper class perform their devotions at home. The girls and women of the people might be heathen were it not for their ritual mutilations and abject social

position – the gifts of Islam. The Moslem Javanese is absolute lord of his wife: he may beat her, kick her and drive her out of the house with impunity. The women of greater means and leisure often achieve a considerable degree of freedom after observing outward forms of faith . . . In the towns, the western influence and examples often lead the daughters of the people to abandon the tenets of Islam and to earn their own livelihood and exercise their own judgement.

Moncelon has given an account of the position of the native women on New Caledonia. They are, according to him, beasts of burden to the men and are inferior both morally and physically. They submit to the caprices of the men and appear satisfied with their condition. They can be sold, generally with their own consent, although the contrary is sometimes the case. They are even deficient in maternal instinct, showing far less attachment and care for their children than the men. Moncelon attributes their general degradation to the oppression they suffer.

On the Admiralty Islands, according to Thurnwald, men and women have sharply distinct property division and inherit from each other. The men own the houses, the herds of swine, the coconut and betel trees, the weapons, nets, baskets and pouches. The women own the cauldrons and pots, the slings for carrying baskets or pouches, small nets, certain baskets, stands for keeping food, needles made of the bones of bats, etc. There is even a special currency for women – the grey, rounded berries of a native shrub (*Lacrima coix*). It is said that the men have no power over the objects owned by the women.

The conditions and customs in New Britain include severe laws against the marriage of blood kin (cf. J. G. Frazer, *Totemism and Exogamy*). In every tribe there are two classes, and only members of these different groups may marry one another.

In spite of these harsh customs and the heavy load of work laid on them, the women of New Britain have considerable influence, both active and indirect. It is very rare for their husbands to conclude any bargain or agreement without consulting the wives, and there is generally some special favour or advantage for the latter in any bargain which is ratified and goes through. They take part in the skirmishes and forays between the tribes, carrying their husbands' spears and shields and encouraging them in battle with applause.

The women and girls are strictly forbidden to enter the assembly houses or to take part in religious rites, and the husband has power of life and death over his partner. Moreover, there is already a distinct prostitute class.

On the Pelew Islands, the women have their own administration as distinct from that of the men. Nevertheless, the head chieftain of all is a man, the *Adjbatul* (Captain H. Wilson terms him the *Abba-Thulle*, Semper the *Ebadul*). He must come from the seat of government *Adjdit*, and his oldest female relative – i.e., the oldest woman of the same stock – is the chieftainess of the women (the chieftain's wife is never the chieftainess of the women, according to Kubary). She has a succession of subordinate chieftainesses and deputies who keep order among the women, as do their male counterparts among the men. They have their own courts of justice and no man may interfere with the procedure or with the sentences they pronounce. The women can become authorized intermediaries between the living and the world beyond, i.e., they may be magicians or *Kalit* as well as chieftainesses. The form of succession goes by seniority, till the older generation is extinct. This female aristocracy is termed *Raupakaldit*.

These institutions are combined with or contribute to a high degree of female independence on the Pelew Islands. No one may strike a woman with impunity or address her in terms of insult, and if such should be used towards an *Adjdit* woman the offender is fined as large a sum of money as though for manslaughter. If he is unable to pay he must flee the islands, and soon, or he is done to death by the women.

There is a strict standard of public decency. No man may behold a woman without her *lava-lava*, or skirt, except in the privacy of the household. Men are therefore expected to shout in warning of their approach when in the neighbourhood of the bathing places along the shore. There is a strict etiquette forbidding men to talk publicly about another man's wife or to mention her by name.

Thus there is a dignity and a certain standard of morals, together with almost complete freedom of sexual relations between boys and girls from their earliest childhood. There is no 'family life' as we understand it, for the sexes live apart for most of the time. There is a certain amount of polygamy, since two women can contribute more food to a household by their field-work than one.

Among the Australian Aborigines, women's status is very low. They are often carried away by force or sold as children, and till death they are at the mercy of their men's caprice, even in its most brutal modes. Polygamy is universally permitted. The work (outside hunting and forays) is done by the women; if they do not perform their tasks to the man's satisfaction or if they otherwise displease him, he beats them mercilessly. The women are excluded from the magico-religious ceremonies of the tribe and may not eat until the men have had their meal. If a man dies his uterine brother inherits his wife and children; the children belong to their mother's totem.

*

In the seventeenth century the women of the Iroquois had their special assemblies, whose decisions and desires were communicated to the general assembly and fully considered by the latter. If a woman was slain among the Huron the family of the murderer was fined more heavily than if a man had been slain: in the latter case thirty articles were exacted, and in the former, forty – for the continuance and increase of the tribe depended primarily on the women (Parkman).

There are also accounts by early explorers of the position and privileges of the women of the Chibcha people, who lived in Colombia and whose civilization is now dying out. According to Zerda, an observer once saw a chieftain tied to a post or pillar in his abode while three of his wives beat him unmercifully, for he had indulged heavily in drink. In the aboriginal civilizations of Nicaragua, the women were also in a good position.

According to the early explorers of the Pacific Coast, Douglas and Vancouver (as cited by Krause), in some of the tribes of that region certain women were so highly honoured that they seemed to be the rulers and leaders of the men. In many tribes the death of a woman was mourned with impressive ceremonial by her widower.

On the coast of British Columbia, among the Koskimo and Quatsino Indians, a woman, the daughter-in-law of the headman, had the office and power of chieftainess, and she was the most powerful and important individual in the neighbourhood. She took the traveller Jacobsen under her special protection and helped him considerably. She was described as already advanced in years, and her skull had been artificially compressed into the conical shape admired by her tribesmen. Jacobsen told M. Bartels that the women of the Tsimshian tribe were also allowed to become 'medicine men' or magicians.

ii. Division of Labour

The division of labour between the sexes is not absolutely rigid in every primitive people. Thus Parkinson describes the constant and inseparable companionship of husband and wife among the Gilbert Islanders. The wife carries her husband's shield and food when he goes on a foray or a fishing expedition. However, she may not accompany him to the Great Assembly House (*Te Maneape*) of the village for dance and sport – these diversions are over for her when she becomes a wife, and she is supposed to stay at home during his absence. If her spouse does not find her there to greet him, she is severely beaten and may not complain about it.

Division of labour and mutual help are often heavily overweighted against the muscularly weaker partner. The man goes to the tribal assemblies, hunts, fishes, goes to war. Prince von Wied gave a striking account of the overloading of the Botocudo women with all the material possessions of the tribe as well as two or three children, when the tribe was on the march. The men carried only bows and arrows, keeping them in readiness for hunting and to ward off attack (Fig. 1).

Fig. 1   A Botocudo family travelling (after von Wied)

Wedell says of the Fuegians that their men showed much attention and demonstrative affection towards the women but nevertheless put all the work on their shoulders. The Samoan girls' life, on the other hand, is apparently mainly *dolce far niente* – a little light cooking, sweeping and plaiting, much personal adornment and gossip, much social life and converse with young men.

In Micronesia the women enjoy a good position. They are not compelled to perform all the heaviest tasks of the daily routine. They devote themselves to household cleaning and adornment, cooking, mat-plaiting, the making of garments and certain accessory help in fishing. In their manners they are gentle and their personal habits are modest and dignified (cf. Cook's experiences in New Zealand as related by Hawkesworth). No chastity is required for the women and girls before marriage. Thus, on the Ratak Islands, they were offered to Kotzebue and his crew, but for one night only.

Hartmann and Junod have given a classic account of the life and work of native women in Africa. Hartmann says that the division of labour follows traditional lines. The man hunts wild animals, tends flocks and herds, wages war, drinks alcohol and takes part in councils and assemblies which discuss the affairs of the tribe or the village. The domestic and agricultural work is mostly undertaken by the women, as well as a certain amount of primitive industrial work, but details vary with the climatic and cultural environment. Thus, among the Funj, Shilluk, Nuer and Bari, the men help till the fields, which is not the case among the South African races. The women build the huts, till the fields, prepare the meals, grind the cereals. They spin, weave and prepare the ox hides for clothing purposes.

It is certainly very difficult to arrive at a just and accurate estimate of the overworking of women in primitive communities since European standards and sentiments may distort perspective. Pechuel-Loesche gives a very clear and graphic description of the customs in Loango (West Africa), bringing forward considerations usually ignored:

> The free man – or the serf who has paid a ransom to his master and is able to work independently – hunts, fishes and barters his goods along the coast. The free woman is busy at her hearth; her hearth fire is usually kindled under the open sky, but it burns for her alone and she may forbid her husband to warm himself beside it and refuse to cook any food for him if she so desires. Then he must roast flesh or fruits at a fire kindled by himself, as though in the wilderness, or let his servant cook them. He has the duty of supplying game, fish, condiments, fruit, palm oil and such goods as can be obtained by barter. She brings vegetables and other necessaries, grown by herself or bartered for; and she often collects shell-fish.
>
> What the woman obtains as produce from the field she tills or from the animals she tends – beyond what is needed for her husband – is hers. Her husband has no right to one root from her basket-load, nor one egg from her hen-run unless they married on the understanding that their goods should be in common. She does not work any harder than he does and sometimes certainly a good deal less. Moreover, in Africa, as elsewhere, the way to a man's heart is through his stomach.
>
> A prosperous and competent woman occupies her time according to her own inclination as she does among ourselves . . . They are much better off than many girls, wives and mothers in civilized conditions who live without sufficient food and in a state of perpetual need, and among whom one can find true beasts of burden such as cannot be seen among savages.

Among the aborigines of North America the division of labour is generally on simple lines. The man feeds and defends his family as a hunter of game and a warrior, while the household tasks are relegated to the woman. She also prepares the food and attends to the children.

iii. Women's Language

Kohlbrugge mentions an ancient legend among the Tenggerese of Java to the effect that their women were originally of a 'foreign tribe'. The first personal pronoun is different among the Tenggerese for either sex: it is *ingsun* for women, *reang* for men.

Spix and Martius have offered a similar explanation of the women's languages spoken by certain South American Indians, i.e., they believe that women were captured wholesale from other tribes. Martius found striking linguistic differences among the Waicuru and other Brazilian tribes, and similar observations have been recorded among the Caribs – especially the island Caribs of the Lesser Antilles. A Carib invasion of these islands has been suggested, resulting in the extermination of the Arawak men and incorporation of the women in the victorious tribe. But Stoll has shown that this particular explanation is hardly tenable, for he says that the Carib women's language has only one word with Arawak affinities. Moreover, Lasch, who has made an exhaustive study of these special languages, including the secret women's language – and to whose treatise we may refer readers interested in the subject – considers it very probable that a special women's language was in use on the West Indian Islands long before the Carib conquest. He finds that there are still traces of such a language among the Arawak Indians of South America today (for instance in Surinam) and cites van Coll: 'If a man of his people says "yes", it must be *ehe* or *tasi*. The woman's affirmative is *tare*. And "to promise" is *bahassida* for men, *babiára* for women.' The same circumstance is mentioned by Prince Roland Bonaparte.

Stoll quotes from the language of the Cachiquel (Maya) in Central American Guatemala:

Men's term	English	Women's term
Hi	Son-in-law	Ali
Ali	Daughter-in-law	Ali
Hi-nam	Father-in-law	Ali-nam
Hi-te	Mother-in-law	Ali-te

There are further examples of different vocabularies. For example, Paul Ehrenreich says of the Caraya Indians on the Araguaya River in Brazil:

Their most remarkable characteristic is the existence of special languages or dialects for either sex as among the Waicurus and Chiquitano. Only a few words, however, are wholly different: as a rule there are different modifications of the same roots. Thus, where in the men's dialect there are two adjacent vowel sounds, there is a *k* between them in the women's speech. 'Rain' is *biu* for men, *biku* for women; 'maize' *mahi* for men, *maki* for women.

In a later publication Ehrenreich says, 'The most remarkable thing in Caraya is the existence of a special speech or dialect for women; a fact . . . ascertained [by me] too late to collect a sufficiently large vocabulary of the different terms.' Examples include:

Men's dialect	English	Women's dialect
Insandenodo	Chieftain	Hauato
Wa-tihui	Pot	Beva
Uo	Coconut	Heeru
Wa-dearo	Nose	Wa daanva
Iramaanrakre	Hunting	Ditiuananderi

According to Lasch, there are also traces of a women's dialect among the Kopagmiut Eskimo on the estuary of the Mackenzie River and the Choctaw Indians. At least, certain terms are said to be used only by women among these races.

A. F. Chamberlain has somewhere pointed out the difficulties arising in the course of Christian mission work from these circumstances. For instance, among the Kutenai Indians in south-eastern British Columbia, the Lord's Prayer had to be translated in two different versions beginning, respectively, *Katitonatla-naeta* for men and *Kasonatla* for women. In the Kele tongue, one of the South African dialects, the ninety-nine sheep that had not gone astray had to be replaced by another simile, as 'ninety-nine' resembled a word taboo to the women. In fact, there have had to be some special women's versions of Scripture, for in the Carib tongue of the West Indies, for example, about twenty per cent of the total vocabulary was different for the two sexes.

One of the causes leading to the formation and crystallization of these special dialects was the rule that women should not utter the name of the king or chieftain, or of their own nearest relatives. They were obliged to use some other word instead, as a 'nickname' or magic formula.

Kranz points out the particular difficulties to which women of the royal household of the Zulu chieftains were subjected. They had to avoid uttering the names of their husbands, fathers-in-law, grandfathers-in-law and of all their husbands' brothers. They had to be constantly inventing new words or syllables of words or altering them, e.g. changing 'water' from *amanzi* to *amandabiu*, etc. Any woman infringing this custom was, according to Kranz, accused of witchcraft and executed. Thus there arose a perfectly distinct special language or dialect of the women, which the Zulus themselves termed *ukuteta kwabapzi* – that is, women's speech.

The same conditions and results are found in the East African Konde district. The women may not utter their husband's personal name or even those syllables which form parts of other words. Thus the wives of Muankenya may not pronounce the word *mkenya* (bachelor). If they have occasion to mention it, they use the term *kekipi* (wood) instead. Nor may they say anything resembling the noun *muañonda*, which is another family name. Thus, instead of *nombe*, or 'ox', they say *nguafi*; instead of *nose* (sheep), they say *ekeampepe* (the tailed one, or that with the tail). The fatal syllable which they must avoid is *no* (Fülleborn).

Vámbéry tells us of similar customs among the Kirghiz of Central Asia. The women may not utter the personal names of any of the men of the household, for to do so is considered highly improper. It is said that a Kirghiz had five adult sons named, respectively, *Köl* (lake), *Kamisch* (reed), *Kashir* (wolf), *Koy* (sheep) and *Pitschak* (knife). One of his daughters-in-law went one day to fetch water from the lake and caught sight of a wolf devouring a sheep among the reeds. She rushed home screaming, 'Down there, beside that which glitters as it sways, a savage beast is eating that which bleats.'

The Swahili women have a special highly developed dialect called *Nenola fûmbo*. It is taught to the young girls in a regular and systematic manner. *Kufûmba* means to close or clench (the 'fist' understood) and *Kufûmba fûmbo* is to speak unintelligibly. Zache maintains that this dialect contains a series of transferable terms; these are not specially invented syllables and sound combinations but words in use for other things and used by the women particularly with sexual significance in their secret dialect.

Sir Spenser St John and Sir F. A. Swettenham give accounts of the secret language (*Bahêsa Balik*, or twisted speech) used by the Malay women at Brunei in Borneo. This system is especially intricate and highly developed. The syllables of words in current use are either rearranged or fresh syllables are added to them as in the secret slang and dialects of our European schoolchildren. Thus instead of *mari* (come), they say *malah rilah*. These expressions are constantly changing, shifting, becoming obsolete and replaced by new ingenuities, invented by the girls and at first confided only to their closest friends.

The same manifestations, in a less pronounced form, may be found in European societies. Thus G. Granier says of the Parisian prostitutes:

Jargon or slang is indispensable to them and is also one of their usual diversions. By adding certain foreign-sounding terminations to all the words they use – such as *mir* or *scof*, they 'talk Russian'. Another variety of secret dialect is formed by taking the first syllable of any noun and putting it in the genitive case at the end of a phrase, while the definite article precedes the second or final syllable of the original word. Thus *la pagne du cam* is their version of *campagne*; *la nette de ca*, of *canette*.

CHAPTER II

Sex

What are the most typical and characteristic sexual attributes of women? We must clear our minds on these points and study their racial and ethno-graphical variation.

i. Historical Background

Among primitive peoples we must not assume any but a very imperfect or rudimentary knowledge of internal anatomy. Even the Ancient Greeks and Romans knew very little about the organs of the female pelvis, for they were not in the habit of making post-mortem dissections of the human body, and the great Hippocrates gave a description of the essential sex organs of women which proved quite clearly that he could never have seen them.

It is probable that the Ancient Egyptians knew more about the pelvic viscera than the Greeks and Romans, for the practice of mummification favoured anatomical observation. Georg Ebers, the Egyptologist, told Hennig the following facts, as recorded on a papyrus in his possession. In the Egyptian script the word *nătú* (Coptic *oti*), when used as a masculine noun, means the uterus; when used as a feminine noun, the vulva. And there is a further term for the uterus – *mut* – which Hennig thinks is the radical syllable from which the Greek, Latin and later European terms for 'mother' originated. The ovaries were called *benti* and depicted as two oval lozenges lying one over the other: ≋ . Recipes 'against falling of the ovaries' are known.

The Talmud gives many glimpses of the medical and anatomical know-ledge acquired by the Jews. Israëls came to the conclusion that the medical authorities cited in the Talmud must have based their views on much dissection and post-mortem examination. Kazenelson states that all the external and some of the internal portions of the female genital tract were known to the Talmudists and that they had a rich and precise vocabulary with which to designate these organs. But there are no references to ovaries or Fallopian tubes in the Mishnah.

Soranus was the first clearly to distinguish between the uterus and the vagina: he owed this knowledge to his observation and dissection of corpses. He also explained that the womb in women had a different shape from that in animals: he described the os externum with remarkable accuracy, as also the two membranes of the uterus. Moschion, who compiled a manual of midwifery in Latin, agreed almost entirely with Soranus and distinguished clearly between uterus and vagina. Then we find Galen reverting to the idea of the bicornuate uterus, an error perpetuated by Oribasius and the Arabian physician Avicenna, who was born about AD 980 in Persia.

In Europe, knowledge of genital anatomy remained extremely fragmentary until the beginning of the sixteenth century, but did show some advance by 1547, the date of J. Dryander's illustration (Fig. 2), and especially in 1565, when the work of Andreas Vesalius appeared. Furthermore, the oviducts, which as Galen informs us had been first observed and discovered by Philotimos, a contemporary of Aristotle, but which had subsequently sunk back into obscurity, were rediscovered around 1550 by the Italian anatomist Fallopio. They are still known as the Fallopian tubes.

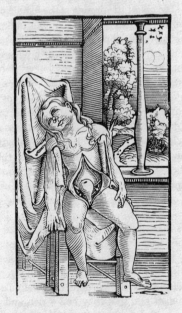

Fig. 2   The internal female sexual organs (J. Dryander, 1547)

We learn very little of the extent of knowledge in Ancient India with regard to the internal sexual organs, though there were prescriptions and suggestions for bringing about conception when it tarried. The term *yoni* apparently referred indiscriminately to all the female organs concerned with coitus, conception, gestation and birth. In the Kamasutra and the Kama-Shastra there are attempts at classifying both sexes into categories according to certain genital measurements. The three groups of women are termed gazelles, mares and elephants respectively, the measurements being six, nine and twelve times the thickness of the thumb; and the corresponding male groups are termed hares, bulls and stallions.

The state of obstetric knowledge in Japan, even as late as 1750–65, when the great physician Kangawa wrote his famous treatise *Sanron*, was very imperfect. However, they had some idea of the bony structure of the pelvis. Similarly, the knowledge and practice of medicine were very primitive in China, previous to the latest revolutionary era (cf. Wong). Among all the ancient medical treatises of the Chinese, some of which are richly and elaborately illustrated, we have hitherto failed to find a representation even of the pelvis. But from certain writings of an obstetric nature, we may deduce that they realized the difference between vaginal passage and uterus, and did not regard the latter as simply a continuation inwards of the former. 'The uterus sits therein, even as a water-lily blossom set on her stalk.' But there is no mention of oviducts or ovaries, nor any indication that their important functions were known.

ii. Sexual Symbolism

Riedel has recorded that in Amboina and neighbouring islands the natives cut rough symbols of the vulva into their kalapa and other fruit trees. This is done with a double purpose: in order to make the trees more fruitful (a form of 'sympathetic magic') and as a spell to ward off robbers, for the symbols represent the parts through which the robbers were born.

Herodotus mentions similar figures carved on stone pillars set up by the Pharaoh Sesostris in Syrian Palestine to commemorate his victories over those peoples. Here there is not the sacred but the opprobrious significance and intention.

The ancient culture of Easter Island commemorated and depicted the vulva with reverence, according to Geiseler. There were many such sculptures and votive plaques, and it has been stated that these representations always accompanied the figure of Make-Make, the duplex and bisexual deity who presides over eggs.

In many parts of Hindustan, the feminine *yoni* receives divine honours, like the masculine *linga*. They are frequently represented together in Hindu art in the shape of an oval or rounded disc, in the centre of which is a short, blunt rod. The rod is the symbol of Mahadeva or Shiva, the male principle throughout nature. The *yoni* portion is the symbol of Bhavani or Kali, his divine spouse, the mother of all living and the female principle throughout nature.

In China there is also widespread symbolism of the genital organs. They are represented as Yang (♂) and Yin (♀) and are, states Katscher, attached to the walls or doors of houses, or above the lintels, in order to avert ill-luck. (H. A. Giles, on the other hand, states that he never saw them in twenty-seven years in China!)

iii. Origins of the Sexual Organs

There are various explanations in primitive folklore of the origin of the sex organs. For instance, the southern Slavs, according to Krauss, declare that St Elias 'clove the woman through the middle and the cleft remains to this day'.

Roth states that the Australian Blacks on the Tully River in Queensland believe that men and women 'came out of' that river in the beginning of things and there was, at first, no special difference between them. Then the spear grass that grows on the banks became the male organ and the long wandering on the river banks gave girls their labia majora.

The Queenslanders also believe that the Great Spirit made little children out of the moist clay of the river banks, and before he put them inside their mothers' bodies he 'clove open' the girl-children on a wooden fork.

Similarly, on Proserpine River (Australia), the natives believe that in the beginning, Kahara, the moon, made man and woman. He was formed of the metallic ore of meteor stones (thunderbolts); she of the wood of the fruitful beech tree. The man was finished by being rubbed all over with black-and-white ashes and provided with a projecting piece of pandanus root. The woman was made smooth and supple by being 'oiled' with river slime and yam juice, and a ripe pandanus fruit was placed inside her body; finally she was cleft open with a slice of pandanus root, 'so that they could be told apart'.

Pechuel-Loesche reports a legend of the Bakongo Negroes on the Loango coast as follows: Nzambi, the Creator, left a kola-nut about and the first woman warned her partner not to eat it. Nzambi praised the woman's steadfastness but did not wish her to be stronger than the man – that did not please him. So he cut her open and took out some of her bones, making her smaller and softer to touch. Then he sewed her together again, but with too short a thread so that a piece remains open to this day.

There is a similar legend, states Krämer, obviously meant partly in jest, among the Samoans. In this story the girl, Popoto, and the three men who try to mate with her have the names of mountains: Mangafolau, Tofuaupolu, and Masa. Finally, Masa 'cleaves through her with a shark's tooth' (the weapons, swords and spears of the islanders are decorated with shark's teeth). Krämer, who gives the story in full, is of the opinion that it 'symbolizes the origin of the first woman'.

iv. The Breasts

FOLKLORE

The African Kabyles of Djurjura have a singular superstition, recorded by Viré. A wanderer across a place of tombs hears a sweet song at night which lures him to follow the sound. Suddenly he perceives a little woman, or rather young girl, quite black all over but very pretty. She flees before him, slowly at first, then quicker, and he is compelled to pursue. Her pace gets quicker and quicker, and suddenly her breasts grow longer and longer and she throws them backwards over her shoulders, leaps into a ditch and her pursuer falls after her and breaks his neck.

The same idea of spectral breasts of unnatural form and length was current in Ancient Peru. J. J. von Tschudi records the local Indians' belief in spectres called *hapiñuñu*. These creatures have women's forms but with long hanging breasts. They fly by night and seize grown men, carrying them off between their breasts.

The Zuni Indians of the Pueblo group in Arizona have peculiar pottery which closely imitates the contours of the breast and nipple. These pitchers are known as *mé he ton ne* (the root word is *mé ha na* – woman's breast). While a Zuni woman is using one of these, the mammillary lip is left open and only closed with a clay stopper when the work is quite done. This she does with averted eyes. Cushing, to whom we owe this interesting information, asked the reason and was told it was dangerous to look at the pitcher while closing the aperture. A woman who did so might become barren or, if she had children, they would die young, and those who drank from the desecrated vessels would fall sick and pine away.

Rosen has drawn attention to the breast-shaped money boxes used for children in Italy, and also found in Greece, Silesia, Mecklenburg and eastern Prussia. Very similar boxes are also found to have been in use in Pompeii and in the Middle Ages. Rosen thinks they were related to the cult of St Agatha, the patroness of suckling mothers, and before that to the Great Mother herself. According to legend, Agatha lived in Catania in the first half of the third century A D. The Consular Quintianus wooed her to be his wife, but she refused him because he worshipped the heathen gods. Persevering in her refusal, despite prayers and threats, she was imprisoned in a brothel –

a frequent fate in these legends. But as she refused and remained steadfast, she was tortured by mutilation of her breasts.

Georg Ebers records the survival of the ideas of pre-Christian times and cultures among the Christian Copts of medieval Egypt:

> . . . they celebrated not only the face but the breast of Hathor, the divine goddess; when her image was borne in procession from Dendera to Edfu, two acts of the festive ritual were the unveiling (*'ap*) of her bosom and its display to her worshippers.
>
> Hathor is always the fair, the good and the kind, and when we behold the celebrations in honour of St Agatha at Catania in Sicily and the waxen votive breasts offered her, we are reminded of the divine bosom of Hathor, the great goddess of Egypt, and of the well-known theory that the Christian martyr is the successor and reincarnation of that nature goddess whom pagan Egypt revered as the mother from whose breasts all creation received life and nourishment.

These associations have also been attached to the Mother of Jesus. Among the relics treasured in certain churches, even in north Germany, are specimens of the milk from her breast. The great Cistercian abbot Bernard of Clairvaux, who died in 1153, received the singular favour of nourishment with the milk of Our Lady. (He was henceforth termed mellifluous, honey-tongued, for his eloquence was irresistible.) Two ancient pictures, both anonymous and dating from the fifteenth century, represent this miracle. In one of them, the Madonna presses the milk from her bared breast in a fine stream towards the adoring saint.

ELONGATION AND BINDING

Among South African natives the breasts are carefully treated and developed; even when the little girls are not more than seven or eight years old, their mothers begin to rub and smear their breasts with an ointment composed of grease and certain roots, pounded to a powder. They then grasp the areola and sensitive portions around the nipples and rub and knead them as though they wanted to tear off the whole gland. At a later stage, the nipple is intentionally elongated and tied round with strips of fibre.

Holländer reports of the Basuto women that they 'pull and knead their breasts long before their confinements so that they may be able to suckle the children who ride on their hips'.

Several African tribes have the custom of constricting the breasts by means of a band fixed just across the thorax where the outward curve begins, and tied tightly so that the breasts are held down, and thus their formation and development are affected. Fritsch confirms this among the South African Bantu; the tying down of the breast is the insignia of the married woman among certain of their tribes.

Fritsch also says of the Ama-Xosa:

> In the prime of life, the breasts are not uncomely, and they are very plump and [not] lacking grace and delicacy of form. As soon as they become wives, the signs of a rapid deterioration appear and their breasts sag and become like empty bags of skin. They consider this normal to woman in her prime, a beauty in itself, and cultivate it by tying down their breasts. The result is that they are soon able to fling the breast over their shoulder to feed the child carried on their backs; or they suckle the child that crouches on the ground between them by lifting their arms. These facts are so often observed that the formation in question must not be regarded as a monstrosity but as normal among these people, and it is taken for granted in South Africa.

Riedel states that the women of the Luang and Sermata groups in the Eastern Malay Archipelago wear a sort of bodice called *kutang*. This garment constricts the bosom and causes a certain amount of malformation.

According to some authorities, the Annamese women in French Cochin-China press down their breasts by means of a double bandage round the neck and shoulders over a triangular 'binder'.

In the South Seas, there is a similar custom among the native women of the island of Uvea, one of the Loyalty group. A woman depicted by Bernard wore a narrow strip of material tied round her thorax so tightly on the upper edge of the breasts that there was a deep visible furrow.

This recalls certain South American aboriginal practices recorded by F. de Azara:

> Among the Payagua on the River Paraguay, the older women tie leather belts across the upper breasts of the young girls as soon as they have reached full natural development, draw the belts tight and fasten them at the back. Thus, before the girls reach the age of twenty-four, their breasts sag to their waists.

The Kalmuck women also wear constricting corsets, whilst Currier says that the Cherokee women occasionally compress their breasts by means of flat round stones in order to hinder their natural growth.

In Europe, during the sixteenth and seventeenth centuries, the Spanish women often practised a strangely archaic custom of which we are, however, unable to trace the origin. The breasts of young girls in the early stages of puberty were covered with leaden plates (cf. Finck), and in many Spanish ladies the result was positive concavity instead of prominence. Extreme thinness was considered beautiful at that time, and the Countess d'Aulnoy describes the display of a long chest and back, which was carried out to the greatest extent possible by the Spanish ladies of the seventeenth century. Indeed, she declares that their breasts were as flat and even as a sheet of paper.

The undue and unhealthy constriction of the breast is found not only in townspeople but also among the peasants of certain districts in Central Europe. Buck made a report of the conditions in Upper Swabia, where the tight clothing and bodices caused complete functional atrophy of the breasts, so that only the remnants of the nipples were left and the women could not suckle their babies – so there was great infant mortality.

Among the Circassians the girls between ten and twelve years old are braced into a broad leather girdle reaching from just over the bust down to their hips. This is then sewn tightly together. The Ossete girls also wear a similar garment. This is first donned between seven and eight years of age (according to Pokrowsky three years later) and not removed till the girl's wedding night, when the bridegroom cuts open the leather tags with his sword or dagger and removes the corselet. After this operation the breasts develop very rapidly. It is said that the Ossetes took this custom from their northern neighbours, the Kabardians (von Seydlitz).

MUTILATION

There are certain possible major operations on the breasts which remind us of the legend of the Amazons. We shall consider them in a later section (Chapter IX), merely recalling for the moment that, according to Strabo, their right breast was seared off in childhood so that they could better throw the spear and draw the bow (hence their Greek name, 'without breast'). Hippocrates, who claimed that they belonged to the Sauromatian stock and lived by the Palus Maeotis (Sea of Azoff), recorded that a brass disc was made red-hot and pressed on the right breast, searing the muscles and flesh to such an extent that the breast could not naturally develop, with the result that all their force flowed into their right arms and shoulders.

In paragraph 194 of the Code of King Hammurabi (i.e., in Babylon, 2250 BC), the breast was to be cut off if a wet-nurse tried to replace a child committed to her care by a changeling.

As late as the nineteenth century, mutilations and self-torments were practised by the Skoptsi, an obscure Christian sect of fanatics who were chiefly Russian in origin (Fig. 3). The detailed accounts by E. von Pelikan

Fig. 3   Twenty-year-old Skoptsi with mutilated breasts (after E. von Pelikan)

and W. Koch mention cases known to the authors in which little girls of ten, nine or even seven years of age had had their nipples cut off. Yet these children insisted, when testifying in the courts of law, that they had thus mutilated themselves.

Similar and worse forms of torture were doubtless inflicted in warfare. The town of Wimpfen, for example, formerly the Roman Colonia Cornelia on the River Neckar (cf. Heid), gets its name from an ancient tradition that the women of Cornelia had their breasts mutilated by the invading hordes of Attila's Huns (*Wimpfen* is said to be a corruption of *Weibs-Pein*). There are also traditions to the effect that an analogous torture was used in the persecution of the Jews in medieval times and later. In a fifteenth-century Hebrew manuscript, women are represented as suspended from low

Fig. 4   Jewish martyrs suspended by their breasts
(after Kohut, from a Hebrew manuscript of the fifteenth century)

branches of trees by cords or ropes looped round their breasts (Fig. 4).
Further details as to whether this agony was meant to be final or temporary
are, however, lacking.

v. The Uterus

THE WANDERING WOMB

Though both primitive peoples and those of classical antiquity had very little
exact knowledge of the uterus, they dwelt much on its purpose and function
in their legends and folklore.

For many hundreds of years, even the learned regarded the uterus as an
independent organism – a kind of animal enclosed in the woman's body.
Even Plato could not free himself from this idea. He considered the uterus a
creature that desired fertilization. If this did not occur, the uterus became
restless and wandered in the body, checking its motions and causing heavy

anxiety, feelings of dread and many illnesses. The same view was expressed in later Greek times by Aretaeus: 'The uterus delights in pleasant odours and moves towards them and shrinks from the foul and evil odours. In this also it resembles an animal: in fact it is one.'

In the Hippocratic collection is found a very extensive notion of the powers of the uterus. We read: 'If the womb leaves its proper place it falls here or there, but wherever it may fall, severe pains manifest themselves.' This is considered a frequent occurrence, for if the uterus is in any way ailing, it may leave its proper place and even wander so far afield as to invade the liver, ribs or brain. Methods of treatment are suggested in great detail, among them fumigations, internal injections and applications of vegetable drugs.

The Ancient Egyptians also believed that the uterus was able to leave its normal position in the woman. In Eber's papyrus, mention is made of healing medicines 'in order to bring back the mother of all men in a woman to her own place'.

Throughout Central Europe and in the Austrian Alps, where folklore has always given much thought and care to the special feminine organs, all the various protean manifestations of hysteria were attributed to disorders of the womb. According to Fossel, the Styrian peasants call the globus hystericus *Hebmutter* (womb lift) to this day. And the ancient belief in the wild creature, incalculable and invisible, ranging throughout the woman's body, striking, struggling and biting, also survives. Handelmann, for example, mentions that, according to popular superstition, the wandering womb creature crawls in and out of the woman's mouth in the shape of a toad during sleep. It goes to water and drinks or bathes itself. But if the woman has shut her mouth, it cannot return and she bears no children.

vi. *The Hymen*

Most nations attach a very high value to the hymen, especially in some Oriental countries (see also 'Chastity', Chapter VI). But in many parts of India and most of China it is completely obliterated and removed in the earliest years.

According to Hureau de Villeneuve, the Chinese nurses wash and cleanse the private parts of the children they tend with such thoroughness that they always insert their finger into the introitus and thus gradually stretch the hymen till it wholly disappears, for in those climates cleanliness is necessary to remove the deposit of matter which is constantly accumulating.

Similar customs prevail in the Moluccan Archipelago and the Amboina group, probably mainly for the same reasons.

In Brazil, among the Machacari, the mothers dilate the vagina of the little girls by introducing large folded leaves and then washing them with tepid water, according to von Feldner's report. Here the original purpose is probably preparation for future sex relationships.

Mantegazza sent Ploss a written account of methods in Paraguay. When the midwives receive boy-babies on their birth they proceed to pull and stretch the male member with their fingers; and, indeed, the natives of Paraguay are very long in this part, according to report. But when the midwives deliver girl-babies, they at once push their finger up the vaginal passage, saying, 'This is a woman.' Thus there are no maidens in the anatomical sense of the word in Paraguay, as the hymen is ruptured by these manipulations.

vii. Pubic Hair

Our speculative forefathers were much puzzled to account for the purpose of pubic hair in both sexes. Opinions varied from that of Galen, who considered their purpose ornamental, to those of Burkhard Eble and the great anatomist Caspar Bartholin, who both preferred the view that the hairs were put there for modest concealment! The same teleological point of view in which human views or morals are attributed to the processes of evolution was expressed by Gerdy. The hair is, he says, modesty's veil, and he notes that it is a remarkable thing that this region should be covered just at the time when the genitals awaken and emerge from their chastity. By thus covering them, nature inflames the imagination and rouses to a high pitch '*la plus impérieuse de toutes les passions*'. Blanchard, on the other hand, thought that the purpose was wholly utilitarian – that of protection of the sensitive mucosae from cold and accident.

The first authority to tabulate such facts as are here available was the late Berlin gynaecologist Eggel, who left his work to Max Bartels to be continued and completed.

One thousand adult women were examined and the results tabulated:

Dark eyes	239
Dark hair on head	333
Dark hair on mons veneris and genitals	329
Light eyes	761
Light hair on head	667
Light hair on genitals	671

Analysis of Eggel's data resulted in the conclusion that the coloration of the pubic hair has a certain tendency to association with the colour of the hair on the head; but that this is a tendency, not an absolute rule. Moreover, there is no such tendency to definite association with the colour of the eyes.

Jacobus X. says that the Moi women in Cochin-China have fairly crisp pubic hair of the deepest black, whilst the Annamese women have only sparse hair on the mons. The same authority reports of the women of Cambodia that they also have sparse hair on the mons: it is dark brown in colour and slightly curly.

In the seventeenth century, the traveller and explorer Tavernier maintained that 'after leaving Lahore and the Kingdom of Kashmir . . . all the women are naturally unprovided with hair on any part of the body'.

Baelz states that the mons veneris of Japanese women is flat and covered with sparse and coarse pubic hair. Doenitz found absolute hairlessness in a surprisingly large number of cases. But this is not considered an attraction by the Japanese, for one of their most offensive terms of insult is *kawaragé*, or 'hair like a brick' (i.e., with a vulva as bald and hard as any brick).

Stratz had the opportunity of examining over 2,300 native women of Java. He wrote:

> The body has generally very little hair. Eyebrows are thin and narrow. The genital and axillary hair is apt to be artificially plucked out, as can be told from the hard surface of the parts. A hirsute mons veneris is rare. In cases where the genital hair has not been removed, it is apt to curl slightly and be lighter in tint than the hair of the head.

The Bushwoman who was celebrated and depicted as the 'Hottentot Venus' had short, woolly tufts, and the same was the case with Afandi, a Bushwoman on whom Luschka and Görtz made a post-mortem and reported fully.

Bässler referred to the genital hair of the native women of the Bismarck Archipelago in an address to the Anthropological Society of Berlin. He stated that the heavy growth was extremely conspicuous, as the hair was usually dyed red like the locks around their faces. The women wiped their hands on their pubic hair when they were soiled or damp, as we are accustomed to use towels.

FOLKLORE

Traditional opinion has always accepted profuse hair in these regions as a sign of strong sexual instincts and functions, and lack of hair as a sign of sterility in women. These opinions can be contrasted with those expressed in folklore and legend. Scientific observations were not always of value in the past!

Among the Siberian Tungus, according to Georgi, thick pubic hair is considered a 'monstrous growth' and attributed to evil spirits. The husband of a woman with such an affliction is entitled forthwith to divorce her.

In Serbia, if a peasant child falls very ill and witchcraft is suspected, a threefold fumigation is performed with hairs shorn from the armpits and genitals of both parents. And the following exorcism is uttered: 'Flee thou away, o weird one and born of a weird one, thy place is not here! Father and Mother created this life and defend it now with this burnt offering of hair and banish all harm from it, for it has no place here! Flee thou away, thy place is not here!' (F. S. Krauss).

Another form of sympathetic magic is associated with pubic hair on the Moluccan Archipelago. Riedel reports that on Serang, Eetar and the Kei Islands, the girls give their sweethearts a few of their hairs from head and pubes as love tokens. This gift is reported as an infallible means to keep a lover faithful and devoted.

Genital and pubic hairs are also remedies against evil spirits. Ribbe says of the Aru Islanders:

> Men, women and children wear charms and amulets hung round their necks to banish sickness and evil spirits. These amulets are little bags or pouches hung on thongs and containing such *pomali* (tabooed) objects as curiously shaped and coloured pebbles, pearls, animals' gallstones, pubic hair from women, and so forth.

viii. The Hottentot Apron

The inner lips or nymphae in women of the Bushfolk and Hottentots are extremely and conspicuously long and pendant. There has been much description and discussion of this peculiarity, which is known as the Hottentot Apron or, in French, the *tablier*.

The early travellers gave accounts of it. Thus W. ten Rhyne described the protuberant nymphae as *dactyliformes*. Blumenbach rejected this statement as an invention, but Lesueur, Sparrmann, Barrow, Péron and others confirmed ten Rhyne's account. It appears from their testimony that the 'apron' consisted in a typical hypertrophy of the inner lips up to 7 inches (18 cm) in extent, and that the prepuce of the clitoris sometimes was involved in this excessive enlargement.

Le Vaillant was the first to propound the theory that the Hottentot Apron was not wholly 'natural' in such extreme cases, but partly 'acquired' or 'artificial'.

Cuvier described the so-called Hottentot Venus and so did Johannes Müller.

She was not a genuine Hottentot, but a Bushwoman, whom a Dutchman had brought to Paris with him and who died there in 1816. Cuvier found that the upper portions of the apron in her case were hypertrophied parts of both clitoris and inner labia, but the pendant elongated portions were labia alone. Virey reported on the post-mortem of this woman:

> The apron is nothing but the two nymphae which are elongated and hang down on either side, protruding from the shrivelled and hardly perceptible labia majora. The nymphae are about two inches long and hide the vagina and urethral orifice; they do not disappear into the perineum, but hang freely and can be turned back like ear flaps.

For some years, a Bushwoman named Afandi had allowed herself to be exhibited in Central Europe, and when she died Luschka made a careful autopsy and anatomical report on her, with illustrations. There was complete correspondence with the cases described by Cuvier and J. Müller as regards the labia majora.

Merensky, a Superintendent of Missions who lived and worked for years among the natives of South Africa, told the Berlin Anthropological Society:

> The Basuto and other African tribes know how to produce artificially enlarged labia minora. The necessary manipulations are performed by the older girls on the younger from their earliest years, as soon as they go together to gather wood or roots, i.e., almost daily. The parts are pulled and twisted and subsequently wrapped round little sticks and twigs.

In the South Seas, this anomaly is also not unknown. Finsch gives an account of the elaborate sexual practices and preliminaries of the natives of Ponapé, one of the Caroline group:

> Very long and pendulous labia minora are considered particularly attractive in women. They are deliberately produced and cultivated from early childhood by manipulations performed by elderly men who have become impotent. These manipulations are continued till the approach of puberty. At the same time and as part of the same training, the clitoris is not only subjected to prolonged friction, but also to suction, and a certain large kind of ant (native to the islands) is applied to this region in order that its sting may produce a brief but acute and not unpleasant stimulation.

Among certain American Indians, there would seem to be similar habits. The Mandan women are said to 'deform their genitals artificially', and among the Hidatsa and Crows, both inner and outer labia are elongated in accordance with custom, according to Prince M. zu Wied.

Dr M. Bartels is emphatically of the opinion that the Hottentot Apron is not by any means such a rarity, even in Central Europe, as medical men have thought. However, he maintains that the reported cases have all been in women who were not averse to 'masturbatory stimuli'. Schröder, the famous Berlin gynaecologist, concurs in this view.

Bartels is further of the opinion that artificial enlargements through manipulation never equal the dimensions of the real 'apron' – though, of course, it is not disputed that this may owe something to the manipulations of the women. On the whole, the German editors are of the opinion – shared by G. Fritsch – that the Hottentot Apron is really a racial peculiarity.

ix. Clitoral Excision

One of the Greek papyri in the British Museum (dated around 163 BC) contains a passage of some interest. In it Harmais, a recluse and mendicant connected with the Serapeum of Memphis, tells of a girl, Tathemis, who earns money by begging. From this money she has saved 1,300 drachmas, which she has given into the charge of Harmais. However, her mother, Nephoris, tells Harmais that her daughter has now reached the age at which circumcision is usual and that as she is now entering womanhood she ought to be provided with dress and dowry. Accordingly she persuades Harmais to hand over the money. Trouble is caused when Tathemis discovers what has happened and demands the return of her money.

This passage is of interest because it suggests that while male circumcision was reserved for the priestly and military castes in Egypt, excision was practised on all women when they were of age to receive their dowries. Herodotus informs us that no woman held any priestly office in Egypt, so we must conclude that excision or female circumcision was either practised on all girls at puberty or was a privilege of those who were reared on the sacred precincts of the Temple of Serapis.

Excision is not confined to Mohammedan East Africa. In Central Africa it is practised among the Wasambara and in the Mahenge district; in the west among the Negroes of Benin, Sierra Leone, Accra and the Congo; among the Fulah, Susu and Mandingo; in Bambuk, Old Calabar and Loanda; and in the south-east among the Wa-Kuafi and Masai, as well as some Bechuana tribes of the south.

Brehm, in discussion with Ploss, expressed the view that excision is intended to set bounds to the extremely active sexual impulse of the women of African race. Other authorities hold that the purpose is mainly *aesthetic* because the labia minora and clitoris are apt to attain unpleasing and inconvenient proportions.

Variations of excision are also practised in Egypt, Nubia, Abyssinia, in Sennar and its environs, in the Sudan and among many tribes such as the Galla, Agau and Gonga. Excision is likewise said to be customary in the smaller oases of the Libyan Desert, and among Arabs the exclamation: 'Oh, son of an uncircumcised woman!' is one of the deepest affronts in their huge vocabulary of insults, according to Wilken.

Bruce of Kinnaird holds that the exceptional development of the clitoris among the Abyssinians was regarded as a positive obstacle to coitus and birth, and that because the increase of the people was considered most essential, the clitoris was always mutilated both there and in adjacent lands. He adds that there was no definite date for the operation but that it was always performed before marriageable age.

Bruce goes on to relate that Christian missionaries forbade their Abyssinian converts to practise excision as they thought it 'a Jewish rite'. The result was that the natural structure of the girls so repelled the men that they would not marry and fewer children were begotten, or they married 'heretics' and unbelievers who had been excised, rather than good Catholic Copts, and lost their faith. The College of Cardinals *de propaganda fide* in Rome sent skilled surgeons to inquire into and report on the matter. On their return, the surgeons declared that either climatic or other causes had so altered the genital anatomy of the women of Abyssinia and such parts that they were very unlike the women of other countries, and that their natural structure caused repugnance which prevented the purpose of marriage. Rome then gave way on this point, but the girls' mothers had to make a solemn repudiation of any 'Jewish propaganda' in excision before it was agreed that this 'obstacle to marriage' must not on any account be preserved. In the course of time, all Abyssinian Christians adopted excision, which takes place by means of a knife or razor when the girl is eight years old.

Finally, the custom has also been found among the Malays of the Archipelago and the Kamchadale; the South American Indians of Peru; the Omagua, the Campa and the Pano; and among those living on the Ucayali River. In Ecuador, natives of the Pano linguistic stock were visited in the eighteenth century by the missionary Francis Xavier Veigl, who learnt that they had been in the habit of circumcising their girls to make them, so it was said, more competent in fulfilling their natural duties.

THE OPERATION

Female circumcision is generally termed excision. It consists in the shearing of the inner lips and a portion of the clitoris with knives of metal or stone. There are, however, great differences of procedure in different races.

Sometimes both labia and clitoris are mutilated, sometimes only the labia, sometimes only the prepuce.

In Arabia, clitoridectomy is performed a few weeks after birth (Niebuhr); among the Somali between three and four years of age (Paulitschke); in Nubia, Sumatra and India in early childhood (Russegger); among the Fulah in West Africa, soon after birth; and among the Abyssinians, the Galla and the Kaffitscho within the first year (Bieber).

On Ceram Laut and Gorong, Riedel found clitoridectomy practised between seven and ten years of age with very festive ceremonial. Death from haemorrhage afterwards was 'not infrequent', but the victims had the satisfaction of entering Mohammed's Seventh Heaven. The operation was performed by the wife of the priest and the girls were bathed afterwards.

The Chuncho and Campa tribes on the Ucayali River practise excision on girls at ten years of age. There is a seven-day festival for all the neighbours, who assemble with dance and song and copious draughts of chicha, an intoxicant brewed from manioc. On the eighth day, the girl is mercifully stupefied by a large drink of this powerful narcotic, and the operation is performed by a woman who staunches the bleeding by rinsing and pouring water on the wound. The songs and dances recommence and the girl is laid in a hammock and borne in triumph from hut to hut. She is considered a grown woman after her operation, according to Grandidier.

Duhousset gives this description of what is done in Egypt:

> Female circumcision consists merely in the removal of the clitoris and is performed on children between nine and twelve years old. The operator, who is generally a barber by profession, rubs ashes on his fingers, grips the clitoris, draws it forward to its full length and shears it with a single razor stroke. Ashes are then sprinkled on the wound to staunch bleeding and it heals after some days of complete repose.
>
> I have both seen instances and heard statements from these barber–surgeons of their laxity and carelessness in operating. The full ritual limits of the mutilation should, strictly speaking, include the nymphae from the level of the clitoris and almost to their junction with the inner fold of the labia majora. Their mutilated remnants then form a cicatrization, rigid and retracted, round a gaping vulva in the circumcised fellah woman. The effect is singular.

Baumstark mentions customary extirpation of the clitoris among the Warangi of East Africa in the Masai territory, when the girls are between six and eight years old. Expert women perform the ablation with little knives of special shape. The girls live apart for a while in a special building. Merker writes of the Masai custom:

As soon as the young girl perceives from certain physical signs that she is about to become a woman, she returns to her mother's hut though she has previously lived in the Bachelors' House in complete and uncontrolled liberty . . .

No member of the opposite sex may approach the places where youths and maidens are respectively circumcised. On the previous day, the girl's mother crops her head and throws the hair under the skins of her couch. All the child's ornaments are removed and she is attired in a long loose garment made by her mother. The mother calls on her child's courage and obedience and washes her genital organs in cold water to deaden the pain. The operation is a simple ablation or removal of the clitoris performed with a sharp piece of iron ore (*ol moronja*) such as is used for shaving. [Among the Bushmen of the Kalahari Desert, according to Dornan, a stone knife is used to perforate the clitoris.] Then the little wound is washed with milk, which, along with the blood, falls to the ground; no styptics are used. The girl remains secluded in her mother's hut till she is healed; she is termed *es siboli* during this seclusion.

The boys adorn themselves with birds' claws and ostrich plumes, while the girls wear wreaths of grass round their brow and stick a single ostrich feather through the circlet in front. Both sexes smear their faces with white clay. The women of the village hold a feast among themselves. The girl's father slays an ox, her mother brews honey mead for them.

The name for a circumcised girl and a young wife is the same: *es siengiki*, and, indeed, as soon as the girl's suitor learns that she has recovered, he hands over to her father the last instalment of the bride-price and the wedding may then take place lawfully.

The Wolof make a festival of circumcision. The whole village assembles, dressed in their best, to the sound of the drum and an ear-splitting orchestra. The girls are clothed with all available splendour and hung with all the family trinkets, and are led through the village in procession, then back again to the square or open space, where a great dance is kept up for hours, all taking part. They are then led into the blacksmith's hut by the old women of the tribe, for it is his wife's privilege to perform the rite, when dawn grows grey. Each young girl takes her seat on a block of wood set at a convenient distance from the wall of the hut, leans back so that her body is supported firmly, and spreads her thighs open as far as she can. The woman operator grips the inner labia between the fingers and thumb of her left hand and slices them off with an old knife which strongly resembles a saw. A plaster is then applied. The girl remains in her father's hut for a week, then for another three or four weeks she goes to the stream, limping on crutches, to bathe herself in the ritual prescribed. At the expiration of this time the bandage is removed.

Dingwall adds:

> Removal of the clitoris has long been advocated by certain writers for masturbation in girls and for such female ailments as pruritus. In 1867 and 1868 the English medical world was convulsed by revelations concerning the opinions and practices of Isaac B. Brown, who performed the operation at his London Surgical Home as a means of curing forms of insanity, epilepsy and hysteria, as well as masturbation. It appeared that not only was the clitoris excised but the nymphae were clipped to their base, and the whole vulva cauterized. The case excited enormous interest and Mr Brown was removed from the Obstetrical Society of London. However, many of his grateful patients, who believed that they had been saved from insanity by his ministrations, combined with others to present him with a silver dessert service in token of his 'singular success in the treatment of female diseases'.

x. Infibulation

The operation which has been termed 'infibulation' or 'sewing up' or, better, 'occlusion' stands in close association with excision of the labia or clitoris, but the two are not identical.

Infibulation does not necessarily imply surgical sutures. Moreover, it appears really to be a specifically African practice, whereas excision is not limited to that continent. North-eastern and Central Africa are, so far, the only regions known to us in which infibulation has been commonly practised (cf. Freimark).

Excision does not necessarily imply infibulation, but infibulation (of one kind at least) must in all circumstances imply excision, and extensive excision, before there can be raw surfaces sufficiently large to form a solid scar. Although the method of executing this mutilation varies in different tribes, the final results appear fairly constant. Either by surgical stitches or – as seems more frequent – by appropriate bandages and attitudes held for days at a time, the raw surfaces are brought into close contact with one another and unite to form a solid scar. The excision is so arranged that this hard scar of connective tissue occludes the whole vulva with the exception of the urinary opening (Fig. 5).

Among the Bedouins of the western Baiyuda Steppe, north of Khartoum, the girls are infibulated between the ages of five and eight years. In Kordofan, excision and stitching are inflicted at eight years; among the Harari at

Fig. 5   Third-stage infibulation in a Danakil girl (right): the operation is finished. Compare with the appearance of the normal vulva, left (Mus. f. Völkerk., Dresden)

seven. Accounts differ about the Somali: some say from eight to ten but Paulitschke says from three to four. Lanzi specifies the third year as that which prevails for infibulation among the Danakil.

In the Middle Ages of the Christian era, Maqrizi related the customs of the Beja. He said that they cut off the inner lips in young girls and then sewed the rimae pudendi together. And this practice still prevails among the tribes south of the Nile Cataracts, the Galla, Somali, Harari and women of Masowah.

Among the Somali and Harari the preliminary excision removes a substantial part of the clitoris and abrades the labia majora or 'outer vulva'. Probably the inner lips or nymphae are cut away at the same time. The operation is performed by skilled women and followed at once by a real 'stitching', according to Paulitschke. The materials used for the sutures are cotton thread, horse-hair or fibres. Only a small part of the vulval cleft remains unstitched. The girls have to rest for several days with bound feet and thus the abraded surfaces unite and are scarred over.

King says that the Somali operate on their girls at eight years old and sometimes earlier. There is always clitoridectomy as well as infibulation.

The clitoris is drawn to its full length and cut off and the membranes of the labia scraped raw with knives, leaving only a very minute section free on either side in the centre of the vulva. Then the labia are pressed together and sutured with two or three stitches, after which the girl's knees and thighs are firmly bound together. The healing process takes a month and is accompanied by fumigations.

Vita Hassan writes as follows about the Sudanese women, after mentioning that the female circumcision common to all Islam means excision of part of the clitoris:

> In the Sudan, most of the tribes extend this operation to a hideous mutilation. This is performed on children six years old with all the festivities customary at a wedding. Clitoris, labia majora and the most projecting edges of the inner lips are shorn off with a razor, leaving the pudendal region a bare flat wound. Then the raw edges are firmly sutured together, leaving one small slit into which a tiny tube of cane is slipped for urination. After some days have elapsed, the edges unite, the wound is cicatrized and closes and the tube can be removed. The woman has become a monster and the sacred and accursed rite has been fulfilled.

Among the Kikuyu, Kenya, the operations on girls have recently been described by Leakey and by local missionaries. The ceremonies are of the well-recognized type and a large crowd assembles for the purpose of witnessing them. The operator is an old woman who passes from girl to girl and performs the operation with what Bowie describes as a 'crude small knife not unlike a safety razor blade'. (See Fig. 6, for which we are indebted to the kindness of Miss A. Brown.)

What is the purpose of this mutilation? There can hardly be any doubt of the answer. Infibulation is performed simply and solely in order to enforce complete abstinence from sexual intercourse on the girls who are subjected to the operation.

Werne is quite correct in pointing out that infibulation and cicatrization are indeed a more certain means of compulsion than any of the locks and springs of the 'girdles of chastity' with which our knightly forefathers in Europe clothed their wives before they themselves rode forth on Crusade or other adventures (see 'Chastity', Chapter VI). Werne quotes the rejoinder, half plea, half excuse, with which these native girls often reply to a stranger's caresses and attempts at approach: 'El bab makful' – 'The gate is locked!'

King, however, states that this purpose is not invariably attained. Although slave-traders often have the operation performed on their freshly captured 'wares' in order to sell them more profitably, even they are sometimes subject to loss on that account. He also mentions that among the

Fig. 6 a) Kenya girls about to be excised, Fort Hall, Izera Areas, Kenya;
b) the interlocked position for the operation; c) the excision in progress;
d) after the operation (photos A. Brown)

Somali, so far from infibulation always compelling abstinence, a form of incomplete intercourse is known to take place for money (twelve dollars).

xi. Defibulation

The almost complete occlusion of the genital cleft in women who have been infibulated makes normal sexual intercourse quite impossible, as has already been explained. Impregnation, however, may sometimes occur as a result of attempted approach and accident. But such impregnation and gestation cannot lead to a normal delivery without further operative interference. So, in order to make both functional intercourse and motherhood possible, the girls whose genital organs have been closed and cicatrized must be defibulated – in King's expressive phrase – or, we might say, ripped open. Let us see what various authorities say of these further operations.

Cailliaud writes of the Sennar women:

Before the consummation of marriage, the unnatural adhesions must be removed. If peril to life ensues, razor and red-hot irons are to hand. The sensibilities of these races seem too much obliterated, too primitive for them to attach any weight to the exquisite suffering and the serious and inevitable injuries of such procedures – procedures invented and imposed by the dominant sex in order to guarantee for themselves the enjoyment of that virginity which is apt in other lands to be so evanescent.

However that may be, it is a serious enough affair to put the girl in a fit state to fulfil her conjugal duties. If there is a woman who, through lack of means, has been unable to prepare herself, then the husband must do what he can. If he succeeds in impregnating her, which is difficult enough, then she has the right to insist on the services of one of the older women, well versed in the cruel trade, who may be able to break down those obstacles which hinder the processes of childbirth. Moreover, the young widow who cherishes a desire to marry again does not hesitate to submit a second time to the operation, although such cases are not common.

Vita Hassan says of the Sudanese natives:

The expectant mother has to face further mutilation. The child at birth cannot pass the cicatrizations in the normal way, so the muscles from groin to reins are severed in order to liberate the infant. And then this laceration is sewn together like the pre-marital wound and the woman is once more impenetrable. Some time after delivery a new *ssehama* (the name of this mutilation) makes the wife and mother available once more.

King gives further particulars about the exact procedure among the Somali:

> In the town of Zayla, an elderly and expert woman of a strange tribe – *midg'an* – accompanies the bridal pair to their chamber. This woman performs the operation on the bride, who is held fast by the husband, so that her convulsive struggles are in vain. Then the woman leaves the room or tent, and the kinsfolk and acquaintances outside the door dance, sing, scream and clap their hands in order to drown the bride's shrieks of pain. And in the interior of Somaliland, the young husband himself generally makes the necessary incision while two of his near male relatives hold down the bride.

Hartmann writes: 'Slaves, too, are infibulated thus. There are cruel masters – and some of them are Europeans! – who have had this thing done even twice or thrice to the same women who have been their mistresses – and then they have sold them.'

Werne says of the tribes immediately south of the First Cataract of the Nile:

> When the girl whose virginity has been preserved in such a revolting manner becomes a bride, further indecent cruelties are practised. One of the women who perform infibulation visits the bridegroom immediately before the marriage in order to obtain exact measurements of his member. She then makes to measure a sort of phallus of clay or wood and by its aid she incises the scar for a certain distance, leaving the instrument – wrapped round with a rag – in the wound in order to keep the edges from adhering again. Then the wedding feast is celebrated with hideous din, the man leads his bride home – every step she takes means pain – and without giving the fresh wound time to heal or scar, he exercises his marital privileges.
>
> Before a child can be born, the vulva has to be opened again throughout its length, but, after delivery, infibulation is again inflicted, according to the husband's order, either to the original or other dimensions: and so the process continues.

CHAPTER III

Beauty

Anthropologists have endeavoured to analyse and define beauty. Cordier, in 1860, maintained – in a thesis presented to the Anthropological Society of Paris – that there was no absolute beauty in human physique, but a variety of racial types and ideals, and that no race could therefore claim a monopoly of beauty.

Delaunay disputed this on the basis of the so-called organotrophic laws formulated by Claude Bernard, who believed that every organ and portion of the human form possessed a special optimum of development and that harmonious proportion and relation of these organs constituted beauty in each human individual.

The aesthetic and ideal aspects of women's bodies have naturally been dealt with inexhaustibly. According to Schopenhauer, the 'beauty' of woman – 'the squat, narrow-shouldered, wide-hipped and short-legged sex' – is naught but a delusion of the 'masculine brain clouded by the fumes of instinct'. But the majority of men remain of a different opinion.

i. The Female Ideal

Many of the distinctive differences between women and men in physique are precisely those which appear especially desirable and lovely to men.

Herr Ernst Loether, of Pössneck in Thuringia, was kind enough to forward Dr Max Bartels the subjoined extract from a collection of German humour and folk sayings on the topic of women's beauty. It appears in many versions in European literature from the Middle Ages till today:

> A lovely maid, I've heard it said,
> Should get from Prague her little head,
> Two sparkling eyes from France,
> From Austria her red mouth,
> Her snow-white hands from Cologne,
> Her slim loins from Brabant,
> Her narrow feet from England's seas,
> Her small round breasts from the Low Countries,
> From Spain her body, from Flanders her arms,
> And her round buttocks from Swabia –
> She who hath all these is worth all gifts.

It would be of greater interest for us, as anthropologists, to be able to delve into the descriptive ecstasies of more primitive and ancient peoples. Unfortunately, we have only few and fragmentary sources, for this mine of human material is hardly worked at all, even in the most recondite anthologies and the most voluminous collections. Nearly all the available examples are of Asiatic origin. The Sanskrit, for instance, provides these verses:

> A face that mocks the moon; eyes that are fit to make water-lilies ashamed; a skin hued more wondrously than gold; dense hair like a cloud of black bees; breasts more splendid than the bosses on the brow of elephants; heavy hips and the sparkling gentleness of speech: these are the natural adornment and graces of a maiden.

> Her face is almond-eyed and luminous as autumn moons; her arms slide softly from her shoulders, her ribs are narrow but carry closely set, prominent breasts; her flanks are smooth and as though polished, her waist may be clasped by two hands, her loins have large buttocks and her feet curved toes. Even as a dancer might wish, so has her body been framed.

The poetry of the Ancient Hebrews, as preserved in the Old Testament, has similar descriptions of and prescriptions for feminine beauty, especially in that great 'Song of Songs which is Solomon's'. The allied Arabic poets also praise the beauty of their beloved, although in verse peculiarly hard for Europeans to translate because of the intricate rhyming and perpetual plays on words. Hariri of Basra, who flourished at the end of the eleventh century of the Christian era, praised his love as 'dark red of lips, hard as cliffs, straight as a tree and in pride incomparable'. T. A. Hartmann quotes another passage by Hariri in praise of 'teeth gleaming like pearls, haildrops or bubbles of rare wine and white as the buds of camellias or palm blossom'.

Baron Junker von Langegg quotes a Japanese on the ideal of his race to this effect:

> To begin with the head: it must not be either too large or too small. Great black eyes surrounded with a fringe of black lashes and over-arched by sharply drawn black brows. An oval face, delicately pale with the faintest trace of rosy colour in the cheeks. A straight, high-bridged nose. A small, symmetrical mouth with fresh lips, that sometimes part and show even white teeth. A narrow forehead on which the long black hair grows in a symmetrical arch. A rounded throat and well-developed but not too plump figure with moderately rounded breasts. Slender hips and small, but not too thin, hands and feet.

There is a striking proverb for exceptional beauty suggesting uncanny delicacy and glitter: 'Like a fairy, with a skin smooth as ice and bones like precious gems.'

Oberländer introduces us to the Singhalese ideal:

Hair to her knees, with curly ends; brows arched like the rainbow, eyes like blue sapphires or the azure blossoms of the manilla. A hooked nose; lips coral-red; breasts conical and firm as coconuts and a waist almost slender enough for a hand to span. Broad hips, tapering limbs and feet without any arch to their soles; the surface of the whole body smoothly firm and rounded with no protruding muscles or bony angles.

The Gypsies have love songs with highly fantastic similes. Heinrich von Wlislocki quotes: 'Her feet are flowers by the wayside, her shoulders white wheaten bread, her eyes are juicy grapes, her lips are blossoms.'

The ancient national epic of the Finns, the *Kalevala*, also has remarkable similes:

> She is like the ripe cranberry,
> The wild strawberry on the hillside,
> Like the cuckoo on the branches,
> Like the nestling in the ash tree,
> Fluttering wings among the birch leaves,
> Like the white throat on the maple!
> Never from the German cities,
> Nor from the Esthonian seashores,
> Came a maiden of such beauty,
> Came a swan of such resplendence . . .

Morice has described the ideal beauty of the Tinne tribe of North American Indians (Athabascan) as having an oval face; large dark eyes; very long, thinly pencilled eyebrows; rich, dense hair; a low forehead; a clear skin, as light as possible; chubby cheeks; full, well-developed chest and large breasts; and, above all, broad hips. The two chief charms are accounted length of face from hair to chin and width of hip. When two women have a quarrel they abuse one another in terms such as 'Lynx!' and 'Blade of grass!' – for the lynx is wide-faced and the blade of grass extremely slender.

J. B. von Spix and von Martius have cited passages from the songs and sayings of the Mauhe Indians of South America:

> I like not her
> That hath her legs too slender
> For fear they twine about me
> As doth a writhing serpent.

> I like not her
> That hath her hair too long
> For fear that it may cut me
> Like swordgrass in a thicket.

In 1884 a troupe of Australian Aborigines were brought to Berlin, where they were visited and studied by Rudolf Virchow. This great anthropologist emphasized his astonishment at the ease, directness and even beauty of movement in these members of a primitive race. He said: 'These women have such a graceful carriage of the head, such elegance of movement – whether of body or limbs – that they might have been brought up in the highest circles of our European society.'

RACIAL MIXTURE

The most trivial details of physique and appearance in persons of mixed race may be of high anthropological significance, and any accurate information on the subject must be recorded and taken into consideration.

The Javanese–European blend produces a conspicuously pretty half-caste, for it modifies the partly *retroussé* nose, the width of the smiling mouth and the peculiar slit of the narrow eyes. Schmarda praises the attractiveness of the half-caste Euro–Malayan woman. And there are extremely pretty women among the half-castes of European and Japanese parentage.

Berghaus praises the mulatto women of South America in comparison with the indolent, apathetic Brazilian women. He says they are incomparably more attractive than the white women, being full of gaiety and animation as well as grace of form.

Finsch found some beautiful girls among the Maori–European half-castes of New Zealand; but none who could be termed beautiful among the full-blooded aborigines.

The children of Europeans and Ponapé women from the Caroline Islands cannot be told apart from European girls, we are told, except by a slightly more swarthy complexion. Another crossing with the white race makes its offspring indistinguishable from full-blood Europeans in features or colouring. The same is said of the Samoan–European half-castes.

Nordenskiold is another witness to the attraction of the half-caste in another region, namely Greenland. He says: 'The women were neatly and carefully arrayed, and some half-caste girls with brown eyes and healthy, chubby, almost European features were rather pretty.'

In North-West America there are people of mixed blood often termed Bois Brûlés, the descendants of French trappers and explorers and the Indians of various stocks. The women of this half-breed race are, as a rule, whiter in colouring than the men and appear pale in comparison. Many of these *métis* have skins as delicate and white as European women, and regular, chiselled features, there being some truly classically lovely girls among them.

Steller writes as follows of the Kamchadale:

> Among the broad-faced women, there are beauties equal to the most admired Chinese womankind. But the daughters of Cossacks from Russia and native mothers are so comely that their beauty may well claim perfection. Their faces are commonly long and oval, and the blackness of their hair, eyes and brows, the whiteness, smoothness and delicacy of their skins, and the rosy pink of their cheeks give them a special charm. And they are notably ambitious, cunning and secret in their ways, know how to keep silent and are much given to the pleasures of love. Thus they captivate even such men as have kept free from illicit dalliance all the way from Moscow till they reached their country.

Of course, this physical improvement and attraction may not be absolute but relative and subjective. It may be an illusion of the white man because half-caste woman naturally approximates more to his own racial type. But there are two arguments against this view. Nordenskiold states that the Eskimo are now learning to regard their own type as less attractive and desirable; and Kropf says that the Ama-Xosa prefer the lighter skins and straighter features of the daughters of women of their own race by white fathers, and that such girls are much sought after. The same is reported in southern India.

THE CULTURAL EFFECT

Degeneration in a people produces slatternly and over-worked women without enough natural vitality to care for their appearance, and incessant hard work will tend to obliterate what is characteristically feminine in mind and physique.

If a people, after having enjoyed a high degree of culture and prosperity, sinks to a lower level, both mentally and materially, this degeneration will be plainly registered in the manners, habits and appearance of its women. Let us cite only one example from the many which history records.

In antiquity, Cyprus was a centre of civilization. The famous shrines of Aphrodite, the Goddess of Love, brought women from all Mediterranean lands to worship and to pray for what they most desired. Excavations have recently brought to light evidence of much prosperity and a comparatively high degree of culture; and the women of Cyprus must have shared in these good things both material and mental.

What is the case today? The main portion of the island, the fertility of which was once so renowned, has been laid waste, and many of its inhabitants are steeped in ignorance and poverty. Samuel White Baker depicts the apathy and misery of the women of Cyprus in 1879. He describes the crowd of women and children who surrounded him and his travelling companions on February 4th, when the temperature was too low to pitch a camp (43 degrees):

> They indulged their curiosity, shivering in light clothes of home-made cotton-stuffs. The children were generally pretty, and some of the younger women were good-looking; but there was a total neglect of physical appearance, which is a striking characteristic of the Cypriot females . . . in Cyprus there is a distressing absence of the wholesome vanity that should induce attention to dress and cleanliness. The inelegance of their costume gives an unpleasant peculiarity to their figures – the whole crowd of girls and women looked as though they were about to become mothers.

Finally, we must not overlook the abnormally early physical decline of primitive women owing to underfeeding and poor living conditions. Reichard thus describes the pitiful effects on women among the Wanyamwezi (Lake Tanganyika):

> The wife and mother ages at twenty-five or even twenty, as a result of the burden of work, and is transformed; her features are deformed and wrinkled, her breasts become slack like pendulous bags and hang almost to her waist; the abdomen is either enormously fat or hollow, and the buttocks are very prominent. The arms are extremely thick and muscular as a result of constant grinding of corn.

Vortisch gives similar descriptions of the Negresses of the Gold Coast; and Müller of the Australian black women.

In fact, the more degraded and unfortunate her social and material position, the earlier the advent of old age in woman. This rule holds good throughout the world.

ii. Painting

All human races try to increase and accentuate the physical characteristics which they consider beautiful, or to produce them by artificial means. Painting of the skin and body is one method.

Sometimes the whole body is smeared with painted designs, as in many Indian tribes, extinct and surviving. But often these designs are concentrated on the face and their meaning is not only aesthetic but ritual as well.

For instance, in some tribes of American Indians the women paint their faces black when their husbands and fathers die. Scott reports that the Li in Hainan have the custom of painting the special sign of the bridegroom's ancestors on the bride's face on the wedding day, so that she may be recognized as one of his tribe. The Hindus wear the symbols of various sects and cults smeared on their foreheads. Moszkorski writes that in the central regions of Dutch New Guinea white paint means peace paint. Bieber reports that blue stains on the lower lip are tokens of marriage among the Kaffitscho women in Abyssinia. Roesicke mentions smears of chalk or white fluid as signs of mourning among the natives of the stretch above Tambunum on the banks of the Sepik in New Guinea.

As a rule, however, paint is a cosmetic among primitive peoples. That is, it is used in order to attract and adorn.

The Andamanese smear their faces and sometimes limbs and bodies as well with broad white streaks. The same is the case with the painted eyebrows and eyelids of many Asiatic women. Vámbéry reports that among the Crimean Tatars, henna (*Lawsonia inermis*) is even more popular than in Turkey, Persia and the Caucasus. The women rub it into their eyebrows, fingernails, palms and necks, and even tint the glossy black of their hair with its red shimmer. This was the custom among the Scythians, according to Herodotus, for the women made themselves cosmetics of powdered cedar and incense. Unfortunately, the smell of henna is offensive to Europeans.

The Javanese and other peoples of the Malay Archipelago stain their teeth black and file them. They despise the white teeth of European women: 'Just like a dog's.' Similarly, according to Joest, certain Madagascan women file their front teeth to points like a shark's (Fig. 7). Mondière says that the Annamite women of Cochin-China not only blacken their teeth by chewing betel nut, but also by the deliberate application of certain drugs. He informs us that the customs here have changed and extended their scope, for it was formerly only from the date of her first menstrual period that the Annamite girl began to blacken her teeth; now she does so from the date of her first sexual intercourse, that is to say, on the average, three years earlier.

Of course ritual, ceremonial or cosmetic paint is not confined to women and girls. Among many tribes men make far more use of this habit, but probably very rarely for purposes of decoration: it is rather to appal their enemies in battle that they decorate themselves thus.

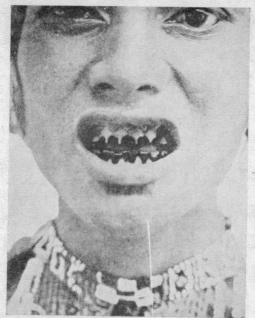

Fig. 7 A Bogobo woman from Mindanao with filed teeth (after Buschan)

iii. Tattooing

Tattooing is a more intensive form of adornment than paint, for the designs are not smeared on to the skin but indelibly stamped into it. Often the designs are very curious and exhibit a high degree of skill in execution, as in Thomson's illustration of the art of tattoo on an Easter Island woman (Fig. 8). The word 'tattoo' itself (Polynesian *tatau*) means, originally, 'right', 'straight' or 'skilled'. As a rule – to which there are significant exceptions (for instance the Ainu, who tattoo women only) – wherever the custom of tattooing prevails, it is common to both sexes. But the patterns and positions differ markedly in men and women. We may regard the custom as often decorative in origin and intention; but the special directions and applications vary considerably. Above all, however, tattooing in many races is part of the discipline and ceremonies connected with puberty.

On many South Sea islands the instruments for tattooing are small hooks with slender blades of bone or shell and serrated edges. These are pressed against the skin and driven in with slight hammer taps after having been

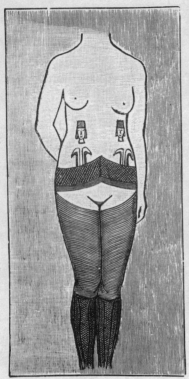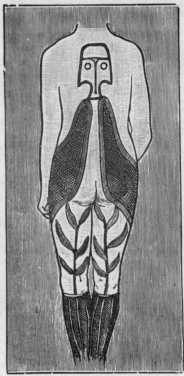

Fig. 8   Tattooed Easter Island woman, front and back (after Thomson)

smeared with the colouring preparation in use. The Japanese and Burmese use needles, sometimes in rows, like the teeth of a comb. Among the Caraya Indians of South America, the design is traced, cut in with a sharp stone and staunched with cotton waste and the juice of the *genipapo* plant.

Among many South Sea Island tribes, tattoo marks are a privilege of the noble and freeborn; slaves may not be tattooed. There is an interesting passage on this topic in Charles Darwin's *Journal of Researches* which also suggests that tattoo marks are perhaps meant to conceal the wrinkles of age.

There is an elaborate tattoo ritual on the Pelew Islands, according to Kubary. The little girls tattoo all sorts of patterns on each others' legs, which are then covered on their hind surface from the ankles to the gluteocrural fold with elaborate patterns. The front of the limbs and the buttocks themselves are left untattooed. Then, with puberty, comes the ritual tattooing of the genital region (see also 'Tattooing of the Genitalia', below). This is a narrow line on both sides of the vulva and extending to the anus. The hitherto untattooed portions of the lower limbs may also be covered with a network of stripes which resemble black tights.

According to Bertherand, the Kabyle girls have a small blue tattoo mark in the shape of a cross on the forehead between the eyebrows, on the cheek, or above one nostril. But this is obliterated before marriage by the *Taleb*, who uses chalk or black soap for the purpose.

In the Moluccan Archipelago breasts are marked with complicated tattoo designs. On the island of Ceram dots are arranged in curved lines, repeating the natural convexity of the mammary outline; while on Tenimber, a star-shaped pattern is preferred with straight or regularly curved rays, and the centre of the star is the nipple.

Abyssinian women, according to Bieber, tattoo their necks 'at marriage-able age'. The skilled operator is called *nekash*, the process, *je anget nekassat*. Petroleum is rubbed into the skin and the patterns pricked with needles.

Friedrich Müller writes of the New Zealand Maori: 'Among the women, the lips and the curve from the corners of the mouth to the chin are tattooed always and the arms and breasts sometimes, but not invariably. As the girl is tattooed, her playfellows sing as follows:

'Lie down, my daughter, to be painted,
  So that thy chin may be adorned!
So that, when thou enterest a strange house,
  They shall not say: "Whence comes this ugly woman?"
So that thou shalt be fair and seemly,
  And when thou comest to the feast,
They shall not say: "Whence comes this scarlet-lipped woman?"
  Come, suffer us to tattoo thee
And make thee lovely!
  So that the slaves shall not say as thou passest by:
"Whence comes this red-chinned woman?"
  We tattoo thee, we adorn thee,
By the spirit of Hine-te-iwa-iwa,
  So that the shore spirit
May be sent from Rangi
  To the depths of the sea,
To the foaming wave!'

The Haida Indians of the Queen Charlotte Islands, off the coast of British Columbia, have their family totems tattooed just above and between the breasts, on the arms above the elbow, and backs of the hands, and just below the knees. Swan observed that during their tribal feasts the Haida men were quite naked and the women clothed only in a kirtle which reached from waist to knees, so that the tattoo marks were visible and proclaimed their rank and lineage to all.

Von Nordenskiold states that the primitive Eskimo women are profusely tattooed in designs somewhat resembling those usual among the Chukchee, with lampblack, fish-oil and graphite, and also comments on the pain experienced in the operation.

Among the Ainu of Yezo, according to von Brandt, women have blue beard-like tattoo marks round their mouths; these disfigurements are begun at about seven years of age and are gradually increased and extended.

TATTOOING OF THE GENITALIA

Tattooing of the visible portions of the external genitalia is, so far as we are aware, only done on certain South Sea islands. Both the well-known authorities on Pacific anthropology, Finsch and Kubary, have given accounts of this practice.

On Ponapé (Caroline Islands), the girls are elaborately tattooed. Kubary describes the tattooing process as very prolonged: it starts when the girl is between seven and eight years old and continues till about the age of twelve, when the hips and lower abdomen are dealt with. 'The adornment of the genitalia is so intricate and careful that both the labia majora and the vaginal orifice are tattooed.'

Kubary also contributes about the Pelew Islanders:

> So soon as the girl has intimate relations with men, she is decorated with the indispensable *telengékel* (tattooing), otherwise no man would ever look at her. The *telengékel* consists of a triangle which covers the mons veneris, and is bounded by a straight line (*gréel*). The area within the triangle is then filled out with black paint (*ogúttum*) and the base of the triangle which lies uppermost is finished off with a zigzag line. This line is known as *blasak*.

The same author states that the women of Núkuóro (Carolines) are less lavishly tattooed than on the Pelew group and Ponapé, but goes on to say:

> In spite of its sparseness, the tattoo patterns of Núkuóro are highly important, for all children born to women who have not been tattooed are put to death. Tattooing is the sign of maturity and membership of the community of women. It is, therefore, performed in company and forms one of the chief items of the Takotona festivities.

N. von Miklucho Maclay's observation confirms Kubary's in a striking manner. He says in a letter to Rudolf Virchow that in order to inspect their tattoo patterns he induced several girls to remove their *kariut* simultaneously, and was reminded of what Virchow said of tattooed nudity elsewhere: 'Modesty is not in any way offended by the sight.' At first glance, the girls seemed to be wearing triangles of some blue textile over the mons veneris.

iv. Scarification

Ritual scars are even more durable than tattoo marks, and just as tattoo marks excel paint in this respect, so tattooing in itself often causes such inflammation that ridged scars resembling keloids appear.

The women of Darfur and Kordofan rub salt into fresh tattoo wounds in order to produce such scars, which are considered attractions. Finsch saw similar scars on the native women of New Britain in the South Seas on thighs and buttocks. The necessary incisions are very painful and take months to heal. The Gilbert Island girls often inflict burns and scalds on themselves, for the scars are considered both beautiful in themselves and a test of high courage, according to Finsch. Avebury and Eyre describe the painful scraping and scarring of the backs of the young girls in the Australian Aboriginal tribes on the Murray River with sharp shells or flints. The Solomon Island women carve and scrape their whole bodies with sharp shells, often causing abscesses and even ulcers. But if the operation is successful, the results are considered supreme charms, according to Parkinson, and greatly raise the woman's bride-price.

Jourdran mentions the highly ornate incised patterns on the lower abdomen, pelvis and sacral region of a Malagasy woman ('*femme de Betsiléo*') which had been executed and endured solely in order to please her husband. There were eight rows of superposed incisions; the topmost row had 104 single strokes and the remaining seven rows 82 each.

A missionary records that he was told by a Magandja woman (Africa), whose body dripped with blood from fresh cuts into old tattoo marks (done in order to cause protuberant scars), that when they healed she would be the greatest beauty in her country. This woman's scars had special names according to their distribution and position.

Among various tribes of Equatorial Africa, tiny longitudinal incisions in the skin of the breasts are not uncommon, arranged in either vertical or diagonal rows. Joest says that the Basuto girls 'also disfigure their breasts, which are often very beautiful, by numbers of horizontal or vertical scars from incisions'.

The habit of scarification has survived among the Bush Negresses of

Surinam, according to Crevaux, who also found cases among Indian women in the north-east of South America, where incisions across the thighs signified the number of children born or, rather, sons.

Scars due to burns (branding) are intentionally inflicted in many cults and customs of the peoples of Hindustan, though mainly on men. But the girls who are consecrated to the temple service in the Bellary region are branded with hot brass instruments. One token or mark, the Chakra (wheel) token, is on the right shoulder, the second, or Chanka (snail-shell) token, on the left, and the third, also Chakra, just over the right breast (cf. Thurston).

The practice of scarification seems peculiar to coloured races and, indeed, mere tattoo marks would not always be strongly visible on a bronze skin. And the primary impulse seems to be the wish to beautify: to please either the eye or the sense of touch. For Fülleborn, in his inquiries among the natives of south-east Africa as to the reason why their women – especially in the Wayao and Makua tribes – were deeply incised and tattooed in the lower half of their bodies, received an illuminating answer: it was pleasanter for a man to stroke and feel an uneven surface than a smooth one.

But scarification may also be a token of mourning and bereavement. Thus Spencer and Gillen have testified that on the deaths of their kinsmen the Aboriginal Australian women often inflict wounds on themselves which leave permanent scars. In New Zealand, among the Maori, these scars are known as *tangi*, or 'dirges for the dead', according to Dieffenbach. (See also 'The Widow', Chapter VI.)

v. Depilation

Probably the favourite and most frequent method of treating, adorning or 'improving' the mons veneris is by the removal of the hair (depilation). Among Mohammedan peoples depilation is enjoined on all women as a ritual, but it is also found in non-Moslem races all over the earth in the most various and unlikely quarters and sections of the community.

Depilation was common in the ancient civilizations of Asia and Egypt, spreading thence to Greece and Italy. Aristophanes tells us that in Hellas depilation was mainly practised by hetaerae and brothel prostitutes; but the custom spread to the women of the ordinary upper class in Athenian homes. In Rome, Martial taunted his countrymen with resorting to depilation in order to make themselves appear younger than they were. Many later writers record the persistence of the habit in Italy, probably for purposes of cleanliness and protection, according to Rosenbaum.

We may say that, on the whole, the available information tends to show that depilation is generally practised by such people and races as are not extremely hairy by nature. Exceptions to this rule are probably ritual in origin, i.e., interwoven with religious or magical concepts.

Epp declares that Malay women in the Dutch East Indies depilate themselves so thoroughly that the mons veneris appears quite hairless. But this is not a universal habit among all Malay women, nor have the Chinese women resident in the Malay Peninsula adopted this habit. There are apparently great differences of custom here.

Jacobs mentions the same customs as occasional among the Achinese women, and Roth among the Dyak women of Borneo, who use little pincers for the purpose.

Maurel gives these particulars of the Cambodian women: that the mons veneris was 'generally shaved; but the women who sought the company of Europeans easily gave up the custom'.

The Annamese women depilate themselves carefully, as do most of the Cambodian women, according to Jacobus X., who adds that in southern China (Canton, etc.) it is practised only among prostitutes.

Krämer says depilation of the pubes and armpits is customary in Samoa.

On the Guinea Coast of Africa, Monrad records of the young Negresses that the unmarried pluck out their genital hair; the wives let it grow freely.

Professor A. Hörll, of the State School of Talca in Chile, was good enough to supply Bartels with the following information, dated November 18th, 1907: 'During my frequent excursions and wanderings through the territory and settlements of the Chilean Araucanians, I have, so far as I was able to observe, found depilation of the mons to be very frequent, if not general . . . the younger women . . . simply pluck out the hairs after lying uncovered in the sun for some time.'

The custom also prevails in various parts and provinces of India. Jagor told M. Bartels that rings of a special shape are used for the purpose of depilation and to this end are worn on the thumb. They resemble unusually large signet rings with flat, sharp-edged discs set with tiny mirrors, which both show the areas in question and reflect the light. The shaving is done with the sharp edges. The name for these rings is *ârsi*.

The favourite Turkish preparation for removing pubic hair is *pigmentum aureum* (*arsenicum sulphuratum flavum*) and burnt chalk in equal parts, moistened to a paste with rose-water. This paste is applied to the hairy areas and removed after a short time, the hairs being removed with it. This is the universal Oriental depilatory, known in Turkey as *rusma* and in Persia as *nureh*, according to Polak.

Polak also declares that the term used for this procedure is *hadschebi keschidev* – to obey the law – but women of elegance and fashion pluck the hairs away with pincers till the growth ceases.

Jacobus X. states that the Wolof women shave their genital hair with pieces of glass from broken bottles, while Zache says of the Swahili women in Tanganyika territory:

> They remove the hair from their genitalia regularly by means of resin from the *mtondôo* tree (*Calopgyllum inophyllum*, according to Stuhlmann), which is rubbed into the skin, and then the hairs are pulled out. A more recent and fashionable depilatory is arsenic, borrowed from the Arab cosmetic lore. It is applied together with chalk in a paste made with water, and then warm fomentations are applied. This is said to be less painful than *mtondôo* resin.

The phrase used for depilation in the secret speech of the Swahili women is 'to sweep the yard clear'.

Finally, we may refer to the habit of plucking out the eyebrows, prevalent in Japan and among the Bongo women (Schweinfurth), as well as among the Sea Dyaks of Borneo. Roth says that the Dyaks pull out the eyelashes as well, and in both sexes.

vi. Piercing

The most widely practised facial mutilation is that on the ears. Even in 'civilized' countries they are often pierced and adorned with jewels and studs. In certain country districts, for instance in the Mark Brandenburg (Prussia), this is considered indispensable and of benefit to the eyesight, 'drawing off bad humours'. It is even recommended as a method for healing eyes which have already suffered from sties or soreness. (This superstition is not by any means confined to Prussia: it is found in parts of Scotland and Ireland as well.) An ear-ring on the left side is reputed to be more efficacious. In some races, the piercing of the lobe of the ear is made the occasion of a special festival.

The shape and material of the ornaments vary greatly among the races practising these mutilations. Sometimes the rings are so large that the lobe is stretched and deformed, or so heavy that they pull the whole ear out of shape, often, indeed, tearing it through and leaving thin strips of flesh hanging to the shoulders. There is also the modification of plugging the orifice through the lobe with sticks and bars of wood, sometimes as large as clothes-pegs, as in Madagascar and Central Africa. The Korumba of the Nilgiri Hills use palm-leaf spirals, according to Jagor. The New Zealand Maori, on the other hand, use flowers as ear-plugs.

Hagen gives an account of the elaborate procedure among the Battak women, who enlarge the hole bored through the lobe 'till it will take a thumb' and place a silver ring in the gaping hole. The upper part of the ear is also pierced and adorned with tiny rings.

Thilenuus has given a detailed description of the extraordinary procedure among the women of the Ancoretas Islands. Great rings of tortoiseshell are fastened or clipped to the ears and a strip torn off the helix so that it droops and can be used as a bracelet; or it is adorned with coconut fibre. The same custom is said to prevail in Popolo, but there it may be connected with puberty ceremonies.

Noses, as well as ears, are sometimes pierced. The Hindu women often wear little studs in one perforated nostril. Both nostrils are never pierced simultaneously and the left side is preferred. But sometimes the ornament is very heavy, a ring, not a stud, and the disfigurement is great.

The alae or wings of the nose are sometimes untouched, while the septum is perforated, but this custom appears to be diminishing. It still prevails among the Queensland Blacks in both sexes. The ornament is a splinter of bone or wood. The Jur women of the Upper Nile often wear iron rings through the septum, or even sometimes through the gristle of the bridge of the nose, according to von Hellwald.

Livingstone has described the rings (*pelele*) worn by the Magandja women through the upper lip, comparing the resultant disfigurement to the gaping maw of a crocodile, as the teeth are filed to match. A headman of the people, Chi-nsurdi, explained that the *pelele* were worn by the women to compensate for their lamentable beardlessness.

The women of the Bongo tribe (Bahr-el-Ghazal) wear metal clips on their upper lips near the corners and thrust grass blades through the upper lip and nostrils and wooden pegs through the lower.

The same custom was observed among the women of a troupe of South American Indians from Guiana (supposed to be Arecuna and Arawak) who visited Europe some years ago and proudly thrust pins and bodkins into the perforations in their lips.

The Eskimo tribes of the extreme north of America, according to Captain Adrian Jacobsen, have similar customs. On the Kuskoquim Estuary, the young girls adorn themselves with beads and shells, threading them through their hair and piercing their lower lip in three places. A sort of stud of bone is then thrust through each perforation with the thicker end inside to prevent it from falling out. The visible portion is then covered with beads. The septum is also pierced and adorned with a short bead chain. The latter custom is prevalent among Eskimo girls on the Lower Yukon and further north among the Malemiuts. The chin is tattooed as well.

vii. Mutilation of the Feet

In some African women the lower limbs from knee to ankle are covered with metal rings. And sometimes the calves and shins are constricted so that they bulge enormously above and below the metal circlets.

Du Tertre, the oldest and fullest authority on the customs of the West Indian aborigines, says that the Carib girls from early childhood constricted their legs from ankle to calf with bandages. The flesh was much swollen between the bandages. Schomburgk found the same custom among the Carib women on the South American mainland, as well as other tribes in Guiana. The same two constricting bandages, one sock-like from ankle to calf and one like a tight garter below the knee, were worn by the Guiana Indian women exhibited in Umlauff's troupe in Berlin several years ago.

There are apparently only two nations who intentionally cripple the action of the lower limbs and extremities: the Chinese and the Kutchin Indians in the interior of Alaska along the banks of the Yukon River.

FOOT-BINDING

Pliny mentions an Asiatic people who had the habit of making women's feet small and were called 'Struthopedes'. The first detailed accounts of the custom were given to Europe in the nineteenth century by Morache, Lockhart, Bingham, Martin and others, who were followed in their re-searches by Welcker and Rüdinger. After the Boxer risings and the further internal troubles much new material was made available. Roentgen photo-graphy has been valuable, especially when used by such authorities as H. Virchow and J. Fränkel. The latter had the resource of radiography at his disposal and took X-ray photographs of the feet of various Chinese ladies resident in Berlin – a fortunate inspiration, as it is extremely difficult to get permission to inspect the unclothed, deformed foot.

What was the origin and purpose of this extraordinary custom? Perthes asked Merklinghaus, the interpreter of the German Legation in Peking, to look up sources for him and was informed that 'Foot-binding is said to have been introduced by the Emperor Chien-hon-djon, who lived towards AD 580 and was exceedingly lascivious. He wanted to create a new feminine charm in diminutive feet.' And there is no doubt that the custom was non-existent at the time of Confucius (551–479 BC). Marco Polo, who visited the brilliant court of China in the thirteenth century, makes no reference to bound feet.

Scherzer and other writers regard foot-binding as the fruit of masculine jealousy lest the women should move about freely and cause their husbands anxiety. Baelz told P. Bartels that he thought the custom was derived from a deformity or peculiarity in some Imperial personage and was a form of courtly flattery, like the *perruques* of the seventeenth century in Europe. Karl von den Steinen, in a discussion of Berlin anthropologists, thought that foot-binding, like long fingernails, was the specific sign of wealth and leisure and of freedom from the need to work.

There may well, however, be an erotic explanation of the foot-binding custom. At the Dresden International Hygienic Exhibition in 1911, a Chinese lady of great culture mentioned this as the *only* reason for its introduction and preservation. And she added that the modesty of the Chinese woman has special reference to her feet to this day. This appears to confirm the theory, and Morache seemed to be also of the same opinion. To quote his own words: 'To those who realize the degree of lubricity natural to the Chinese, it is evident that the smallness of the foot excites them and causes this trend of associations.'

Moreover, Christian converts among the Chinese confessed that they had gazed wantonly at the little feet of ladies, regarding it as a sin, according to their new faith. Morache adds that he was assured that persons exhausted by opium were in the habit of practising a form of foot and shoe fetishism and obtaining enjoyment by the sight and touch of 'tiny and very dainty shoes'. Even women who were all professional prostitutes of the lowest grade refused to uncover their feet, though otherwise they were quite naked. Naecke thinks that we have here a case of specialized and relocalized modesty, and that the crippled foot is a fetish – 'less a fetish aesthetically than sexually'.

The severe restrictions on the growth of the Chinese women's feet are a form of feminine 'beauty culture' in the strictest sense of the term. Never, and in no circumstances, is this crippling torture applied to boys. But it should not be overlooked that the custom does not prevail over the whole of China. The Manchus – including the members of the late Imperial family – detested and refused the mutilation, according to Bastian. Whole districts in various parts of China were immune from it. The Chinese women resident in the Sunda Isles, for example, do not bind their feet at all. But Keitner recounts that in the Singang-fu and Lantscho-fu districts, the calves are constricted as well as the feet. The bandages are knee-high 'and the effect is accentuated if a strip of flesh, an inch wide, protrudes in the middle like an old ragged garter'.

Among the poorer classes the mother herself binds her daughter's feet. Wealthy people have specially trained women experts who work in the families on this task.

In the first years of childhood, the little girl is spared and runs about in loose slippers like her brothers. The earliest stage at which the operation begins is four years; in other families it is deferred till six or even seven. (A Chinese lady informed Professor H. Virchow that in the first cases the child was of very high birth and would not need to walk; but if the children are plebeian they must have attained the full use of their feet before they are bound.)

Morache describes the first stage as a persistent kneading and moulding of the foot. The great toe is left in its natural position, but the four other toes are forcibly bent downwards and pressed over and on to the sole of the foot with steadily increasing force. They are kept in place by means of a bandage 5 cm wide. This bandage is changed daily and as it is removed the foot is 'aired', bathed and rubbed with spirits of sorghum. If this precaution is neglected severe ulcers are apt to develop.

The child wears a laced boot reaching rather high up the calf, and with a pointed toe. The sole is quite flat and heelless. This procedure alone results in the kind of structural modification usual among the majority of women in the northern provinces of China.

The more elegant and aristocratic form is yet further complicated (Fig. 9). When the toes have been permanently bent over the sole, a metal cylinder is placed under the sole and bandaged firmly in place. The instep, ankle and lower leg are tightly constricted with firm bandage supports, and the mother or attendants force the toes and heel together under the cylinder so that the bones of the foot are displaced. Finally, the maltreated extremity is forced into a shoe with a thick convex sole. And the bandages remain in place for days, in spite of inflammation, tears, cries and feverish symptoms. The children are forced to stand upright and to walk on their crippled feet, as otherwise they would lose the use of their limbs. The mother and nurses are said to console the tortured child with promises of beauty in the future and of a husband's approval.

Perthes has described a third degree of this mutilation, quoted from the statements of an educated Chinaman, who told him that in southern China the great toe was sometimes wrenched upwards and over on to the instep and bound tightly down.

If the girls survive the ordeal and the bones and tissues 'set', the walk is permanently altered. They sway or, rather, wobble from side to side with stiff knees, as though on stilts, for the whole weight of the body is balanced on the point of the heel and the ball of the great toe. They have to use sticks for walking or to lean on the arm of their attendants. Morache points out that the extensor and flexor muscles of the foot atrophy, so that 'the leg assumes the shape of a cone pointing downwards'. And he compares the method of progression of the Chinese woman with that of a man whose two legs have been amputated and replaced by wooden limbs. In both, the lower

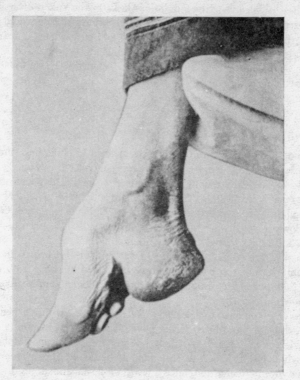

Fig. 9 Foot of a Chinese woman showing displacement of the bones; the toes lie bent under the sole (Anthrop. Ges., Berlin)

half of the leg has become a 'rigid lump of matter' – at least so far as walking is concerned. Gray and Virchow recount the pain and difficulty entailed in this. Some Chinese ladies are carried like children on their slaves' backs. The lady consulted by Virchow crawled on all fours when she thought herself unobserved.

The poetical imagery of China has christened the feet of Chinese great ladies 'golden water-lilies' – *kien-lien* (cf. J. F. Junker). In the collection of Dr M. Bartels is a plaster cast of a 'golden water-lily' measuring 8 cm (3 inches) from the tip of the toe to the tip of the heel.

As already mentioned, the only race apart from the Chinese to bind women's feet is that of the Kutchin Indians, according to Stoll. Of Athabascan

stock, these people live in the interior of Alaska by the Yukon River. Kricke-
berg describes them as indefatigable and adventurous traders, and it may
be that they have in some way discovered and copied the Chinese habit.
Richardson recounts that the babies and children are carried in a sort of
litter on their mothers' backs. Their feet are encased in warm fur leggings
and tight bandages in order to dwarf their growth, as small feet are naturally
beautiful.

viii. Fat

Near and Middle Eastern taste is greatly inclined to plumpness and fat in
women, so much so that extreme adiposity is cultivated by special diet in the
harems of Arabia and among many African peoples. The wives and concubines of African chieftains, for example, are fattened with curdled milk or
broth and soup of cornmeal, while in southern Nubia the girls are compelled
to swallow a revolting diet of durra (meal), a little sodden meat and goat's
milk for forty days before marriage, the mother or other relative standing
over them with a whip and showing no mercy. This diet is combined with
continual external applications of fat or friction of the body with oil and
grease. Paulitschke gives similar facts about the Somali, and the custom is
well known in Nigeria.

Excessive corpulence and laziness lead, of course, to many bodily ills.
Speke, Schweitzer and Emin Pasha have given amazing examples of girls
who had been so fattened that they had lost the use of their limbs, or of
others who were treated as a kind of family heirloom. They were fed on a
milk diet with no water and, once a week, on a salted meat broth.

Chavanne comments on the enormous obesity of the milk-and-butter-fed
girls of the Trarsa, a people of the Sahara between Talifet and Timbuktu, an
obesity all the more conspicuous as the men of their tribes are gaunt and
bony.

Indeed, wherever Islam has held sway, the preference for fat women
appears. But, curiously enough, the ideal beauty of Ancient Arabia
stressed other features than rolls of obesity, and even now the Himyarites
are never plump or stout. By Mohammed's time, however, a superabund-
ance of fat was admired as, for instance, in his favourite wife,
Ayesha.

The dietetic rules for producing fat in Egypt are elaborate and combined
with hot baths. In the sixteenth century Alpini described this system in
detail.

Among the Tunisian Jewesses extreme obesity is common and emphasized
by their peculiar costume, while among the Hindus extreme plumpness has

been admired since the days of Manu, who recommended his faithful to seek brides 'graceful in gait as young elephants'. Great obesity is also cultivated and admired in Oceania by the Hawaiians, Tahitians and people of New Ireland.

STEATOPYGIA

Steatopygia ('fat rump', in Greek), a condition in which the hindquarters are extraordinarily large and prominent, has been observed to a peculiar degree among certain races in South Africa: the Bushmen, Koranna and Hottentots (very pronounced, according to E. H. L. Schwartz). In steatopygous peoples the women are naturally the most conspicuous, and their peculiarity is said to begin at the earliest date – in childhood, not in puberty, as Blanchard, Le Vaillant and others have confirmed.

The famous so-called Hottentot Venus described by Cuvier was steatopygous to a high degree; the measurement is given as 16.2 cm. Luschka and Görtz made an autopsy on the woman Afandi, described as of Bushman origin. The thickness of her adipose cushion when preserved in spirits for a year was between 4 and 4½ cm at its maximum point, and the disposition of this extra layer of fat was not on the European plan but particularly marked over the glutaeus maximus, so that the sides were proportionately flatter and the posterior more prominent than in European women.

The cause of steatopygia is not muscular but adipose, as has been demonstrated by many autopsies. It is out of the question that the phenomenon can be mainly due to the bony structure or pelvic inclination. Theophil Hahn declares that the young Hottentot boys who were his playmates were steatopygous as well as the women, and that their dimensions waxed and waned according to the season, becoming 'almost incredible' when the rains brought an abundance of game and roots for food. Sokolovsky, in fact, believes that human steatopygia is analogous to the layers of fat on the hindquarters of the fat-tailed sheep (*Ovis aries steatopyga*). He considers that they represent an adaptation to life on the African deserts, supplying nutriment to the system when exhausted by lack of food.

Certainly the impression that steatopygia (in its pronounced forms) makes on an unaccustomed European observer is extraordinary and aesthetically repulsive. Even the slighter protuberance common in some Bushwomen is ugly in our eyes. But the Hottentots themselves consider their steatopygia, which they term *aredi*, supremely beautiful.

PART TWO

The Life Cycle

CHAPTER IV

Maidens

Among many races the birth of a daughter is accepted as a misfortune and even in some cases as a discreditable and shameful affair.

The Asiatic aversion to female children is well known, and the most pronounced example is perhaps to be found in China, for here ancestor worship comes into play (as also among the Japanese). Unless a son is able to perform the ritual sacrifices, his father must hunger and thirst perpetually in the world of shades. The people of Peking gave an only daughter such names as 'Call a boy!', 'Make a son come!', 'Beckon for your brother!' and so forth (Grube).

The Ancient Hindus justified their contempt and oppression of women by a modification of their doctrine of reincarnation and transmigration of souls. If in former lives, states Schmidt, much guilt had been incurred and evil deeds done, the soul was punished by rebirth in a woman's form.

The Turks of Central Asia, when Vámbéry visited them and reported their customs, had the following verses as a popular proverb:

> If a daughter is born to thee, better she should not live;
> Better she should not be born, or, if born,
> Better the funeral feast be with the birth.

The Kirghiz say: 'Keep not thy salt too long or it melts away to water; keep not thy daughter or she becomes a slave.'

The Jugo-Slavs of Montenegro also used to receive their new-born daughters with grief and almost scorn, and this view was even held among the rulers. The mother of several daughters and no sons was expected to summon seven orthodox priests to exorcise evil spirits from the house with holy oil and by replacing the threshold of the house with a new one.

There are races, however, among whom the girl is more welcome than her brother. Roth quotes Low to this effect in reference to the Sea Dyaks of Borneo, who pray for girls in preference since they are more useful to them than sons. The same is true of the Battak, and has been observed among the

Malays of the Aru Islands – due perhaps to the future bride-price and marriage portion, for all those present at the bride's birth then receive 'largesse' which they spend in a tremendous feast. Pigs are killed and an incredible amount of arak is consumed on these occasions. The son has no such welcome, and reproaches are even cast against the unfortunate mother. An Aru girl is often promised in marriage at birth, and the amount of her dowry is settled in advance (von Rosenberg).

The same is true of the African Hottentots and other South African tribes. The reasons may be strictly utilitarian, for the girl, when she becomes nubile, will bring her father many cattle as her bride-price. Many daughters thus mean wealth, actual or prospective.

i. Infanticide

Deliberate destruction of male infants is found in the Amazon legends, but infanticide is more common when applied to female children.

According to Hauri, the pre-Islamite inhabitants of Arabia were in the habit of burying their new-born girl-babies alive in the sand.

As to the extent which female infanticide has reached in many parts of India, we read in Schweiger-Lerchenfeld's work:

> When in the year 1836 the first inquiry into this matter was made by the Anglo-Indian authorities, it was shown that, for example, in Western Rajputana, in a group of 10,000 of the population, there was not one girl! In Manikpur, the Rajput nobility admitted that in their district for more than 100 years no girl-baby had lived longer than one year. However, these horrors were not exhausted by a long way. About twenty years ago, investigations were again made. A government official ascertained first the existence of the practice of murder in 308 districts which he had visited; in twenty-six he found not one girl under six years of age; in twenty-eight, not one under nubile age. In a few districts, no marriage had taken place within the memory of man, and in one the last marriage dated eighty years back.

And there seems to be no doubt that female infanticide was and is frequent in Hindustan (Mantegazza), in spite of the efforts of social reformers, religious missions and the Infanticide Act of 1870. The answer to the reproaches of Occidentals is: how is the infant to be fed and supported till puberty, and who will pay her marriage portion?

According to Eitel, the slaughter of girls is habitual among the Hok-lo, Hak-ka and Pun-ti, three agricultural tribes of southern China in the province of Kwang-tung and on the frontiers of Cochin-China. The Hak-ka themselves estimate the number of children thus slain at birth as amounting to two thirds of the total female births.

At the other side of the world, in Greenland and round the Cumberland Sound, female infants are often killed. Schliephake is of the opinion that female infanticide is responsible for lowering the population.

Von Hellwald states that before the arrival and settlement of the various Christian missions among the Athabascan tribes on the eastern slopes of the Canadian Rockies, female infanticide, either by strangulation or exposure, was customary. The same practice prevailed among the Eskimo of the Bering Strait, according to Nelson, but was sometimes deferred till the children had reached the age of four or six years. The parents took them to a desert place and filled their mouths and nostrils with snow, or else left them on pack ice or in the tundra, where frost soon ended their sufferings.

Perhaps the widest diffusion and prevalence of this practice is in Oceania, and especially, states F. Müller, among the natives of Australia, perhaps because of hunger and lack of sufficient food to rear the children.

In New Guinea the favourite method is to break the baby's neck by forcibly bending its head forward with a sharp jerk. The matter is left in the hands of the women, and the men neither dictate nor interfere. Cripples and deformed infants are thus disposed of, and also sometimes perfectly normal infants whose birth has been very prolonged and painful and risked their mothers' life.

Moncelon states that the New Caledonian women kill their female infants in order to escape the burden and tie of lactation. The fathers keep an eye on their sons, who generally survive.

ii. Menarche

The distinctive signs of puberty have been recognized and referred to in all ancient civilizations, from Ezekiel, who wrote, 'Thy breasts are fashioned, and thine hair is grown, whereas thou wast naked and bare,' to the Emperor Justinian, although sometimes one or sometimes another has been emphasized or ignored. Thus Susruta, the ancient physician of Hindustan, mentions only the monthly period as the proof of feminine maturity, whereas in Rome the test in both sexes was the appearance of pubic hair.

The medical Talmudists paid much attention to the signs of puberty and recognized many other symptoms besides menstruation, such as changes in the breasts, elasticity of the nipples and mons, the growth of pubic hair, etc. Primitive peoples, on the other hand, direct all their attention in this respect to menstruation, and they celebrate the occasion by rites and ceremonies to which we shall refer later with greater detail.

We are, as yet, comparatively ignorant as to the precise factors which determine any changes or irregularities in the usual sequence, or any conspicuously early or late onset of the whole process of puberty. Is it interwoven with particular constitutional characteristics, such as are shown in the colouring of eyes, hair and complexion? Is one course of development 'normal' or more frequent in blondes, and another in brunettes? We can say nothing definite on these matters, for we have insufficient data.

We do know, however, that *pubertas praecox* was known to Pliny, Seneca and the Greeks. By the year 1862, Kussmaul had established and recorded thirty-two cases, and in 1913 J. Lenz published a work in which he enumerated 130 cases, the earliest of the year 1658. Among these cases, which were recorded by various observers, Zeller notes one of menstruation at two months, and Comarmond one at three months. Another child, who was seen by A. van der Veer, was born in February 1880, menstruated at four months and then regularly every twenty-eight days, the flow lasting four to five days. Cesarano reports a case at six months and d'Outrepont mentions another who began at nine months. Sally Deweese, who was born in Kentucky in 1824, menstruated at one year and, according to Montgomery, was pregnant at ten.

In genuine *pubertas praecox* there is not only pelvic but also mammary development. The general outlines of the body become fuller and rounder and the pubic hair grows. Then, also, there are girls whose general physique and pelvic, pubic and mammary development are completely 'adult' before they have their first menstruation.

The earliest available material led us to suppose that climate and especially temperature were the main factors in retarding or hastening the first menstrual period. According to Susruta, menstruation generally began in girls at the twelfth year in Hindustan. The Talmudist Rabbis gave thirteen as the most frequent year when referring to the Jewesses of Asia Minor, and Soranus of Ephesus gave fourteen as the usual age for Roman girls. But such Europeans as dealt seriously with the subject before the fifteenth century favoured the twelfth year as the decisive date. Albrecht von Haller agrees with them. He says that in Switzerland and other lands of the temperate zone, menstruation begins at twelve or thirteen. It is retarded the longer, the further we go north, while in tropical Asia, etc., it is accelerated and appears as early as the tenth or even the eighth year.

In 1869 Krieger, a Berlin medical man, compiled a tabular synopsis which gave mean annual temperature, geographical latitude and race or ethnical stock. Climate showed a preponderant influence, although summer and spring did not usually bring on menstruation in European women. Many more than half the number of cases he studied and recorded had menstruated for the first time in the months of September, October or November.

Engelmann, however, gave a table of the age of the first menstruation from various sources in which the figures illustrated the climatic factor as probably little influencing the age of onset. We may therefore conclude, especially in view of testimony from Krieger, von Baelz, Glogner, Engelmann and Novak, that climate plays but a small part in the appearance of menstruation, and that internal secretions, food, habits of life and racial stock play a considerable one.

Social class and urban or rural environment may thus be considered to have some influence on the onset of menstruation, as was shown by Bensenger's minute study of 5,611 women who had lived in Moscow for ten years. He distinguished three groups. The first began to menstruate between nine and twelve years of age, the second between thirteen and sixteen, and the third between seventeen and twenty-two. Social class and profession of parents were carefully noted.

It was found that the majority of the first (early) group were either foreigners or members of the nobility. In the second group, the majority were of mercantile class or daughters of the Russian clergy. And the third were mostly of the peasant class. No doubt food, rest and manner of life generally, as well as the accumulated effect of physical environment on the nervous system, all interacted in these cases.

Weber's Russian researches also showed that class and occupation were important. He found that domestic life and a sheltered childhood at home favoured early development, while proletarian life with hunger and overstrain retarded it. He also found that menstruation tended to appear at exceptionally early ages in girls who later showed a marked inclination for study and intellectual professions, and also among teachers, singers and actresses.

As early as the seventeenth century (1610), the physician Guarinonius, who lived in Hall, near Innsbruck, made a similar observation and attributed it to the richer, daintier and 'more heating' food which the wealthier familes could afford.

Finally, we must not lose sight of such facts as may be produced by heredity and by constitution. Thus H. N. and M. R. Gould, in a study of the relation between first menstruation in mothers and daughters, found that the age of the mother at first menses has a demonstrable effect on the appearance in the daughter.

iii. Rites of Passage

An important part of the ceremonial of puberty is found in the sharp divisions between the sexes among primitives. Men and women in some primitive societies spend much of their time apart, have different occupations and even, sometimes, different dialects. In each of these two main sex groups there are often age groups, and puberty rites are essentially initiations from the youngest age group into the adult.

There is a marked difference between the initiation of boys and girls. The boys are primarily: a) released from the maternal tutelage and brought into the male world, and b) tested against pain, fear and peril by homeopathy. The girls are often directly instructed and prepared for sexual intercourse and child-bearing, and often marriage follows on their ceremonial initiation.

The following are the leading concepts and purposes of puberty ceremonial for women in the primitive sphere of thought and custom:

1. As soon as menstruation occurs, the girl or woman is reckoned 'unclean'. Among the Bakairi of Brazil, for example, pubescent girls are considered to be ill, and treated with incisions, fumigations, special diet and confinement in seclusion.

2. The woman, being possessed or overshadowed by an ancestral spirit, must be shut away from others. (This line of thought may also be manifested in the nights of ritual abstinence at the beginning of married life – see 'Nuptial Abstinence', Chapter VII – and in the repeated seclusion of menstruating women – see 'Seclusion and Purification', Chapter V.) During her seclusion the girl 'dies to the world' and passes into the Beyond; has dreams and trances, and learns the will of the ancestral spirits.

3. The woman is prepared for sexual activity and maternity by detailed instruction, fasting, blood-letting, ordeals, tattooing, stretching or breaking of the hymen, clitoridectomy, defloration, etc. (see also 'Clitoral Excision' and 'Infibulation', Chapter II, and 'Tattooing', Chapter III).

4. The woman is prepared for marriage. In this context there is a whole mass of obscure survivals in the Carnival legends and customs of all Europe – the masking, dancing, general licence. These customs were especially associated with such seasonal festivals as Valentine's Day, Easter, Whitsun, Midsummer (John the Baptist's Day) and Lammastide. It is probable that at no very remote date in Europe these seasonal festivals were celebrated with sexual congress as well as song, masks, mimes and some kind of procession or exodus.

The following is a résumé of rites of passage, organized generally according to geographical area.

THE AMERICAS

Koch-Grünberg mentions that amongst the tribes of Rio Ariary in Brazil, the girl's hair is cut short and her back rubbed over with *genipapo* paint by her mother. (Her hair is probably subsequently used as a head-dress and decoration by young men, as on Uaupés.) There is a great feast, with dances and drinking. The girl must fast from all animal food and large fish and may eat only *beijú* (manioc) and pepper with small fish till her second menses have concluded. Then she has a great cauldron of animal food and is painted all over with *karayurù*. A general feast follows.

Burmeister describes the strict seclusion of girls among the Coroado Indians of Brazil at their first menstruation. They are shut into a sort of case or cupboard made of tree bark. Among the Passé, the girls fast for a month, lying in their hammocks in the upper chamber of the hut. The Arawak of Surinam shut up the girls for three weeks in a special building on the first occasion, but they are guarded by their own mother and not by a special official. A great feast is celebrated on their release and there follows a second seclusion of a month, but less rigorous than the first.

According to Grinnell, Cheyenne girls were kept close to the fire, bathed, painted red all over and fumigated by means of a live coal from the fire, on which fragrant grasses, cedar chips and a special white salve were thrown. The girl bent over this smouldering scented heap and caught the fumes in her clothes. Then, with her grandmother, she left the hut and went to another where she remained for four days. Her father, standing at the door of the hut, announced his daughter's arrival at womanhood to the tribe, and after the four days were over, the girl returned to her home and was again fumigated with grass, juniper and salve, standing across the fire with her legs apart.

In British Columbia the Clayoquot Indians dress their girls in a curious costume of cedar-wood bast which shrouds them from head to foot. Among the Nootka and neighbouring Hesquiat tribes the elaborate costume has become a head-dress, worn for four consecutive days on the first eight menstrual occasions. This head-dress is made of cedar bast with beads and the beaks of parrot fish, and is depicted in Fig. 10. The girls must use their own bowls and spoons during their period, and for eight successive months they must eat alone, abstaining from fresh fish, especially salmon.

H. R. Rust has given a graphic account of the initiation ceremony known as the 'roasting of girls' among the Mission Indians of southern California. The girls are wrapped in blankets and placed in a pit about three feet deep by five feet wide, containing a fire which steams them. Here they remain for four days. The older women surround the pit, singing, dancing and performing mystical gestures of propitiation to the good spirits and exorcism to the evil. The atmosphere of this festival is friendly and happy. Finally, the girls are led before a yoke-shaped stone which is believed to symbolize or have reference to the female organs of generation. Rust and Kroeber have

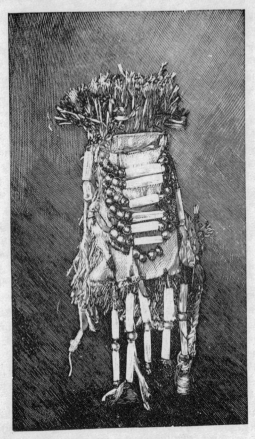

Fig. 10 Head decoration worn by a nubile Hesquiat girl,
made of cedar bast and hung with cloth, glass beads, fish bones, etc.
(Mus. f. Völkerk., Berlin; after photo by M. Bartels)

described similar stones in American museums and Rust believes they also
are genital symbols.

Among the Hopi Indians of southern California and Arizona, states
Powers, the *Kin Alktha*, or dance of the maidens, follows the attainment of
puberty. For nine days in succession the men of the tribe meet and dance
amongst themselves – women being excluded. Meanwhile, the girl is concealed in the hut, fasting from animal food and hiding from the eyes of men.

On the tenth night two young men and two elderly women come to find her and lead her forth. They are chosen from among her kinsfolk. The youths wear large masks of dried rushes or hide pulled over their heads and bearing a grotesque resemblance to a sea-lion's muzzle. The girl is led forth with the youths on either side and the two older women flanking the latter. Before the assembled tribe the girl walks solemnly backwards and forwards ten times, raising her arms to shoulder level and chanting. Finally, all five leap high into the air and the tribe greets the new woman with loud cries of welcome.

On the Aleutian Isles, before the introduction of Christianity, the women and girls had a full week of menstrual seclusion. Captain Zagoskin saw girls with faces blackened with paint or soot sitting behind a leathern curtain in a tent in 1842, during his sojourn with the Athabascans. Canadian and British Columbian Indians also seclude their girls at puberty. G. A. Erman gives three days as the time for seclusion for women among the Tlingit.

According to Parker, the Chippewa girls had to leave not only their parents' wigwam but their village as soon as menstruation began for the first time – even if it were midnight in midwinter or a blizzard were raging. They made their way to a little hut in a lonely place not far from the village. The hut was made as comfortable as possible for them and they remained there, alone, for some days and nights. The families brought food, but nothing cooked. Parker adds that ritual fasting at puberty was strictly observed by the Chippewa. The girls were encouraged to fast for five whole days during their seclusion. Many did so, drinking only cold water and eating no solid food. The dreams they experienced under this regime were considered highly important and they were urged to remember them and learn from them throughout life.

Nelson reports that the Malemiut Eskimo girls are taboo for forty days after their first menstruation. They sit crouching in a corner with their faces to the wall, and must draw their hoods over their heads and let their hair hang down over their faces. They may only leave the house at night when all are asleep.

Koluschan Indians seclude their girls for three months, according to the season, in a bower of leaves and branches or a house of frozen snow. Formerly the seclusion lasted for a year.

AFRICA

According to Ankermann, the Bakuba people have a whole series of terms for the different types of disembodied spirit: *nshonga* and *mophuphu* (life soul or breath soul), *ido* and *edidingi*. The *nshonga* leaves the body after death, enters a woman's body, grows and is born as a child. From the time of her first menstruation a girl is ceaselessly liable to invasion and possession by these ancestral spirits, and if she has not gone through the puberty ritual of her tribe her children may be the incarnations of strange and hostile ghosts, and are often put to death on that account.

Büttiköfer has published a valuable account of the rites practised in Liberia. According to him, the 'magic country' (or greegree bush) is a sort of novitiate through which both sexes must pass at puberty – but in strict separation. He has traced greegree bush institutions among the Vey, Kosso, Godah, Pessy, Queah and western Bassa, but has no idea of their existence in eastern Africa. Almost every village of any size has its greegree places.

Among the Vey, the girls' greegree bush is called the 'sandy'. Their teachers and initiators, who are called greegree women or devil women, are distinguished by small tattoo marks on the back of the calf or lower leg. They are women advanced in years and the leader is generally the head wife of the chieftain. The girls enter the sandy at ten years of age or sometimes sooner and occasionally remain till after puberty. Payment in kind and foodstuffs is levied on their parents by the greegree women. The girls go about naked in their sandy and on entry are tattooed and undergo clitoridectomy, the tip of the organ being removed with a special knife, mummified and hung round their necks in a little bag. Scarification is performed on both boys and girls.

Men and all initiated girls may not enter the sandy which, together with the 'belly' – its analogue for boys – is under the protection of the N'janas, or ghosts of the dead. Older women who visit the sandy must strip and leave their garments on the edge of the wood. The neophytes may visit their homes occasionally, but before doing so are smeared with white clay so that they look like circus clowns (Fig. 11). Neither they nor the boys may wear woven cotton, but are clothed in skirts or aprons of wood fibre, leaves or palms. They learn to dance, play and sing, and it is said that some of the songs are of a nature quite contrary to their usual modesty and decorum in conversation and behaviour. They learn how to catch fish, do all household tasks, weave nets and cook.

The Bakongo of the Loango coast take the girls to special remote huts, the daughters of wealthier persons and chiefs each in her own hut, the daughters of the less prosperous majority together in one building. They are known as ukumbi or tchikumbi until they marry. They are instructed by a woman whom the parents choose for duty.

Falkenstein says that the Negroes of Loango lead the girl in procession through their villages with song and dance, accompanied by her playmates, and even lead her before Europeans. The whole ceremony is one of pride and

Fig. 11   Greegree bush girls smeared with clay, Queah River, Liberia (after Büttiköfer)

joy, with no shame and no furtiveness. Others confirm this account and add that songs are sung in praise of maidenhood and wedlock.

According to Fritsch, the Bechuana *bojale* seems equivalent, for girls, to the male circumcision or *boguera*. The girls are taught their future duties by an older woman in strict seclusion. They go into the desert in sixes and sevens, trotting in single file to the sound of curious monotonous chanting. They smear themselves with white clay and wear a great girdle of canes, rather like a lifebelt, and chains of dried pumpkin seeds (Fig. 12). The canes are gathered into aprons round the loins and rolled into sausage-like tubes round the thorax. The pumpkin seeds, which hang between the canes, give a sharp dry rustling which proclaims the girls' approach and is very loud when a troop comes running along. If they are disturbed, in spite of this warning sound, they may use the thick, long staves they carry to beat any man most severely. The initiation also includes tests of skill and ordeals of endurance. When it is over, the girdles are collected after nightfall, in the presence of the assembled neophytes, piled in a heap and burnt in the village square. As they flare up, the girls dance fantastically and chant, while the men, sitting in a ring, make music.

Fig. 12 Bechuana *bojale* (photo G. Fritsch)

Endemann says Basuto girls have a special ceremony called *Pollo*. Conducted by an older woman, they go into the water far enough to be able to immerse themselves completely and have to find and pick up a bracelet from the bed of the stream. In the daytime they are taught their future duties and dance and sing. At night they are secluded and smeared with ashes. It is reported that they seem 'crazy', 'beside themselves', commit all sorts of mischief and 'dress themselves up'. They must perform many ritual ablutions.

Velten and Zache give accounts of a mysterious East African stone 'of anointing', a smooth fragment of coralline rock which is used to rub spices into the skin and plays a role in the marriage ceremony. It may never be uncovered outside the house, nor seen by men. Zache says it is termed *Jiwe la msio* – the stone of the secret. The head matron strews powdered sandalwood on the stone and the girl's body is rubbed and perfumed all over by her adult friends. The outer epidermis falls off in flakes during this friction. After this symbolic 'shedding of the serpent's skin' the girl enters womanhood fully prepared as 'one who knows'. Evil spirits are feared and exorcised, good spirits summoned, and the flat stones which are brought into contact with the body are specially powerful vehicles of *mana*.

Reichard describes the Wanyamwezi girl's puberal initiation as an exclusively female festival with song and dance and libations of native beer. The girl has already, in almost every case, lost her virginity. She is bathed and washed all over with herbal concoctions by the medicine women or *wagangna*. Then she is anointed with oil and sprinkled all over with meal. Further, there is a sort of examination or test of efficiency in an important direction. The girl has to perform the movements of coitus in various postures before a jury of matrons. Men are most strictly excluded.

The missionary Schloemann, who worked in Malakong, informed M. Bartels that among the Bavenda of the northern Transvaal a miniature human image of clay was put before each neophyte and solemnly announced as the *koma* (Merensky heard the same word among the Wakonde on the shores of Lake Nyasa, who used it to designate some supreme and divine being). On one of his journeys, Schloemann passed by a tract of bush in which the women were celebrating their *koma* rites.

Certain images were set up, and the driver of Schloemann's cart, a baptized native boy, saw those which stood nearest the edge of the wood. The celebrants realized this and forthwith there arose a violent tumult. They rushed after the cart, pursuing it with shrieks and abuse up to the doors of the mission station. Then, to the number of several hundreds, they assembled around the station and attempted to set the buildings on fire, shrieking the while: 'He has seen it, he has seen the *koma* of the basket' – which means that the *koma* should be secret and concealed as though under a basket. Finally the missionaries summoned the local headman and the women were dispersed.

Zache says that every Swahili settlement or town has a special building known as a *kumbi*, large enough to house about 100 persons, to which girls are conducted on the first appearance of the menses, and where they remain in ritual seclusion for three months. They are conducted to the *kumbi* after nightfall. For the first twenty-four hours after arrival the girls abstain from food. Then their mothers bring them victuals while 'a sort of godmother', ripe in years and knowledge, protects and instructs the little maidens in all that is most necessary for wives and mothers to know.

Velten tells us that the Swahili girls have a great dance festival at the end of their seclusion in the *kumbi*. They are carried after nightfall on the backs of older women to the *muyombo* tree, where the *unyago*, or fertility dances, are performed. Some of the expert matrons of the tribe dance before the neophytes (*mwari*), displaying the twisting movements which this people have brought to a pitch of mastery in the sexual act. The girls must copy the adepts until they are themselves expert. These movements are called *tikitiza*. Songs are sung, urging the girls not to 'hide their hips'. The *kungwi*, or wise woman, also sings, inviting them to 'grind the corn' otherwise than with their stone querns.

According to Zache, the women move in close single file, describing a circle round the crouching girls. They advance slowly with a shuffling tread, and from time to time they turn round completely. Their arms hang loosely, their eyes are half closed or gaze dreamily into the distance. Meanwhile, they execute a twisting movement of the buttocks and hips, sometimes flexing their knees at the same time, the Manyema women being especially apt at this. Zache quotes some of the verses they sing, dramatizing the girls' timidity and exhorting them not to be afraid to join 'those who know'. Thus they repeat, 'Oh! on the day my c— is open, Mother won't be there, little sister won't be there! Oh! Mother! It's the old story! It's something hard and long, that old story!'

Furthermore, these rites include a puberty ordeal by fire. Each girl has to dance up to the fire and lift a vessel, set in the midst of the flames, without spilling any of its contents. The girl must also go through certain physical exercises proving spinal suppleness and agility, for example catching and lifting in her mouth a small silver or bead chain hung round her neck while lying on her back, and pass an examination on the sexual terms and allusions of the songs. If she guesses right she is applauded '*Chereko!*' (my child knows a thing or two!). If she is shy or stupid, blows are her portion. Finally she is adorned and led back to her home in triumphal procession.

According to Hahn, the Nama Hottentot girls go about quite naked till puberty. Then they are clothed in a richly decorated *kaross* (mantle of wild beasts' skin with the fur) to show they are nubile. They hold a sort of reception, sitting cross-legged for three days in a sort of stockade of wood posts a foot high, opposite the entrance to their fathers' huts, and receiving visits from kinsfolk and neighbours, who are also entertained to a feast.

Brinckner has given some account of the *Efundúla* festival of the Ovambo. The mothers of the pubescent girls bring them to the royal compound, or *Eúmbo*, and watch over them for one night. Then the real feast begins. The youths freshly initiated, and many married men as well, come with drums and songs to the royal residence at sunset and all night long there is wild dancing, singing and the throb of drums. The girls' hair is interwoven with white beads and berries; they wear girdles of beads and husks of fruit on their feet and wave ox-tails in their hands. They are under strict surveillance, and any physical intimacy with any of the men or boys means death for the girl and life-long slavery for him. The dancing is continuous and the owners of the *Eúmbo* must vacate their usual quarters while it lasts.

Then the crowd disperses. The girls are undressed by older women, head-dresses put on them and ashes rubbed over their bodies. Then, singing a curious recitative, 'Ho hui, Ho hui,' they emerge in single file from the *Eúmbo* and for a month they are free of the whole tribal domain. They are known as *Oihanangólo*, and all men and boys – even the chieftain himself – must avoid their company and flee before them under penalty of hard knocks from their sticks. When they return to their homes they bathe and are anointed afresh. They are now regarded as marriageable, but the *Efundúla* is an indispensable preliminary.

ASIA

The Veddah of southern India seclude menstruating girls in special huts for five days. Then for five more they repair to other huts, halfway nearer their homes, where there are daily ritual ablutions. On the tenth day they are fetched from the hut by their sister and their husband's sister and solemnly conducted to a ceremonial bath. Person and garments are washed, their body rubbed with turmeric, again washed, and finally anointed with oil. Then their escorts lead them back to their home. Schlagintweit says that the Veddah believe that any mistakes or omissions in the ritual imposed at such times would bring fearful retribution from the *tchawns*, who are ancestral ghosts of demoniacal character.

In Cambodia, the puberal rites for girls are termed 'stepping into the shadow' (the pregnant woman as well as the pubescent girl 'steps into the shadows', and the bonzes profit largely from the offerings of the faithful). Aymonier tells us that they are associated with adoration of the deity of darkness, the star devourer *Rahn* or *Ranh* (the Indian *Rahu*). There is much perfuming and burning of incense, which lasts from three to five days among the poorest classes to sometimes over a period of years among the wealthy. Sacrifices to the ancestral spirits and a formal announcement to them take place. A banana tree is planted, of which the fruit may be eaten by the girl alone or given by her to the temple bonzes. She may not look at any male person, eat any animal foods or go abroad, even to the pagodas.

PACIFIC ISLANDS

Antonie Herf has given an account of a festive procession in Java, where about a dozen young native men, naked and powdered with a yellow substance which gave them the appearance of wearing saffron-coloured tights, carried a costly jewelled mirror, a red fan, a brush and comb in an ivory case lined with red velvet, plates of gold with transparent sachets of native cosmetics and a variety of other such luxuries and toilet requisites, some unknown to her. They were followed by musicians and then by floating white banners and snowy flowers and tables loaded with fruit and confectionery. A fantastically decorated open carriage, drawn by white horses, followed with a much-bedizened little brown-faced girl about ten years of age, who looked very unhappy. A crowd in their gayest garments and another band brought up the rear. It was all in honour of a maiden, whose maturity and nubility were thus proclaimed.

There are various accounts of Melanesian puberty seclusion. Powell gives the time as four weeks in New Ireland, and says that the girl is shut into a cage-like structure or annexe to her home and hung with fragrant wreaths round her shoulders and hips. This 'cage' is generally two-storeyed; the girl is in the upper room and a child or old woman inhabits the room below. The girl's quarters are so extremely small in all dimensions that she cannot stand upright, but must sit or lie. She may only leave her cage by night while her seclusion lasts.

Hahl's account also refers to New Ireland, but differs in some important particulars. He says that the 'little house' or *mbak* is built as part of the large women's quarters. The girl is kept there, hidden from the public gaze, and may only emerge at night. She must squat or crouch so that her condition is not perceptible and must remain in the *mbak* for ten months (twelve to twenty months, according to Parkinson). He adds that the elder women who look after her are entitled to bring any of the men of the community, married or single, whom the girl prefers to the *mbak* so that she can have intercourse with them. But when she leaves the *mbak*, this promiscuity ceases and she keeps herself from all but her betrothed husband. At the end of her seclusion, in the course of which the freedom from hard work and the shelter from the sun's beams will have made her plump and lighter in complexion, characteristics which are considered highly attractive, a great feast is set before her by the men of her tribe and a special wooden stand set up on which food is served to her. These feasts are called *gutpok*, and are followed by ritual dances.

Danks gives a detailed account of the very prolonged seclusion of the Melanesian girls in New Britain. The missionary Romilly confirms Danks's account and gives further details of a festival which inaugurates an incarceration of about *five years'* duration.

Romilly reports the 'ceremony of caging' as described by an eyewitness. The poor little girl was laden with necklaces and chain belts of glass beads, red, white and blue, and looked very frightened. In the forenoon she had been elaborately tattooed in the painful native manner. A part of the ceremony was a very vigorous fight between the adult women of the two groups to which the native population of these islands belongs (the Maramara and the Pikalaba). These contended for the honour of guarding the captive in her seclusion. After having hurled every and any missile they could lay hands on, the victorious women made a rush at the house in which the girl was 'caged' and there was a furious mêlée in the narrow doorway of the house.

The Rev. G. Brown, as quoted by Danks, was able to obtain permission to visit these strange temporary prisons in New Britain. He had to overcome great reluctance on the chieftain's part, disapproval from the guardian duennas and, finally, extreme timidity on the part of the girls themselves, as the huts, which are situated deep in the woods, are absolutely taboo to the male sex, even to the fathers and brothers of their inmates.

The building was about twenty-five feet in length and surrounded by an enclosure of reed and bamboo. Across the entrance hung a bundle of dried grasses, a sign of most solemn and complete taboo. In the interior of the building were three conical structures about seven or eight feet in height and from ten to twelve feet in circumference at the base. These cones tapered to a point at the roof and were about four feet above the surface of the ground. They were so firmly sewn together from the wide and tough leaves and bark of the pandanus tree that no light, and a very minimum of air, could penetrate into their recesses. They had each one narrow entrance closed by a double door of plaited coconut-tree and pandanus-tree leaves. In each of these structures was a young woman who would not be released for a term of from four to five years.

Brown persuaded the old female guardian to open the cage doors and the girls peeped shyly forth, holding out their hands for the glass beads he had brought as presents. But he stood at some distance, so that they were obliged to creep out of their cages. The old woman helped her charges to circumvent the taboo on putting their feet to the ground by putting pieces of wood or bamboo as stepping-stones and holding the girls' hands so that they could walk up to Brown and receive the coveted beads.

He also examined the interior of the cages. The atmosphere was oppressively hot and close, but the little cells were perfectly clean and quite without furniture except for a few short lengths of bamboo for holding water. The girls had no room except to sit on the floor or lie in a crouched position, and when the doors were closed the cages must have been quite dark. The ritual routine was said to allow these women to come out of their cells once a day and wash themselves all over with water in a large wooden vessel. The heat of the cages evidently caused strong and frequent action of the sweat-glands. The girls entered the cages quite young and remained there till they were 'young women'. On their release each one had a great marriage feast prepared for her.

One of these girls was between fourteen and fifteen years of age and her release was imminent. The other two were between eight and ten. It was said that no deaths of girls had been known to occur while they were thus immured.

On the west coast of the islands, the period of seclusion is much shorter and less rigorous. It may be added that Danks himself never set eyes on any of these cages during the whole of his ten years' sojourn in New Britain.

Erdland gives an account of the festivities which followed the week of seclusion when a chieftain's daughter on the Marshall Islands reached puberty:

> All the subjects throughout the atoll came bringing food, flowers and mats as gifts. The girl had the half of a roomy special hut near the beach of the lagoon reserved for her. The lesser half of this building was occupied by the sorceress or wise woman and by various friends of the chieftain chosen by their families as a special honour; those favoured guests included both men and women. They were known as *rubik in kabit*.

Ceremonial ablutions were performed, and all the garments worn and utensils used during menstruation were destroyed. Erdland mentions the hieratic postures in which the girls were compelled to remain during the period, and the custom of fumigation and lustration with perfumes and flowers. He adds that the hymen was perforated, whether by some older relative or by the girl's own father, after a festival of two or three weeks' duration.

According to Krämer, the first menstrual period of Samoan girls is cele-brated quite quietly. He writes, 'The parents collected finely woven but otherwise inexpensive mats and fabrics, and invited the *analuma*, or unwedded girls of the village, to a festival; during this festival the mats were given as presents and the daughter of the house received as an *analuma*.' The girls' long hair is, however, cropped at puberty.

The missionary Keysser thus described the customs of the Kai, a Papuan tribe: 'They must abstain from many sorts of food and may not eat boiled grain and vegetables, but only baked; nor must they drink of running water but only of still. Otherwise their menstrual symptoms might become per-manent.' The Kai girls are only allowed to leave their special abode for natural needs, and they cover themselves with mats and walk on coconut shells or wooden blocks tied to their insteps with thongs; thus they are, as it were, insulated and protected against evil influences. Older kinswomen keep them company and prepare their food – especially a liquid brewed from various pungent leaves and roots and seasoned with salt and ashes, for this is supposed to be efficacious in preventing unwelcome pregnancy. They must also lie or sit on banana (*gong*) leaves and rest their heads on a block of *gong* wood.

AUSTRALIA

Among the Australian Aborigines of Queensland on the Pennefather River, the girls are led by their mothers from the camp to an enclosure where there are shady trees. The mother draws a circle on the ground and digs a deep hole into which the girl steps. The sandy soil is then filled in, leaving her buried up to the waist. A woven hedge of branches or twigs is set round her with an opening towards which she turns her face and where her mother kindles a fire. The girl remains in her nest of earth in a squatting posture, with folded arms and hands resting palm downwards on the sandheap that covers her lower limbs. She must only scratch herself with a little stick of wood and may only speak to her mother, who brings her food. When she returns to the camping place of the tribe at night, where she may converse with her husband – active sexual life begins long before puberty among these people – she must hoist herself up by the staves or poles on either side of her 'grave'. In the daytime she returns to her inhumation, and when the period of five days is over the grave is filled with ashes and stamped down.

The mother then decorates her daughter with certain insignia – a girdle round her body, a necklace of oyster shells and a frontlet or garland round her hair. Sometimes she also wears a sort of breastplate of beads. Moreover, she also wears crossed bands from the shoulder to the opposite armpit, fastened at the waist behind, and bracelets on wrists and elbows decorated with the feathers of the greenbill parrot.

CHAPTER V

Menstruation

The onset of menstruation is a profoundly disturbing occurrence to girls and is apt to cause both anxiety and a feeling of shame. It is often referred to indirectly or in veiled and ambiguous terms.

The Old Testament in English, for example, speaks of 'the manner of women', while the peoples of Ancient India termed it 'the flower growing in the house of the god of love' (Schmidt). Vatsyayana in his Kamasutra advised the maiden to speak to her too importunate lover of 'that illness which comes without being called, cannot be concealed, cannot be revealed, and yet is not always present', and Manu speaks of the 'four days which are condemned by the Illustrious Ones'.

The Japanese have many distinct phrases and expressions for this function. The most usual is *gek-ke*, which is the equivalent of our 'monthly period'. *Mengori* or *megori* means 'recurrence', return of the seasons. A term much used in the folk-songs and proverbs but too unrefined for conversation is *akane Son-ke*, 'redness'.

The Swahili women, according to Zache, call the first period *kuvunja ungo*, a term referring to the husking of grain on the flat basket-work, *ungo* or disc.

The Serbs use the simile of blossoms and seeds, and so do the women of Latvia, according to Alksnis. The term used is *seedi*, and the womb is called *seddu mahte*, i.e., the mother of seeds and blossoms.

The women of Central Europe use the equivalents of the current English phrases 'monthly time', 'periods', 'courses' and being 'unwell' or 'poorly'. The only striking expression peculiar to modern Germany is *roter König*, 'the red king', which is, however, considered impossible except in very humble circles.

i. Myths of Origin

In an account of the Sokotri texts, J. H. Müller has printed this story of the origin of menstruation:

> In olden times there was a man and a woman. The woman had no menstrual flow, but the man had blood in his armpit. These two were married and the man had always the blood. Every morning he scraped off the blood with a knife, put it into a pot and hid it from his wife.

One day his wife saw him at the place where he was hiding it and waited till he went away. When he had gone she went to the pot, took it away, unfastened the lid and took it off. She dipped her finger inside, drew it out and, thinking the blood was honey, licked her finger.

When she tasted the blood she spat it out on the ground. She looked at her finger and still saw some blood on it. So she went and washed her finger, but could not get it off. Then she took water and heated it over the fire and washed her finger, but she could not wash the blood off. So she came to her husband and said, 'What have you done with that pot there?' And he replied, 'What I have there is blood!' Then she said, 'What will get it off my finger?' He replied, 'Go to the Sage, he will get it off.'

Then the woman went to the Sage and said to him, 'I have touched my husband's blood which he scrapes off from his armpit, and I have tried to wash it off, but it won't come off.' Then the Sage said to her, 'Go, and when you get home put your finger into your vulva and then suck it.' And she did so, and the blood came off her finger and entered into the woman and from that day it flows from every woman once every month.

The ancient Hindu belief (as recorded by Schmidt) involved guilt and expiation for the death of the demi-god Visvarupa slain by Indra's thunderbolt.

Among the Omaha, menstruation is ascribed to Wakonda. In the struggle between the rabbit and the black bear, the rabbit threw the bear's mutilated member at his grandmother, wounded her and originated the catamenial function.

Archibald Hunt states that the Murray Islanders of the Torres Straits believe menstruation to be due to the amorous attacks of the Moon, a youth who periodically possesses all women.

Seligman has quoted the Sinaugolo myth (from the Rigo area of New Guinea), which also introduces the moon as the originator of menstruation. According to the story, the moon lived on earth as a tiny youth covered with silvery hair, cohabited with a woman, was slain by her husband, and has punished woman ever since.

The Tuhoe Maoris have, states Goldie, another version of the same motif. A Maori term for the period is *paheke*, which means 'ancestral spirit', 'deity' or 'mystery'. It is believed that no woman can menstruate at the new moon, but some are able to do so when it wanes, some at full and some after the first quarter or turn. The women call the moon 'husband of all women on earth'. An aged native man said, 'The union between spouses is nothing. The real husband of women is the moon.'

The New Guinea Development Company has given certain long planks of wood, decorated with carving, to the Ethnographical Museum of Berlin. According to the district superintendent they had been used in the village of Suam near Finch Harbour (New Guinea) to decorate a building whose function was to sequestrate young girls between eight and twelve years of age. This was probably one of the menstrual dwellings so frequently mentioned in our study. The planks in question are several yards long and apparently form part of a continuous pattern of figures showing the concept of menstruation as the work of supernatural or external deities.

On one plank (Fig. 13) we see a large crocodile, which seizes in its mouth the top of a tall, rectangular head-dress from which four feather ornaments project sideways, worn by a disproportionately small grotesque female form. Her face is long, her chin descends almost to the pit of her stomach, and her shoulders are on a level with her temples. Her nipples are indicated by little round holes on either shoulder, her navel by a slightly larger circular hole. Her hands are placed between her thighs as though to drag open the rima pudendi; her short legs are straddled, and her vulva is wide open. A second crocodile of equal dimensions to the first approaches her from in front and thrusts its long narrow snout into her vulva. All the figures are coloured red, black and white.

ii. *Taboos and Superstitions*

Pliny himself believed and perpetuated the belief that the very approach of menstruous women to new wine or ripe fruit caused these products to ferment and become uneatable, the seeds in the garden to become withered and, if they stood or sat in the shade of a fruit tree, the fruit to fall to the ground. Their reflection tarnished or dimmed mirrors and rusted and blunted blades of steel. Metal objects became covered with rust and malodorous, and if dogs licked such objects they became rabid and their bite fatal (*Nat. Hist.*, VII, 64 ff., XXVIII, 77 ff.).

In 1610 Guarinonius gave detailed advice to women on menstrual hygiene and precautions in doggerel verse. His injunctions were that the young girls should not frequent balls and festivals at such times, and that the wives should keep away from contact with their husbands. They should not 'whine and whimper' nor 'lay about them' in anger, or 'the poison' would 'strike up' into their limbs and make them crooked. They should avoid caressing or touching babies and young children, not prepare any cooked food themselves, not enter the wine or beer cellars, nor serve these drinks. They should even avoid the neighbourhood of vineyards and young fruit trees, 'nor look into their mirrors'. They are admonished to 'sit at home

Fig. 13 Carved wooden female figure on a plank
from a hut for menstrual seclusion, Suam, Finch Harbour, New Guinea
(Mus. f. Völkerk., Berlin; after.photo by M. Bartels)

quietly sewing', to take care of themselves and not be too sparing of 'cloths of linen' as a necessary precaution.

The superstition about wine cellars is old and widespread. Certain emanations or exudations are supposed to turn the precious liquid sour, and this superstition is extended to all stewed or distilled liquid products, jams, jellies, sauces and cordials. The wine taboo is mentioned in the Talmud (*Midrash Wayyiqra*), in the tale of Rabbi Gamliel and his maidservant Fabritha.

In Bari (southern Italy) Karusio states that menstruating women are forbidden to pickle under a cherry tree, otherwise the tree will go rotten. Their mere presence in a house at such times prevents milk from setting into butter or cheese as required. The superstitions in Belluno and Treviso are even more extreme. It is believed that grass withers where the woman treads, and if her husband sleeps beside her he has severe lumbago. Moreover, all the soiled underlinen is carefully packed and washed separately (Bastanzi). Among the peasants of the Po, the menstruating woman may not, according to Mazzuchi, visit or help any nursing mother or the milk will dry up.

H. von Wlislocki states that among the Gypsies of eastern Europe the woman at such times may neither bake bread nor make pickles, nor churn butter nor spin thread, 'for they would all go wrong'. Similar beliefs have been current for centuries among the peasantry of Germany. Saint Hildegarde declared that menstruation was particularly fatal to vegetation and noxious to wine, pickled vegetables and fruits of all kinds.

The laws of Manu are especially emphatic in warnings and prohibitions on the subject of menstruation. Intercourse or even contact between spouses at such times 'destroyed the man's brain, energy, eyesight and manhood'. Similar ideas are crystallized in Moslem texts and traditions.

'Faithful Eckarth', moreover, the popular obstetric writer of the early eighteenth century, was very emphatic on the 'dangerous and poisonous' nature of the menses. In his collection of medical and pseudo-medical folklore, it is recorded that 'some believe that the hair of a menstruating woman, if pulled out and buried in a refuse heap, will turn to serpents'. The glance of a menstruating woman prevents any wound from healing, and her bite is as fatal as that of a mad dog, especially in Cyprus and Crete. She can cast the evil eye or 'overlook' both poor children and grown people, 'which is even worse', says Eckarth.

Among the Portuguese, states Rey, there is a belief that menstruating women are bitten by lizards, and they wear trousers or knickers at such times for protection (a similar fear prevails among the Macusi Indians of British Guiana, but refers not to lizards but snakes (Schomburgk)).

In the Königsberg district of east Prussia, among the countryfolk, Hildebrandt mentions that if a girl's period falls on the day of her betrothal it is a sign of ill-luck for life.

Among primitive races, these ideas have led to murder. Thus, in Townsville, in 1870, an Australian native is reported by Armit to have killed his wife because she had wrapped herself in his blanket while menstruating and he feared some evil might result.

Special fears are entertained by primitive peoples for their hunting gear and weapons. Morice relates that Captain Back was appealed to by an Athabascan Indian squaw with a six-year-old child who had stepped over her husband's rifle by mistake in the dark during her period. The woman was in acute terror and begged for protection. Shortly after the accident, however, the hunter fortunately shot a deer with his rifle and she could return to him without hesitation. If his hunting had been unlucky, she would have risked mutilation and the loss of an ear or the tip of her nose, according to the accepted code of her people.

Hiekisch says that the Samoyed hunter must avoid contact with weapons or tools touched by the women when menstruating, for they are considered actively noxious at this time; and Pallas gives a detailed account of the fumigations of the sleds, clothes and household goods when the huts are set up. Women have to unfasten the loads bound on to the sleds *from below*, creeping between the sled poles under the reindeers' bellies. When on the march, the women may not pass between one sled and another, but have to go all the way round or crawl between the poles.

In Uganda, states Roscoe, the new moon or the moon on the wane is associated with menstruation. A woman who does not menstruate is thought to be fatal to her husband – unless he scratches her with his spear so that the abrasions bleed. Thus he ensures his safe return from battle. If a woman during her period touches her husband's gear and implements, he falls sick; if she lays a hand on his weapons, he will be slain in his next fight.

Grinnell describes typical hunting and fighting tribe taboos among the Cheyenne. The women may eat only food roasted in the warm ashes, and may not eat or sleep with their husbands for fear of bringing ill-luck in chase or foray. Furthermore, they may not touch any weapon, gun, knife or bow, and if they venture into a special hut where sacred bundles have been left, they are expected to be smitten with fatal haemorrhages.

Boas confirms the seclusion among the Nootka and says that the Shushwap women are forbidden meat at the period and must subsist on roots, and live apart from man, otherwise the bears he hunts will slay him.

VISUAL WARNINGS OF MENSTRUATION

In northern China, states Grube, especially in the Peking district, women and girls are in the habit of wearing a large ring (known as a *chieh chih* or 'ring of warning') on their finger during menstruation, thus definitely, though silently, indicating their condition.

De Rochebrune, in describing the Wolof women, states that they wear a distinctive scarf, shawl or large handkerchief, crudely and brightly coloured, folded triangularly and knotted loosely across the breast, as a sign of their condition.

Roth reports that the Queensland natives allow their young women to remain in the camp after the third recurrence of the period, but in addition to avoiding their husband's fire and lighting their own, they must also proclaim their availability for coitus by carrying a large basket of shells on their back. (At one time, the Queensland natives considered menstruation a source of fatal infection to men.)

TOXICITY AND BENEFICIAL PROPERTIES

The belief in the toxicity or poisonous properties of the blood lost during menstruation is very ancient and deep-seated. In the eighteenth century it was vehemently maintained by learned doctors of medicine, for instance by the court surgeon of the Great Elector, Timoeus von Güldenklee, whose work, published in 1704, expressed superstitions and advocated remedies now practised by the most backward European peasants. And such superstitions are equally prevalent among primitive peoples, who believe that demons rise from the menstrual blood and that these evil elements may seek to re-enter the body of the girl – or of other women – and render them diseased or sterile. Among the Gypsies, for example, menstrual blood is used as a poison, and if mixed with earth and strewn in food is believed to deprive a detested husband or lover of genital potency and to inspire hatred of the object of his desire. Similarly, Schurig, in his *Parthenologia*, states that, when mixed with wine, menstrual blood makes people moon-struck or turns them insane and 'mad with love'.

In 1920, Alois Czepa published an article (in the periodical *Umschau*) in which he referred to an address by Professor B. Schick to the Medical Society of Vienna. Professor Schick had handed a magnificent spray of roses to one of his domestic servants in order that she might arrange the flowers in a vase, but the next morning they were withered. He was amazed, but the girl said she ought to have foreseen what would happen for such was always the effect of menstruating women on flowers which they handled.

The professor thereupon attempted a simple comparative experiment. He gave two bunches of similar flowers (in this case anemones and chrysanthemums) to two domestics, one of whom was undergoing her period and the other inter-menstrual, and asked them to hold the flowers in their hands for sixteen minutes each. The non-menstruating girl's bouquet remained fresh and unspoilt; in the other case the flowers drooped and were seamed with brownish streaks after sixteen hours and withered after twenty-four. The leaves fell away after forty-eight hours.

On the third day, however, the test flowers in the hands of the menstruating girl remained in better condition than those held by the non-menstruating control, and on the fourth day no damage to the flowers was demonstrable. Professor Schick maintains that 'menotoxin' is at its greatest virulence on the first day of the period.

Schick also found that his menstrual test cases often could not prepare dough with yeast and that even when they partially succeeded their dough was half as high as that of the non-menstruating controls.

It has been stated that cases of hysterectomy in which the ovaries were left intact and functional suffered from morbid symptoms which could only be attributed to self-poisoning through menotoxin in the organism. In such cases, ovarian preparations were useless, but blood-cleansing and purgative methods were beneficial. Menstruation is thus in one aspect a cleansing liberation from what we now term menotoxin.

We have already mentioned the primitive conviction of the extremely noxious and dangerous nature of menstrual blood. To the primitive mind there was only one step between this conviction and the attempt to use menstrual blood homeopathically as an antidote to the bad magic of disease. Moreover, this trend of thought was not confined to the peasantry and the uneducated classes but also received support from physicians of experience and repute. Pliny, for example, reports that applications of menstrual blood were considered curative of podagra (gout), goitre, sore throat, erysipelas, boils, puerperal fever, the bites of mad dogs, epilepsy and even mere headaches, while Saint Hildegarde recommended ample baths of menstrual blood as an infallible preventive against leprosy.

A special – or sometimes sole – efficacy was attributed to the first menstruation in this respect. Garments stained with this fluid were soaked in Rhine wine or vinegar, according to Welsch, and the result used as a medicament and considered useful against epilepsy. Others thought it efficacious as an emmenagogue or in curing stone; others again, mixed with bread and theriac against tertian fever.

In Pliny's time, menstruating women could disperse storms and hail, and their presence on board saved many a ship in peril. Insects fell from trees if a naked menstruating woman approached. Metrodorus of Scepsis, whom Pliny quotes (*Nat. Hist.*, XXVIII, 7), has described the Cappadocian custom whereby women during the period walked at night naked below the waist or with unbound tresses, bare feet and girdles unloosed through the fields to destroy insect pests. But Pliny warns us that after sunrise this method lost all its efficacy, for even young vines and climbing plants such as ivy withered at the touch of the menstruous woman.

In Ancient India menstrual blood was an ingredient in magic potions promoting virile force and length of life. The Kausika Sutra was emphatic on this point – but it had to be the blood of the first menstruation.

The Ancient Goths, Finns and Lapps used it on their venturous sea voyages, smearing sails and ropes therewith. Young maidens were safe from harm if they wore a shred of their own stained linen and a morsel of fern root in a little bag round their necks. To the lusty and the worldly it brought luck in games of hazard and victory in battle; to the sick, healing, both among men and cattle, and especially in cases of mange or itch.

The Gypsies of Transylvania, states von Wlislocki, practised a primitive kind of organotherapy, bathing the male organ before coitus in asses' milk and menstrual blood, or drinking the powdered testicles of a fox and menstrual blood, mixed with food. The full moon appeared repeatedly as a necessary accessory in these rites.

A. von Henrici's collection of traditional Russian folk medicine has examples from Novaya Uschytza and Ryshancvka, especially against warts and birthmarks. The blood mixed with water was to be drunk, or stained clothes laid on the affected parts.

iii. Seclusion and Purification

The belief in the perilous and 'unclean' properties of menstruating women was held firmly by the Iranians 5,000 years ago and is perpetuated in the teachings of Zoroaster. The Medes, Persians and Bactrians had rigid rules in this respect. Zoroaster prescribed nine days' abstention from coitus in addition to five further nights if the menses lasted over four days. The incarceration of menstruating women in dark *Dachtansatan* rooms, in silence and with insufficient food, is still the law of the Indian Parsis' Zoroastrian faith.

In Ancient India the existence of women during menstruation was one series of deprivations, degradations and prohibitions, some of the most fantastic character. Should any of these be infringed, the woman's children and descendants were believed to be in danger or afflicted in some way.

Mohammed expressly forbade coitus in marriage until the woman had gone through her ritual purification, and all Islam to this day regards menstruation as unclean. In some respects this stringent taboo favours personal hygiene. Thus in Persia and Turkey women are expected to wash all over at such times thrice in twenty-four hours and to abstain from religious exercises.

Jewish women are forbidden to work in their kitchens, sit at meals with others or drink water from a glass which another person may happen to use during the period. The time of seclusion and taboo lasted a fortnight in the code as first given to Israel. Any contact with the husband during this time made him 'unclean' or *tame*, and the punishment for actual coitus during menstruation was death for both partners.

The Talmudists decreed that there must be careful ablutions after menstruation and then a plunge bath. The water had either to be 'natural', i.e., from a lake or river, or else rainwater. According to Weill, even the smallest Jewish colony had its special *mikveh*, which was arranged so that the water could be warmed. The ablutions and plunge bath were taken in the presence of two women specially selected and generally paid by the community. Whether in summer or winter, the woman had to immerse herself completely three times. Only after bathing and dressing in her usual attire was she recognized by her husband as 'clean'.

Dubois states that the Hindus have a series of graduated stages of 'uncleanness' for the successive days of menstruation. According to the regulations in the ancient scriptures relevant to the subject (the Nittia Carma and the Padmapurana), the seclusion is absolute for three days; then, on the fourth, there are elaborate ritual ablutions. Among the endless prohibitions for the first three days, she must not weep; she must not fall asleep in the daytime or clean or rinse her mouth and teeth; she must not let her thoughts dwell on prayer and sacrifice, nor on the divine sublimity of celestial things; she must not greet any persons of higher rank. Even the *wish* to cohabit with her spouse is a deadly sin.

Even among the very primitive indigenous tribes of northern India there is an elaborate menstrual taboo. The Gauri, a Sanskrit-speaking people in northern Bengal, according to Tavernier, have the following custom: all women or girls, as soon as their periods begin, retreat with all haste to a little hut standing in the fields made of branches woven like basketwork and with a long woven curtain before the doorway. There, so long as their sickness lasts, they are given food. When their time is past, they send to the priests a goat, a pullet or a dove as sacrifice. Then they bathe and summon their kinsfolk to a meal which they have prepared.

When the Nayars of Malabar build a house, there is always a special room for the women's residence during menstruation, birth and the puerperium.

In Travancore, states Jagor, the ranees have a palace of their own.

Throughout primitive Africa we find these ideas and customs of menstrual seclusion in various manifestations. The Ibo Negress of Old Calabar, for example, is forbidden, states Hewan, to leave her home during her period and must sit on a specially constructed chair resembling an old-fashioned 'commode', while on the Guinea and Ivory Coasts, for instance at Issini, there are, according to Loyer, special huts some hundred yards or so from the rest of the buildings. The women and girls retire to these buildings and their food is brought to them there.

In parts of the Congo, states Degrandpré, the menstruating woman is secluded most strictly for six days; if anyone catches sight of her she is further secluded for another six days. Afterwards, she cleanses her body all over with red earth and then with water.

The term used by the Ewe Negroes of southern Togoland for menstruating women is *gbototesitri* or *dudatsitsi* – 'stay apart from the village'.

Pechuel-Loesche mentions the separation from homes and husbands during the period among the Bakongo of the Loango coast. He also informs us that the women pound a vegetable product from a tree growing in the Majombe district into a powder which is called *takulla*, and colour their bodies red with this substance. Moreover, they practise extreme cleanliness by extensive bathing and washing, and appear generally to suffer very little during their periods.

Holub mentions a seven-day seclusion of wives among the Makololo and other Marotse peoples on the Zambesi. The curious cone-shaped structures in the palace precincts are the menstrual abodes of the chieftain's harem and of the princesses.

We find similar customs among the free 'Bush Negroes' whose ancestors were transported as slaves from Africa to Surinam. The women, writes Riemer, are debarred from social companionship and converse even with their own sex. They must leave their husbands' huts until they have recovered and must particularly avoid turning their backs on or walking before anyone. They must call aloud '*Mi kay, mi kay!*' ('I am unclean').

Alberti mentions the rigid separation of the sexes among the Kaffir women, and Le Vaillant, speaking of Hottentots and Gonaqua alike, states that the women retire at once to a special hut set apart, or build one for themselves, and remain there till menstruation ceases. They then have a ceremonial ablution. He believes that the aesthetic motive, the wish to please and the fear of exciting disgust is very strong among these peoples.

Among the Wandonde (East Africa), the women may not cohabit with their husbands or eat with them out of the same vessel during menstruation. They have to fold a large leaf together and drink water from it as from a funnel. Nor may they follow in the footsteps of any men. They may not bathe during menstruation, but at the end of each period, states Fülleborn, there is a ritual bath and purification conducted by a medicine woman.

Vaughan Stevens has given particulars of the customs of the various tribes in Malacca. Among the Orang Laut, for example, menstruating girls and women may neither drink out of the same water vessels as the men nor cook and prepare food for them. (In practice, however, this means that they may dig up the roots which the men then peel and prepare.) The women have definite rules about ablution and post-menstrual purification. They wash their genital organs and lower limbs in water carried in specially capacious bamboo tubes known as *chit-nort*, which are painted with mystic designs to avert mischief from the evil spirits and spectres and kept hidden from the men. Indeed, no man will touch one, believing that coitus or even contact with a menstruating woman will damage his virility.

On the islands round Ceram Laut the natives not only avoid coitus but also forbid social converse at such times. Nor may the women dye thread or fabrics, help with the fishing or visit gardens or plantations.

Very similar ideas and customs prevail elsewhere. Mertens records them in Micronesia (Carolines, Marshalls, Gilberts and Marianas) and others testify as regards almost the whole of Polynesia.

The Australian natives, according to Schürmann, regard their womenfolk as taboo for a week during their periods and keep them secluded in a hut apart.

There are many records of seclusion at menstruation among the Indians of North and South America; sometimes this is limited to the first occasion, sometimes it is recurrent and lifelong. Coitus and even slight contact is avoided, and the woman lives in a hut or tent apart during the period (Fig. 14).

Among the Chevsurs of the Caucasus, the menstruating women have to dwell apart in remote huts of slate known as *samrevlo*. They wear their oldest and shabbiest garments and, if the sun shines, they sit on the low roofs of the huts and devour an immense amount of raw herbs and greenstuff, chervil especially and all varieties of thyme. These are eaten uncooked and unsoaked and a considerable quantity of sour milk is sipped. (The women are not, however, considered too 'unclean' to milk the cows and take them to the stables.)

In certain Japanese provinces, especially in Hida, women may not visit temples or pray to the gods or invoke the good spirits during menstruation. In other districts, they are secluded in their apartments and may not share the meals of the household.

Fig. 14 Tent used among the Indians of North America for secluding women at menstruation (after Schoolcraft)

iv. Tampons and the Like

It is probable that special precautions (and possibly special ceremonies) are observed in disposing of the discarded bandages and necessary occasional garments, but very little is definitely known about this. We learn, however, from Goldie that the Maori women use as pads (which they call *kope*) clumps of fine soft moss (possibly *Hypnum clandestinum*) which are crushed up and pressed against the vagina and then burned secretly in the woods. Each woman has her own 'burial place' and any intrusion on her privacy in this matter would be considered so grave an insult that her humiliation would probably lead to suicide.

Among the Kai of New Guinea there are similar customs, and not only in respect of menstruation but also of the placenta after birth. The missionary Keysser gives a curious account of primitively logical animism here, stating that if the wild pigs of the islands were to find and devour any such objects it is feared that they would visit the fields and plantations and devastate them. Moreover the *mana* of the women, whose daily duty it is to visit and dig in the fields, would pass into the pigs' bodies and if this occurred often the animals would die.

In Indonesia, where coitus is avoided during menstruation, the native women use tampons, balls or pads of soft vegetable fibre which are inserted into the vagina, while in Central Africa the Azimba women wear pads or lumps of the same material as bandages. These are held in position, according to Angus, by a soft oval piece of goatskin and twisted thong.

The ladies of Japan, in all classes, practise a form of personal hygiene at such times. They always carry a large store of thin paper about with them. This paper is rolled, pinched and kneaded into balls the size of a walnut or large almond and inserted into the vagina, especially before visiting the theatre (although menstruating women are forbidden to work hard, bathe or have sexual intercourse and must avoid chills – *shimokase*, or 'wind blowing from below' – they are allowed to divert their minds by visiting the theatres). As soon as they feel that the absorbent paper has become saturated they retire and insert another. In order to keep the tampons in place, the women wear a well-made T-bandage known colloquially as *kama*, 'the pony' or 'the little horse'. A thorough bath is usually taken after the period.

Both Virey and Steller state that the Kamchadale used vaginal tampons of grass or vegetable fibres during their periods and wove special bandages to keep them in place.

According to Pallas, there is a similar custom among the Ostiak women, who

> constantly wear a twisted roll of soft schappe silk pushed up as far as possible and frequently changed for the sake of cleanliness. And because this would fall out if it were not kept in place, the Ostiak women have invented a belt shaped almost like the girdle of chastity inaugurated by the jealousy of southern Europe, and a bandage is passed between the thighs with a special shield of birch bark.

v. Anomalies

Yamasaki quotes an interesting case which has more than one significant aspect:

> Among the Japanese prostitutes, whose menstrual history I was able to study, there were two women who were twin sisters and grew up under exactly similar conditions. They entered the same elementary school on the same day, left it on the same day, did the same work in their home, which was also a confectioner's and baker's shop, became inmates of the same brothel on the same day, and began their menstrual period on the same date. Moreover, since then, their menstrual periods have almost synchronized.

Goldie reports a case of vicarious menstruation among the Ruatahuna natives. A woman of the Hamua tribe had severe nose-bleeding at every new moon but never menstruated in the normal manner.

Habits of life may, it appears, either promote regular menstruation or cause direct injury. Uterine disease is frequent among the Hindus, and Rigler found much menstrual irregularity – metrorrhagia, amenorrhoea and dysmenorrhoea – among the secluded and hygienically neglected women of the East. On the other hand, Polak declared menstrual irregularities extremely rare in Persia and noted that they occurred only among those women who were neglected by their husbands.

According to Blyth, menstrual anomalies are not unknown in Fiji. He attributes these to the habit of bathing in the rivers and wading in the sea in order to catch fish.

Ravn says that suppressed menstruation is common among the Faroe Islanders. The women go about barefoot and their feet often become soaked or chilled to the bone, thus causing severe shocks and cold.

Olafsson has made very similar observations and comments on Iceland, especially as concerns the unmarried girls. He attributes these disturbances to their lack of exercise, to their very sedentary life at the loom or the spinning-wheel during the long winter, to their habit of crouching or squatting on a mat or rug or on the cold floor, to their lack of mental interests and distractions, their apathy and melancholy. He adds, 'Perhaps there are many other reasons for the ill-health of the female sex which no one considers or thinks worth while to discover.'

Keating was informed by a Red Indian chief of the Pottawatomi tribe that irregular and suppressed menstruation was common among the women of his tribe. Bernoulli also reports the same symptoms as 'frequent' in Guatemala. Similarly, in Sierra Leone, the practising surgeon, Robert Clarke, found amenorrhoea, dysmenorrhoea, haemorrhages and leucorrhoea as common among the native Negresses as among the resident English women.

It has been asserted that changes of climatic environment may cause great and rapid menstrual changes. Blumenbach was one of the first to mention that European women who went to the Guinea Coast were at once troubled with uterine haemorrhages, a well-known effect of residence in the tropics that may be due to anaemia, arising through malarial infection.

Hippocrates held that such women as had never been pregnant were far more subject to menstrual irregularities and sufferings than those who had borne children, for the post-partum lochia was beneficial to the whole circulation. He also noted that the average mean temperature was slightly higher in women than in men and considered that the normal monthly period prevented this temperature from reaching a dangerous pitch.

vi. Remedies

Neither Hippocrates nor his immediate successors had any exact knowledge of internal human female anatomy, in spite of their recipes for curing both obstructions and haemorrhages. Paulus Aegineta recommended blood-letting, ligatures round the thighs, fumigations and a draught of myrrh. The Arab masters of medicine took the same line; both Avicenna and Serapion advised blood-letting, ligatures and such supposed emmenagogues as musk, castor oil and myrrh.

A prolonged menstrual period (over nine days) was attributed in Iran to evil spirits and treated with four hundred strokes, and all kinds of purifications with water and cow's urine were undertaken. Ants and other insects had to be slain in sacrifice as well.

In the East Indies and in the Malay Archipelago, states Epp, a favourite method of hastening delayed menstruation is by rubbing and kneading various parts of the body, then consuming various herbs and vegetable brews which are reported to have excellent effects.

The favourite emmenagogue among the Japanese is a plant of the genus Madder (*Rubia cordiflora*), which the women call *shenkong akane*. Further recourse is now had to iron and quinine preparations, hot foot-baths and mustard poultices, and both pepper and mustard are taken orally in various dilutions and combinations. Williams reports that *key-tu-sing* is employed for amenorrhoea among the Japanese. This tincture, made from the leaves of a tree belonging to the *Ternstroemiaceae*, is drunk at full moon with mysterious ceremonies.

The Chinese women have a large collection of remedies, some of a curious kind, for example mixtures of the urine of boys with old wine and herbal drugs. For pains in the heart before menstruation they use decoctions of grass roots and rotten lemons. For blackish menstrual blood, peony rinds and symphytum, saffron and green lemons. Excessive losses are countered by a mixture of sea-kale (*Crambe maritima*) and white spear thistles.

Goldie states that the New Zealand Maori are wont to isolate their women when suffering from dysmenorrhoea, treating them with a decoction of the New Zealand flax lily (*Phormium tenax*) and the *Rubus australis*, a variety of brambleberry. They attribute great influence to the phases of the moon, and, since the moon rises in the east, they pluck the twigs and shoots of these plants from the eastern side of the plantation.

The Algerian women have many different methods of dealing with suppressed menses. Sometimes they throw some ammonium chloride, which they term *nchader*, on the fire and squat or straddle above the fumes, or they use other materials for fumigation, immediately after various ceremonial ablutions. Or they introduce tampons of wool or cotton smeared with black sulphide of antimony into their vagina. But sympathetic magic is considered more efficacious. The woman writes the names of her father, her mother and other near kinsfolk on four or five poplar leaves and puts them into a copper box, which is then laid on the fire. If smoke rises thickly and hides the receptacle, all will soon be well.

If the menses are punctual but scanty and painful, the woman drinks a decoction of black cumin (*Nigella sativa*), according to Bertherand. But if she suffers from too profuse losses, a compound of vinegar and diluted vitriol or of honey mixed with vitriol and the rind of pomegranates is inserted into the vagina.

If a Fezzan girl is of full womanly physical development but without menstrual periods, she is given, according to Nachtigal, a brew made of barley meal, butter and sugar for three days in succession and a paste made from madder.

The Swahili regard a girl or woman with delayed menstruation as ill and treat her with *dawa* – that is, with relaxation and alteration of previous food taboos for seven days. Her food is cooked specially for her and she drinks the liquid gravy.

Blyth has given some facts about the Fiji Islanders. The bark or rind of the *vesi ndina* (a tree of the greenheart species) is grated fine and an infusion made therewith. This is often efficacious in bringing on menstruation; if it fails, then nothing else can avail. The midwives say that there are sometimes fatal cases involving *suppressio mensium* as a symptom. There are also cases of painful and excessive losses which the Fijians call *dravutu*. The native wise women treat these with another infusion of the grated leaves and stem of a climbing vine called *wa Ndamu*. The wise women visit and 'treat' their patients at intervals of four days.

Specifics for the regulation of menstruation play a particularly important part in popular medicine. Not only fear of possible pregnancy, but also certain ideas of the harmful effects on the organism of the absence of the monthly elimination of blood, cause their use. As supposedly proven and reliable specifics of the populace we know ground ivy, hazelwort, saffron, the onion, iron filings softened for twenty-four hours in a warm place, chalk taken in the form of a fine powder, salt, magnesia and soda or ground mustard as an admixture in hot baths. Physicians are known to have used sodium, salicylic acid and potassium permanganate, the latter as a pill, as specifics for restoring menstruation.

The Serbs, according to Krauss, have a form of sympathetic magic by which the woman with suppressed periods drinks 'the juices of red flowers and berries'. But those who suffer during their periods must wash themselves and pour the water over a red rose bush (Petrowitsch).

Bastanzi says that in Belluno and Treviso, mallows and maidenhair fern are used as emmenagogues. In Bari, according to Karusio, uterine haemorrhages are treated by tying waist, wrists and ankles with cords and even the fingers with black wool. The bleeding will then soon cease.

In Swabia, the popular remedies include savine and feverfew, as well as rue, columbine and the urine of goats. Mare's milk is also drunk, diluted with rainwater. Bitter almonds are, according to Lammert, the favourite remedy for menorrhagia.

CHAPTER VI

Marriage

It was Lubbock first of all and then McLennan, Lewis, Morgan, Post, von Hellwald and Wilken who advanced the opinion that, originally, no actual marriage, and consequently no families, existed, but only tribal societies and tribal fellowships in which communal marriage existed. In this all the men and women belonging to the little community would have regarded themselves as married uniformly to each other. These peculiar conditions in the tribes of primitive mankind Lubbock designated 'hetaerism'.

Bachofen endeavoured to defend the idea of the original type of tribal society as the cementing of a group of blood relations through their tribal mother. Following Strabo, he designated this as gynocracy; and he collected examples from Greek and Roman writers to support his view. Similar conditions are to be found among the very different North and South American tribes; among numerous communities of the South Seas; among Hindu primitive peoples; and in many African tribes.

Giraud-Teulon states that in Australia, when war breaks out between two tribes, it is the signal in each for the departure of a great number of young men, who go to join the tribe of their maternal parent, so that it is not unusual to see father and son in opposite camps.

Stevens also found matriarchy among the Orang Laut in Malacca, but sees in this no preference for the female sex, the women being very badly treated in this tribe particularly.

Among the nomad Gypsies in Hungary, maternal government still prevails. H. von Wlislocki writes that

the tent gypsy, as soon as he takes a wife, must join the clan to which his wife belongs; further, that after his marriage, he is still reckoned as a person or unit among the kinsfolk or clan to which he belongs by birth, but he and his issue belong only to the kinsfolk of his wife ... Probably the reason for this peculiar relationship is ... that the young husband gets the whole outfit of a gypsy 'household' – tents, wagons, horses, tools, etc. – from his wife, whose relations watch carefully that he who has married into their troupe does not waste the 'wealth' of his wife. He has, accordingly, to travel with his wife's clan, and if necessity requires it, has even to separate from his nearest relations by birth, whom he then meets only sometimes in the common winter quarters.

i. Family Relations

There were several forms of marriage in Ancient Egypt. Some comprised simple intimate love-relations, even including the less rigid form of marriage. The wife or female partner received a certain sum of money and had her choice of living with the man in his household. Her eldest son was entitled to inherit from the father. In this case she could, it seems, be formally and finally repudiated.

In another form, the wife became the official partner with a share in all the man's property and equal rights. These alliances were concluded in contractual form and the woman could not be repudiated arbitrarily, though a divorce could take place. If it did, the woman's dowry or its equivalent was returned to her.

In yet another form, which probably originated with the custom of inheritance through the daughter, the *Nebt-pa*, or lady of the house, obtained formal possession of the house and control of the household arrangements. In certain cases the man appears to have made over his property to her and only stipulated that she should provide him with good treatment and keep. The *Nebt-pa* was entitled to leave her husband.

Most of the demotic marriage contracts which have come down to us were found in the ruins of Thebes. Many of these arrangements stipulated the payment by the man of a dowry to the wife and also a yearly allowance.

One can contrast with this the position of women in primitive patriarchal societies such as those in Africa or Oceania.

According to Merensky, each Zulu woman has her own hut, enclosure, garden and household goods. Nevertheless, the Zulu are extremely patriarchal. They are herdsmen, and girls are bought from parents for so many head of cattle. Sometimes marriage by purchase is modified into marriage by service, but once a wife, the woman is a servant.

Waitz says of the social position of women in Fiji:

> The wife is her husband's property; property bought by him from her parents. As a rule, he is at liberty to drive her into the wilderness, lend her, exchange her, or sell her outright for the wherewithal to purchase new wives, etc. Among the common people ... the women are ... simply wares, bought and sold in the market, and may be slain and eaten by their husbands with complete immunity from either communal punishment or private revenge. A man's wives are often inherited by his son, like a house or a piece of furniture.

POLYGAMY

The polygamous impulse exists more strongly in man than in woman. His love-life falls, if we leave 'cultural' suppressions out of the question, to the woman who has the strongest erotic effect on him, a circumstance to which prostitution pays very careful attention; marriage, however, does not. Therein lies the deep gulf, the very cause of unhappy marriages.

So long as our wives understand how to keep their attraction for their husbands, marriages will be happy: on this subject our wives could learn from the prostitutes. The difference between them is most clearly shown by a feminine characteristic: *love of underclothes*. The better prostitutes and the Frenchwomen of good position love beautiful linen, and have very good taste in it. They also, however, use it consciously as a sexual stimulus. Quite different is the German 'Gretchen'; with her the urge for cleanliness has become a neurosis and the erotic sensation has been repressed.

Polygamy literally means multiple marriage, although it is generally used only for multiple wives (polygyny), i.e., matrimonial union of one man with several women.

The Koran (Sura 4) expressly permits the Mohammedan to marry several wives (although the Persian, according to law, may not have more than four lawful wives at the same time with whom he has contracted a permanently binding marriage). According to Vámbéry:

> In the Mohammedan countries – I am not afraid to make this bold assertion – among thousands of families there is at most one where legal permission for polygyny is claimed. Among the Turkish, Persian, Afghan, and Tatar people (i.e., among the lower ranks) it is unheard of, even unthinkable, as several wives necessitate also greater expense. It occurs just as rarely . . . among the middle classes. In the higher classes, and in the highest of all, this social evil is, of course, terribly rampant.

Von Maltzan, on the contrary, found that in the towns of Arabia there were as a rule several wives in one house, and that, of the Arabs in Jerusalem, even the poorest had two.

According to Chavanne, the nomadic Arab tribes of the Sahara treat and view women as slaves but give them a certain amount of freedom. Polygamy is customary and welcomed by the wife as it means that her burden of household toil is lessened.

Polygamy on a large scale is characteristic not only of Islam, but of primitive paganism as well, whether in Africa or elsewhere. Dobritzhoffer, for example, remarks that the South American Indians change their wives more frequently than Europeans their clothing, but almost always the women have their own separate huts or tents. Among both the Carib and the Chilean tribes, the rights and duties of the polygamous wives are arranged and systematized by immemorial usage. Frezier says that in Chile the Indians have an alternate system: the particular wife who has spent the night with the man cooks for him on the morrow, as well as saddling his horse and cleaning the hut. Among the Carib, the wives, according to du Tertre, take turns, a month at a time. Among the Peruvians, on the other hand, the men undertake a share of the domestic work, which is usually left to the women.

Among the tribes of the Juri, Passé, Miranha and others the first wife is mistress and superior to the rest, and her hammock is hung next to her husband's. There may be five or six other wives, but they are economically expensive. Each woman has her own hammock and generally her own hearth as well, especially when she has borne a child. The husband is generally feared by these women, and he only acquires a semblance of peace from their intrigues by extreme strictness.

Polygamy is frequent in Polynesia, but poor men can only support one wife. Their chieftains generally have half a dozen, and others according to their rank and station.

The Germanic peoples, too, had polygyny. Adam of Bremen tells of the Swedes that they were temperate in everything except the number of their wives. Each had two or three, or even more in proportion to his wealth. The wealthy and the princes had no limitations as to number, and these were genuine marriages, for the children had full legal rights. As well as among the Scandinavians, polygyny also occurs among the distinguished Franks: Clotaire I took two sisters as wives; Charibert I had many wives; Dagobert I, three wives (and innumerable concubines). These were real marriages contracted by purchase, betrothal and 'leading home'.

POLYANDRY

The union of one wife with several husbands is most widespread among the tribes in Ceylon, in India, especially among the Todas, the Nayar and other tribes in the Nilgiri Hills; further, also, in Tibet; among the Eskimos, Aleuts, Koniago and Tlingit. This custom has also been found among the Australian Aborigines, in the Marquesas Islands and among the Iroquois.

About polyandry among the tribes of the valley of the Upper Indus, Rousselet says:

> The marriage of several men to one wife is probably the oldest type of
> social organization among the natives of the Indus and the Western
> Himalayas . . . As a rule, when the eldest brother marries, all his brothers
> thereby become husbands of his wife. The children who result from this
> alliance do not belong to anyone singly, but give the various husbands of

their mother the title of father without distinction . . . a woman sometimes has four husbands at once; but the number is not limited in any way. Besides this regular form of polyandry, the wife has also the right to choose one or more husbands (not lovers) in addition to the group of brothers . . . Among the polyandrous people in Kulu the wife forms the head of the community. She manages the property which is worked by the husbands, the income from which they hand over to her. She alone establishes the children and bequeaths her property to them.

A. Brandeis reports from the South Sea island of Nauru that polyandry is rare, although sometimes several brothers have one wife together.

On the Isle of Lancerote, in the Canary Islands, polyandry was practised by the indigenous inhabitants, but the head of the household was always a man. Each one of the joint husbands occupied this position in turn for a lunar month.

In Caesar's time, almost the same conditions existed among the Britons, ten to twelve men ('*et maxime fratres cum fratribus parentesque cum liberis*') having a wife together. The children were considered the issue of the one who first co-habited with her (*De Bello Gallico*, V, 14).

TRIAL MARRIAGES

Of the Hurons (Wyandote) in the seventeenth century, the Jesuit missionaries are quoted by Parkman as reporting:

> There was also a period of trial marriage which lasted a day, a week, or longer. The sealing of the contract consisted merely in the acceptance of a present of wampum (pearl money) which the suitor made to the object of his desire or whim. These presents were never returned at the dissolution of the union. As an attractive and enterprising young lady could enter into twenty such marriages before her final marriage, and frequently did so, she collected in this way a wampum ornament with which to adorn herself for the village dances.

In Persia marriage is either *akdi*, i.e., permanently binding so long as there is no valid ground for divorce, or *sighei*, i.e., only for a stipulated period of time. In *sighei*, the woman is married on payment of a certain remuneration and of a settled sum on the appearance of pregnancy; during this stipulated time, she enjoys the full rights of a legal wife. On the expiration of the contract, however, she is forbidden to the man by law.

In northern Dalmatia there existed, and still may exist, according to A. Mitrovič, the trial marriage, or, as he calls it, the period marriage (*zeitehe*):

The lad cannot or may not . . . be married at once, before he has taken home the bride. He wants to test her, first of all. He wants to see and be convinced that she will give birth to children. If she brings children into the world, especially if they are boys, then he marries her – if he himself does not die beforehand. If she brings no children into the world, she can and must leave the man's house.

Of the Igorrote in the Philippines, Hans Meyer says:

If two lovers have their parents' consent for their marriage, then a feast takes place at which roast pig and rice play the chief part. During the feast the couple to be married are shut alone in a hut, where they stay, provided with food, till the end of the feast – four or five days. After this trial period, either of the parties is free to abandon the marriage. If the man withdraws, he has to present the girl with a dress, a piece of feldspar, a cooking kettle, a bracelet and ear-rings, and he has to bear the cost of the feast. If the girl withdraws, then the cost of the feast falls upon her. But if the girl becomes pregnant as a result of this trial marriage, then the man has to build her a hut and give her a pig and some fowls.

ii. Age at Marriage

At this point we should acquaint ourselves with what, in civilized countries, must be considered the legal age for marriage.

Among the Ancient Hindus, girls seem to have been married early: according to the law of Manu, a man of twenty-four would preferably be given a girl of eight, a man of thirty a girl of twelve (Duncker).

Early marriages were also arranged for girls among the Ancient Medes, Persians and Bactrians. Celibacy from choice, even when it lasted only till the girls' eighteenth year, was threatened with the longest punishment in hell; and girls were ordered when they had reached their eighteenth year to ask their parents for a husband. There were, according to the decrees of Avesta, only three kinds of uncleanness for which any atonement and purification were an impossibility, either here or in the life beyond. They were: a) if anyone ate of a dead dog; b) if anyone fed from a human corpse; and c) if a girl up to her twentieth year had not yet entered into the married state.

Among the Romans the girls were married between their thirteenth and sixteenth years. A woman who had reached twenty without being a mother incurred the punishment which Augustus had inflicted on celibacy and childlessness. Hence the age of nineteen was the uttermost limit to the conclusion of marriage.

In the Middle Ages, in Lombardian, Frisian and Saxon law and in the Swabian Code of Laws, we find the same age limit as that decreed by the Church, i.e., twelve for girls and fourteen for boys.

The less civilized peoples of Europe, especially in the southern parts, still have the custom of marrying the young girls early. For example, Cleghorn writes that on the island of Minorca the girls marry at the age of fourteen. Among the Mainotes of Greece, the girls marry as early as their twelfth or thirteenth year. It is also stated that among the Hungarian Gypsies there are mothers of twelve and thirteen years.

It is quite different in northern Europe. Esthonian women, for instance, seldom marry at a very youthful age: in the years 1834–59 only between 4 and 15 per cent of marriages were concluded before the twentieth year. Wappaeus, in 1859, reckoned as the average age of marriage of all women married: in England, twenty-six; France, twenty-six; Norway, twenty-eight; the Netherlands, twenty-nine; and Belgium, twenty-nine.

Among the Warrau (Guarauno) Indians of British Guiana, on the other hand, the girls enter into matrimony as early as their tenth year (in the Guato tribe of Paraguay at five to eight, according to Rhode); at ten to thirteen among the Smoo in the Mosquito territory of Nicaragua; at fourteen among the Delaware and Iroquois Indians of North America; at ten to twelve among the Aborigines of South Australia; at twelve to thirteen among the Maori of New Zealand; at ten among the Samoyed; and at ten to twelve among the Javanese. In North Africa, twelve- to fourteen-year-old brides are reported, for example among the Egyptian women, the Beni Mezab of the Sahara and the Kabyles, while the Mande-Maningo of Sierra Leone and the Ama-Xosa, Basuto, Bechuana and Ovaherero are among those African tribes whose females marry at about the age of twelve. The girls of the Bushmen are often married when they are seven, and are sometimes mothers at twelve or even ten (Burchell).

All Mohammedans are permitted to enter into matrimony at ten years of age. In Persia, although the girl may legally marry only after menstruation has appeared and the pubic and axillary hair begins to grow, the poorer classes do not abide by this and buy a dispensation from the priest.

iii. Courtship and Betrothal

Hagen reports that among the Papuans of Astrolabe Bay in New Guinea, if a young man wants to woo a girl, he rolls a cigarette in which he has entwined a hair of his head, one from his shoulders and one from his pubic region. This he smokes half through and then gives to his mother, requesting her to take it to the lady of his choice. Then, if she smokes it to the end, the suitor is accepted.

Among the Hottentots in the neighbourhood of Angra Pequena, the lover goes to the parents of his choice, sits down silently and, still silent, makes coffee. When it is ready, he pours out a bowlful to hand to the bride. If she drinks half of it and gives the bowl back to the suitor so that he may drink the other half, then he is accepted. If she leaves the drink standing, the lover does not grieve unduly; rather he wanders on to another hut to try his luck again (Sigismund Israel).

Among the Ama-Xosa, however, if the girl refuses the bridegroom whom her parents prefer, there is a drastic ceremonial. When his emissaries come to fetch her from her father's kraal, she smears her body with human dung instead of the festive ochre and this nullifies the contract.

If one of the Kamchadale wants to marry, reports Steller, the only way he can get a wife is by serving her father. When he sees a maiden he likes, he goes and, without uttering a word, settles down in her home as if he has long been known there. He begins to take part in all the work of the house and tries to make himself more pleasing than other suitors by dint of strength, labour and hard work. If, after one, two or four years of service, he succeeds in getting so far as to please not only the parents-in-law but also the bride, he is permitted to speak to the father about his daughter. If he does not please them, then all his service is lost and in vain, and he must go away without payment or revenge.

The Battak, who inhabit the interior of Sumatra, often show great spirit in repelling unwelcome marriage ties. The missionary Simoneit says that if a betrothed girl resolutely refuses her suitor it becomes the duty of her parents to compel her. The first stage of force is a kind of stocks and the second torture by ant bites, while in the stocks a whole nest of these insects is poured over her. If she persists her hair is shorn. After this her father is no longer liable. But if the father refuses to torment his recalcitrant daughter he must repay the bride-price at double the rate.

It is not always the youth who woos the girl, but sometimes the girl who woos the youth.

On the island of Eetar in the Malayan Archipelago, for example, a girl, when she is kindly disposed towards a man, sends him a snuff-box made of intertwined koli-leaves and filled with tobacco, which is supposed, symbolically, to represent her genitals.

Among the Osage, too, according to Waitz, a girl wooed a famous warrior by offering a maize pipe without surrendering anything by so doing. The marriage was mostly concluded by this means, and it was publicly declared by both parties at a festival that it was their intention to live as husband and wife. Then a hut was built for them by the combined forces of the community.

Of the Zulus in the north of the Zambesi, Wiese says:

> Among the pure-bred Angoni, the woman has the right to choose her husband. The girl, after the [puberty festival], accompanied by her girl-friends armed with green twigs, betakes herself singing to the house of the chosen man and discloses to him in song that he is her heart's choice. If the man shows no readiness to accept the wooing, then they all go back to their home village, weeping loudly. But if the proposal is accepted they greet the news with tremendous jubilation, and the girl, now considered a bride, is accompanied to her family amid a thousand manifestations of joy. Next day the chosen man presents himself to the girl's father, and then begin the extremely difficult negotiations over the price of the young lady, who is to be paid for in cattle.

Reports from Chinese sources say that when a girl among the Hongsao tribe in Formosa reaches marriageable age, she builds herself a house and lives alone. The youth whom she wishes to obtain plays a musical instrument, called a 'beak-lute', and remains standing before her house. If this pleases the girl she comes out and invites him in, whereupon they live together. This is called the 'sign manual'. After a month, they each inform their families; the girl's parents bring meat and wine, gather their kinsmen together and receive their son-in-law.

iv. Chastity

TESTS TO ESTABLISH VIRGINITY

According to Ovid, a thread with which a maiden's neck was measured indicated an increase in size if she had lost her virginity. Even today, according to Karusio, such a thread oracle exists in the province of Bari. The maiden is measured from behind over the neck and lips. If the thread will then not let itself be taken off over her head, she is still in possession of her virginity.

In the fourteenth century, Konrad von Megenberg, writing of the *Aitstein*, or black amber, recorded that the water in which it had rested for three days could be used as a virginity oracle. If a woman drank the water and nothing happened, she was a virgin. If she was not a virgin she would not be able to hold her own water. In the Old Wives' philosophy of north Germany, it is a proof of virginity if a maiden, blowing on an extinguished candle, makes it burn again.

In Russia, according to Schrader, there still exists the solemn ceremony of the inspection of the bridal nightgown or sheets.

If stained with blood, the bride has passed the chastity test and . . . it is borne in triumph into the courtyard amid singing and dancing. Vessels are broken nearby and the husband bows before the mother. If the garment is unstained, the bride's father or brother is bound with a halter; the husband does not bow before the mother and no vessels are broken. Instead, a vessel with a hole in it is brought to the parents.

Among certain of the Chinese of Peking, on the wedding eve the bride is undressed by a female attendant. She retains her stockings, knickers and belt, in the pocket of which is a white cloth. The bridegroom must not take off her underclothes, but takes the white cloth from her pocket and spreads it over the couch so that, at the coitus, it may absorb the *hsi-h'ung*, the 'luck-bringing red'. If the latter is absent, it is a misfortune and a great disgrace.

Clot reports that in Egypt, the husband obtains unmistakable proof of virginity by manually destroying the hymen, i.e., wrapping a piece of white muslin round the index finger of his right hand and forcing it into the bride's vagina, and then showing the bloodstained cloth to the relatives. Among some of the Arabs the betrothed is bereft of virginity in the same way, but not by her husband. A matron performs the defloration instead – and prudently, for she does so at a time when the girl is menstruating. Indeed, with rules so strict that they threaten a maiden's whole future happiness – if not her life – if she has lost her virginity, it is easily understood how she or her relatives may devise means of simulating, or apparently restoring, the lost virginity for the testing period. Different methods are used. In Persia, for example, a little sponge soaked with blood is said to be put with benefit into the vagina on the nuptial night, and surgeons may even put a few stitches in the maiden's labia a few hours before the wedding. The stitches are torn out by the man's attempt at cohabitation and blood flows, which the man regards as a sign that the bride was *virgo intacta*.

DISREGARD FOR VIRGINITY

Max Buch says of the Votiak, primitive people of Finno-Ugrian stock, that men and maidens have intercourse without constraint, and so-called chastity sets no barrier against love. Indeed, it is even a disgrace for a maid to be unsought by a young man. They have a characteristic saying: 'If no young man loves her then God does not love her.' Authors' descriptions in regard to this are by no means exaggerated. It is said that a game is played by young men and maidens called the marriage game. Each lad chooses a maid, not always without a struggle, of course; and each couple then hides in a dark place where the play is conceived very realistically. Thereafter, the 'family couples' reassemble for the continuation of the game. Children born out of such games are under no disgrace. After marriage, according to Buch, the wives are treated as property and may be lent to guests of special importance.

Seligman reports of the Sinaugolo, in British New Guinea, that sexual intercourse is very frequent before menstruation has appeared, and that in many cases the maidens before marriage bestow their favours as they please. Many keep an account of their love adventures by making knots in their girdle, which they usually wear as a necklace.

Von Tschudi says of the Old Peruvians:

> Among many of the Quechua tribes, young men who loved a maiden used to throw sticks or stones at a big stone or rock in order to get their missiles into a split in it. When they succeeded, the maiden was informed and had to bow to the will of the victor who, as Villagomez says, was rarely refused, since it was a great honour to which many superstitious traditions clung.

The missionary Grützner says of the Basuto women that only when a girl becomes pregnant, which strangely enough does not happen very often, must a fine be paid. The man concerned then pays in some places one or two goats, in others as much as seven cows. So long as the girl is not pregnant she is still, in spite of all unchastity, quite proper. Indeed, unchastity among children is called nothing but playing.

DEFLORATION

Among some races we meet the custom of defloration of the bride *lege artis*, i.e., by the exercise of coitus. This is done not by the bridegroom but by some other man in his stead. The root idea of this custom lies in the superstitions attached to menstrual and defloration blood.

The loss of blood was believed to be dangerous because through it 'evil spirits' might spring forth which might injure the husband as well as the wife and their offspring. Hence the 'malignity' of blood is spoken of, and men arrived at the idea that defloration must be performed either by instruments or by indifferent or specially powerful persons. The Phoenicians, according to a statement of St Athanasius, kept a special slave on whom devolved the duty of defloration, while among the Bisayas in the Philippines there existed individuals who carried out defloration as a profession (Blumentritt). Similarly, virgins in Samoa used to be deflowered by a rod.

But defloration can also be regarded as an honour which is given only to a man of high position (*jus primae noctis*) or as a sacred gift which must be offered to the Godhead and which only the image of God himself or of the representative of God upon earth, the priest, is fitted to undertake. An example of the first case is to be found among the Balantes in Senegambia, a very barbarous Negro tribe. Here the chief, according to Marche, has the responsibility of deflowering the bride, a favour without which no maiden is permitted to marry and which he often condescends to do only in exchange for handsome gifts. Roman brides placed themselves in the lap of the god Mutunus, by means of whose phallus the hymen was rent and the vagina widened. Similar ceremonies were connected with the linga cult in India, and even in modern India it is said that the bridegroom sometimes takes his bride to a Brahmin for him to take her virginity.

NUPTIAL ABSTINENCE

The institution of nuptial abstinence was known to the Ancient Hindus. The Grihya-Sutra says, for example: 'For three nights both shall eat nothing pungent or seasoned with salt; they shall sleep upon the ground and preserve chastity ... On the fourth night, a food offering is to be made and the marriage consummated.'

In Esthonia neither the physical union nor anything approaching it may take place on the wedding night. In some districts they even take care that the husband does not touch his wife's breast for fear of milk tubercle, inflammation and abscess of the mammary glands developing in later calmness.

On the Kei Islands in the Banda Archipelago the young married people may accomplish coitus only after the expiration of three nights, and to guard with certainty against a transgression of the prohibition an old woman or a young child must sleep between them for the first three nights.

According to Graafland, on the island of Roti, the newly-weds retire accompanied by two old women. The husband must undo a girdle on the bride, the nine knots of which are covered with wax, using only the thumb and index finger of the left hand. The old women watch this. Until the girdle is completely undone the husband must not enter into married relations with his bride. Graafland was told that often a month, or indeed even a year, passed before it was accomplished.

Among the Swahili in East Africa the bridegroom must not consummate the marriage on the first day. After gently destroying the hymen and expanding the vulva of his wife, he devotes himself to a woman slave for the purpose of coitus (Zache).

The missionary Spiess informs us that, on the coast of Togo, the bride, before she is considered really a wife, has to spend several weeks in a hut which she is not allowed to leave during the daytime. In one district on the coast this time amounts to six weeks, elsewhere to four.

v. Adultery

There can be no question of adultery where the husband himself resigns his wife to other men for sexual intercourse. It is the wrong done to the husband, the suppression of and encroachment on the right handed to him alone, which is what we must consider when we speak of an infringement of marriage.

CHASTITY BELTS

The moral purity of European women has not always been in accordance with Christian requirements, and it has long been known that instruments of torture were used in Europe to prevent infidelity. Probably we have to thank the Crusades for these barbaric inventions, which were condemned even by contemporaries.

In the Arsenal at Venice an instrument is to be found that comes from a lawsuit against Carrara, the Governor of Padua, in the year 1405. It served as evidence for his offence, for which he was imprisoned by order of the Senate. In spite of the exemplary punishment of this man, the instrument seems to have spread not only in Italy but also to France. The first attempt to introduce it was made under Henry II by a tradesman who offered iron girdles of chastity at the fair at St Germain, but was unsuccessful. Indeed, the merchant had to flee for his life.

Later, however, the use and employment of this instrument perhaps became familiar, at least in secret, for in the Musée de Cluny in Paris is an instrument which, judging from its worn condition, was probably very often in use. It consists of an ivory plate fastened to a steel girdle, which is red with rust and can be closed in the middle by a lock (Fig. 15).

In the famous collection of weapons in Erbach Castle in the Odenwald, M. Bartels saw two such girdles of chastity made of sheet iron. One was covered with red velvet but otherwise unornamented; the outer surface of the second (corresponding in most respects to the upper example in Fig. 15) showed somewhat roughly etched pictures in the style of that period, the sixteenth century. From an iron belt in four parts and about 1 cm wide, two narrow pieces of iron plate, bent to fit the curving of the body, went from back and front downwards. These were joined to the girdle by a hinge and had a broad base, then tapered to a point, like a lancet. These lancet points met in the perineal region of the woman and here also were joined together by a

Fig. 15 Girdles of chastity (Musée de Cluny, Paris)

hinge. The back plate had a clover-leaf-shaped opening 5.2 cm wide and 4.5 cm high, corresponding to the anus. (In the unornamented girdle, this opening was round and only 3.1 cm in diameter.) The anterior portion was provided with an opening corresponding to the vulva. This formed a spindle-shaped slit 7 cm long by 1 cm at the widest. In both girdles this slit was set with fine teeth.

On both back and front plates of the finer girdle were etched designs and inscriptions. These represented an intertwining network of tendrils which opened out towards the top and framed a picture. In front of this was a kissing couple with their arms round each other. The woman sat on the man's lap, as if in deep conversation. Below it was the following inscription: 'Alas, this be my complaint to you, that women are plagued with the breeches.' The back plate had a picture of a woman sitting in half profile and holding in her hand the erect brush of a fox which was creeping between her calves. Under this, too, there was an inscription: 'Stop, little fox; I have caught you! You have often been through there!'

As late as the middle of the eighteenth century, a wife in France proceeded against her husband because he had put such a girdle on her. The speech of her advocate in Parliament is reproduced in the work of Caufeynon. Dingwall and Caufeynon also cite several cases of legal proceedings from more recent times, and publish the advertisements of Parisian instrument-makers at the end of the nineteenth century who offered girdles of chastity at from 300 to 500 francs.

Since their books were published, other cases have occurred. In 1930 a girl entered a Parisian hospital wearing a girdle of chastity. She was said by her parents to be an inveterate masturbator and an examination indicated that she was not a virgin. The girdle, which had been purchased at a dealer's establishment, was of the single plate type, well padded and with a slotted hip band.

In March 1931, a further case was revealed from Batavia, New York. John B., on account of certain dreams he had had, forced his wife to wear a girdle of chastity. The discovery was made at the hospital where Mrs B., the mother of nine children, had entered for treatment. Mr B. was charged with assault in the second degree. The belt was made of leather and steel and secured by padlocks. It is said that Mr B. had insisted on its use for twenty years.

In December 1933, the League of Awakened Magyars put forward as Point 19 of their National Programme that all Hungarian girls of twelve upwards and unmarried should wear girdles of chastity, the keys being kept by the fathers or other competent authorities (*Time*, December 4th, 1933; January 29th, 1934).

PUNISHMENTS FOR ADULTERY

We read of the Ancient Germanic peoples in Tacitus, Chapter 19:

> Adultery is very rare with this populous nation. It is followed by immediate punishment which is executed by the husband. In the presence of relatives the husband drives the wife out of the house, naked and with her hair cut off, and whips her through the whole village.

Boniface of the Saxons writes in *Monumenta Moguntina*:

> Sometimes a whole crowd of women assembles and they lead the [adulteress], who has already been flogged, round the district, whilst they strike her with switches and tear off her clothes to the waist. With their knives they thrust at her and chase her from village to village till she is lacerated and bleeding from little wounds. Fresh scourgers keep on joining them till they leave her lying dead or half dead, so that the rest shall fear adultery and licentiousness.

Punishments vary from place to place. Among the Apache Indians, the husband puts the adulteress out of his house, but first he cuts off her nose and has his purchase money paid back (Spring). Radde relates that the Chevsurs in the Caucasus also punish the wife's unfaithfulness by cutting off her ears and nose, and sometimes also her cheeks. The tribes on the Orinoco, however, have the right to punish adultery with death, as do the Orang Belenda in Malacca, the Angoni in the north of the Zambesi, the Chinese, the troglodytes of the Matmata mountain range in southern Tunisia, and many others. On the islands in the south-east of the Malay Archipelago, on the other hand, whilst formerly the husband could immediately kill the seducer and his unfaithful wife (or the latter alone), now the affair leads generally to separation, along with which the purchase-price of the bride must usually be refunded by the wife's parents. Of the Wamakua, Adams reports that wifely unfaithfulness is branded by a vertical slit being cut through the middle of the upper lip, and the seducer is made a slave or put to death.

The punishment meted out to the adulterer and the adulteress in New Britain is, according to Danks, extraordinarily severe. The wife is transfixed with a spear immediately and without mercy. The man, however, falls into an ambush prepared by the husband and his friends. They fall upon him, beat him with great force with a stick and twist his neck as violently as they can. Then they leave him lying in terrible agony in the road. He can no longer speak, he is parched with thirst for a few days, whilst his tongue swells to a great thickness. He dies a frightful death.

Among the Konde in East Africa, the hair of the adulterer's head and the penis itself are singed or burnt, according to Fülleborn, and the wife's genitals are burnt with fire. The cutting off of the ears which Merensky mentions, but of which he was doubtful, Fülleborn confirms from having seen a wife thus mutilated. Another severe punishment, according to Merensky, consists in the adulteress being compelled by her husband to bury alive the child conceived in adultery.

The Law of Mohammed against the adulteress is very strict. According to the commands in the Koran, the woman who was convicted of adultery by three witnesses was originally imprisoned in the house till death set her free or God put a means of deliverance into her hand. Later the woman was given a choice between imprisonment and stoning.

vi. Divorce

The Mohammedan may decide on divorce at any moment he likes and without stating any reason. He must then, of course, hand over the dowry of his wife and allow her maintenance for the *iddah* period, i.e., the period of three months during which she may not remarry or until her delivery. However, if the wife has brought about the divorce by disobedience or if the man fears that 'he is unable to fulfil the laws of God' if he remits the dowry, then he may keep part of it or even the whole.

The idea that the wife can press for divorce is absolutely foreign to the Koran.

Among the Persians it is customary for adultery to lead to divorce, but as a rule divorce results only if the wife remains childless (and this, moreover, can be proved to be her fault) or if she is a loose woman or if the husband believes that with her entry into the house bad luck has come upon it. She is then considered an evil omen.

About the Jews in Fürth at the beginning of the eighteenth century, Kirchner says:

> Divorce is not unusual among the Jews. The causes, however, must be both important and serious. They consist chiefly in the following points: if she is considered a pure virgin and afterwards proves to be the opposite; or as a widow had not behaved well and had been a whore; or if an evil smell came from her mouth; or if she had a running sore on her arm and had concealed it from her husband; or if she did not keep the Judaic laws, for instance if she did not keep her fourteen days of warm and cold baths ... if she is defiant and refuses the marriage bed; also if she speaks or plays cards with strange married men or bachelors without her husband's will and knowledge; or when she repeatedly gives her husband spoiled food.

The grounds for divorce in China were, according to the rules of Confucius, as follows: disobedience to the husband's parents, sterility, adultery, dislike or jealousy, serious disease, garrulity, theft of the husband's property. In three cases, however, the husband could not divorce his wife: if her parents, who were still alive at the time of marriage, were now dead; if she had worn mourning for three years for her husband's parents; if she had been poor and lowly and was now rich and respected.

A Japanese saying runs: 'A wife leaves in seven ways.' According to Ehmann, this refers to the seven grounds for divorce which appeared in the Taihō code, a law book drawn up after the Chinese pattern in AD 701: childlessness, adultery, disobedience towards the husband's parents, gossip, theft, jealousy and hereditary disease.

On the Marianas Islands, a marriage lasts only so long as both husband and wife want it. If the husband is not submissive enough, the wife leaves and goes to her parents, who then are accustomed to fall upon the husband's property and destroy it. On the Pelew Islands, if the husband wishes to separate from his wife he simply sends her away. The children, who inherit the position of their mother, follow her (Kubary).

Among the Bechuana, the husband can easily get a divorce, but he has to provide for the divorced wife if she was not found guilty. Among the Wan-yamwezi, according to Reichard, divorce can be obtained through the chief if there are sufficient grounds for it, for instance if the wife gets no children on account of syphilis, or if she leaves her husband with evil intent. In all cases, however, whether husband or wife is the guilty party, the purchase-price of the bride must be refunded. Among the Ashanti, only the chiefs may divorce or dispose of their wives.

vii. The Widow

> Now hast thou given me my first pang
> With thy last breath!
> Thou sleep'st, thou hard unfeeling man,
> The sleep of death . . .
> Loved have I and lived but now no more
> Am living here.
> I retire within myself from emptiness;
> Let the veil fall,
> There have I thee and my past happiness,
> O thou my all.

Thus Adelbert von Chamisso makes the widow lament at the death-bed of her husband. He could not sketch a more apt and finer picture of the situation of the true wife.

At the opposite pole are conditions such as Powell has described from New Britain. A chief had carried off a woman from a hostile tribe to take her as his wife, and in so doing her existing husband was killed. At the wedding feast the latter was eaten and his widow calmly shared in the horrible meal.

Although in this case we do not find any mourning, among other tribes it is customary for widows to be obliged to mourn the departed husband for a prescribed number of years, or even for the rest of their lives. This mourning, apart from loud lamentations, chiefly consists in the habitual adornments and pretty clothes being laid aside and replaced by ugly and coarse clothing, and the cleanliness and care of the body and hair being neglected. Sometimes the body is also smeared, injured and mutilated. In New Caledonia, for example, widows blacken their whole body with soot as a sign of mourning and draw tears on it with white chalk (Moncelon), while in the Los Pinos Indian Agency in Colorado they smear their faces with a substance made from pitch and coal. Among the Kaffitscho (Abyssinia), on the death of a man the wives lash their bellies below the navel with thorny wild-rose twigs till they bleed, and also shave their heads (Bieber). Before 1860, records McChesney, at the death of a Sioux warrior, the whole tribe gathered in a circle. The widow hacked her arms, legs and body with a flint and cut off her hair. Then she went round in the circle and as often as she went round, so many years she had to remain unmarried. While doing this she had to lament and wail.

In New Guinea (among the Kai), the widow (and, in the reverse case also, the widower) is obliged to spend a few weeks (among the Bukaua until the mourning dress is ready) in a mourning hut hastily erected at the grave. When the weeks of the strictest mourning are past, the widower appears in a mourning hat of bast, and the widow with a long mourning net (Fig. 16). The grave is hedged round and with this a feast is connected. The length of the whole period of mourning varies from six months to two years.

Among the Tautin Indians in Oregon, according to Ross Cox, the widow has special obligations. After the cremation, she collects the bigger bones in a container of birch bark which she is obliged to carry on her back for at least a year. She now has to do slave service for all the women and children, and if she is disobedient is severely punished. The ashes of her husband are collected and laid in a grave which she has to keep free from weeds; if weeds appear she has to dig them out with her fingers. In this she is supervised by her husband's relatives and tormented. If she survives the torture for three or four years (often she takes her life instead) she is released from it, and a great feast is given. Her husband's bones are taken off her back and put into a box which is fastened with nails and set up twelve feet high. Her behaviour as a faithful widow is praised, and she may marry again.

Among the Chippewa Indians, when a woman's husband has been carried off by death, she blackens her face; in addition, she has to fast and may not wear ornaments or comb her hair for a year. Besides these mourning customs, we learn some very strange ones from McKenney. He states that he often saw women walking about with a roll of material (Fig. 17). When he asked what this signified, he was told that they were widows who carried these things and that this was the badge of their mourning. For a Chippewa wife who loses her husband it is absolutely necessary to take her best dress, roll it up and tie it together with her husband's sash and, if he had ornaments, as is usually the case, to fasten them at the end of the roll, round which a piece of cotton is tied. This bundle is called her 'husband', and people expect her not to let herself be seen anywhere without it. When she goes out, she carries it with her; when she is sitting in her hut, she lays it at her side. This sign of mourning the widow has to bear until the family

Fig. 16 Widow's dress, Bukaua (after Neuhauss)

of her dead husband thinks she has mourned long enough, which is generally the case after a year. She is then, and not before, released from her
mourning, and is free to remarry.

The souvenirs of the dead husband which the Mincopi widows on the
Andaman Islands have to carry about with them are still more remarkable. A certain time after the death the skull of the dead man is specially
prepared, painted red and ornamented with fringes of wood fibre. This
skull the widow now has to hang on herself and is obliged to carry it
with her until she remarries. The skull is fastened in such a way that the

Fig. 17 Chippewa widow with the model of her late husband on her arm
(after Yarrow)

band holding it passes round the neck and left breast and hangs from the
right shoulder.

In New Guinea a bunch of the dead man's hair and his penis covering are
part of the widow's mourning garb; the covering the widow wears under
her knot of hair, the bunch of hair on a string round her neck.

There can be no doubt that there is a superstitious motive at the root of
such mourning customs. The married woman in the period of patriarchy is
exactly like the servant. She is the property even of the dead man, and has
to follow him into the grave and beyond. Chu-hi, the most famous com-
mentator of the classical canonical works of the Chinese who lived in the
twelfth century AD, says, according to von Brandt:

> Woman is born to serve man with her body, so that the life of a wife
> comes to an end with that of her husband and she is said to die with him.
> After the death of her husband she is therefore called 'the woman not yet
> dead'; she is merely awaiting her death and she is supposed never to
> have any desire to become the wife of another man.

SUTTEE

Among some peoples, widows were not allowed any period of mourning but were compelled to follow their deceased husbands to death.

The classic land for killing widows is, as everyone knows, India: even Cicero and Diodorus recorded the practice. The custom of suttee is said to have arisen when Sati, the wife of Shiva, the great god contending with Brahma for precedence, threw herself into the sacred fire at her father's sacrifice, grieving because Brahma had not invited her husband to attend. Since then, every wife who mounts the stake on which her husband's corpse is to be burnt to ashes is called *sati*, and the custom itself *sahagamana*, 'the going with'. A verse of Sanskrit, quoted by Böhtlingk, lauds the wife's faithfulness, which continues even after death: 'A man later discontinues the amiable attentions which he has paid wives in secret; the wives, on the other hand, embrace the inanimate husband from gratitude and ascend the funeral pyre with him.'

In Nepal it is said that the widow who has not followed her husband to death always loses caste. One Hindu, Madhowdas, according to Ryder, declares that it is easy to see why a widow should prefer death to the state of widowhood, for 'if she falls ill no doctor will attend her; if she dies nobody will take her unclean corpse to burn it; nobody will talk with her; nobody looks at her, and the persecution of her never ceases. Her children are exposed to the same afflictions; no school will receive them, no priest will instruct them.'

Another Hindu, Rama-Krishna, denies, however, that the lot of a widow is so wretched that it is a reason for her choosing death in preference; the real reason, according to him, lies in the Indian woman's romantic sense!

Schlagintweit states that the burning of widows now occurs only in quite isolated cases and in remote districts. It is prohibited by an Indian law of 1829, and the Penal Code punishes all participants with imprisonment of up to ten years. Nevertheless there are still one or two suttee burnings to be dealt with annually, and it is of interest that the custom came actively to life again during the First World War, under the influence of the priests.

The Hindus are not the only people among whom the killing of widows is to be found. According to Dolittle, widows in China are likewise accustomed to kill themselves so as to show publicly their faithfulness to their husbands. Some take opium and lie down to die by the side of the corpse of their husband. Others commit suicide by starving themselves to death, or by drowning themselves or taking poison. Another method is to hang themselves in a public place, having given notice to the effect so that those who desire may be present and behold the act. In New Zealand, too, on the death of a chief, they used to give his wife a rope with which she was to hang herself in the woods, while among the Basutos the widows are beaten to death with clubs after the corpse of the deceased husband is buried.

According to Tylor, among the Kwakiutl Indians in north-western America, the widow is obliged, while the corpse of her husband is being burnt, to lie with her head beside it. Then, more dead than alive, she is pulled out of the flames, and when she comes to herself she has to gather up the remains of her husband and carry them about with her for three years. A confirmation of the opinion that in this custom is a residue of the rites of a real burning is contained in a statement made by E. von Hesse-Wartegg about the Nataotin Indians in British Columbia. He says:

> I need mention only the peculiar custom of burning widows which Paul Kane discovered . . . in 1858, and which has now, fortunately, been abolished. The burning of corpses, however, is still a common custom, and the widow of a dead man has to mount the funeral pyre and stay with the corpse till it is enveloped in flames. Until then she may not leave the pyre.

Until recently there also existed among the Fiji Islanders the custom of strangling the wife of a man of rank at his death. Her corpse was then anointed and arrayed as for a feast and laid beside the dead warrior. When Ra-Mbithi, the pride of Somosomo, was wrecked at sea, seventeen of the wives were killed; and after the news of the massacre among the population of Namena, in the year 1839, eighty women were strangled to accompany the souls of their murdered husbands (Tylor).

REMARRIAGE

There are two rights which are of the greatest importance for the further life of a widow; these are the right of inheritance and the right of remarriage. With some peoples, we see the widow quite deprived of these, and particularly of the latter.

Thus, in India, the widow who has not followed her husband to death is strictly forbidden to remarry, and not only by the Brahmins and Rajputs but by all religious castes, even the singers and beggars. The Japanese, according to Ehmann, have the saying, 'A faithful wife has no meeting with two husbands,' and in China, if a widow remarried, her own children renounced her and did not mourn for her at her death.

Among the southern Slavs, according to Krauss, a widow's second marriage is regarded as an insult to her deceased husband, while a woman who has children rarely marries a second time with the Croats and Serbians, for

she is not allowed to take her children with her into the second marriage
and they are regarded as orphans. Similar views prevailed in western Europe
during the Middle Ages. Hüllmann writes of this:

> In France a special outbreak of coarseness was the barbarous uproar
> which is called *charivari*; in front of the house of a widower or widow
> who was going to marry again, the neighbours, on the eve of the wedding,
> played licentious, insulting pranks, beating kettles, basins and pans
> against each other and behaving wantonly at the wedding ceremony in
> the church.

Among many peoples, however, we find quite the opposite custom. A
widow often has to marry again whether she will or not, moreover the right
of marriage with her usually appertains to a relative of the husband.

In Israel, marriage with the widowed sister-in-law is prescribed by law,
but is to take place only if the widow is childless and if the brother-in-law is
in agreement. This type of marriage, which is called the levirate, occurs in
many other countries, for example in Persia, where although it is not legally
obligatory, it is considered proper and praiseworthy. Among the Abyssinians
it is regarded as an absolute rule, and after the death of the husband his
brother must in any circumstances marry the widow (Hartmann). Among
the Chippewa Indians, too, according to McKenney, the deceased husband's
brother has the right to take the widow to wife. This takes place at the grave
of her husband.

A limited form of levirate is known in a number of Indian tribes and castes
and also in some parts of the Indian Archipelago. Here, marriage is permitted
only with the younger brother of the dead husband. Indeed, among the
Battak on the west coast of Sumatra, marriage with an elder brother is
looked upon as incest and results in the man being killed.

Other customs also prevail. There is, for example, an ancient law of the
Arabs which requires that the son marry his widowed mother. This holds
good in Nias, where a son often takes all his stepmothers in marriage unless
they are pregnant (Modigliani). In Korea, on the other hand, if a man but
proves that he has had sexual intercourse with a widow he has the right to
claim her as his property.

STATUS AND INHERITANCE

In many countries widows are treated kindly and benevolently, and when
they are old and without means people willingly provide them with all that
is necessary. In the Amboina group, widows, when they have many children,
are even held in great respect. In Ceram Laut and the Gorong Archipelago,

in the Tenimber and Timor Laut islands, as in Halmahera, widows are supported by the husband's kin.

Among the islanders in the Amboina group, the widow gets the free disposal of the personal property and real estate. With her consent, the weapons, fishing gear and conveyances may be divided among the sons; the daughters' share and the gold and silver articles remain in her care. In the Tenimber and Timor Laut islands the widow inherits everything and has, at the same time, the guardianship of any children who are minors. In the Luang and Sermata islands she inherits conjointly with her children, although if she marries again her claims pass to the eldest son. In the Ceram Laut and Gorong islands, if a widow wants to marry again during the period of mourning, which lasts 140 days, she forfeits all rights of inheritance.

Among the Iroquois and Delaware Indians, on the other hand, a widow inherits nothing at all, as the relatives of her dead husband distribute everything that belonged to him to strangers, so that they may not be continually reminded of the dead man by the sight of his possessions. Among the Ostiaks also, the widow inherits nothing, and in other tribes she may even become common property: on Duke of York Island, for example, it is customary for the men to claim the widows for themselves, while in the Nissan islands in Melanesia, the chief takes them under his 'protection' and uses them freely for sexual intercourse. The 'property principle' also applied among the Ancient Germans: if the husband had not paid for his wife the price agreed on, then after his death the ownership of the widow fell to her father or to a male relative on her father's side (Grimm).

The widow in India has a particularly unfavourable position, according to Schlagintweit, while Helene Niehus describes the life of a widow in the East Indies as unspeakably wretched:

> They take all the poor widow's ornaments away from her, depriving her even of the natural adornment of her hair, and give her shabby clothes. But not content with this, they have her eat one meal a day only and fast twice a month. 'They have to go through a cold widow burning,' a Hindu once said, and he was only too right.

CHAPTER VII

Pregnancy

For the primitive individual and race, sexual functions, especially those of women, are extremely mysterious. Women are supposed to exude a kind of force which might almost be likened to a virulent contagion. Primitive customs of unmeasurable antiquity are interwoven with pregnancy, birth and childbed: the more mysterious the manifestations of sex, the more peculiarly and exclusively feminine will be certain of the results.

In pregnancy lies the eternal, unalterable division of labour of man and woman, for this work man cannot do, whilst woman can only *apparently* take over the work of the male. Hence it is quite in order that, in this work done by woman, a thorough consideration should be given to the circumstances and activities concerned.

i. Fertility

The Talmud says that he who wilfully abstains from marrying in order to avoid parenthood is morally the equivalent of a murderer. It is even stated that 'he who preserves only one human life has done as much as though he had preserved the universe'.

Amongst most people in the world an abundance of children is desired, and the fertility of the wife is regarded as a special mercy and as a great conjugal good. Sterility, on the contrary, is considered an imperfection in a wife, and she is regarded as incapable of fulfilling her conjugal duties. If the evil cannot be removed, the marriage is very often broken up. In Kordofan, for example, the husband treats a sterile wife with contempt even if he has once loved her, while among the Galla the wife herself helps her husband to get a second, third or fourth wife, by suggesting and introducing to him 'beautiful and fertile girls'. Among the peoples of Africa, too, sterility is a disgrace for the woman, and among many Negro peoples it is regarded as a proof of earlier gross excess; the childless woman in Angola is generally despised, and therefore she sometimes makes an end of herself by suicide.

Childlessness is a misfortune for the Chinese woman even while she is dying and after her death. Katscher reports:

> If a second or third wife remains childless, then when she is near death she is taken to another dwelling; she may not die in the house of her

husband. The ancestral tablets of first wives who die without having left children are not put upon the altar in the ancestral hall but on a pedestal fixed in an adjoining room.

The Ancient Hindus, because there was little difficulty about food, also put a high value on children. The Laws of Manu (Book IX, 59) ran: 'If one has no children, the desired descendants can be obtained by the alliance of the wife empowered thereto with the brother or a relative.' The child thus produced was regarded as if he were begotten by the real husband, for 'the seed and the produce belong by law to the owner of the soil'. In these cases male issue was particularly desired, and a woman who after eleven years had borne only girls might be divorced. In Ancient Greece, too, the desire for children led to the custom of a substitute being used in the case of an impotent husband.

But this great esteem for fertility is not common to all nations, and in many peoples very great fertility is even regarded as contemptible and animal.

Among the Greenlanders, a woman has from three to six children at intervals of from two to three years, so that when the Greenlanders hear of the fertility of other nations they compare them with their dogs. Similarly, the Indian women of British Guiana made a grimace of mockery when they learnt from Schomburgk that with European women twin births were not rare: 'We are not bitches who throw off a heap of young,' they said.

Among the Australians in Queensland fertility cannot enjoy any great respect either, for Roth reports that a husband often prays to the spirits which form children to send a child as a punishment when his wife has annoyed him. In former German New Guinea, too, an abundance of children does not appear to a Papuan wife as a desirable object of her marriage, in this case because of the attendant woes and pains. Thus it happens that a husband plays a wicked trick on the wife who scorns him by inflicting children upon her.

ENCOURAGING FERTILITY

We can easily understand, especially among peoples where a barren woman is exposed to shame and contempt and all kinds of insults, that the bride and her friends are beset by anxious fears on the conclusion of marriage lest such an unhappy fate be destined, and all kinds of preventive steps are taken. Naturally, if these magic measures are to be properly effective the right moment must be chosen for their use.

People proceed with the 'sympathetic' magical measures as early as possible, and there are three times which are especially preferred – the wedding day, the wedding night and the morning after the wedding.

In Aegina, immediately after the blessing is over, the marriage witnesses are accustomed to pelt the young bride with peas and pomegranate seeds in order to ensure her fertility.

The Serbian woman hangs her chemise upside down on a grafted tree so that the sleeves are hanging downwards. Under the chemise she puts a glassful of water. Next morning, the woman drinks all the water and puts on the chemise. Others put some leaven in their waistband and, having slept with it for one night, eat it the next day for breakfast.

The tent Gypsies in Transylvania, according to von Wlislocki, throw old boots and peasants' shoes at the newly married as they enter their tent, thus increasing the fertility of the marriage, while the Esthonians throw money and ribbons into the well and into the fire 'for the propitiation of the water and fire mother'. As late as the end of the eighteenth century gifts were thrown by them into a great fire round which barren women danced naked, whilst sacrificial feasts were held and orgy reigned (Böcler).

Among the feasts customary with the Masai is one which is celebrated only by married women in order to beseech God to give them children. Merker reports:

It is called *iruga 'Ng ai ol adjo*, i.e., 'may God listen to the word'. In or near the kraal, the women meet in the forenoon, together with a magician (*ol goiatiki*) round whom they place themselves in a circle. Each woman then receives from him an amulet which she hangs on the hip-string of her hide apron. Then he sprinkles their heads and shoulders with a medicine which, besides milk and honey-beer, contains another secret ingredient of his own, for which he is rewarded with a few sheep. Then the women dance and sing all day long in the shadows of a tree and, at night, in the kraal until day dawns. In the songs they repeat continually the following prayer: 'God, I implore thee; I beg; we beg thee alone, we beg for children, for fertility for the barren woman.'

ii. Barrenness

Sterility is regarded by most peoples as a special misfortune, a curse weighing heavily either on both the husband and wife or, which is much more frequent, only on the unfortunate wife.

The Talmudists thought that fertility or sterility depended upon the will of God, as did the Mohammedans: in accordance with the Koran, 'God causes, according to his will, one woman to get girls, another boys, another children of both sexes; according to his will, he also makes woman sterile.'

According to popular belief, however, it is not only God who causes sterility but also demons and wicked sorcerers (see also 'Demons', Chapter V). In Bosnia and Herzegovina, for example, people believe that a woman is sterile because she has had intercourse with evil spirits.

The idea that childlessness is due to a curse or spell or some other pernicious cause is shown in the burial customs of the Wachaga, of whom Gutmann reports:

> If a childless wife dies, she is thrown into the stream with all her things, her cooking pot and her ladle. She is carried to the forest or to some place that is never tilled. Also, they do not take her corpse out by the door but break a hole in the cottage wall on the opposite side through which they carry the corpse and all her things. The bearers, her relations, receive three goats as reward for their labour. One of these is killed for her gratification.

Brough Smith reports that the wizards, or medicine men, in southern Australia are much feared by the women because they firmly believe that they have the power to make them sterile.

Among other nations, also, it is considered possible that wicked people have the power to obstruct the fertility of women by magic arts. Among the Magyars, if someone wants to make a woman sterile, 'then one smears the genitals of a dead man with the menses of the woman in question' (von Wlislocki).

The women of the Bakhtiari in western Persia are accustomed to hang amulets on themselves which have the power of spells to make their rivals sterile whilst guaranteeing the fidelity of the husbands and ensuring abundant issue for themselves (Houssay). Also among the Bakhtiari it is considered enough to make a woman sterile if she has touched the flesh of the pig anywhere without her knowledge.

Among the Chippewa and a few other Indian tribes, the sterility of women is regarded as proof of marital infidelity and of artificial miscarriages (J. de Laët: Keating).

The Japanese, on the other hand, find the reason for sterility in the temperament of the woman. One of their sayings runs: 'Sensual women are often sterile' (Ehmann).

REMEDIES

It is a common trait of the human mind not to rely solely upon the power of suitable medicines to restore lost health. Hence the help and support of God or of demonic powers is invoked and recourse taken to peculiar forms of treatment, which are supposed infallibly to bring about the desired cure by some quite inexplicable 'sympathetic' means.

Schmidt says of the Hindus:

> Certain gods of the Hindu pantheon are said to be accessible to the prayers of barren women who, to entreat the earnestly desired blessing of fertility, often undertake long, wearisome and expensive pilgrimages to certain shrines. The seven pagodas between Madras and Masulipatam are especially favoured for that purpose ... The rites and ceremonies are, however, according to old reports, of a somewhat mystic and phallic kind, so that it is perhaps best not to inquire too closely into the acts of sacrifice which have to be done on these occasions.

In Java, an old Dutch cannon which lies in the open near Batavia (Fig. 18) has a special power and significance. The women, in their best dresses and adorned with flowers, are accustomed to sit astride upon it, often two at once, and at the same time they put down offerings of rice, fruits, etc., which are then pocketed by the priests.

In the Tyrol, so-called *muettern* are hung up among miracle images. These

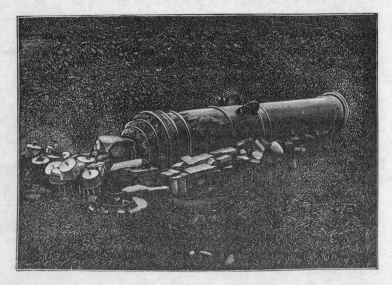

Fig. 18 Ancient Dutch cannon at Batavia, on which barren women ride and before which offerings are laid (after photo by F. Schulze)

are little waxen toads which are intended to represent the uterus. Zingerle says that barren women make offerings of these wax figures to images of the Madonna and to the Holy Sorrow.

The barren Nishinam (southern Maidu) woman in California is given a grass doll by her friends which, in order to remove her sterility, she lays on her breast, singing cradle songs (Powers). A similar practice is found among African tribes. Fabry reports from the life of the Wapogoro in Tanganyika:

> For women who would like to have a child ... there is a doll, a dry bottle-gourd bearing at its upper end a bundle of short strings to which dried seeds of the wild banana are fastened. This ... doll is tenderly rocked and fondled, and if one treats it with special tenderness one soon gets a child.

On the Slave Coast of Guinea, among the Tshi, the childless woman is assigned to a fetish as its property in case it may give her children; if this happens the child is a fetish child and is the property of the fetish.

Many peoples also believe in a sympathetic connection between the life substance of certain trees and plants and the destiny of human beings. On the most important thing in a woman's life, namely conception, the soul of a tree is often able to exert its influence.

The wives of the Chin in the Himalayas, for example, direct their prayers for children to the chili tree (von Ujfalvy), while among the Kara-Kirghiz apple trees are regarded as places of refuge for barren women.

The Maoris in New Zealand, according to Goldie, regard both human beings and plants as descendants of the god Tane-nuia-rangi, although coming from different wives. The trees of the forest were first-born, and they too were given souls, to which the sterile apply for help. The barren woman goes to a tree which possesses a male and a female side and embraces it whilst a priest sings incantations: if she embraces the male side (east), a boy will be born to her; in the other case, a girl. Another tree has a sterile and a fertile side. With closed eyes, the wife goes to the tree and embraces it for a long time; then she goes away without seeing the place she has embraced. The accompanying priest, however, sees it; if the woman has embraced the barren side she will never have a child.

To the same group of ideas belongs also the following spell from Bosnia, recorded by Truhelka. The woman who wants to get rid of her sterility must, on the first Sunday after the new moon, look for three grubs in a wild dog-rose hip. If she is lucky enough to find them, she climbs on a willow tree, looks towards the sun, and devours them. While doing so she says thrice: 'The sun was setting behind the mountains and I shall become expectant.'

However, it is above all on the medicinal power of vegetable and herbal products that men have relied. In the great mass of these popular medicaments there have sometimes been found remedies really useful and effective, but most nevertheless seem senseless.

Among those plants regarded as healing there is one above all which in ancient times was held in high esteem and even ascribed divine properties by the Bactrians, Medes and Persians – the soma plant (*Asclepias acida*), mentioned in the Avesta. In the time of Hippocrates women who wished to have children were advised to take silphium with wine, that mysterious specific which the ancients prized so highly, while in the seventeenth century barren women with 'a cold and too damp a complexion' had to take drinks made from clove-pinks (*Caryophyllon*) with balm mint and orange peel. Rosemary also with grains of mastic was a favourable remedy.

At the present day in Styria, asparagus seed with wine and young hop shoots prepared as a salad is still used as a remedy for sterility, according to Fossel. The wife must also avoid conjugal intercourse for two months, have herself bled and then have coitus the following day. In Bohemia the young wife drinks an infusion of juniper berries in order to get children, in Russia a solution of saltpetre. Popular remedies in Bosnia and Herzegovina include the drinking of sour milk in which dill leaves have been soaked and the eating of the fruit and seeds; a soup made of an old cock and the dried, baked and powdered testicles of a wild boar; or ordinary water containing some powder from the cleaned and dried uterus of a hare.

Among the Turkish Gypsies the corpse of a dead man is sprinkled with the blood of a black hen. When the drops of blood on the dead body are dry, they are carefully scraped off. Sterile women mix this blood with asses' milk which they then drink out of a pumpkin cup (von Wlislocki).

In Fezzan, according to Nachtigal, people try to increase the fertility of women by plentiful consumption of the dried entrails of young sucking hares, while in Algiers, if a woman has already had a child and then does not conceive again for a long time, she must drink sheep's urine or water in which wax from the ear of an ass has been pounded (Bertherand).

As a cure for sterility on the Fiji Islands, the woman has to bathe in a river and then both husband and wife have to take a drink made from an infusion of the grated root of the *mbokase*, a kind of bread tree, and of the nut of the *rerega* or *kago*, a kind of turmeric. Coitus must be performed immediately after this drink has been taken.

A medicament used in Japan for menstrual troubles and sterility, called *kay-tu-sing*, is recommended by Williams. It is the tincture of the leaves of a perennial tree of the class *Ternstroemiaceae*. After only a few hours the specific is said to affect menstruation and to remove sterility. In China and

Japan it is taken whilst magical formulae are repeated and at the time of the full moon.

Nowadays an important method of removing sterility in women is the use of medicinal baths and springs. Indeed, one important spring in Ems has, as is well known, received the name of *Bubenquelle* (baby spring) because of its happy effect. But the prescription of medicinal waters is by no means a discovery of recent days. In Ancient Greece, many springs and wells were recommended as a cure for sterility, as, for example, the Thespian spring on Helicon, and baths also played a part in Hindu and Chinese mythology.

In Algeria, not far from Constantine, there is a bath situated in the rocks with the spring of Burmal er-Rabba, which Jewesses and Moorish women have been frequenting from the earliest times in order to seek a cure for barrenness. On several weekdays the native women come down from Constantine to Sidi-Mecid, kill a black cock by the door of the grotto, and offer up inside a wax candle and a honey cake. Then they take a bath and are sure that their desires will soon be fulfilled.

Among the Yoruba on the west coast of Africa the water which is kept in the temple of the goddess of nature, who is represented as a pregnant woman, is also renowned, and is used as a remedy for barrenness and difficult delivery.

iii. Contraception

One of the most widespread artifices resorted to for contraceptive purposes is *coitus interruptus*, which was stigmatized in the Old Testament as the sin of Onan, who had to atone for his conduct with death. Equally widely diffused is the process of introducing foreign bodies, such as absorbent substances, into the vagina in order to prevent the penetration of the sperm.

More interesting from an ethnological point of view, however, is the contraceptive use of internal and magical specifics.

In Ancient Greece it appears that *Vitex agnus-castus* L. played an important part in this respect. Attic matrons, when celebrating the festival of the Thesmophoria, used to strew it and other plants which were supposed to be anaphrodisiacs under their beds (Frazer). The Greek physician Soranus also gave the advice that the wife should, if a birth threatened to be dangerous to her, beware of having coitus just before or after menstruation. Before coitus she should smear the os uteri with oil, honey, opobalsam or wormwood mixed, and insert pessaries with astringent qualities. At the moment of ejaculation she should hold her breath, and after coitus sit with bent knees.

In Ancient Rome attempts were also made to cause sterility in women by specifics. According to the ideas underlying sympathetic magic, the seeds of fruitless trees, drunk as tea, were said to produce sterility – especially those of willows and poplars growing in the grove of the childless Persephone (H. von Fabrice). Indeed, willows figured very similarly among the German peoples until comparatively recent times.

In Esthonia the women take mercury, and in the district of Kiev the aqueous infusion of the *Paeonia officinalis*. The fresh juice of the celandine (*Chelidonium majus*) is also famous; and the Tatar women use an infusion of male fern (*Lastrea filix-mas* Presl.).

In Styria it is generally believed that water from the smithy-trough will cause sterility. Likewise the taking of tincture of zinc, English balsam, honey and aperients of all kinds, particularly aloes and myrrh.

According to Klunzinger, the women in Upper Egypt take, fasting, three mouthfuls of powder of burnt cowry shells in order not to become pregnant. In Algiers, if a woman does not want to conceive so soon again, she drinks for a few days some water in which the leaves of the saltwort and the peach tree have been cooked, or she drinks the juice of the fig.

Blyth reports of the Fiji Islanders that 'the native midwives ... use an infusion of the leaves and the peeled and grated roots of roga-wood and samalo. If coitus has taken place at night, then the drink is taken next morning.'

Mechanical means are also used.

According to Riedel, the women of the Malay Archipelago keep themselves very indifferent during coitus in order not to become pregnant, while those of the Australian Aborigines get rid of the injected sperm by a jerking movement of the pelvic region. There also occurs in Australia the cutting out of the ovaries as a preventive, and the same thing happens in Indonesia. Indeed, N. von Miklucho-Maclay reports that the Australian Aborigines remove the ovaries in certain girls in order to supply the youth of their tribes with a special kind of promiscuous companion who can never become a mother. Further, a dumb native woman whom the naturalist MacGillivray saw near Cape York with scars proving the extirpation of her ovaries had been thus treated in order to prevent the birth of dumb children.

In India and the Dutch East Indies people know how to avoid conception by intentional changes in the position of the uterus. The missionary Jellinghaus says that poor women among the Munda in Chota-Nagpur, India, have their wombs compressed and displaced without the knowledge of their husbands in order to free themselves from the worry of pregnancy. Similarly, van der Burg reports from the Dutch East Indies that

a *Doekoen*, one of the numerous old women skilled in medicine for avoiding conception ... seems to know how to bring about a change in the forward or backward position of the uterus by external manipulations; by pressing, rubbing, kneading the abdomen without touching the vagina. It must be admitted that the results are no worse troubles than slight pains in the loins and kidneys and difficulty with micturition during the first days of the procedure. If a girl wants to marry and later to become a mother, the uterus is prepared again in the same way.

iv. *Conception and Rites*

Pregnancy is, in many nations, the occasion for giving thanks to God with religious sentiment and for recommending to the further protection of the Godhead, by a special consecration, the woman herself as well as the new life germinating within her.

In Ancient Mexico, when the first signs of pregnancy were found in a young wife, the fact was celebrated with a feast. At a later feast, amid discourses similar to those delivered at the previous one, a midwife was installed with her, by whom, Waitz reports, she was bathed and from whom she received much advice.

Among the Ancient Jews, the child was prayed for during pregnancy and special forms of prayer for the different stages of pregnancy were prescribed by the Talmudists.

Roman women sacrificed to two sister goddesses, Porrima (or Prorsa) and Postverta. The former could bring about the proper presentation of the child at delivery and the latter took care that, if the child had unfortunately assumed the wrong position, the confinement should still have a happy ending.

Of the Hindus in Madras, Best reports as early as 1788 that husbands used to arrange a feast of rejoicing on the occasion of their wives' first pregnancy, and that in the seventh month the whole family made offerings to the gods.

In Java, as is mentioned in the report of the voyage of the *Novara* (*Anthrop. Th.*, III, 79), when the woman is in her third month of pregnancy, this is announced to all her friends and relations, and then various presents are offered. In the seventh month, all the relatives are invited to a gala dinner. After it, the wife bathes in the milk of an unripe coconut which her husband must have opened. On the shell two beautiful figures, a male and a female, have been carved beforehand, so that the pregnant woman may contemplate them and bring a beautiful child into the world. She now puts on a new dress and presents the old one to one of the women with her who has been helping her with these arrangements. In the evening, a shadow play is given for the guests, which has for subject the life and adventures of an ancient hero (Raffles).

On Tenimber and Timor Laut, when a woman feels herself pregnant, she must bring an offering and have her teeth filed, if this has not been done at marriage. If she does not do so, then she is despised as one who insults the *mores majorum*. On the islands of Romang, Dama, Teun, Nila and Serua, the pregnant wife, as soon as she perceives her condition, must kill a fowl and offer the head, a piece of the tongue and the liver to Upulero at the usual place of sacrifice.

Last states that among the Masai in East Africa, if a woman has conceived, her husband fetches a big pot of honey, mixes other things with it and stirs it until the mass is quite thin; then he calls the headmen together. Husband and wife sit down, and the headmen take some of the honey and spit it out over them. After this they say a prayer for the welfare of the parents and the expected child, and then each makes a speech, after which the rest of the honey is drunk.

Not far from Malange, in Angola, according to Lux, pregnant women always carry with them a little calabash which is filled with earth, nuts and palm oil, in order to be sure of an easy confinement, while among the Negro tribes of West Africa the pregnant woman hangs magical symbols and strings on neck, arm and foot, and she has bracelets made of bast put on her hands and knees by a priestess, which are supposed to guarantee her a successful delivery.

v. Superstitions

DEMONS

The belief in evil spirits which injure the pregnant and their offspring is very ancient and deep-rooted in the mind of man, and is even preserved among nations of a high degree of civilization, particularly among the less cultivated classes. The means of banishing and appeasing demons are extraordinarily varied. Amulets, exorcisms and magical specifics, but also the noise of weapons and the use of smoke, all play a prominent part.

Among the Ancient Babylonians and Assyrians the *labartu* was especially dreaded. This was a demon horrible in appearance but divine in origin who dwelt in mountain regions and reed-grown thickets, and wherever she went she spread terror and desolation. However, she was expressly dangerous to little children and their mothers, and caused abortion and miscarriage. In the so-called Labartu texts from the library of Ashurbanipal, means of fighting her are given. These include incantations, talismans and sacrifice, and prescribe that a young pig be killed and its heart laid in the demon's mouth (Weber). Alternatively a figure of the demon is made, placed for three days at the head of the sick, then destroyed and buried at the corner of a wall.

European nations, too, are not free from such superstitions. In modern Greece it is believed that the Nereids possess a harmful power over the pregnant, and women expecting a child try to make themselves secure by means of amulets, among which jasper plays a prominent part. It is unlucky if anyone steps over a pregnant woman, for he thus opens the way for the Nereids; likewise a pregnant woman must not go under a plane tree or poplar or encamp by streams or other running water, because these are the places where the Nereids are in the habit of staying.

Among the superstitions of northern Europe is that encountered in Esthonia, where the pregnant woman is in the habit of changing her shoes every week in order to put the devil off her track. According to popular belief he is always pursuing her in order to get the child into his clutches.

In Bali, the pregnant woman everywhere sees evil signs for her confinement. Jacob writes:

> In her thoughts, she peoples her surroundings with hundreds of *kalas* (evil spirits) which have designs upon her life and that of her child and which will make her pregnancy difficult. The howling of a dog, the croaking of a bird, the working of a crater, etc., terrify her. Her personal enemies, or the neighbours with whom she is not on a very friendly footing, try to bewitch her in every way to bring her life and that of her child into danger; and in despair she resorts to one of the specifics known to her and sacrifices her new-born child in order to save her own life.

Demonology has fashioned the spirits which occupy themselves with pregnant women in many varied forms. Not infrequently they are aerial spirits which surround the house of the pregnant woman and threaten her banefully. This is the case among the Kalmucks, the Persians and also a few other peoples.

There exists in the Philippines a peculiar tale:

> They say that Aswang was a Visaya (an inhabitant of the islands between Luxon and Mindanao) who made a pact with the devil. He set foot neither in churches nor in any other holy places, and under his armpit he had a gland full of oil which enabled him to fly wherever he wished. He had claws besides, and an immensely long black tongue, soft and shining. His chief duty consisted in tearing the foetus from the body, and this was done by touching it with his tongue. In this way the death

of the pregnant woman was achieved, so that Aswang could then quietly devour the foetus. A night bird, called by the Tagales *tictic*, gave warning of Aswang: when it sang, people knew that Aswang was about [*Oceania Esp.*, 1884].

Of the Dyaks in Borneo, Hein says:

> The *kamiak* is a very evil-intentioned spirit who has the gift of flying, and he is feared intensely by pregnant women as he always endeavours to penetrate invisibly into their bodies and either to make the birth of the child difficult or else quite impossible. Sacrifices are made to him in little huts [which are either sunk in the river or hung on the top of a tree near the house].

In another passage there is a report by Hein about the offering by pregnant women of fowls. This has, he thinks, its reason in the belief that the female *hantoes*, while dying in childbirth, are changed into evil spirits, *kamiak* or *kangkamiak*, which generally try to enter pregnant women in the form of a fowl to hinder their delivery; even the voice of the *kamiak* resembles the cry of a hen. Howell states that the period of pregnancy is passed in great fear of the *hantoes*, and they must be appeased by offerings of fowls at every opportunity, for instance when dreams occur. Offerings are also made to the water spirits, *djata*, who protect the pregnant from evil spirits and facilitate their confinement. But despite all these precautions, according to O. von Kessel, the Dyak woman seems not to feel herself safe, for the young wife, as soon as she is pregnant, never leaves the house without taking with her a talisman – a little basket hung with leaves, roots and bits of stick, and particularly with numerous snail shells.

The women of Ceram Laut often wear a piece of paper with a passage of the Koran written upon it and wrapped in linen in order to be proof against the injurious influences of evil spirits.

The pregnant women of Orang Panggang in Malacca, as Stevens reports, lay flowers down beside a tree which belongs to the same species as their so-called tree of life. On this tree the soul of the future child waits in the form of a bird until it is eaten by the pregnant woman. Women who omit to eat the soul bird during pregnancy bring a dead child into the world, or else it dies soon after birth.

PROHIBITIONS

It is regarded as a very serious offence among the Magyars or the Transylvanian Saxons if the pregnant woman denies her condition. Among the former the children are, as a result, late in learning to speak; among the latter they do not learn to speak at all. Similarly, the tent Gypsy woman of Transylvania, during pregnancy, is supposed to tread underfoot every snail she sees, or else her child will have difficulty in learning to walk. The Saxon in the same place must, when in this condition, avoid treading on an animal which has been killed, otherwise her child will not learn to walk at all. If the former spits at a toad her child will have difficulty in learning to speak; and if, on hearing the cry of a corncrake, she does not cover her mouth quickly with her left hand she will give birth to a child which will cry day and night.

Flowers must not be thrown at the pregnant Saxon in Transylvania, or her child will have a birthmark at the place where she is struck. She must not put beans in her apron and also not urinate on hemp leavings, otherwise the child will get a skin rash. Further, she may not wind thread or wear pearls round her neck, otherwise the navel cord will wind round the child's neck at birth.

In the Amboina group, the woman during pregnancy avoids sitting with her back to a cooking pot because otherwise her child will be black. In Samoa, as von Bülow reports, birthmarks with which new-born children come into the world are a consequence of certain transgressions of the mother:

> The Samoans maintain that if the pregnant woman steals food in order to eat it in secret, or if she pilfers any of the food common to the members of her household in order to eat it secretly, or if she takes an egg from a hen's nest and devours it in secret, all these objects which she has secretly used for herself without giving any to others are delineated in black pigment somewhere on the body of the unborn child, and so make the mother's faults public.

All tying, knotting and joining are thought to bring about a closure, and must be omitted by the pregnant woman unless she wants to be closed herself, or, in other words, if she wants to avoid a difficult confinement. Hence, on the Luang, Sermata and Babar islands she must not weave cloth, and on the last-named she must also not weave mats. Probably also for this reason the Songish Indian women in Vancouver, as well as the wives of the Nootka Indians, when they are pregnant take off all their bracelets, anklets and necklaces, as Boas reports. Likewise the pregnant woman in Achin must not sew clothes on her body, for by so doing she will bring about a long confinement (Jacobs).

The pregnant Mentawei women, according to Maass, must not fetch water from the river in 'a bamboo vessel in which there is a knot on the outside of the bottom; it must be quite smooth if the woman wants an easy confinement'.

Another idea is that all crawling and wriggling make the navel cord twist round the child (Majer). Hence, in the Palatinate and in Brunswick, the pregnant woman avoids creeping under a clothes-line; in addition she may not weave, wind a reel or twist yarn (Pauli, R. Andree). In Bavarian Franconia also, she must not creep under a rope or a plank, and the same fear causes pregnant women among the Esthonians to make no circular twisting movements when washing and rinsing clothes.

vi. Sexual Seclusion

There are a great number of peoples in all parts of the inhabited globe among whom coitus with a pregnant woman is most strictly forbidden. In most cases this rule is kept by the husband with the greatest punctiliousness and strictness.

Sexual intercourse with a pregnant woman was strictly forbidden by religious law among the Ancient Iranians, Bactrians, Medes and Persians, and anyone who had such intercourse received, according to the Vendidad, 2,000 strokes. Moreover, in expiation of his crime, he had to bring 1,000 loads of hard wood and as many of soft wood for the fire; to sacrifice 1,000 head of small cattle; to kill 1,000 snakes, 1,000 land lizards, 2,000 water lizards and 3,000 ants; and to put thirty foot-bridges over running water. The seed of life was not to be wasted, and the already existing new life was not to be injured (Duncker).

The Rabbis of the Talmud drew up similar rules: 'In the first three months after conception coitus is very injurious both for the pregnant woman and for the foetus. He who does this on the ninetieth day commits an act like that of annihilating a human life.' The careful Rabbi Abbajé adds: 'Since one cannot always know this day exactly, may God protect the innocent.'

Among the Hindus, Susruta also advised against sexual intercourse during pregnancy, and the Chinese likewise stated as 'the first and most important rule' during pregnancy the total abstinence from physical love (von Martius).

Among the Parsees it is, on the other hand, permitted to have sexual intercourse for the first four months and ten days after the onset of pregnancy, but coitus after this time is regarded as a crime deserving death (according to A. du Perron they believe that it may injure the foetus). Among the Swahili in East Africa, as Kersten states, this period is even longer, for the woman is used sexually by the husband till the sixth month after conception. Then he must certainly exercise restraint because it is supposed that otherwise the consequence will be a difficult confinement.

In other tribes, however, the husband must carefully abstain from his wife during the whole period of pregnancy. Such abstinence is practised by the Ashanti and the Basutos, and also by the Indians of North America and the aborigines of the Antilles. In Florida, the separation even extends to a period of two years after the confinement.

Among the Masai, according to Merker, husband and wife are separated until the end of the period of lactation, which lasts from one to one and a half years. Neither the husband nor any other man may touch the woman during this period, and in order to discourage advances she takes off all the ornaments which she has hitherto worn and avoids everything that is likely to attract men. Polygamy would seem to be a blessing in this respect, for it protects the pregnant woman.

Abstinence from sexual intercourse during pregnancy is also general on the little islands of the Malay Archipelago, and so strictly carried out that the desire to be free from this irksome prohibition sometimes makes the wives resort to artificial abortion.

Similarly in Peking, according to information given by Grube to M. Bartels, it is customary for the woman, when she feels she has become pregnant, to separate from her husband and sleep in a special bed. From this custom pregnancy is also called by the Chinese 'bed separation'. Moreover, in early times in China, the woman was completely isolated from her husband during the last period of her pregnancy. The *Li-chi*, part of the Confucian canon, says: 'If a woman is about to give birth to a child, she lives in a house apart for one month. The husband sends somebody twice a day to ask for her, and he himself asks for her. His wife, however, dare not see him, but sends the *mu* to answer his questions until the child is born.'

Thus, and in not a few countries, the separation is not always solely that of the bed: just as in menstruation the woman is often not permitted to have her meals with her husband, or even also with the other members of the family, so also during pregnancy she is sometimes not even allowed to stay under the same roof with him, a custom from which it can be deduced that, according to the belief of some peoples, the pregnant are in a state of *uncleanness*. Of a few tribes – the Siamese women (Schomburgk), the women of the Marianas, Gilbert and Marshall Islands (Keate), and the women of New Caledonia (de Rochas) – this is actually stated.

Schütt says of certain natives in West Africa: 'Every Negro regards the woman who is going to have a child as unclean; three weeks before her confinement she has to leave the village, and nobody may associate with her. She generally goes through the difficult hour without any assistance.'

The Yakuts, too, regard pregnant women as unclean and do not allow them to eat at the same table as the rest. They are believed, says Sierochevski, to spoil the huntsman's bullets and lessen the strength of the manual worker.

Among the Pshavs in the central Caucasus, the uncleanness during pregnancy, according to a statement of Prince Eristow, extends in a certain respect also to the husband. Both husband and wife are, at this time, excluded from all festivities, and that is why they try to keep a pregnancy secret as long as possible.

A similar belief is found in the Mandated Territory of New Guinea (Bukaua), where the husband of a pregnant woman may not go fishing: he has *gina* (fish taboo). The foetal blood is supposed to accompany the husband, and as soon as the fish perceive its appearance they vanish into the depths.

vii. Duties of the Husband

In many nations the onset of pregnancy imposes quite definite obligations on the husband, obligations other than those merely of abstention from intercourse.

During the pregnancy of a Mentawei islander the husband must do certain work which otherwise falls to his wife, such as cleaning the dishes after eating whilst his wife sits in peace on the verandah of the house. 'The husband,' states Maass, 'performs all the little household functions so that the mother's child does not turn around in the womb, and that the mother should have no pain when the child moves through the mother working.'

The Achinese must not leave his wife alone from the moment that the pregnancy is diagnosed till the forty-fourth day after the delivery, and especially in the interval between sunset and sunrise, in order to protect her from all kinds of ghosts which threaten to endanger the pregnant woman. If the man has two wives, then the rule is that he stays the night, or most of the night, with the pregnant wife. If, however, both are pregnant, then he divides his nightly society between the two. In the first five months of pregnancy he must not kill an animal, not even a snake or tiger, otherwise the confinement will be difficult and the child will assume the characteristics of the slaughtered beast (Jacobs).

Of the Jakûn in the Malay Peninsula, Stevens reports: 'A Jakûn husband never, if he can avoid it, goes out of sight of his wife when she is pregnant ... The presence of the husband is supposed to contribute to a certain extent to the growth of the unborn child in the womb.'

During the pregnancy of a Kota woman in the Nilgiri Hills her husband must have neither his hair nor his nails cut, according to a report by Mantegazza. Similarly, Brandeis states that on the island of Nauru the husband who is otherwise accustomed to wear his hair short leaves it uncut till the child is born.

In the Amboina group, the husband may not urinate in the moonlight, for, by exposing his genitals, he offends the women in the moon, who could as a result bring about a difficult confinement for his wife. The husband is likewise prohibited from constructing tables, chairs, doors, windows and the like, and from driving a nail, etc., because this also will impede the confinement. Further, he must not split bamboo cane to make an axe, as otherwise the child will get a harelip, and he is not permitted to open coconuts, to cut hair or to hold the rudder of a boat (Schmidt).

In Greenland, too, the husband must refrain from work until the confinement, as otherwise the child will die. And in Kamchatka a husband was made responsible for the wrong position of a child at birth because he had bent wood over his knee at the time of his wife's confinement (Steller).

In several South American Indian tribes the husband as well as the wife refrains from eating meat during her pregnancy. Among the Guarani, for example, the man does not go hunting so long as his wife is pregnant. In other tribes, for instance the Mauhe (according to J. B. von Spix), the husband has to fast and live only on fish and fruit, while among the Yap Islanders (Carolines) he may not eat bananas, fallen coconuts, plaice, turtles, crabs or speckled fish.

viii. Abortion

METHODS UP TO THE MIDDLE AGES

The old Hindu physicians used abortifacients mostly of vegetable extraction, which they gave when the abdomen swelled abnormally in pregnant women. They considered special means suitable for each month of pregnancy. Thus for the first month: *Glycyrrhiza glabra* L., *Tectonae grandis semen*, *Asclepias rosea* and *Pinus devandaru*; for the second month: wood sorrel, *Sesamum orientale* L., *Piper longum*, *Rubia munjista* Roxb. and *Asparagus racemosus* Willd.; and so on to the ninth month: *Glycyrrhiza glabra* L., *Panicum dactylon* L., *Asclepias rosea* and *Echites frutescens*.

Among the Ancient Greeks and Romans, *Mentha pulegium* and saffron (*Crocus sativus*) are said to have been used as abortifacients. Soranus declared every abortion to be dangerous, although he himself made use of it in isolated cases of physical affliction. For bringing on abortion he, as well as Aetius and others, recommended the compression of the abdomen by binding, severe shaking, injections of astringents, *fel tauri* and *Absynthium*; friction of the genitals, baths, astringents for internal use, plaster of cyclamen, *Elaterium*, *Artemisia* L., colocynth, *Coccus cnidius*, natron, opoponax, etc., and also specifics for causing sickness and sneezing. Further, one was to insert a pessary of *Iris*, galbanum, *Thymelaea* berries, turpentine mixed with oil of roses and cypress, and on the following morning to steam the genitals with an infusion of fenugreek and *Artemisia* L.

Bleeding, lifting and carrying heavy burdens, fasting, irritation of the orifice of the womb by a roll of paper, a quill, a piece of wood, etc., were used by Arab physicians to bring on a miscarriage when the normal delivery might be dangerous to pregnant women owing to their small size. At the same time, a great many internal medicines were used (we find these enumerated in Avicenna, *Lit. can.* 12, 13), as was a peculiar long-necked *instrumentum triangulate extremitatis* whose purpose it was to open the orifice of the womb and to inject it with material for causing the abortion.

The abortifacients of the old Arab physicians have been summarized by Pfaff. Among them are: *Calendula officinalis* L., ammoniac, *Anagyris foetida* L., *Juniperus sabina* L., *Iris florentina* L., *Cyclamen europaeum* L., *Artemisia arborescens* L., *Adiantum capillus-veneris* L., *Amyris gileadensis* L., *Daucus carota* L., *Gentiana lutea* L., *Lepidium sativum* L., *Cucumis colocynthis* L. (carried in the vagina kills the embryo), *Cheiranthus cheiri* L., *Aristolochia rotunda* L., *Crocus sativus* L., *Gnaphalium consanguineum*, *Aspidium filix-mas* Sw., *Seseli tortuosum* L., *Saponaria officinalis* L., *Stachys germanica* L., *Ferula persica* Willd., *Laurus cassica* auct., *Sesamum orientale* L., *Pinus cedrus* L., *Anchusa tinctoria* L., *Nigella sativa* L., *Laurus nobilis* L., *Bryonia dioica* Jacq., *Rubia tinctoria* Salisb., *Mentha* L., *Momordica elaterium* L., *Veronica anagallis* L., *Costus arabicus* L., *Hedera helix* L., *Clinopodium vulgare* L., *Centaurium majus*, *Apium petroselinum* L., *Bubon macedonicum* L., *Daphne gnidium* L., myrrh, and *Thymus serpyllum* L.

These specifics were sometimes used internally, or sometimes introduced into the vagina as irritant pessaries; or sometimes abortion was achieved by the introduction into the uterus of little pads of wool sprinkled with irritant powder after an opening of the orifice had been effected by means of softening pessaries.

According to Duncker, among the Bactrians, Medes and Persians there were old women who brought on abortion in pregnant maidens by means of *baga* or *fraçpata*, or other 'decomposing' kinds of trees the nature of which is not, however, known.

The German physicians of the sixteenth century, among other medical specifics for bringing about miscarriages, mention the smoke from ass-dung, an adder's skin, or myrrh, castoreum, sulphur, galbanum, dyer's madder, and hawk and pigeon droppings. They gave the woman wine with asafetida, rue, myrrh or savine, also an infusion of figs, fenugreek, rue or marjoram, and put plugs of cotton into the vagina with ammoniac, opoponax, hellebore,

Aristolochia L., colocynth, cow gall and rue sap. They also smeared these plugs with rue sap and scammony with birthwort, savine, garden cress, etc. The pregnant woman had to drink the milk of another woman; also dittany juice with wine. Then followed baths with water mint, mugwort, bitumen, etc. Not until fairly late did more effective medicaments come to the knowledge of doctors. According to Richard, ergot was not used by obstetricians till the year 1747.

PRESENT-DAY METHODS

We come now to a survey of the procedures among modern peoples.

F. de Azara reports that he asked the Mbaya women in Paraguay what they used to effect abortion. 'You shall see immediately,' they replied. Thereupon one of the women lay down on the ground quite naked and two old women began to deal her the most violent blows on the abdomen with their fists until the blood ran out of the genitals. This was a sign that the embryo was about to be expelled, and indeed Azara heard a few hours later that it really had occurred. At the same time, however, he was told that many women experience the most harmful effects from this procedure throughout their lives, and that many even die during the operation itself, and some from the results of it.

Of the Eskimo women Bessels reports:

Just as in Christianized Greenland the pregnant make use of the heart stick (a piece of wood for stretching wet foot-gear), so the Ita women of Smith Sound use either a whip-handle or some other object, and knock or press against the abdomen with it, which procedure is repeated several times daily. Another way of producing abortion consists in the perforation of the foetal membranes, an operation which is rather astonishing.

A thinly cut walrus or seal rib is sharpened at one end like a knife edge, while the opposite end is rounded and blunt. The sharpened end has a cylindrical covering of dressed sealskin open at both ends and corresponding to the cutting part of the piece of bone. At both the upper and lower ends of this covering is fastened a thread of reindeer sinew from 15 to 18 inches in length. When this probe is introduced into the vagina, the blade part is covered by the leather sheath. When the operator thinks she has penetrated far enough, she gently pulls the thread fastened at the lower end of the sheath. By this means, the blade is, of course, laid bare. Then a half-turn of the probe is made and, at the same time, a push upwards and inwards. After the rupture of the foetal membranes has taken place, the instrument is drawn back again. First, however, the thread at the upper end of the probe is pulled in order to cover the sharp end of the probe and thus to avoid injuring the genital canal.

Bessels learnt that this operation is always performed by the pregnant women themselves.

The Shasta Indians in north California, according to Bancroft, used as an abortifacient great quantities of the root of a parasitic fern which grows at the top of their fir trees.

In Armenia, where artificial abortion is very common, Minassian states that decoctions (for example of saffron, juniper, oleander) are drunk, or it is induced in a very crude manner by the introduction of a piece of wood.

In Japan the artificial induction of abortion is not permitted; it is regarded as a great disgrace among the higher classes. Nevertheless, it is very frequently carried out in illegitimate pregnancies, and even among married women of the lower classes by a kind of midwife, who is, moreover, quite ignorant. Stricker states that the procedure consists in inserting between the wall of the uterus and the foetal membranes a piece of the flexible root (resembling a goose quill in thickness) of a certain plant and letting it remain there for a day or two. The root, before being introduced into the vagina, is smeared with musk; and musk is also given internally. The result of this is said to be certain. There also occurs the rough method of pushing a pointed twig of some shrub into the orifice of the womb, a method which not infrequently leads to death. The proper time for doing this is supposed to be the fourth or fifth month of pregnancy.

In Karikal, a French possession on the south-east coast of India, the seeds of *Nigella sativa* L. (the fennel flower), powdered and taken as a paste with palm sugar, are used in doses of up to fifteen grains as an emmenagogue, and in larger doses as an abortifacient (Canolle). A rod or pointed reed is also sometimes introduced into the uterus and allowed to remain there.

In other parts of India the induction of abortion is very common. On the methods used there John Shortt reports that the juice of fresh leaves of *Bambusa arundinacea* Retz., the milky juice of various euphorbias (for instance *E. tirucalli* L. or *E. antiquorum* L.), also asafetida mixed with various scented and aromatic substances, are much used. Moreover, *Plumbago zeylanica* L., which can be employed internally, is also used locally, its pointed root being pushed into the womb with great force. Indeed, Shortt found it still there in several cases when the embryo was already expelled, and in the dead body of a woman who had aborted he found the fundus uteri pierced in three different places. Such cases are said to be not uncommon, as indeed are other affections of the womb, in consequence of such treatment.

In Galela and among the Tobelorese on Djailolo, abortifacients are prepared from kalapa oil and lemon juice, and the roots of various trees are also much used. On Bali, the women employ, among other things, a little extract of *Sterculia foetida* L., a tree whose unripe fruit is used for the same purpose in Java.

According to de Rochas, the inhabitants of New Caledonia have great skill in the art of inducing abortion. The most usual method they call the 'banana cure', which apparently consists in devouring boiled green bananas. Since the bananas are quite harmless, they are used, in the opinion of de Rochas, to conceal the true but as yet undiscovered abortifacient. Moncelon also states that their specifics are unknown but vegetable in nature, and in his opinion certain kinds of bark are used.

Abortion is very common among the Murray Islanders in Torres Strait. A. E. Hunt reports that in order to induce abortion the leaves of certain trees are chewed or sometimes mixed with coconut milk and drunk. If this medicine fails, less gentle methods are resorted to. Sometimes the abdomen is struck with big stones, or the woman is placed with her back to a tree whilst two men take one end of a long post and press the other end against the woman's abdomen until by continued pressure the foetus is squeezed to death. It is hardly necessary to add that the woman also is often killed by this treatment.

Similarly, among the Sinaugolo in British New Guinea the person who wants to have the abortion brought on lies on her belly and another woman sits on her back; or the abdomen is pressed, or hot stones are laid on it. This, however, is only done before the bones of the child have formed, because then the child is still *rara*, i.e., 'blood'. They put this period in the first three or four months of pregnancy (Seligman).

All kinds of magical cures are used in New Guinea. One interesting abortifacient of the Kai, according to Keysser, is a pip from the dung of the cassowary. It is cooked with the vegetables which the woman is to eat. The pip itself is kept back, for it is only the life substance from the pip expelled from the cassowary's bowels that is to be imparted to the vegetables. This life substance in the woman's abdomen effects the expulsion of the nascent being.

Blyth learnt from native midwives that in the Fiji Islands the method of abortion consists purely and solely in taking herbal decoctions, which are used when movement is first felt. For this purpose five plants are used: two *Malvaceae* (*Hibiscus diversifolius* Jacq. and *Hibiscus abelmoschus* L.), a *Tiliacea* (*Grewia prunifolia*), a *Convolvulacea* (*Pharbitis insularis*) and a *Liliacea* (*Dracaena ferrea* L.). The sap and the leaves, and of the third and the fifth the surface of the stem as well, are used. The last is considered the most effective and is used when the others fail.

Fig. 19   The *kapo*, a wooden image presiding over miscarriages, Hawaii
(Mus. f. Völkerk., Berlin; after photo by M. Bartels)

The women of Hawaii have a special image (the *kapo*) of the god whose function it is to bring on miscarriages (Fig. 19). This image, now in the Ethnological Museum in Berlin, is carved from a brown wood and has at the top a fantastic head with a cock's comb-like crest. Towards the other end it forms a rounded, slightly conical tapering stick shaped like an awl, of the approximate thickness of a medium-sized index finger. Its whole length is now 22 cm, but the instrument was originally somewhat longer. Its lower point appears rough, irregular in shape and very much worn, an unmistakable sign that this god had performed his bloody office very industriously. There can be no doubt that the pointed end of the figure was introduced into the uterus in order to perforate the foetal membranes, and in this way to induce abortion.

In Ethiopia the wood and resin of the cedar and the savine tree are used for the induction of abortion (Hartmann), and in Massawa, according to Brehm's report, an infusion of a species of thuya.

The Arab midwives, according to Rique, induce artificial abortion by perforating the membranes. In the case of a woman delivered in this manner, where the inexpert hand of the midwife had missed its mark, Rique, according to Bertherand, saw two or three wounds near the os uteri caused by some sharp instrument. If the child is thought to be dead, the pregnant woman has to take a drink consisting of honey and warm milk in which powder of vitriol is dissolved. Should the child be not quite dead, however, it will turn on its side and then be certainly expelled.

According to Oppenheim, saffron and savine are known as abortifacients among Turkish women. Besides these they often use orange leaves with jalap, which they infuse with boiling water and drink as tea, a specific which they prefer to all others because of its certainty, even though its use is said to result in dangerous haemorrhages. According to Eram the midwives also introduce foreign bodies into the womb, for example pipe mouth-pieces.

Although in every country in Europe intentional abortion has hitherto always been considered a penal offence and punished accordingly, it is practised everywhere.

Numerous popular remedies and specifics are used, and also baths and blood-letting, over-exertion, intentional falling and pushes and blows on the abdomen. Electricity has also been tried, as well as the insertion of sharp objects into the womb.

In Russia, corrosive sublimate, white bryony and savine are said to be used internally as abortifacients; in Esthonia, mercury mixed with fat; in Greece, rue, savine and amber; in France, squills, sarsaparilla, guaiacum, aloes, balm-mint, camomile, saffron, absinthe, vanilla and juniper; in Bohemia, beer with peony or *Asarum europaeum*, or a decoction of rue and a solution of sodium sulphate; in Swabia, savine and mugwort; in Styria, strong purgatives, ergot, savine, the twigs and leaves of rosemary, and infusions of tar; and in Frankenwald, balm-mint, rue, savine, vinegar, cooking salt, and all harsh and poisonous things, as well as Peruvian balsam and gunpowder, of which they say, 'It makes an opening as it must get out through a hole.'

With regard to chemical and herbal preparations Köhler has stated that really nothing is to be expected from these medical specifics, and that although one portion of them leads not infrequently to the expulsion of the product, the other portion is, however, quite ineffective. Moreover, because of the great danger to the pregnant woman owing to their uncertain action, it would never enter a physician's head to make use of any of these specifics when reasons of health make an interruption of pregnancy necessary.

CHAPTER VIII

Birth

i. Is Birth Easier Among Primitive Nations?

Aristotle says, in his book on the generation of animals:

> In regard to pregnancy, the differences between man and the animals are known. Among the latter, for instance, the body is mostly in a condition of well-being, whilst most women at the time of pregnancy are ailing. To some extent the mode of life is to blame for this. For, in a sedentary mode of life, too much secreted matter is accumulated, whereas among the peoples where the women work hard, even in pregnancy, no special symptoms appear and . . . the act of birth is easy. That is to say, exertion dissolves the secreted matter, while in a sedentary mode of life much of it remains in the body for want of activity . . . and the pains at birth are severe.

If we cannot, on this basis, help awarding the prize for easy births to the savages, we are still more strengthened in this view if we try to make a survey of the individual peoples. Nevertheless we should fall into a great error if we were to assume that serious disorders in the course of birth did not occur at all among savages, or that, because a woman uttered no sounds of distress, the labour pains were not present at all. We may quote here as an example the North American Indians, among whom it is a point of honour not to allow the least sound of pain to be heard. Indeed, as Morton says, 'If the woman betrays any such weakness she is held unworthy to be a mother and her children are regarded as cowards.'

In the question of easy births we must, of course, refer preferably to the records of physicians who have had the opportunity of being present frequently at the parturitions of women of less civilized peoples and of becoming acquainted with their mode of life.

Engelmann learnt from one doctor who had been among the Canadian Indians for eight years and from another who had been among the Oregon Indians for four that, during these periods, they had heard neither of an interrupted birth nor even of a case of death in childbed. The latter authority had at most had to rupture the foetal membranes. Engelmann seeks to explain the favourable results in these tribes by the fact that the structure and development of the women's muscular system is strong. He also refers to the circumstance that the women marry only within their own tribe or race, so that the head of the child, in respect of its compass and diameter, conforms completely to the maternal pelvis through which it must pass.

One of the authorities in this field, Professor Dr Külz, who was for a long time active in medical affairs in the German Colonies, says:

> Only very rarely does a confinement not end in the natural way. Too narrow a pelvis does not exist, because, in the first place, rickets is unknown, which is the most frequent cause of this in childhood. Further, should there ever have existed a tendency to this in any woman, she would have died for want of medical help, and, therefore, her defective tendencies could not have been transmitted. In a numerous clientele in Africa and in the South Seas, I have had to interfere on only one single occasion owing to a misplaced transverse presentation. Far more common than irregularities in the mechanism of birth are the possibilities of an infection, either because of dirt, or of the foolish manipulations of the people assisting, for instance pulling the umbilical cord and tearing it, or causing an *inversio uteri*, etc. It is remarkable, however, that in spite of great want of cleanliness, serious septic puerperal fever does not appear to occur ... it is the opinion of all colonial doctors that both irregularities in birth and still-births are rare.

In Central America generally, births seem to proceed easily. We learn through Bernhard that the women of Nicaragua are well built and have a wide pelvis, 'therefore the births there are generally easy and normal'.

Marr asserts emphatically: 'I have seen parturitions among the Indians where the woman in childbirth lay on her knees, smoked a cigar and, at the same time, let the rosary slip through her fingers.' Moreover, he extols the 'enormous pelvis' of these women.

The Patagonians, according to Guinnard, who lived in captivity with them for three years, make their wives work hard during pregnancy, 'for which nature makes amends with an easy confinement'.

Of the Brazilian Indian women, Marcgravius stated in the seventeenth century that they give birth extraordinarily easily. Yet it appears that at least in one case of birth, which Lery had the opportunity of observing in an Indian woman in Brazil, the affair seems to have proceeded not without considerable pain and great wailing, for he writes: 'Another Frenchman and I were sleeping in a village when, about midnight, we heard a woman screaming, so that we thought there was a wild animal trying to devour her. When we rushed there we found that it was not so, but that the travail of bringing a child into the world made her cry out in that way.' Moreover, according to many reports, very barbarous methods of delivery are in use among the Brazilian savages (hanging women between trees, etc.), so that we must presume that births are not infrequently difficult and proceed with the help of foolish artificial aid.

Among the Melanesians, and particularly on the Fiji Islands, births take place 'easily' (T. Williams and J. Calvert) and the women seldom die at confinement (de Rienzi). Similarly among the Polynesians on Samoa, according to Gräff, births take place for the most part so easily that the mother is seen soon after going to the river to bathe herself and her child. On Hawaii, too, the native women give birth to their children without pain, except in quite uncommon cases. Indeed, when they saw the wives of missionaries delivered with pain, they were surprised at this suffering and laughed about it, for they thought that the crying out of the women of white race was only one of their habits or customs. And on several Micronesian islands, for instance on the Caroline Archipelago, correspondents and travellers never heard of any unsuccessful confinement among the native women. Troublesome mishaps, they say, seem to be quite unknown.

As to the process of birth in Australian women, J. Hooker has collected from various parts of this continent records which agree that confinement is, in general, quick and easy, and that only in exceptional cases does a difficult delivery occur, sometimes, according to Searanke, extending over two days. According to other statements, it varies between a few hours and five to six days (Parris).

Goldie, certainly a very reliable judge, states that among the aborigines in New Zealand births in general proceed very easily, seldom lasting more than two hours, and that the young mother returns from the bath and soon goes on with her work again. As an example, he brings forward the case of a Maori woman who, acting as a carrier, was overtaken by labour pains on the march, was confined and walked four miles afterwards.

In the Levant generally, birth, according to H. J. Türk, proceeds with great ease, so that skilled assistance is hardly ever required. He adds: 'Many would like to attribute the reason for this not only to the climate but also to the fact that the women are accustomed from childhood to sit on their knees with their legs crossed and their knees apart.'

In his *Voyages and Travels in the Levant* (London, 1706), F. Hasselquist also states that the women in the country have easy births, 'and one seldom hears of a woman having a difficult birth, much less that she lost her life over it; and this is especially true of the Turkish women'. Oppenheim, too, states that 'women's confinements, as over-civilization and fashion do not distort and cripple the body, are not attended with the difficulties and troubles common in civilized Europe'. (In this respect, what Hille said a long time ago about the Negress slaves in Surinam, to whose birth processes he was able to devote years of attention, also seems relevant: 'Just as in the whole world generally the women of the lower uncultured classes, where the body has not been disturbed in its development from childhood onwards by incorrect, cramping and distorting clothes, usually bear children easily, so in this case with Negresses.')

Rigler, on the other hand, observes that Turks and Armenians experience irregular births relatively more frequently than Europeans, this no doubt having regard chiefly to the women in Constantinople and other large towns in Turkey where not only rickets and deformities of the pelvis are common but also bad midwives may bring about troubles in confinement.

In Persia, as Polak, physician-in-ordinary to the Shah, reported to Ploss, parturition is nearly always normal, because the body is not cramped by corsets and because the women wear their clothes fastened round the hip-bone ridge and not round the abdomen. The women are broadly built in the pelvis and ride a great deal in man's fashion.

However, of the inhabitants of the Persian province of Gilan, on the Caspian Sea, Häntzsche says:

> According to all the information I could get, I am no doubt not far from the truth if I assume that abnormal births must be just as common with them as with us, and that the women's diseases are caused by unskilful delivery (which always occurs because there the so-called midwives do not even know what an examination is). Cases, which with us can be brought at least to some extent to a successful finish, always end fatally there.

Births in Java are usually wonderfully quick and successful: one often sees the young mother with her child go to the river to cleanse herself and her clothes half an hour after the birth, states Metzger. Kohlbrugge, too, heard that the confinement of the Tenggerese on Java, from the beginning of labour to the birth of the child, seldom lasts longer than an hour. Only a few women have labour pains lasting several hours; these are supposed always to be the result of heredity.

In Siam (Quaritch-Wales) births in general are easy. The women are, as a rule, well developed, and wear no clothing which cramps the body. The breasts are left uncovered, and a girdle only is wound round the abdominal region. In the Philippines, on the other hand, the process of birth is in no wise easier than in civilized nations, according to D. Bell. Owing to the unsuitable manipulations by the assistants, the consequences for mother and child are often lamentable. In 38 out of 105 cases, serious lacerations were caused in the perineum and cervix.

In China, the process of birth may vary considerably according to social position and province. The Chinese women of high position who, owing to having had their feet cramped by binding, are condemned to almost continual sitting and are therefore weakened, appear to go through the labour of birth much less easily than those of the lower classes, who, as we know from several examples, give birth to their children quickly and easily. Cases of death in delivery are said almost never to occur (Stenz). The painter Hildebrand saw the confinement of a farmer's wife in Shanghai: she gave birth to a healthy little boy without the help of a midwife; kind neighbours put a bundle of rice straw under her head, a young girl brought a dish of curry and rice, the woman in childbed sat up and polished off the ample quantity to the last grain; then she wrapped up the child (which till then had lain naked on the tiles in the sharp December air) in her rags and took herself off.

Theophilus Hahn says of the pure-blooded Hottentots, among whom he was born and brought up: 'Hottentot women have extraordinarily easy confinements. It often happens that a woman delivers herself and takes up her work again shortly after the birth as if nothing had happened.' And he writes further: 'A woman was once overtaken by childbirth and was alone in the house without any assistance. She simply chased away a cow ... from the place where it was lying, lay down in the warm hollow and was delivered there by herself.'

As G. Fritsch informs us, the Bechuana women also have easy births. Here, too, it happens that the women work in the fields up to the last minute, are overtaken by birth, bring the child into the world without any help and go back to the village with it. Birth troubles, owing to their infrequency, seem to these women something quite horrible and thoroughly upset them. (Indeed, among the Ama-Xosa, where birth on the average proceeds very easily, according to Kropf, a difficult delivery causes the woman to be looked upon as bewitched and to be forsaken by everybody.)

Even the wives of the colonial settlers at the Cape of Good Hope are said to give birth to children with less pain and risk than the Europeans at home, and their confinement is said to take place more quickly. Kolben, who reported this in the eighteenth century, heard of no case in the ten years he stayed at the Cape in which a woman died in childbirth.

On the other hand, while the Negresses in the Nile Territories seem, according to Hartmann, to give birth to their children easily, as they are often confined in the open fields and soon after return calmly to work, very young slaves who have been infibulated are said to suffer severely in being delivered (see also 'Defibulation', Chapter II). In Egypt, weakened urban women also suffer frequently in childbirth, and need skilled help; moreover they often die during delivery. These troubles are probably due mainly to the fact that Egyptian women marry too young, i.e., at the age of eleven to thirteen.

In Europe there are relatively few nations (and it must be admitted that these are chiefly the less civilized) where, according to consistent reports, the women in general enjoy a particularly easy parturition.

The women of Iceland 'get rid of birth soon', as Baumgarten expresses it, and in Lapland also the women have an easy confinement. Krebel reports the same of the women in Esthonia, and Gaunt in the seventeenth century of those in Ireland.

Sicilian women are likewise said, according to Finke, to be distinguished for easy births, as are the women in Minorca. The same is true of the Basque women, who, because they take a considerable share in agricultural work and are physically strong, also bring their children into the world with great ease. Indeed, Eugène Cordier, speaking of the Basques, states that among them more than one new-born child has spent the first day of its life in the shade of a tree under which it first saw the light of day whilst the mother has calmly gone back to work again.

Southern Slav peasant women are also said to go through the process of giving birth with great equanimity. According to report, it often happened that a pregnant woman who had gone to the hills to collect firewood was suddenly overtaken by labour pains and, without ado, acted as her own midwife and brought the child home in her apron; in addition, she sometimes also brought back a load of wood with her.

ii. Birth Alone and Out of Doors

Prochownick has tried to refer childbearing accomplished alone to the realm of fable – incorrectly, as it happens, since we possess records of this from different travellers whose statements we have no reason to doubt.

According to Riedel, many women give birth to children quite alone, in the woods or on the seashore, on the islands of Buru, Ceram, Kei, Tenimber and Timor Laut, as well as in the Babar Archipelago and on the islands of Keisar, Eetar, Romang, Dama, Teun, Nila and Serua. In the woods, they like to choose the neighbourhood of a stream, in which they bathe themselves and the child immediately after delivery; on the seashore, after the birth, they take a bath in the sea. On the Tenimber and Timor Laut islands, they are even accustomed to be confined sitting in the sea.

A similar custom is also found among the Maori women in New Zealand, who give birth alone beside a stream, in a thicket, whither they withdraw in order to be able to wash themselves and the child just after the delivery (Tuke).

The Negrito and the Montesca in the Philippines, according to Mallat's report, likewise give birth almost always without any help, and are often quite alone when labour sets in. Then, having found a suitable place, they support and press the abdomen down hard on a bamboo. The child is received in warm ashes, whereupon the mother lies down beside it and cuts the navel cord herself. Immediately after this, she rushes into the water with the child (this is certainly contested by Reed), goes home and covers herself with leaves.

The native women on the Moluccas give remarkable examples of how little troublesome the business of birth is for their women. Thus we read:

> A woman alone in a boat who had set out for the other side of the bay was overtaken by labour when she was a good sea-mile away. She was confined but continued to row to the far shore. There she washed herself and the child and returned home the same day. Another time the missionary baptized a child which had been born whilst its mother was alone in the middle of the river.

Of the wives of the Iroquois, the missionary Lafitau says that, if they are overtaken by birth pains on the march, they manage the delivery for themselves, wash their children in the nearest water and go to their huts as if nothing had happened.

The ease with which Indian women go through confinement is also described by Engelmann:

> Choquette tells that once an Indian troop of Flatheads and Kootenais, consisting of men, women and children, set out on a hunting expedition. On a bitterly cold winter's day, one of the wives left the troop, dismounted from her horse, spread a buffalo skin on the snow and gave birth to a child whose arrival was followed by that of the placenta. Having seen that everything was well, she gathered up the child, which was wrapped in a cloth, mounted her horse and overtook the troop before anyone had become aware of her absence.

The missionary Beierlein, who lived for many years among the Chippewa, informed Ploss from his own observation: 'With them, the woman, when she feels the labour pains, leaves her work, gathers some grass and hay, and goes quite alone into the wood in order to give birth to her child . . . Then she goes to the water and washes herself and the child, and immediately after continues her work.'

We find the same custom among the women of a few South American Indian tribes. Of the Tupi and Tupinamba, for example, Thevet recorded in the year 1575 'that in labour they are neither helped nor relieved by any person whatever'. And Father Gumilla relates of the Indian women on the Orinoco that, when they feel the first pains, they go secretly to the bank of the river or the nearest stream and there give birth to their child alone. If a boy comes into the world, then the mother, greatly pleased, washes herself and the child carefully, and recovers from birth without any more rest. If a girl is born, however, she breaks her neck or buries her alive, then washes herself lengthily and goes to her hut as if nothing had happened.

Schomburgk says:

> The Warrau (Guarauno) Indian woman in British Guiana, when the time of her confinement approaches, goes away from the village which her husband and relatives inhabit. Alone in a hut in the wood, she awaits the moment, which is without danger for her, and then returns with the new-born child to her people without having called in outside aid. On one of my excursions, I myself found one such woman in childbirth.

A similar custom, according to Speke and Burton, existed among the Wakimbu and the Wanyamwezi at Ujiji in Central Africa, where, when a woman noticed that her confinement was near, she left the hut, retired into the jungle and, having delivered herself, returned, carrying the new-born child in a sack on her back.

Felkin records of confinement among the Acholi that a block of wood is placed immediately in front of a tree-trunk. On this $3\frac{1}{2}$-foot-high block, which is covered first with grass, then with a hide, the woman sits. About $2\frac{1}{2}$ feet from the block and the same distance from each other, two poles are driven into the ground; each of these has a fork about $1\frac{1}{2}$ feet from the ground, on which the woman plants her feet, while she holds the poles fast with her hands. When once she has taken her place, she hardly ever gives up till the child is born (Fig. 20).

Of the Bedouins in south Tunisia, Narbeshuber says:

> ... as I myself have seen, the event of birth is enacted even more simply than with the town Arabian woman of Sfax. The woman crouches down somewhere, gives birth to her child, cleans herself and the child superficially and returns to the *duâr*. People hardly notice that she has had her 'difficult time', and she generally takes up her hard work again immediately.

The Ostiaks, a nomad tribe of Asia, are also quoted by J. B. Müller as thinking very little of birth, often having to go from one place to another in winter. If there is no yurt in the vicinity and no convenience for the woman in childbirth anywhere, she manages her affair as she goes along, buries the child in the snow to harden it, etc.

Fig. 20 Acholi woman during delivery (after Felkin)

Similarly, it is recorded by Mme Dora d'Istria of the women in Montenegro that they do not even stay in their miserable huts to wait for their confinement, but deliver themselves unaided in the fields or woods, neither sigh nor plaint escaping from them. As soon as they have recovered a little, they take the child in their apron and wash it in the nearest brook.

iii. Parturition in Public

Whilst the women among the peoples already mentioned generally go a little apart for their delivery, we find in many others a total lack of regard in this respect. A confinement to them is an act at which anyone, even children, may be present, and it usually takes place in the public street.

According to Nicholas, women in New Zealand are delivered in the open air before an assembly of persons of both sexes, without uttering a single cry. The bystanders watch with attention for the moment when the child comes into the world and, when they see it, cry, *'Tane! Tane!'* The mother cuts the umbilical cord herself, and then resumes her usual activities as if nothing had happened. (This description does not, however, agree with those of Tuke and Goldie, according to whom Maori women are supposed to be confined quite alone in the bush.)

Of the Aru Islands, H. von Rosenberg reports that when a woman is on the point of being delivered, friends and relatives are summoned in order to be present at the birth of the child. The guests make an infernal noise throughout, shrieking and beating gongs and *tiffas* (little drums). And E. V. Vollum states that, when called to an Umpqua chief, he found the female patient lying in a hut filled to suffocation with men and women. The assembled people shrieked in the wildest manner, lamenting the misfortune of the sufferer. It used to be not much better among the half-civilized inhabitants of Mexico at Monte Rey; but in these cases men were as a rule excluded (Engelmann).

Among the Munda in Chota Nagpur (India), during labour, both her own and even strange children, big and small, remain in the room with the mother till the infant is born. Jellinghaus adds that 'this barbarous naturalness (as it appears to us) seems not to have any bad influence on the morals of the children'. Further, in the Brahman village of Walkeshwar, not far from Bombay, Haeckel saw a delivery carried out under difficult conditions and with the strangest instruments in the open street. A Hindu constable kept the assembled onlookers in order, and was good enough to explain to Haeckel the significance of the act.

Similarly, Steller records that in Kamchatka the woman is usually delivered lying on her knees in the presence of all the people of the village, without distinction of position or sex.

Of the Guinea Negroes, Purchas recorded in 1625 that when confinement begins, men, women, youths and children stand round the woman, and she brings her child into the world 'in most shameless manner' before the eyes of all. In Central Africa, Felkin (1879) also found many onlookers at delivery in several tribes, but the presence of children was not tolerated.

Among the desert tribes of Algeria, when the woman is seized by labour pains, she is at once laid down in the street, for custom does not allow of a birth taking place in the house. Von Maltzan was present at such a birth in the open street in the little oasis village of El Kantarah.

In America, too, we come across similar customs, for the Caripuna Indian woman on the Madeira in Brazil gives birth to her child in the presence of her fellow tribesmen (Keller-Leutzinger).

iv. Birth at Home

In ancient times, the Roman woman resorted to a special room where rich coverings were spread. She washed herself, bound her head, took off her sandals and lay down covered with the pallium on the couch prescribed for her confinement. Soranus, who wrote a book on obstetrics, stated the regular preparations for equipping a room in conformity with all requirements regarding hygiene: in winter, the woman in childbirth had to stay in a spacious room with pure air; in the room there had to be standing ready various requisites, such as oil, infusion of fenugreek, liquid wax, warm water, soft sponges, cotton binders, pillows, perfumes, a delivery chair and two beds. It may be imagined that no such arrangements were made for the lower classes.

The old book *Shorei Hikki* records the place where the Japanese woman gave birth. According to Mitford, the furnishings of the lying-in room consisted of: two tubs in which to put underclothes; two tubs for the placenta; a low armchair without legs for the mother to support herself; a stool used by the midwife for support when she grasped the loins of the woman being delivered and afterwards for washing the child; several pillows of various shapes and sizes with which the woman in childbirth could support her head as she pleased; twenty-four baby garments, twelve of silk and twelve of cotton, whose hems had to be coloured saffron yellow; and an apron for the midwife.

In Achin, confinement also takes place in the house. The woman in labour is put on the floor over which bamboo laths have been spread. The woman must remain lying on these during the whole period of confinement, however long it may last. The amniotic fluid can flow at once down through the crevices in the floor, and here, under the piles, it is received in a leaf sheath of the *aren* tree in which some salt and ashes have been put. This vessel, when the fluid and the blood have run into it, is very carefully covered with the big rough leaves of a kind of pandanus (Jacobs).

On the Gilbert Islands, the woman looks out for foster parents for the expected child, who adopt it. The child is then generally born in the house of the foster father, the *Djibum* (Krämer).

Birth in south Shantung, as Stenz records, must always take place in the pregnant woman's own house; it must not even take place in the house of her parents. In accordance with this, if the confinement comes unexpectedly quickly and the wife is staying with her mother, she must at once go home, even in the last hour. If in spite of everything the child is born in a strange house, then ill-luck befalls the family. To avert this, the husband of the woman in childbirth must plough up the floor of the family's barn, carefully clean the bed and, on leaving, fill the family cooking-pot to the brim with wheat.

In Germany the arrangements of the room in which urban women of high position, or even middle-class women, are confined can in no way be compared with those of peasant women. From the Bavarian Upper Palatinate, the following facts, which are certainly true of other districts also, are reported by Brenner-Schäffer:

> In most cases a peasant house contains only one room in which stay husbands and wives, menservants and maidservants, children and neighbours. Under the colossal farm stove, which radiates the same heat

day and night, summer and winter; in which the cooking is done year in year out for men and cattle; under this stately erection, which no peasant room is without, geese cackle, hens cluck, pigs grunt. Here the food for the cattle is boiled, there the potatoes for the pigs washed, an ever-open water-pot, the so-called hell-pot, is continually sending forth clouds of vapour whilst, from the stove pipe, the smell of burnt fat, roasting potatoes and a thousand other kinds of gas pervades the room. In this medley the child comes into the world!

In somewhat better families among the poor, they try sometimes to help matters by changing the bed which is to be used for the lying-in into a kind of canopied bed. This is done, for example, in Istria, where the Slav woman, when she feels her confinement approaching, goes to the church to pray and returns home to find her bed hung round with bedclothes and coverings. (There the houses, except for those of very wealthy families, generally contain only one large room, so that the beds in it are very close together and are not separated from each other by curtains or hangings.) In this case the husband also surrenders his bed to the woman for her lying-in.

In parts of Hungary the birth does not take place in bed but on the floor in the middle of the room, on some straw covered with a linen cloth: 'because Christ was also born on straw' (J. von Csaplovics). A similar custom is found among the Gurians in the Caucasus, who put the woman in childbirth into a room without floorboards, the floor of which is strewn with hay. Birth likewise takes place on the ground among the Parsee women in Bombay and among the Hindus in the Punjab – it is only afterwards that the woman is placed on a mat. For her first confinement, the young wife very often returns to her parents' house (Rose).

If the Ama-Xosa woman gives birth to her child in the house, 'then she crouches stark naked on a heap of loose earth so that neither her clothes nor the floor of her house are soiled by one drop of blood' (Kropf).

v. Birth Huts

It must be admitted, however, that not many peoples allow women to be confined in the dwelling-house, but erect a special hut or tent for them in which the delivery is to take place. This practice is very old and widespread, and may be reckoned among the many customs that cannot be explained otherwise than by supposing that people try by means of them to lead the pursuing demons on a false scent. Equally, an idea of the uncleanness of women in childbirth may also be at the root of this custom.

Among the Ancient Hindus, the women of the Brahman, Kshatriya,

Vaicya and Sudra castes repaired to the parturition house where, with the help of four courageous women, the delivery took place amid many cere-monies. The birth chamber of the Brahmans was, according to Susruta, constructed of the wood of the bel-fruit tree, banyan, ebony and *Semecarpus* L. The bed was of woven camel's hair. Brahmans had charge of the whole hygienic procedure, and the observation of the regulations as to diet. Here the woman in childbed remained for half a month after the arrival of the child.

Even in the present day, the Hindu wife in childbirth is taken to a birth hut, but here she is tortured by unskilled women with heat and smoke. This isolation of women in labour exists also among the Todas in India. Among them, when the time of delivery approaches, the husband leads his wife to a little hut erected in the woods and takes her food to her there daily. She lives in complete isolation and has intercourse with only a few female friends, who give assistance at the birth of the child.

In north Malabar, on the other hand, the woman, after being taken to a shelter at some distance from the house, is left for twenty-eight days without any assistance. Even her medicines are thrown to her from afar, and, apart from a jug with warm water, which is taken to her about the probable time of her confinement, nothing is done for her (Schmidt).

In New Zealand, a similar isolation of women in childbirth prevails among the aborigines. Even during pregnancy the woman is declared to be taboo. She is therefore cut off from all association with other people and banished to a crude shelter made of leaves and twigs which is scarcely capable of giving protection against rain, wind or sun. However, she is attended by one or more women, according to her rank, and these, like her, are taboo. The isolation lasts for several days after the birth, and during this time the new-born child is exposed to every inclemency of the weather. According to other information printed in the report of the voyage of the *Novara*, the hut erected for the Maori woman in childbirth is situated not far from the family dwelling and is regarded as sacred.

The northern Asiatic peoples also have special birth huts. The 'unclean tent' in which, for example, the Samoyed woman must be confined is called *samajma* or *madiko*. Among the Ostiaks, when a confinement is imminent, the woman goes to a special yurt and lives there till five weeks after the birth of the child (Alexandrow). The Gilyaks, who live on the Lower Amur and in northern Sakhalin, relegate the pregnant woman to a birch-bark hut before her confinement. J. Deniker states that

the pregnant woman is surrounded with every possible care, but about ten days before the expected parturition she is taken from the house to a cabin of birch bark, where a small fire is kept up. This custom is strictly observed even in the coldest weather. Its meaning is not clear; there seems no indication that the woman in childbirth is regarded as unclean, for after parturition she does not undergo any ceremony of purification. During the whole of her stay in the cabin the woman is attended only by persons of her own sex, who help her during the delivery and bathe the new-born child in the same cabin, often in a temperature of 40 degrees below zero.

We come across similar phenomena in Central America. The Wulwa (or Ulua) on the Mosquito Coast, a good-natured but very uncivilized Indian tribe, do not live in villages but in scattered communities of two or three huts. One hut is generally occupied by three or four families, each of which has its own fire in a corner at which the members cook their bananas and round which they sit talking, the women in their decidedly incomplete toilets. Births occur very seldom, but when they do the women are always obliged to go to a hut in a remote part of the woods, where they are provided with food and looked after by the other women alternately.

Among the North American Indians, the customs vary. The wives of the Chippewa and Winnebago, for example, are confined in winter in a special tent near the family hut, whilst in milder weather they go to the woods for this purpose. The Comanche, on the other hand, build a special refuge for the pregnant woman at a little distance from the settlement, near her family tent (Fig. 21).

Engelmann says of the Indians in the Uintah Valley Agency (Ute):

At the first sign of approaching birth, the woman in labour leaves the hut of her family and, at a little distance from it, puts up for herself a small wickiup, in which she stays during her confinement. Here she cleans the ground and then makes a shallow groove in which a fire is to be lit. Stones are put round this and warmed, and a kettle of water is heated, of which she drinks much and often. The wickiup is made as compact as possible to guard against variations in temperature and to promote perspiration. Women from the neighbourhood give assistance.

Among the eastern Eskimo, the birth of the first child takes place in the usual igloo. In all later confinements, however, the wife has to go to an igloo specially built for her (Hall). The husband may not be present at the birth. In western districts, the woman is shut up in a little hut with the carcass of some animal, generally a dog, and here she stays quite alone and without help.

The place in which the Annamite of Cochin-China is delivered varies

Fig. 21 Comanche parturition hut (after Witkowski)

according to the social position of the woman in childbirth. Nevertheless, in no circumstances can this be within the house. The wives of labourers and servants are generally granted a dirty little corner, which may have been cleaned a little according to circumstance, whilst wealthy people construct in the courtyard a little bamboo hut which has only a door and a tiny window. Here a bed of bamboo laths on four posts is prepared and with that everything is ready. After a month, for which period the woman stays in this hut, it is torn down and often burnt. This is certainly a very good hygienic measure.

In Ukinga on Lake Nyasa, Fülleborn found that pregnant women had to have their confinement in solitary birth huts, and he succeeded in taking a photograph of one of these with the pregnant occupant, also carrying an older child on her back, alongside it (Fig. 22). The 'miserable pointed grass hut' had as its only furniture a primitive couch.

We find the usage of a special birth hut also in South Africa, although only in isolated cases. According to Damberger, special huts for women in childbirth exist in every native village; no man may go near these places, and when a woman is confined her husband may not enter the hut until three days have passed.

Girschner's record of the customs in the Caroline Islands must certainly be regarded as originating in the desire to hide from evil spirits. According to

Fig. 22 Parturition hut, Ukinga, Lake Nyasa (after photo by F. Fülleborn)

him, when the woman feels the hour of delivery approaching, she repairs to the birth hut, which no man may enter. Of any real help in birth the natives know nothing; they only try by exorcisms and magic to ward off a mishap which, in their opinion, is always caused by evil spirits. The most powerful of these is the 'black spirit' called Lukaisonup. He is a wood spirit, entirely covered with hair and of terrifying appearance. To keep him off, an exorcist takes his place before the hut, and six torch-bearers guard the place at night. People also throw food, breadfruit and fish, into the wood nearby, or hang it up there; this the spirit devours. If he is heard chewing and the food has disappeared next morning, that is a favourable sign. There are also two female spirit sisters, Inapwane and Limerakis, who approach invisibly and try to kill the woman in childbirth by making a hole in her breast and eating out her eyes.

BATH-HOUSES

We have to recognize as a special and exclusive peculiarity of certain Russian peoples that they have their women in childbirth delivered neither in the dwelling-house nor in a hut erected for the purpose, but in the bath-house. This is reported not only of the women in Great Russia, but also of the Letts, the Esthonians, the Finns, the women of Viatka and the Votiaks (M. Buch). It is also customary in White Russia.

The bath-house, which is not infrequently the property of the whole village, takes the form of a detached little windowless house with a stove, the smoke of which emerges into the open air through small openings in the walls. It contains no other equipment, other than platforms or benches, and thus presents an excellent place for confinement, much more suitable than the cramped and disturbed family rooms in the village houses. The hot stove also means that the warm water necessary for cleansing the woman and the new-born child can easily be procured.

According to Alksnis,

> the idea that warmth mitigates the labour pains, as well as the fact that people did not want the mysteries of birth to take place in the presence of a number of possibly young people, no doubt brought about [this] custom of pregnant women repairing, when the birth was near, to the well-warmed bath-house, where all the necessary procedures of the midwife could more easily be carried out. There was warmth there, and warm water for baths, and they were not bothered by disturbing relatives, and had more space to act.

This view is, of course, quite correct and proper, but need not express the original and primary causes, for it may simply have been the belief that the woman in childbirth was unclean and that she had a defiling and pernicious effect on the dwelling-house and its occupants that brought about her banishment to the bath-house, where, after the confinement, her uncleanness could immediately be removed by a purifying bath. Only afterwards would it have become clear to the people that they had in fact chosen a very suitable place for the woman. In spite of this, as we learn from Alksnis, the bath-house has now gone out of fashion among the Letts as a place for lying-in.

vi. *Midwifery*

Parturition among many peoples is so very much an exclusive concern of the female sex, a thing to be kept from profane male eyes (not from modesty but from belief in magic and for social reasons), that it cannot be wondered at that when help is given it is usually by a female hand. Generally it is one or more friends who stand by the side of the woman in labour, and we must regard it as very human that these are, as a rule, of somewhat riper age.

The beginnings of a regulated midwifery are to be recognized wherever we find stated as helpers at parturition not simply women friends or relatives, but 'experienced women', ones moreover with a special name giving expression to their talents and capabilities.

As early as in the Talmud the midwife was called *Majalledeth*, 'the wise woman'. The wise woman was supposed to be able to give advice in all cases of distress and illness, and by no means only where diseases of women and children were involved.

According to Baas, midwives were called *meschenu* among the Ancient Egyptians. The Greeks had the *Maiai* or *Jatromaiai*, who were also called by their names, such as 'dividers of the umbilical cord'; the Roman midwives were called *obstetrices*, also, quite commonly, *matronae*.

Each nation has its own designation for a midwife. Thus the Japanese call them *samba-san*, which means 'impoverished women', or else *toriegababa*, 'the taking, lifting granny'. The Turks call them *ebe-caden* or *mamy*; the Persians, *mama*; the Basutos, *babele xisi*; the Swahili, *kungwi*. On the Philippines the midwife is called *mabutin gilot*; on the island of Ceram, *ahina-tukaan*; on Nias, *solomo talu*; among the Siamese, *yi* and *mohrak-sah-eran*, also *mo-tam*, i.e., 'nettle doctors'.

Bastian writes in his *Reisen in Siam* (1867):

> Midwives are called *mo-tam* (nettle doctors), either because they have constantly to be on the point of departure, and may also be summoned

hither and thither at night, or because their hands come in contact with things which others would not know how to take hold of. Also the use of the urticatio as a stimulus is not unknown.

The French have their *sage-femme*, or wise woman (although it must be called to mind here that, in the opinion of some, the word derives from the *sagae*, the witches, who were notorious in particular for their skill in inducing abortion); the Poles their *babka*; the Swedes and Danes their *Jordgumma*, *Jordemoder*, literally 'earth mother'. The Russians used to call the midwife the 'clever Dutchwoman' because the first trained midwives came to Leningrad from Holland.

In every country where such midwives pursue their vocation professionally they are not without considerable influence on the general life of the people, not only because they are at the side of the women in childbirth at the hour of danger, but also because they remain in close contact with those families in which they have helped children into the world. Owing to their long and trusted intercourse with such families and a certain degree of knowledge of humanity, as well as their energy and decision in their personal conduct, which brooks no contradiction and which they gradually learn from experience and practice how to adopt, they obtain in a moral respect no little esteem and a superior position and influence on the whole population. The profession of the midwife thus becomes a very significant social element.

The importance of midwives in the history of civilization should by no means be put too low. While the professional representatives of medical science, the doctors, did not practise midwifery, then, naturally, the welfare and travail of pregnant women and those in labour, as well as the fate of the coming generation, remained solely in the hands of the midwives. This was a power they did not give up willingly, and the doctors and surgeons had a hard and difficult struggle to wrest it from them. How difficult this struggle was can be understood from the fact that even learned men ranged themselves with the midwives. In the year 1705, for example, Hecquet published in Paris a work which bears the significant title *De l'indécence aux hommes d'accoucher les femmes*.

But all civilized nations today are at one in agreeing that the science of obstetrics can no longer be confined to the midwives, who for so long have obstinately claimed childbed and lying-in as their exclusive domain.

HISTORY

It was in Italy that the most important groundwork for the progress of the science was done, for it was here that the anatomical examination of the human corpse was for the first time introduced into the resources of medical science.

In the seventeenth century Italy had a special influence on the obstetrics of other countries through certain publications for the instruction of midwives. Among them the work of Scipione Mercurio, published in Venice in 1621, deserves special mention. Mercurio's work is of importance in the history of obstetrics because it records his experiences of Caesarean section, which he accumulated in his travels in France in 1571 and 1572 (the first quite indubitable case, described by Donatus, of a Caesarean section on a living woman was in fact performed by Christophorus Bainus in Italy in 1540; a dead child was extracted and the woman gave birth to children four times more in the natural way).

As far as the ancient times of the German people are concerned, we have but little knowledge of matters connected with midwifery. The midwives, skilled in magic, exorcised and cured by magical means the very great pain of the women in labour: mechanical help was probably confined to the reception of the child, the ligature and division of the umbilical cord and the further attendance on the new-born infant. During the Middle Ages the realm of medicine, like every other, was governed by crass superstition.

From this time onwards, however, we can see a very favourable turn for the better. One of the important improvements as regards the profession of midwifery in Germany consisted in the fact that by degrees midwives began to be paid from the public purse; moreover, regulations for midwives were drawn up, and it was decreed that women who applied to be established should submit to a systematic examination. Certain doctors were commissioned to give them the necessary instruction. We may regard it as a good result of this attention and supervision that doctors were induced to publish obstetric text-books for the benefit of midwives, of which the first is dated 1480.

In the second decade of the sixteenth century, Katharina, hereditary princess of Saxony and widow of Duke Siegmund of Austria, caused Dr Eucharius Rösslin in Worms to write a text-book for midwives. This was printed in 1513, and in a short time achieved an extraordinarily wide circulation. The book was a collection of the teachings of Hippocrates, Galen, Aetius, Avicenna, Albertus Magnus, etc., and differed from previous medical works in that it was illustrated. In his dedication to the Princess Katharina, the author expressed the request that the book be distributed among respectable pregnant women and midwives.

Further advances in the evolution of obstetrics were achieved in Munich towards the end of the sixteenth century. A lying-in room was established in the hospital of the Holy Ghost in 1589, for the first time in Germany, and the authorized and official instruction of midwives began not only to be extended to technical practice, but also to make a serious effort to combat the superstition still deep-rooted, and particularly noticeable in this class. The Augsburg regulations for midwives, for example, prohibited all 'pronouncing of blessings, useless customs, sayings and sinful wages'. The Gotha regulations, too, stated: '... making character or letter signs, strange gestures and the sign of the cross, dividing the umbilical cord with certain questions and answers, hanging up any strange things ... sprinkling before or after the bath and the like are strictly prohibited.'

In the seventeenth century the doctor who wrote a number of text-books in the form of a romance under the pseudonym of 'Faithful Eckarth' had no inconsiderable share in obstetric instruction in Germany. In 1715 he published in Leipzig a book called *Die unvorsichtige Heb-Amme* ('the careless midwife'). The general condition of midwifery in Germany was indicated here as still at a fairly low stage, and the frontispiece (Fig. 23) shows a midwife holding in her hand part of the body of the woman in childbirth which has been torn out. At her side stands a table on which lie two newborn children; an arm and a leg have been torn off one, and even the head of the other.

In England, according to Aveling, women in the middle of the sixteenth century appear to have been rather dissatisfied with their untrained midwives. Then, in 1537, one man (probably Jonas) undertook the translation of Rösslin's text-book for midwives, and this was published under the title *The Woman's Booke*. Rösslin's work was for a long time the only source from which English midwives could acquire their knowledge.

They seem not to have learnt much, for in the last part of the sixteenth century Andrew Borde wrote about inexperienced midwives in his *Breviarie of Healthe* as follows:

> In my tyme, as well here in Englande as in other regions ... every Midwyfe shulde be presented with honest women of great gravitie to the Byshop, and that they shulde testify, for her that they do present shulde be a sadde woman, wyse and discrete, havynge experience, and worthy to have the office of a Midwyfe. Then the Byshoppe, with the consent of a doctor of Physick, ought to examine her, and to instructe her ... and [this] ... is a laudable thynge; for and this were used in Englande, there shulde not halfe so many women myscary, nor so many chyldren perish in every place in Englande as there be. The Byshop ought to loke on this matter.

At the beginning of the seventeenth century, Peter Chamberlen practised in London as the first, and indeed very distinguished, obstetrician; he recog-

Fig. 23 German popular midwife at the beginning of the eighteenth century (frontispiece to Eckarth's *Die unvorsichtige Heb-Amme*, 1715)

nized the evil state of the profession of midwifery, and in 1616 made the humane and sensible proposal to the king 'that some order may be settled by the state for the instruction and civil government of midwives'. This well-meant proposal was not, however, listened to.

As in medical science in general, so also in the history of English midwifery a new and better epoch began with Harvey, whom Aveling and Spencer call the father of English obstetrics. His own studies and the work of another prominent 'man midwife' (as Aveling expressed it), Dr Percival Willughby, were of great importance.

Gradually it became customary in England to call in doctors as obstetricians in confinements. This, however, did not take place to any great extent till about the middle of the eighteenth century, at which time a violent struggle was going on between Smellie, Hunter and the midwives. Sterne took part in this struggle, for he attacked the man-midwives, and the character 'Dr Slop' has been recognized as an example of the type to which they belonged.

In France, an important change for the better was achieved in the sixteenth century by Paré, who endeavoured to get recognition for medical assistance in midwifery. The improved teaching of Paré appears to have influenced the great mass of midwives only slowly, but that his efforts were not without effect is proved by Louise Bourgeois, called Boursier (born 1564), who was trained in Paré's school for midwives in the Hôtel-Dieu and who wrote a text-book for midwives. This work, first published in 1609, had a very good influence on the knowledge and skill of midwives in France.

French doctors first came into power as obstetricians after Jules Clément delivered La Vallière in 1636, and had honours heaped upon him for it by Louis XIV. From then on, surgeons who practised midwifery called themselves *accoucheurs*, and male midwifery became fashionable. At the other European courts it was good form to be delivered by a doctor; surgeons were sent to Paris for instruction in obstetrics, and Parisian obstetricians were sent for.

THE MIDWIFE IN SUPERSTITION

The exceptional and undisputed position which midwives occupy in human society, their riper experience and their greater knowledge of all kinds of physical and spiritual needs, have given support to the superstition that they possess knowledge of supernatural forces and that they have an innate capacity for curing diseases by all kinds of secret remedies. In this respect they are linked with shepherds, blacksmiths, huntsmen and executioners. Especially in rural districts many of them practise quackery extensively.

But there is another belief which we find associated with midwives. It is they who dispatch earthly beings from the unknown dwelling-place of the unborn into their existence on earth. This place which other mortals may not enter must, therefore, be accessible to them. Usually it is some pond or other from which the midwives must draw the young children (a later conception). In this connection a belief prevalent among the people on the island of Amrum, according to the periodical *Am Urds-Brunnen*, is of great interest:

> From *gunskölk* (goose water) and sea-foam, the Amrum women, accompanied by the midwife, fetch their babies. The nurse in charge of the babies, however, who rules over the water with the babies living in it, will not let the latter go and lays about her with the scythe when the women approach ... Nevertheless, the women usually succeed in catching a baby, but those seeking it must let themselves be wounded in the leg by the guardian of the many children swimming in the water.

Riccardi reports a curious superstition from Modena: 'Two must always go to summon the midwife, or if only one can go, she must carry two loaves of bread with her so as to have *la grazia di Dio* with her, otherwise the Devil will cause confusion on the way and thus delay the arrival of the midwife.'

The tale is still quite common in Germany that dwarfs or subterranean beings, also water sprites or pygmies, used to fetch midwives to deliver their wives. Thus it is told, for example in Thuringia, that a water sprite came to fetch a human midwife to his wife, who was about to be confined; he then presented her with a thing of apparently little value, which, however, later turned into gold. If a midwife refused to go when summoned, she was taken by force and afterwards her dead body was found floating on the water (Wucke).

These tales are not confined to European territory. An interesting example occurs among the Annamites (Landes):

> There was once a tiger whose wife was in labour and could not be delivered. Then the tiger ran to the house of a midwife, watched till she came to the door, and carried her off to the place where the tigress was. There he made the midwife understand by signs ... that she had been brought to deliver his wife. She said to him: 'Look away, for I am terrified when you look at me.' The tiger turned aside and the midwife set about the delivery. When it was all finished, he carried her home again. The following day he stole a pig and took it to the midwife to show his gratitude.

METHODS

The help which women in childbirth in the desert tribes of Algeria get from midwives is limited to this: the midwife seizes the child when it is half-way out of the womb; she holds it with both hands and keeps it fast in this position for quite a quarter of an hour. The poor woman thus gets an increase of pain not ordained for her by nature, but imposed on her by a superstitious prejudice of these desert Arabs. Von Maltzan thinks that the aim of this custom is either a misunderstood hygienic measure or that it has a mystical significance, man being kept on the threshold of existence between being born and not being born.

The midwives in Egypt are generally very ignorant women; their manipulations, pressing and kneading of the abdomen of the woman in labour, as well as the insertion of the finger at the expulsion of the child, are said to be carried out in the crudest manner.

Among the Swahili, according to Kersten's verbal reports to Ploss, there are professional midwives (*Kungwi*) who charge one to one and a half talers, paid in the clothes of the pregnant woman. They confine themselves to kneading the abdomen, cutting the umbilical cord and dressing the child's navel, etc. According to H. Krauss, they are so far intelligent as to refrain from unnecessary manipulations, especially as regards internal interference, and also see to a certain cleanliness of their hands. The woman in childbirth, too, is cleansed by them in quite a rational way inasmuch as they remove the pubic hair. For this a knife must not be used; it is singed off with ashes.

The North American Indians, according to Engelmann, have also, to some extent, their special midwives; for instance the Klamath, the Mandan Indians, the Gros Ventres, the Nez Percé, the Arikara, the Clatsop, the Pueblos, the Navajo in Arizona and the Indians of the Quapa Reservation in Mexico. The help of these midwives is confined almost entirely to external manipulations together with compression of the abdomen in order to press out the child: in addition to these there are incantations and exorcisms by the medicine man. Only a few of these tribes, the Umpqua, the Pueblos, the natives of Mexico and the Pacific Coast ever undertake manipulations inside the vagina. The introduction of the hand into the vagina and uterus is something unknown to the rest. The dilation of the perineum or the removal of the placenta hardly ever occur. The placenta, if retention happens, has to remain in the uterus.

The midwives in Mexico work at the pregnant woman's back and abdomen with their fists as early as the seventh month of pregnancy. This is done for half an hour at a time, so that the poor woman writhes with pain.

The midwives among the Annamites in Cochin-China Mondière describes as extremely ugly, old and lean, with grey or white hair which is often shaved. They are, he says, like witches. Usually they visit the pregnant woman for a month twice daily before parturition is expected, and finally daily, in order to prescribe some articles of food for her, which consist chiefly in infusions of leaves of the papaw and a species of mint. However, they do not touch or examine the woman.

In Achin, according to Jacobs, they have a special class of midwife. Such a midwife is always an elderly woman who is acquainted with pregnancy and confinement from personal experience. Her influence is great, extending far beyond the lying-in room. It extends to all questions of the nursery, of the life of the young married couple, and not seldom also to abortion. Along with them there is, however, still another class of midwife, which has a very small number of representatives. These might be called 'head midwives', for they are called in for advice and help only in very hopeless cases. They are the *bidan dalam*, whose name signifies that their hand assistance extends to the internal genitals.

Among the Mohammedans in Baghdad the influence of the midwives is very great; they are generally very highly paid. From wealthy people they receive usually a honorarium of from 50 to 100 gulden. They are by no means satisfied with this, however, but impose a tribute when the child begins to teethe, to walk or to talk. In the illnesses to which it is subjected they alone are consulted, and they usually prescribe a universal powder made up of bitter and astringent ingredients.

In the Finnish tribe of the Syryenians, every woman who has reached a certain age must become a *gegin* (midwife) and give help to anyone, otherwise she must, in the opinion of some, act as a midwife to a bitch in heaven. In the opinion of others, however, such a woman never reaches heaven at all.

Among the Teutonic peoples, midwifery was a matter for women among themselves. Along with the crouching position, the sitting on the husband's knee and the massage and kneading of the abdomen, or drawing the woman through holes and clefts in trees, etc., people had recourse to incense-burning (juniper, etc.), also the fruits of the ash tree, and herb potions and fomentations. Then they tied on the appropriate herbs as amulets and, above all, they used magic words and runes to bring forth and banish obstructive or otherwise injurious demons.

Krebel, in 1858, writes of the procedure followed in Russian confinements:

> The woman in labour hangs on cross-bars swaying over her like a kind of swing, and awaits delivery in this half-lying, half-sitting position, assisting by making jumps, or trying to shake the child out, as it were. The child then often falls out before the midwife can catch it; and the umbilical cord is often torn off, or the uterus is pulled down and out. These evil occurrences also take place if the midwife pulls the umbilical cord too hard, in order to remove the afterbirth. If the uterus is drawn out in this way, the poor woman is taken to the bath-house, laid on a

board which is placed on the steam-bench steps, so that the feet are higher than the head, and then the board ... is raised quickly several times ... in order to shake the uterus back into place. According to the popular conception, the child comes into the world all curled up, as it were; therefore it is actually stretched by the midwife; she rubs and heats it with a bunch of birth-twigs, presses the head on all sides, stretches the limbs and, finally, takes the poor little thing by the feet so that the head hangs downwards and shakes it hard and quickly several times in succession to bring the intestines into the proper place.

Of the Esthonians, Holst reported in 1867 that among them a popular midwifery has been indigenous since ancient times. The midwives, untrained old women, are said to do the ordinary services not unskilfully, but when the course of delivery deviates from the normal they do not know what to do, and maltreat the child and the mother in the most horrible way. In such cases they are very clever at delaying the calling in of the doctor by intimidating the relatives. Their measures include hanging the woman by the arms, dragging her up and down a bed with cross-pieces like steps on it, squeezing the abdomen, the premature rupture of the membranes, etc. 'In a face presentation they squeeze the eyes out of their sockets, break and lacerate the lower jaw; whilst in transverse presentations they tear off the arms, tear open the breast and abdominal cavities, etc.' Krebel also confirms the fact that the midwives of the lower classes of Esthonians in difficult confinements try to expedite the course of birth by tying the abdomen, and by suspending and shaking the woman in labour.

In Galicia there are thousands of primitive midwives, old women who, for the want of any other occupation, call themselves midwives; but midwifery is practised also by young women whose mothers were considered midwives and to whom, therefore, the art has been transmitted. These women, whose whole technical skill hardly extends beyond the ability to tie up the umbilical cord, know that in normal birth the head should come first. At the very beginning of parturition they smear the woman's abdomen with a mixture of brandy and fat; then they knead it and perfume it. In addition they let the woman bear down till her strength is exhausted. If, in a transverse presentation, there is prolapse of an arm they try to draw out the child by it. About a retained placenta they do not bother; they leave it to decay.

Reports of the midwives on the Caroline Islands in the Pacific are more favourable. They are called proficient, and it is said that only a few unsuccessful cases occur through unskilful midwifery. The women in charge lift up their voices in song or shrieks so that the husband may not hear his wife's cries of pain.

Blyth reports that the Fiji Islanders have had from ancient times native midwives called *alewa vuku*, or wise women. They keep their art secret and surround it with mystic usages. A short time before they think of retiring from their profession, they instruct a successor in their art. In remote districts they also give help to European women.

In Hyderabad and Delhi, according to Smith, the midwives usually belong to the Telegu tribe. They are extraordinarily ignorant and the result of this is an enormous mortality among women in childbirth. The midwives torture the woman in labour in the lying-in hut by heat, smoke, thirst and irritant drugs (pepper, ginger, etc.). If they think it necessary to have surgical help, they send for a woman barber, who carries out extraction and embryotomy; both kinds of women practise abortion.

Miss Billington also gives a very unfavourable description of the activity of midwives in India. She calls their ignorance and methods of treatment simply barbarous. Many of them interrupt their necessary manipulations to press for higher payment and refuse to go on with their duties until a guarantee is given them that their impudent demands will be complied with.

vii. Supernatural Help in Labour

Owing to the expressions of pain, the moaning and groaning, the efforts to be quit of the foetus, the bearing down and resistance – phenomena almost always observable in greater or lesser degree in women in childbirth – parturition, especially among peoples of low civilization, is a highly alarming process for those nearby, one moreover threatened by inimical powers, demons, spirits and gods. The feeling of anxiety seeks and finds comfort in the belief that supernatural forces can help, and various means are employed to summon or banish the spirits and demons according to their nature, whether good or evil.

Among the Ancient Hebrews, Lilith was regarded as a specially dangerous demon for women in childbirth and those lying-in. According to legend, after the separation of the first couple of human beings she bound herself to Adam. But soon she wearied of the affair and fled from him. At Jehovah's command, however, she was sought out by three angels, Senoi, Sansenoi and Samandelof, who commanded her to unite with Adam again and warned that, if she refused, she would lose one hundred of her children daily by death. She refused. Now, to avenge the loss of her children, she constantly tries to strangle new-born children in the first days of their life, and only where she finds the names of those three angels does she make no attack.

This ancient belief in Lilith and the angels has persisted. In Germany

many Jewish families still draw a chalk-line round the woman in labour and write on the door: 'May God let the woman bear a son and grant him a wife who resembles Eve, not Lilith,' while others hang placards on the walls of the lying-in room on which the names of the angels are written.

Among the Ancient Hindus, according to Susruta's report, the woman in labour was given the fruit of the *Myristica moschata* in her hand to make the delivery easier; she was also surrounded by boys and saluted with blessings and good wishes. If the child could not be extracted, the doctor pronounced an exorcism: 'May the divine ambrosia, Moon, Sun and Indra's horse dwell in thy house, O deeply afflicted mother!' Anila, Pavana, the god of the wind, the sun and Vasava (Indra), as well as the gods to whom salt and water belong, were also invoked for relief for the woman in labour. Only when this was without result did they proceed to dismember the embryo.

It is well known that Teutonic female demons (Holda, Perchta and Freya) were regarded not only as the patron goddesses of lovers but also of marriages, and likewise as guardians of women in childbirth. *Galium verum* L., a plant still called among the common people 'our dear lady's bedstraw', was specially sacred to them, and was put in the bed of pregnant women to make delivery easier.

Supernatural specifics to promote delivery were also used in medieval Italy. Trotula recommended holding a magnet in the right hand, putting strings of coral round the neck, wearing the *Album quod invenitur in stercore accipitris*, a stone found in the belly or nest of the swallow, etc., and Franciscus de Pede Montis, who taught at Naples about 1340, praised with great confidence as promoting delivery such specifics as magnesia sprinkled with the ashes of asses' and horses' feet. In cases of dangerous labour, consecrated images of the saints or relics were hung round the room or swallowed (von Siebold), while on Easter Sunday among modern Italians in the provinces of Belluno and Treviso, according to Bastanzi, people used to throw into a warming-pan filled with red-hot coal, all mixed up together, consecrated olive leaves, wax candles, paper images of saints and Madonnas, cock feathers and hairs from the husband, fumigating with these the woman in labour. In Bologna, according to von Reinsberg-Düringsfeld, women in difficult labour use the rose of Jericho (*Anastatica hierochuntica* L.), which is there known as the *rosa della Madonna*, so called because it is supposed to have sprung up where the Virgin Mary set her foot in the desert on her flight to Egypt. When the first pains begin, it is put into water in a withered state, and people are convinced that the pains will pass away in the time necessary for the plant to expand in renewed freshness.

Among the peoples of Russia, as Sumzow states, there still prevailed in 1882 many kinds of mystic customs for making childbirth easier. In the province of Vilna, for example, the midwife, in addition to holding a lighted taper before the patient's eyes, also applied to the house spirit, the protector of the family, by knocking on the ceiling of the room with a broom, while in many parts of Russia and Serbia they opened all the locks in the house, untied all knots and loosened plaited pigtails. The woman in labour generally tried to hide herself in order to escape the 'evil eye'.

Gluck quotes of the customs in Bosnia:

> If labour is protracted for some reason . . . a raw egg is put unexpectedly on the back of the patient's neck so that it rolls down her back. Of sympathetic expedients, a few more are mentioned here: tearing the front opening of the chemise; untying all the knots on the clothes and loosening the patient's hair . . . untwisting a girl's plait over the patient; laying a comb on the abdomen; taking a mouthful of water from the husband's boots; licking the ashes of a wooden shovel; and, finally, strewing nuts between the patient's legs, probably as an enticement for the child, which is supposed to play with them.

Vámbéry says of the nomad Turks of Central Asia:

> As the wife among the nomads is spared no exertion during the whole pregnancy, even in the last days, she is sometimes overtaken by the first labour pains in the midst of her work. The first help is given as a matter of course by the older women of the *aul*, who have taken good care, by means of magic, to rid the patient of the harmful influence of the *albasti*, the evil-bringing spirit. For this purpose the *tumars* (amulets) which the pregnant woman has been wearing round her neck for a long time were duly prepared and breathed upon. When the pains become stronger, a favourite *nuszch* (talisman), kept in readiness, is dipped in water, which is then given to the woman to drink, on the assumption that the miraculous power of the words has passed into the black ink and that this will now be immediately efficacious.

In Kazwin, in western Persia, guns are fired when a woman is in labour in order to drive away the demons, while the women lay a sabre beside the woman in childbirth and, on the flat roof of the house, set in motion by means of threads a row of dolls dressed as soldiers. If, in spite of this, the child will not appear, the husband makes a white horse eat barley from his wife's bare breast. (Many horses have in truth acquired quite a reputation by their fortunate influence on parturition, and it sometimes happens that, when in a village two peasant women are overtaken by labour pains at the same time, their husbands come to blows over the wonder-working animal (Dieulafoy).)

Among modern Parsees, a great fire must burn for three nights during labour in order to drive away the *daeva*, the evil spirits (Duncker). The usage is ordained by Zoroaster's religious laws, and the same custom appears again among the nomad Gypsies in Transylvania.

Among the Battak (Sumatra), the pregnant woman blackens her face as soon as she feels the first pains of labour, so that she will not be recognized by the many evil spirits which torment pregnant women (Römer).

On the islands of the Sawu Archipelago, in the Dutch East Indies, the *wango* is regarded as a spirit which obstructs labour. People try by means of thorn bushes to keep it from pushing its way into the house (Riedel).

A demon very dangerous to women in labour in Achin is, according to Jacobs, the ghost (*boeroeng*) called Tenkoe Rabiah Tandjoeng, who, herself childless, is filled with envy for pregnant women and constantly endeavours to make delivery impossible or at least as difficult as possible for them. She is able to creep through the smallest cracks and clefts, and once she is in she forces her way through the big toe of the woman in labour, turns the child in a wrong direction, prevents complete dilation of the womb, and torments the poor woman in every way, even to madness and death.

Every effort is made to keep her from entering the house. For this purpose, and most important of all, a branch of the thorny *mamake* or *moeroeng* tree is hung from the ceiling of the lying-in room. Then, especially if parturition takes place at night, four little wood fires are lit at the four corners of the house, and into them, from time to time, salt, pepper, sulphur and horn are strewn. These give out a horrible stench. Finally, the midwife has to rub the patient's big toes with a mixture of finely ground pepper, white onions and asafetida. In protracted labour they take a rose of Jericho, let it open in lukewarm water, and give it to the woman in labour to drink. (We have already seen that the same plant is used in Italy to encourage delivery, and in the Rhine Palatinate it also has the same effect if the woman in labour smells at the 'freshly blown rose'. Interestingly, Jacobs adds that the plant grows in the Arabian desert and that the Achinese owe their knowledge of it to the Arab priests, who esteem it highly for its effects. Thus it is not improbable that it was transplanted to the European lying-in room by the Crusaders.)

In easy as well as in difficult labour in China, amulets play a great part. Sorcerers, both male and female, have to banish the evil spirits. The woman in childbirth puts on special stockings which have been ordered from the Dalai Lama and have been consecrated by him beforehand; or she swallows pills of paper on which special incantations have been written (Staunton).

As to the help in difficult labour which is customary among the Cheyenne,

Arapaho, Kiowa, Comanche and eastern Apache, a doctor gave the following information to Engelmann:

> ... the chief doctor of the tribe made great efforts ... to help the woman ... The ceremony was performed apart in a closed hut and consisted, as far as I have discovered, in drum-beating, singing, shouting, dancing, running round the fire, jumping over it, manipulating knives and other tricks. This kind of medical help is very common among the Indians and is always carried out seriously and ceremoniously and with full confidence in its efficacy. The main idea is that illness is an evil spirit entered into the sick person, from whom it must be driven or frightened away by magic powers or by flattering words.

Engelmann adds that among the Coyoteros (Apache) mechanical aid is also given in almost all confinements. One such confinement is portrayed in Fig. 24.

Fig. 24   Difficult labour among the Coyoteros (Apache) (after Engelmann)

According to Rohlfs, the procedure for a difficult labour in Morocco is as follows:

> First a fakir is brought to the woman in labour, and he tries to cast out the devil by burning incense and by pious quotations, for in Morocco ... the devil is the cause of every ill, including protracted labour. If this is to no avail, they write passages from the Koran on a wooden tablet, wash them off, and make the patient drink the water used for the purpose. If this procedure too proves vain, then passages of the Koran, written on

paper, pulverized and mixed with water, are administered to the patient. However, Satan is sometimes ... not to be cast out even by the Sacred Book. Then all kinds of amulets are arranged, for example the hair of a great saint, sewn into a little bag, is put on the woman's breast; or they make her drink water from the Semsem well (which is situated in the middle of the grounds of the sacred temple of Mecca and ... contains a slightly bitter water); or dust from the temple of Mecca is put on the woman's couch. Then the devil sometimes abandons his prey, and the labour proceeds to a successful conclusion.

In quite a number of cases, however, the *Iblis* (devil) will yield to no expedient. The woman helpers then engage in battle with him, and amid exorcisms and invocations they undertake mechanical manipulations.

viii. Woman as Mother

The true love of a mother for her children, which we find almost universal in the animal kingdom, we can show to be a common instinct in the women of all nations. A glance round the world shows that innumerable women of uncivilized nations are accompanied by their children as baggage in all the duties of their daily life. They hang on their backs, ride on their shoulders or hips; they are put, as with the Eskimo, in wide fur boots; packed in a cradle, carried in the arms, on the back or on the head. We often see that mothers have to carry the hammock, cradle or bed for their child to the fields with them as well as the child itself.

Of the Aht (Nootka) and Makah, Indian tribes of Vancouver, Malcolm Sproat records that they love their children greatly, and, according to Krause, this is true also of the Tlingit Indians.

N. A. E. Nordenskiold cites of the Greenlanders that they

are very fond of children. The freedom of their children is as unrestricted as possible anywhere. They are never punished, indeed not even talked to sharply. They regard as extremely barbarous the old European method of bringing up children, and in this opinion they are in agreement with the Indians in Canada who, when the missions reproached them for the cruel torture to which prisoners of war were subjected, answered: 'At least we do not, like you, torture our children.' In spite of this undisciplinary method of upbringing, one can bear witness that the Eskimo children when they have reached the age of eight or nine are as well bred as possible.

Merensky says of the Basutos: 'They love their children tenderly. The little baby is caressed, shaved, rubbed with red pomade by the mother and carried about everywhere with her in the carrying cloth so that one sees that it is the mother's greatest treasure.'

The Barolong in South Africa, on the other hand, give clear proof of their love for children by their strict upbringing of them, and beat them when they deserve it. In spite of this strictness the mothers enjoy very great respect.

A fine example of self-sacrificing mother love, fearless in the face of every danger, is recorded by von Schweiger-Lerchenfeld:

The Khonds in the hill country of Orissa still offered human sacrifices to the earth goddess at certain festivals in the middle of the last century. Those destined for sacrifice were called Meriah, and were first well fed and looked after for a long time. Often they had been bought or stolen when still little children, enjoyed careful attention, and were even allowed to marry. Their children, however, then became Meriah also. They were fully aware beforehand of their own and their children's fate. When the day appointed for their sacrifice arrived, they were drowned with great ceremony in a pool of blood, squeezed to death between boards, or had their living bodies dismembered.

The English Government had repeatedly to equip military expeditions to check and suppress these atrocities. By this means, one Meriah and three of her children were rescued, and after some time she begged that they should rescue her fourth child, which had been left behind with the Khonds. This, however, was not practicable, for the season was advanced and the tribe in question very hostile to the English. They put the pitiable creature off with hopes for the following spring. Then she disappeared quite suddenly from the camp. She had left the children behind, which led to the conclusion that she had undertaken the mission of rescue herself. In fact, after forty days' absence, she returned to camp leading her rescued boy by the hand. She had made her way right in the rainy season through primeval forests and swamps, living scantily on roots and fruit and, owing to the fear and anxiety, had scarcely slept the whole time; i.e., only when exhaustion made her sink down in the woods in which poisonous snakes crept and tigers roared. Thus she reached the last village, and she made use of the accidental absence of the inhabitants to find and carry off her child. The return journey was beset with the same difficulties, and it is not surprising that she reached the camp ill and wasted to a skeleton. The Government found accommodation for her and her children at once.

Hendrich found it touching to see a young mother in south Borneo, wherever she walked or stood, holding a bundle of stunted bits of wood over her suckling in order to protect him from evil spirits. And the scientists of the *Novara* expedition alleged that, in spite of infanticide, the Australian native woman lavished touching love on those of her children which had been left alive.

CHAPTER IX

Venus's Satellites

i. The Prostitute

The word 'prostitution' is nowadays used as often wrongly as rightly. In many spheres any extra-marital intercourse is designated prostitution. That is quite incorrect. By prostitution is understood the surrender of a young woman to several men for *recompense*.

A female who lives with a man as his *concubine* is thus not necessarily a prostitute, and free love and the so-called 'liaison' must also be eliminated from the discussion. On the other hand we must reckon among the harlots even the greatest women artistes if they give themselves to men in return for diamonds, etc. – but only if the gain thereby is the first consideration.

Prostitution is not a phenomenon of modern times; its roots lie rather in antiquity, and it may be viewed as a deterioration of free sexual intercourse which has existed from the time of the nomadic tribes. Further, it is the result of a false morality, especially of the struggle for monogamy. Woman herself is not the party least guilty in the matter. The gift of her body is her greatest *capital*, by which she is assured her future in marriage; hence she has an instinctive dislike for the young woman who claims not a lasting alliance but merely money. Wulffen expresses a similar idea when he writes: 'Many hold women at least partly to blame for the ineradicable condition of prostitution because they demand monogamy before everything, thus misunderstanding the polygamous nature of the male and driving him to a sexual satisfaction which he can buy.' Thus, so long as marriage exists, prostitution will exist also. Since we cannot eliminate marriage without the abandonment of our civilization, we cannot eliminate prostitution, however much it may be called an evil.

Similar to concubinage, but still not identical with it, is a form of prostitution such as we find in Ancient Greece. This was *hetaerism*. The legitimate wives were confined to a domestic life and the husbands found a stimulating pleasure in free intercourse with women who, by their cultivation, refinement of manner and witty conversation, together with the surrender of their female charms, exercised an irresistible power of attraction over men of higher standing. It was mostly freed women who resorted to the position of hetaerae, but free-born citizens also, driven by poverty, entered into such alliances with men. They became the intimate associates and the fashionable hostesses of the leaders of the people, of artists, of statesmen and of philosophers.

Wulffen's estimation of this phenomenon is very striking:

> The classical age of the Greeks . . . is so closely interwoven with prostitution that without knowledge of it the finest flowers of genius would remain unintelligible. All the arts and even philosophy sprang, to some extent, out of prostitute soil. The great exploits of the artists, sculptors, painters, poets and philosophers . . . were inspired not by their legal wives, but by hetaerae.

Among the various schools of philosophy the Epicureans and Cyrenaics explicitly accepted the hetaera in theory as well as practice; and such men as Plato, Socrates and Aristotle saw no shame in it.

Herodotus wrote of the Lydians (I, 93):

> The country . . . can show . . . the greatest work of human hands in the world, apart from the Egyptian and Babylonian, namely the tomb of Croesus' father Alyattes. Its foundation consists of huge stone blocks; the rest of it is a mound of earth. It was erected by tradespeople, craftsmen and prostitutes, and on the top of it there survived to my own day five pillars with inscriptions cut into them to show what each class had done in the construction. Calculation revealed that the prostitutes had done the most. All the working-class girls in Lydia prostitute themselves in order to acquire a dowry, and they do this until they marry.

Solon is said to have made the vocation of hetaerae legal out of regard for public morality, for he hoped in this way to restrain men from the prohibited intercourse with married women.

In Rome, as in Greece, the Venus cult contributed not a little to the development of prostitution. The Romans had public pleasure-houses (*Lupanaria* and *Fornices*) as well as independent 'women of pleasure' (*Meretrices* and *Prostibulae*), and prostitutes used to appear at the baths.

The aversion from mercenary love which was peculiar to the women and girls among the Ancient Teutons was lost in great measure as a result of the penetration of Roman culture and contact with other races as well as with the ideals of an ascetic Christendom. Indeed, the female sex had a remarkable share in the increasing degeneration of morals in the Middle Ages. Prostitution became extraordinarily prevalent in spite of the efforts of jurists and rulers who were still imbued with the old Germanic spirit to repress it.

In the twelfth and thirteenth centuries the towns issued regulations for the public houses of ill-fame. The licensed landlords of these were heavily taxed. According to Schultz, the rules laid down for low women in brothels by the Nuremberg Council in the fifteenth century begin with the words:

Although an inheritor councillor of this town by praiseworthy descent is more inclined to increase his estate and encourage good morals than to permit the activities of sinful and criminal persons, yet for the sake of avoiding worse evils in Christianity, low women will be tolerated by the Holy Church.

Indeed, the high ecclesiastical authorities in many cases did not fight shy of undertaking the protection of these houses, supported by a dictum of St Thomas, who says: 'Prostitution in the towns is like the cesspool in the palace: take away the cesspool and the palace will become an unclean and evil-smelling place.'

On special occasions, such as government meetings and councils, crowds of wandering women were to be found, and all campaigns at that time were accompanied by a powerful gang of such females, whose discipline was officially maintained by an inspector of harlots. Leonhard Fronsperger, in his *War-book*, has described in detail the duties of the whore-usher:

Item, when a regiment is strong in numbers, then the camp followers also are not few; there should be appointed by the colonel an official, an able, honest, sensible warrior ... one who has helped in battle and attack ... for such an officer must know how to order and lead such troops just as ordinary or straying troops have to be kept in order and led.

He must see to it that they do not hinder the troops on the march, and that they do not come into camp before them, where they would take away everything usable from the combatants. Besides, he must see that whores and loose fellows keep clean the latrines, and further, that they wait upon their masters faithfully and that they are kept occupied when necessary with cooking, sweeping, washing and especially attendance on the sick; and that they never refuse either on the field or in garrison, running, pouring out, fetching food and drink, knowing how to behave modestly with regard to the needs of others ...

Under the officer for the harlots is a provost, whose duty it is to establish peace and order. When he cannot make peace by other means, he has a conciliator about the length of an arm with which he is authorized by their masters to punish them.

We see from Fronsperger's remarks that these women were not taken with the army for the sole purpose of sexual enjoyment, but that they also had many other duties.

Long journeys were attended with such great hardships that the princes of that time could not expect their wives and daughters to accompany them. Only courtesans were hardened enough to be able to follow the princes on foot or on horseback, or when they marched with the army. Thus these women became a necessary part of the princely retinue, and in war were regarded as an indispensable part of the camp followers. The army which the Duke of Alva led to the Netherlands, for example, was followed by 400 courtesans on horseback and 800 on foot. A description of an army on the march is given in *Parsifal* (I, 459):

> Of women, too, one saw enough;
> Many bore the twelfth sword girt
> As pledge for their sale of lust.
> They were not exactly queens;
> Those same paramours
> Were named women of the war canteen.

It has already been made clear that the soil of prostitution is not unfruitful when the state understands how to cultivate it. This is also shown by the example of the Republic of Venice, that grand centre of European culture. Among the courtesans of Venice we find, for instance, a poetess of significance, Veronica Franco, whose work Schaeffer considers the best of its kind in the whole of the sixteenth century. He writes:

> In Venice the ancient sensuousness awoke from its thousand years' sleep into which it had been sung by Christian anthems. As always when a culture is under the influence of sensuous pleasures, as in Athens and Alexandria, woman was in the ascendant in Venice in this century. And just as in Athens and Alexandria, not the married woman but the courtesan.

PROSTITUTION IN PRIMITIVE SOCIETIES

According to Bloch, writing in 1912, prostitution appears among primitive peoples wherever free sexual intercourse has become limited or restrained. It is nothing but a substitute for, or another form of, primitive promiscuity.

On the Pelew Islands, prostitution is quite a common phenomenon. When a girl is ten or twelve years old and still has no husband, she goes as 'Armengol' to a strange district, and there enters a Baj, where she lives as the paid mistress of a native. In secret, she has to cohabit with all the other men of the Baj for money. If she does not find a husband, then she goes to a second Baj, then a third, etc., until at last she becomes the wife of a native.

In Achin (Sumatra), prostitution occurs more frequently in harbour and fishing districts than in the villages of the interior. It is held in such contempt that it can be carried on only in secrecy, and if the affair becomes known the headman of the village usually banishes the women concerned, who are almost always fully developed girls and young widows for whom marriage or remarriage is impossible. In the Lampong district of Sumatra, on the other hand, many men marry second and third wives in order to hire them out for payment.

Among the Olo-Ngadjoe, a Dyak tribe in south-east Borneo, a husband gets the proceeds of a fine imposed on the man with whom his wife commits adultery. In order to gain this money the Dyak sometimes drives his wife to the same offence, to *hadjaivet* (work), as he calls it, with other men, who are led on by the wife just enough for the husband to be able to claim the corresponding fine when he appears, which he always does at the right time.

On the Gilbert Islands, according to Krämer, girls of the middle class are quite prepared to surrender themselves; in fact, the fathers take pains to offer their daughters to men of high position for payment in money. Hence they have the same word for a girl of the middle classes and a courtesan. It is characteristic of their morality, which is quite different from our own, that in yielding herself the girl is not thought to have done anything scandalous, although it is considered shameful and mean if she gives herself without receiving a reward for her family.

Although prostitution is contrary to the laws of Islam, the ancient moral trait of the Numidians still continues among the tribes of the Sahara. The girls of the tribe Ulad-Nail, called Nailia, and also those of other tribes, are accustomed to go in great numbers to the oasis-towns visited by foreigners and nomads in order to pursue the profession of an *alma* (originally 'dancer'), which they do until they have earned so much that, as women of means, they can get a distinguished husband in their native place. Von Maltzan knew much-respected Algerian chiefs decorated with French orders who married such prostitutes.

BROTHELS

Prostitution in Japan has been much described, most vividly and clearly, perhaps, by Crasselt, whose account we shall follow here:

> The daughter takes it as a matter of course that she shall sacrifice herself for her parents if their means are precarious . . . She becomes a prostitute with the full knowledge and consent of her parents, and enters a brothel, changing her name for the duration of her employment.

According to the number of years for which she has engaged herself, she receives a fixed sum ... which, minus the considerable expense of her agents, goes into her parents' hands. After she leaves the brothel she resumes her original name and is now not regarded as in the least dishonoured. On the contrary, by her heroism as an obedient daughter she has earned the respect of her fellow-men ...

The glittering misery of the famous brothel quarter, Yoshiwara, in the capital should be seen. This is an enclosed quarter, with a special entrance gate, and conceals thousands of these unhappy creatures in its houses ... Behind the wooden bars of each brothel, in the light of electric lamps, sit from ten to thirty girls in splendid old Japanese costumes, with a smile on their lips, offering a welcome to the passers-by. It is a sight of strange splendour; nothing else like it exists in the whole world. And yet it is a tragedy when one recalls from what motives most of these girls have to act this sad part, a part which they play smiling.

As Hintze reports, brothels were originally scattered all over the towns. The Yoshiwara of Tokyo, which in 1899 accommodated altogether about 3,000 girls, was founded in 1626, after almost ten years of building. Towards the end of the eighteenth century the custom was formed of classifying the houses externally by the height of the bars behind which the girls were exposed to view (Fig. 25). In houses of Class I the wooden bars reached to the ceiling; in Class II they were shorter and narrower; and in Class III they ran not vertically but horizontally. This distinction continued until 1872, when the buildings were also limited to two storeys. The houses of the first and second classes no longer exhibit their girls, but affix photographs of individual occupants to the outside of the house; others do not even do that. Prospective visitors must first go to a tea-house which undertakes 'delivery' inclusive of maintenance and charge.

In China the state of prostitution is very much developed, and special laws do not harass the harlots. They are often lodged in brothels which are furnished with great luxury. On account of their blue blinds they are sometimes called 'blue houses' (*Tsing Lao*). In those towns which, like Canton, lie on the river, specially built, firmly anchored ships, called 'flower-ships' (*Hua Ch'uan*), are also frequently used as brothels. The girls accommodated in these places are the slaves of the brothel-owner, and their position, as well as the fate awaiting most of them, is truly lamentable. They are usually trained systematically for their profession, and just as systematically exploited by their owners. At the age of from six to seven they have to wait on the older girls and their male visitors; at the age of ten to eleven they learn to sing and play, also to read, write and paint; but as early as the age of ten

Fig. 25 Exhibition of Japanese prostitutes in a kind of cage with gilded bars (after Bienvenu)

they are used to earn money for their masters: first of all outside the house, afterwards in the institutions themselves, when two or three years have elapsed. These unfortunate beings fade early. In later life they are to be seen in every street in the big towns sitting mending, for very little reward, the torn clothes of soldiers and labourers. According to official reports, Amoy, a coast town with a population of 300,000, had in 1861 3,650 brothels accommodating 35,000 girls.

In the early history of China the 'flower-girls', i.e., the occupants of the flower-boats, played a similar part to that of the distinguished hetaerae in Greece. They were the epitome of all beauty, good education and culture, and were sought by male youths to complete their own education. But the ideal which formerly gave an ennobling touch to this arrangement (if we may believe Colquhoun's descriptions) has been completely lost. He says that the young ladies, though some of them are not wanting in good looks and a certain gracious bearing of their own, are very illiterate and incapable of reading and writing – much less of improvising poetry, as they are said to have done in the good old times.

The former military attaché of the Chinese Embassy in Paris says that the flower-boats are not places of excess, and serve this purpose just as little as the concert halls of Europe: on the boats is to be found everything that an epicure could wish for; and in the cool of the evening, with a cup of deliciously perfumed tea, the women's harmonious voices and the sound of musical instruments are not considered a nocturnal debauch. It is, however, admitted later that the platonic friendship in which this Chinese authority would have us believe is not absolutely consistent.

ATTEMPTS TO SUPPRESS PROSTITUTION

Regardless of the dictum of St Thomas and in spite of the tenet of faith laid down by St Augustine ('Abolish prostitution and you will see confusion') in Europe in the Middle Ages, rulers of church and state repeatedly tried to suppress prostitution. As is to be expected, there was no lack of refined cruelty in accordance with the spirit of the age. Not infrequently prostitutes were publicly whipped, as under Charles the Great, and in many places they were led ignominiously through the streets, sometimes naked, sitting reversed upon an ass. In England people used to throw filth at them. And even where these women were tolerated they became liable to punishment if they did not submit to the rules and regulations decreed for them. The question was also attacked by prosecuting landlords and landladies who kept prostitutes in their houses. Flogging, branding with hot irons, banishment and confiscation of their property played a great part in this campaign, and in cases of a second offence capital punishment was decreed.

In the civilized states of the present day people endeavour in an increasing degree to restrict prostitution. In general, two opposed systems are to be observed: on the one side 'conditional tolerance'; on the other, the most rigorous efforts for total suppression. A widespread movement has arisen in the last decades which, under the name of 'abolitionism', is, in a misdirected philanthropy, trying to resist the police regulation and supervision of prostitutes. It clearly sails under religio-political colours supported by the movement for women's rights. As Dingwall notes, the work of these abolitionists is unfortunately marred by their ignorance of the practical side of prostitution and also by the emotional fervour of their propaganda. Any candid examination of this readily reveals the motives behind their work, which is inspired not only by a desire to suppress prostitution but also by a desire to suppress the manifestations of sexual life altogether. They are dominated by Christian traditions and Pauline asceticism; and, whereas they fulminate against the prostitution of the female body for gain, they are singularly silent on the subject of the prostitution of the male mind for the same purpose, which is one of the significant features of Western civilization.

ii. The Virgin Dedicated to God

From time immemorial, we find among the most different civilized nations the custom of removing certain female representatives of the female sex from profane everyday life in order that, prepared by special ceremonies, lodged in special houses and trained in a special way, they may be dedicated to God for the whole of their life. In most cases, these virgins of God were condemned to everlasting celibacy; they had to do duty in the temples, to glorify the festivals of the gods with their singing and dancing, to act as priestesses of the sacrifice and sometimes to prophesy.

Among the Ancient Egyptians there were virgins in the service of Ammon who were kept under special supervision in his temple, and the Babylonians had temple virgins (as distinct from the girls destined for temple prostitution) who were regarded as the sisters or wives of Marduk; but perhaps most famous of all were the vestal virgins of the Romans, who, as everybody knows, had to make a strict vow of chastity in memory of the goddess Vesta, who had sworn the oath of eternal virginity when Apollo and Neptune wooed her.

The priestesses of Vesta in Rome were first two, then four and afterwards six in number. According to Minckwitz, the vestal virgin could not be more than ten years of age, had to be a native of Italy, without external deficiencies, and the issue of living parents who belonged to the free class and pursued an honourable calling. If she satisfied these conditions the father could give her up voluntarily to be a priestess. If choice was necessary, it took place by lot at a meeting of the people. The girl elected had to learn the service of Vesta for ten years, practise it for ten and teach it for ten (that is, up to her fortieth year). Only then did she have permission to leave the temple and even to marry if she wanted to give up her sacred calling.

Infringement of the vow of chastity was punished terribly. The criminal was, like the nuns of the Middle Ages, buried alive amid horrible ceremonies, whilst general mourning prevailed in the town, people looking on such an occurrence as a heavy infliction by the angry gods. Because of this, however, these priestesses also enjoyed the highest respect and a number of privileges. As soon as the Pontifex touched them with his sacred hand on the day of their ceremonial initiation, they were regarded of age and capable of making a will; they had seats of honour in the theatre below the first town councillors; when they went out, the fasces were carried before them by the Lictor, and if a criminal who was being taken to the place of execution met them on the way he was granted his life.

The Teutons also had their virgins dedicated to God on whom the gift of prophecy was conferred. Tacitus speaks of them in his *Germania*. These virgins were called *Wala*.

NUNS AND NUNNERIES

To the sphere of consecrated women belong the nuns, with the variations of nursing orders and those of deaconesses' orders. For the last in particular, self-denial, neighbourly love and self-sacrifice were necessary.

The convents originated almost simultaneously with the monasteries about the second century in our reckoning of time. The first impetus to these was given by crowds of hermits who, as St Jerome records, came to the West in daily immigrations from India, Persia and Ethiopia. Around these, believing disciples flocked in great numbers, who were then gathered into bigger groups by prominent clerics. St Pachomius (*fl. c.* 320) is considered to have been the first to found an actual convent.

These convents, which consisted of a great many individual houses united under a supreme direction, made their way over all Christian countries, and from all classes of the population pious souls streamed to them in crowds. But the life of pious ecstasy and self-mortification gave place, after a few centuries, to a freer conception of human existence. If there still exists in many places a popular tale that this or that famous convent had an underground passage connecting it with the neighbouring monastery, there are, in not a few cases, only too well-founded reasons for this.

We must likewise not fall into the error of regarding certain houses for women built like convents as true nunneries. Although they were set up and established exactly like nunneries and even had an abbess at their head, yet nothing was changed in their character, and they remained what they were, namely public places, without any supervision, to which anybody had right of entrance. The brothel of Toulouse was even designated in a royal decree of Charles VI as a *grant abbaye* (Dulaure).

In sharp contrast with the above-mentioned liberties within the convents is the terrible severity in many of them towards the unfortunate virgins of God who had broken the vow of chastity. The more severe penances, fasting and whipping, awaited them, and in many cases they expiated their sin with death, which was brought about usually by their being buried or walled up alive.

It is no doubt less well known that the Buddhist church also has the institution of convents, which no doubt rose from the same root as the Christian. In China, a large number of young girls become Buddhist nuns in order to avoid a marriage not desired by them, but in spite of this many an imprisoned virgin heart may die of longing for the joys of the world within those walls where she remains by her parents' command.

Of the Bhotea, who inhabit the most northerly part of Sikhim on the frontiers of Tibet, Mantegazza says: 'Some women are close-cropped and are nuns, but before they consecrated themselves to the gods they had usually enjoyed earthly life even to excess.'

The honour of priesthood is denied to the female sex by the majority of savage peoples. It is not an absolute rule, however, and here and there it is possible for women to become priests. The Javanese women, for example, are permitted to attend a Mohammedan school for priests, and if they are successful they may enter the mosques, which are strictly barred to all other women.

iii. *The Sorceress, the Prophetess and the Fortune-teller*

Actually, only very slight differences separate the witch from the sorceress. To their kind also belong the prophetess and the fortune-teller, for do they not know how to foretell the future from every possible thing; how to cure diseases and injuries by incantations, that is, by murmuring magic formulae; and how to make enchantments harmless by sympathetic expedients?

In the belief in the supernatural powers of sorceresses and in the methods by which they use their powers, we once again find cause to marvel at the way in which human beings in different centuries and in the most various parts of the globe have yet hit upon similar ideas and analogous expedients for their performance.

Speke found that special women called *Wabandwa* functioned at the court of the king of Uganda. These women had to be present at every audience the ruler granted in order to keep the evil eye from him. Also in East Africa, among the Wachaga, Gutmann found that there were female as well as male witch-doctors, who, decked with gnu-tails, magic horns and amulets, wandered through the country. Women fortune-tellers were also known, for example among the South African natives (Fig. 26).

Krämer describes an Araucanian witches' tree (*rehue*). In the trunk, which has been denuded of most of its branches, steps are hewn. The tree is climbed by the witches on certain occasions, for example on the death of a chief, 'so as to announce from there in a dream from a higher inspiration the person who was guilty of the death: this person is then put to death'.

Pallas records of the sorceresses of the Kalmucks, who are called *Uduguhn*, that they are not to be confounded with religious or holy persons, but are of a lower class, and that they

> are held in abhorrence and are accustomed to be punished for practising their forbidden arts. They are supposed to practise magic only once a month, on the night on which the new moon rises. They do not make use of magical drums, but have a dish of water brought, immerse a certain herb in it and then sprinkle the hut with it. After this, they take certain roots in each hand, kindle them, and with outstretched arms make all kinds of gestures and violent motions of the body, during which

Fig. 26 Native soothsayer from South Africa (from *Anthropos*)

they sing in constant repetition the syllables *dshi, eje, jo, jo,* till they fall into a kind of frenzy in which they answer the questions asked about lost things or future events.

Wizards and witches also play a great part among the Siberian tribes. The witches do not differ in their magic arts from the male shamans; in their costume and outfit they are almost exactly like the latter, and like them they use peculiar hand drums at their official functions (Fig. 27). If a Goldi woman wants to be a shaman, the oldest shaman has to carve in wood a female figure about half an inch high to represent her. As soon as the work is finished the woman attains the honour of being a shaman. From this it appears that it rests entirely with the chief shaman whether he will receive the woman into the ranks of the initiates. If he has anything against her, he need only never succeed in carving the figure.

Fig. 27 Tatar shamaness dancing round the fire (after Rechberg)

Among the Scandinavians there are likewise women who practise the black arts and possess knowledge of secret powers and things. In Norway and Iceland, women with the gift of prophecy used to go from farm to farm in the winter, foretelling the lot of those they visited. Because of their gift, people believed that something divine was innate in these women. Indeed, there arose a belief that women determined the fate of human beings which none could escape.

In the Saga of Nornagest soothsayers of this kind are spoken of. There it runs:

At that time there went about the country women soothsayers called *Volven*, who prophesied people's fates. Many men invited them to their houses, entertained them lavishly and gave them valuable jewels when they left. My father did so, too, and they came to him with a great train of followers in order to tell my fate. I was in the cradle at that time, and . . . two wax candles were burning over me. They spoke favourably about me and said I would be a very fortunate being, and so it was to be with me in all things.

The youngest Norn felt herself slighted because she had not been questioned. Also there was a rough mob there who pushed her from her seat and knocked her to the ground. She was annoyed at this, cried loudly and angrily, and made the others cease with their great promises, 'for I destine him not to live longer than the candle burns which is alight here by the boy'. Upon this, the older Volva seized the candle, extinguished it and bade my mother keep it and not light it until I was in the last days of my life [Edzardi].

Weinhold describes one of these fortune-tellers, a Volva named Thorbiörg who went about in winter to prophesy at feasts. According to him she wore a dark mantle laced with a thong which had knots in it from top to bottom, glass pearls round her neck, and on her head a cap of black lambskin lined with white catskin; her hands were in catskin gloves, and on her feet she had rough calfskin shoes with long laces. She held a staff with a brass knob set with stones, and round her body was a cork girdle on which hung a leather purse with her magic instruments.

The Teutonic soothsayers, who along with the gift of prophecy also had the power of performing magic, used certain wooden staves scratched with runes to foretell the future. Hence, according to Weinhold, all names of women in which the word *run* appears were originally women who had the gift of soothsaying.

The *covalyi*, the sorceresses among present-day Gypsies, enjoy quite a special power and an extraordinary influence. Von Wlislocki writes of them that they are in the front rank as helpers and, indeed, as physicians for human beings as well as animals. They know the magic formulae by which the *misiçe* (the evil demons of disease) can be banished from the bodies of the sick. They have the strength and power to put in bondage and release the souls of men, to arouse and to destroy love and hate, and to combat psychic affections as well as those of the body. Thus, they still have the same role which priests had among primitive peoples before the care of the soul was separated from the care of the body. As in healing sickness, whether of body or mind, the sorceress has to prove her ability in other forms of knowledge so as to be able to dispense talismans and fetishes to the people. She must know not only how to banish the dead, but also how to regulate the weather in order to demonstrate her connection with supernatural beings.

HYPNOSIS

Siberian sorceresses place themselves in a state of ecstatic excitement reminiscent of hypnotic processes by lively movements of the body, monotonous songs, the banging of the magic drum and noise of tin rattles. It was no doubt much the same in the case of the famous Pythia in the temple at Delphi, who was transported into a state of semi-torpor by the frightful noise made under her feet and, it appears, by the sending out of gases.

We still find the use of hypnotism for the purpose of fortune-telling in some islands of the Moluccan Sea. For instance, Riedel records of the island of Buru that, if they want to find out who has made someone ill or to have a glimpse of the future, they call two of these experts, generally elderly widows, into the house or to a big tree in the woods. Here a seat of *gabagaba* or a stone is set up for one of them to sit on, whilst the other stands amid the deafening noise of tuba and drum, grasps a sword (*parang*) and, with her eyes staring open and her hair hanging loose like a fury, leaps wildly, looks above, to the sides and also into the eyes of the second woman, whilst perspiration pours in streams from her body. While doing this, she cuts herself with the *parang* and then picks up a stone with which she hacks at her bare breasts until her companion, who remains seated, falls into convulsions and becomes cataleptic, loses the sense of her personality and falls into a kind of torpor and hypnotic state. In this condition she is questioned by the other about everything people want to know.

There are likewise women on the islands of Leti, Moa and Lakor who have themselves hypnotized by the banging of drums and can then foretell the future and explain dreams. They are held in great respect and people ascribe their gift of divination to a union with the chosen spirits.

In China also, where the people in general are inclined to believe in all kinds of magic, hypnotism is brought into use for certain procedures.

iv. Witches

The oldest literary works of the Babylonians and Assyrians speak of witches who, as the ghosts of night, are credited with being excitants of disease and mishaps, evil dreams, slanders, in fact of any affliction.

There is no end, says Weber, to the names by which witches (who seem often to represent the whole family or guild) and magicians were called in exorcisms. The witch is the tramp, the harlot, the woman consecrated to the goddess Ishtar, etc. In her mind is the baneful word devised; on her tongue is magic; on her lips bewitchment; death follows in her footsteps. Eyes, feet and hands are quicker and more active than with other people. Like a demon, she is fond of staying in abandoned houses, but when she has spied a victim, she follows him through the bustle of streets and squares, entangles his feet in a net, and causes his downfall. But she likes best to practise her activities at night.

Foreign women, particularly from the lands on the mountain frontiers of Babylon and Assyria, had a special predilection for appearing as witches. Their weapons were the 'evil eye', which exposed the victim to every misfortune, and the 'evil word', the baneful formula which was full of magic and raised every evil power in the service of the witch. Along with these, they used the knotted string with which they filled men's mouths. That witches used amorous arts for the corruption of men is an ever-recurring belief which existed even in Babylon. The magic arts which Circe practised on Odysseus and his companions are known to everybody, as well as those with which Medea brought aid to her guest Jason. The Romans too were firmly convinced of the magic power of witches, as can be seen in the works of Virgil.

The strangest activity of witches was the making of images of the persons to be bewitched out of all kinds of materials like clay, asphalt, honey and wax. With these images witches performed symbolical manipulations which were destined to have the same effect simultaneously on the original. The images were placed among the dead, thrown into ditches and wells, laid in much-frequented places to be trodden on, etc.

Although witches could have social communion with the devil at all sorts of times, yet, as is well known, there was one appointed time, Walpurgis Night, when the general meeting of all the witches with the devil took place. This was the great witches' Sabbath, busy preparations for which are shown in an interesting painting by F. Francken (1581–1642) in Vienna (Fig. 28). In a room decorated with all kinds of magical characters, a great many womenfolk have assembled. A well-built witch, quite naked, riding on a broom, is just going up the chimney. Three kneeling women are praying to a hairy devil on a small platform, who holds a dish from which fiery rings and sparks ascend. Other women are cooking a ram's skull in a giant cauldron, while snakes, dragons and all manner of monsters swarm overhead. In the middle of the room an altar has been set up at which an old woman is reading incantations from a book of magic. A perforated human skull lies on the altar; snakes, frogs, human and animal bones and scratching creatures are heaped on the floor before it. A young standing person is unlacing her bodice; another sitting on a stool is in the act of taking off her stockings. The purpose of these two in taking off their clothes is explained by the three women standing behind them. One of these is already quite naked, and has a broomstick in her hand which she intends to use as a horse. Beside her stands another well-built young maid, likewise naked, whose back is being rubbed by an old woman with a pot of salve in her hand. This is no doubt the witches' salve which gives women the power to go through the air on a broom.

Fig. 28   The witches' kitchen (oil painting by F. Francken, Kunsthistorisches Museum, Vienna)

Belief in witches is not yet completely extinct in Europe, and even in Germany there are still many pious souls for whom the existence of witches is an established fact.

F. S. Krauss has made thorough investigations with regard to the belief in witches prevalent among the southern Slavs:

> In general, people regard witches as swarthy, evil, ragged old women with curly white hair ... malicious old women who cannot get away from this world and therefore prefer to inflict sorrow on their fellow-men ... In every witch is lodged a demonic spirit which leaves her at night and turns into a fly, butterfly, hen, turkeycock or crow, but best of all a toad. If the witch wants to inflict particularly severe harm on anyone, she turns herself into a beast of prey, usually a wolf.

Other ancient ideas crop up as well in this Slav belief:

> There are three kinds of witches. First, there are the witches of the air. These are of a very evil turn of mind. They are hostile to mankind, strike fear and terror into them and set traps for them on every highway and byway. At night they are accustomed to waylay people, and confuse them so much that they lose all clear consciousness. The second kind are the earth witches. These are ingratiating, noble and affable by nature, and are in the habit of giving wise council ... They like best to tend the flocks. The third kind are the water witches who are most malicious, yet, if they wander free about the country, they even treat kindly the people they meet. But woe to anyone they get at in or near water – then they pull and whirl him about in the water or ride him successively till he drowns miserably.

People have certain signs for knowing whether anyone is or is to become a witch, and one of them, according to Krauss, even shows itself at birth: 'If a child is born with a caul, it must be made known generally. If the caul is red, then the girl will be a *mora* (nightmare) but after marriage a witch.' In Herzegovina people recognize a witch by her dull, deep-set eyes and eyebrows that meet, and by her little moustache. On the island of Lesina in Dalmatia all women are regarded as witches who are not on the best of terms with God and who are born under a particular star; these are old, shrivelled women with grey hair, a long turned-up chin and sunken eyes. In Russia, too, it is easy to acquire the reputation of being a witch, according to Löwenstimm. One can see this from the number of signs by which a witch can be recognized: in the province of Vilna, for example, the people in the Molodetshno district believe that a witch, on the evening before Mid-summer's Day, cannot refrain from begging something from her neighbours, especially fire and matches. Other signs are that she is a woman advanced in years, lean and bony, slightly hunchbacked, with tangled hair or hair hanging out from under her headcloth, a wide mouth and a prominent chin. According to tradition in southern Russia she has besides a little tail and a black stripe down her back from the nape of the neck to the shoulder.

Belief in witches occurs even further north, in Greenland, where Cranz observed it. He says:

> When a woman becomes very old, she has to pass for a witch, something they often like doing. The end, however, is that at the least sign of enchantment they are stoned, thrown into the sea, stabbed or cut to pieces ... Indeed, there are examples of a man who stabbed his own mother or sister in the house in the sight of all the people and nobody even reproached him for it.

The supernatural power of women is also known in South Africa. Natives in the Orange Free State believe that when a man curses anybody it does no harm to the person concerned, but that if a woman curses seriously then the curse is certain to take effect.

Witches are much feared among the Wachaga in East Africa, and with a certain justice, since, according to Gutmann, they do not exist only in the popular imagination but lead their diabolical existence in the midst of the people as mixers of poisons and agents of all knowledge of life-destroying forces. The superstition of the people has divided them into three classes: 1) the witch who causes swelling: to her people trace swelling of the abdomen and symptoms of dropsy; 2) the real poison witch, of whom people maintain that she tests her drugs on little children by giving them food in secret; 3) the 'consuming' witch, who causes death with wasting phenomena. The latter might also be called the 'sympathetic' witch, for she is said to cause death by collecting whatever she can from the body of the person concerned: hair from his head, spittle, nail cuttings, urine, threads from his clothes, etc. All these she buries with curses.

Among the Ama-Xosa, according to Kropf, belief in witches is widespread. They even have two kinds of witch-priests: the *Amagqira awokumbulula*, who discover and remove objects, and the *Isanuse* or *Amagqira abukali*, the 'sharp-doctors', who smoke out the witches. It seems as if the *Isanuse* smoke out men much oftener than women. The explanation is simple: the property of the individual found to be a witch is confiscated by the chiefs and therefore it is a matter of course that wage-earning rich men are smoked out rather than poor women.

On the Gold Coast, belief in witches is so deep-rooted that even conversion to Christianity is powerless against it. Vortisch relates that a teacher of the

Basel Mission had to be dismissed because he constantly accused the wife of a catechist of witchcraft and always hid his child from her.

Katscher records of the Chinese:

> As in other lands, there are in China also persons, old women, who pretend to be allied with certain supernatural spirits and to conjure up the souls of the dead and to be able to make them talk with living people. In all the bigger Chinese towns, there are an immense number of witches ... Their services are mostly resorted to by married women who, because of cruel treatment or for other reasons, want to get rid of their husbands. The witch to whom they resort collects the bones of sucklings in graveyards and prays the evil spirits to accompany the bones to her [dwelling], where she grinds them to a fine powder. This she sells to her clientele, who are given instructions to give it daily in water, wine or tea to the persons to be killed ... The authorities have made repeated attempts, and with success, to remedy this evil. Gray records several cases of mass execution of these witches.

Von Goltz also mentions an association of women bearing the name *Mi-fu-chiao*, i.e., 'the science of casting spells on men'. He says:

> The head of this association is an old woman who, by her magical influence, induces many women and girls to become members. When once they have entered they have to carry out the peculiar customs of the association. In the silence of midnight, they repair secretly to a remote burial ground and, after they have discovered the grave of a boy or youth who has died while still in possession of his virginity, they burn incense before his grave; then ... they open the grave and each of the women takes one or a few of the bones home with her ... The new members are also taught the songs which are sung whilst practising witchcraft. Thus instructed they can bewitch their husbands when they quarrel with them ... The man thus bewitched is supposed to become insane in a short time, or he is seized with a violent illness for which there is no cure and of which he soon dies.

Among the Kirghiz, too, Pallas came across all sorts of magicians, and after having told of this, he continues:

> Finally, there are two kinds of witches, who are generally women (*Dshaadugar*) and who bewitch slaves and captives so that they either get lost when escaping or fall into the hands of their owners again, or, if they succeed in escaping, yet soon fall again into Kirghiz slavery. They pull a few hairs out of the captive's head, ask his name and place him in

the middle of the tent on hearth ashes, which have been scattered and strewn with salt. Then the witch repeats her incantations, during which she makes the captive step back three times, spits on his footprints and springs out of the tent each time. In conclusion, she sprinkles on his tongue some of the ashes on which he has stood, and with this the working of the spell ends.

The lamentable confusion of mind which for centuries made thousands of people in Europe unhappy and after indescribable torment and anxiety brought them to a terrible death because of a supposed alliance with the devil, raged and stormed among the female sex particularly, and infinitely more witches suffered death by burning than wizards. This terrible period of witch persecution has had so many exponents that we need not go thoroughly into it here.

Johannes Wierus, in spite of his belief in a personal devil, deserves our admiration for having been the first daring opponent of the superstitions about witches and of the incredible cruelty involved in their persecution. He examined the details of the belief in witches with a vision surprisingly clear for that unreasoning period, and at every point sought to indicate its untenableness, physical impossibility and absurdity. Although the captured witches, he argued, had confessed all these misdeeds, yet they had been partly deluded by the devil, partly also they had confessed to the shameful deeds laid to their charge because they preferred to suffer death rather than undergo longer the indescribable tortures of the rack.

Unfortunately, as is very well known, the voice of this man went unheard, for the minds of even the most cultivated people in Europe were still not sufficiently enlightened to realize the enormity of these horrible trials of witches. More than two centuries were to pass before the evil would be remedied.

Nevertheless, these beliefs have required more victims even in recent times. Löwenstimm quotes several cases which have occupied the attention of the Russian courts. Thus on February 4th, 1879, in the village of Wratshevka in the Tichvin district, a soldier's widow, Katharina Ignatjev, who was regarded generally as a witch, was shut up in her house and burnt alive in the presence of 300 onlookers; the jury acquitted fourteen of the accused, and three were condemned to church penance. In the Ssuchum district in the year 1889, a widow, one of whose sons had died suddenly and the other fallen ill soon after, was designated as a witch by the fortune-teller whom the sick son questioned. Thereupon, with the consent of her own son, the old woman was formally cross-examined by the peasants, tortured, bound to a pole, and on this roasted as on a spit. Löwenstimm cites a few more of these cases and points out how here 'in good faith' all the ties of kinship, even the most sacred, are ignored.

v. Amazons

By a trend of thought connected with the patriarchal organization of the community and male dominance, it became both ignominious and disastrous not to have achieved parenthood of at least one son. How could this misfortune best be met? Among the choice of methods was the nurture and education of daughters on masculine lines, so that they might play the part of sons.

It was, of course, impossible to obliterate the girl's primary physical attributes, but the mammary glands could be removed or, to some degree, constricted and arrested in growth, as is still practised among certain races of the Caucasus (Fig. 3, p. 61). Thus the archaic habit of mutilating or disguising the female breasts became associated with the recognition of the daughter as her father's successor and representative, and this is the theme of legends and sagas in many lands.

The classical legends and references go back to beyond recorded history. In Homer's *Iliad*, the aged Priam, king of Troy, tells Helen of Sparta that he went at the head of a band of warriors to Phrygia as a young man to help his allies Otreus and Mygdon, 'on that day when the Amazon warrior-women invaded their land'. There is no more suggestion of anything mythical here than in any other deed of arms or warlike tribe mentioned in the great epic. And Herodotus mentions them as well, though he, too, says nothing about their original home; although they must at one time have dwelt near the Phrygians and Hellenes, as they were engaged in war with both these peoples.

Strabo regarded the foothills of the Caucasus as the homeland of the Amazons, and gives the well-known particulars about the mutilation of the right breast – by cauterization – in early youth, so that they were the better able to use their right arms, especially to throw the spear. They had also bows and arrows, shields and small battle-axes. In the springtime they went among the Gargareans, from whose land their own was separated by a mountain, 'in order to obtain progeny'. They sent the boys back to their fathers and kept the girls, who were incorporated in their tribe (Hüsing).

Diodorus (III, 53) mentions African as well as Asiatic Amazons, according to the version of Dionysios of Mytilene:

In the western parts of Libya, on the edges of the world, a people is said to have lived under the rule of women. The women waged war, vowing themselves to this for special times, and during their vow they kept apart from men. When they had fulfilled their vows and the time was past, they mated with men and bore children but kept public offices and the rule of the state for themselves. The men lived in the house, as the women do among us, and took charge of the children ... When a girl-baby was born, both her breasts were cauterized so that when they grew and rose they would not interfere with the use of weapons. Because of this, these women were called breastless – Amazons by the Greeks.

As is well known, the female regiment of the ruler of Dahomey persisted till quite recent times. John Duncan mentions ten regiments, each consisting of 600 women; these were the ex-wives of the ruler, who left his harem on attaining their twentieth year. Sir Richard Burton has also described their uniform, appearance and habits in some detail. The women performed intricate dances and hunted wild animals as well as engaging in warfare and forays.

Maqrizi is particularly definite in his account of the Beja, among whom the women were skilled in the craftsmanship of making lances. They lived in a mountain fastness which a man might only visit at certain times of the year to buy lances. On these occasions there was intimacy between the sexes and children were often born in due course. They were reared if girls but killed if boys. The tale is recounted by Hartmann and we also find something similar among the Agni tribe in western Africa.

Jacob found highly curious material in the writings of the Arab geographers and travellers. Thus Kazvini speaks of 'the city of the women', a mighty town set in wide lands in an island of the western ocean. Tartuschi says that its inmates are women, free from all men's rule, who understand horsemanship and themselves take the field in warfare, showing great courage in action. They have male slaves who visit them in secret by night. If one of the women should bear a son, she slays the child at once, but if a daughter, she rears her. The same author adds that this city is a fact beyond all doubt.

The same tale appears on the eve of the Middle Ages, but here again the geography of this women's state has changed. Eneas Sylvio de Piccolomini, traveller and author, and later also Pope Pius II (1405–64), recounted the ancient Bohemian tradition of the women's kingdom under the queens Libussa and Valasca.

Krünitz refers to another medieval legend of an Amazonian race. The authority here is Adam of Bremen, the indefatigable chronicler who lived in the latter half of the eleventh century. According to his record, a community wholly composed of women dwelt on the shores of the Baltic Sea. He relates the same stories that are recorded in other Amazonian legends, but exaggerates in a fantastic manner; for example, he describes pregnancy through drinking magic brews, or through intercourse with monsters, and states that if they became mothers, they either brought forth beautiful girls or 'Cynocephali', monsters whose heads were where other men's chests were.

In the account by Edward Lopez of his travels to the kingdom of Congo in the year 1578 he describes the land of the Monomotapa:

> Among his chief stalwarts are the crack regiments of women, picked troops whom the ruler thinks his best fighters.
>
> They burn away their left breasts in order to shoot more effectively with bows and arrows. They are expert, rapid, bold and fine archers and, above all, they stand their ground in battle and do not easily take to flight . . . They reside in districts specially set apart by their Emperor for the purpose, and at certain times and seasons go among men and mate with them.

Fig. 29, which accompanies Lopez's account, is probably a work of the seventeenth century. In the immediate foreground is the nude figure of a young Amazon with a bow and arrow and a quiver suspended from her right shoulder. Her left breast is quite obliterated. To one side is a group of three women by a blazing fire. One of them, a young girl, sits across the knee of an older woman, who presses an iron instrument like a tube or seal against her left breast, whilst a third holds her firmly down.

Fig. 29 Amazons at Monomotapa (after Lopez)

During and just after the great discoveries in the southern continent of the New World in the sixteenth century, there was a revival of Amazonian legends, and the giant river discovered in 1541 by Francesco d'Orellana was called after the warrior-women and bears their name to this day. Stricker and Fischer give full contemporary accounts of this discovery.

Orellana was told by a Cacique that a tribe of women lived on the banks of the river, apart from men, skilled in the chase and tilling the soil themselves. At certain times every year they allowed the men of neighbouring tribes to visit their hunting grounds; their sons were handed over to the fathers, their daughters they reared themselves. After Orellana had travelled some way into the interior of the country he heard a similar story. The name for the strange women, he was informed, was *Coniapu-yara* – 'great women', or 'tall women'. Some hundreds of miles further on their journey into the unknown the Spaniards were greeted with a swarm of arrows in flight and had to defend themselves against a band of Indians, including ten to twelve women who not only took part in the battle with the utmost ferocity, but urged on their menfolk and struck down the laggards with great clubs. These women are described as tall and of powerful build, but with comely features; their hair wound round their heads in long braids; their clothing very scanty; and their weapons bows, arrows and clubs. Seven of them were killed in the fray, whereupon the Indians took flight.

Many later explorers of the Brazilian and Venezuelan forests heard and recorded stories of Amazonian women. A man of the Tupinamba tribe told C. de Acuña that, as a child, he had accompanied his father on a visit to the Amazons and seen the handing over of the little boys to their fathers' tribes.

La Condamine, who wrote in the eighteenth century, also met persons who claim to have seen or known the Amazons. At Topay he found the curious pieces of nephrite or jade which are known as *muirákitans* or 'Amazon stones'. The Topay tribes declared that they had received these 'from their fathers', who, in their turn, had received them from the *Congnontainsecuma*, the 'women without men', who possessed many such pieces.

Rodriguez also was told of these stones, obtained from a beautiful lake called Yacuaruá, which lay at the source of the Yamunda River and which was dedicated by the Amazons to the moon. (Here as elsewhere we find the association of these mysterious women with a lunar deity.) At a certain season of the year and phase of the moon, the Amazons assembled on the shores of the lake and celebrated a festival in honour of the moon and the mother of the *muirákitans*. If, after some days of ritual festival, the lake appeared smooth and clear, reflecting the light of the moon, the Amazons dived into the water and gathered *muirákitans* from the bottom of the lake, thus receiving them from the Great Mother's own hand. They presented these to the men who found favour in their eyes.

Schomburgk received detailed accounts of Amazons and sought for them but did not find them, though he went as far as the Corentyne. He says:

> The kernel of fact on which this widely spread tradition has been built up must certainly be the fierce and active character of the women of various native races of the New World. Columbus, in the course of his second voyage, encountered a canoe near Santa Croce, and the women on this canoe fought the Spaniards with as much obstinacy and vigour as the men. And he was even prevented from landing on Guadeloupe by armed women.

Even in antiquity certain authors expressed doubt in, or disbelief of, the full Amazonian legend, especially Strabo, who, while recording what was believed about them, was very sceptical. But he mentioned that such famous and prosperous towns and cities as Ephesus, Smyrna, Cumae, Myrina and Paphos were believed to have been founded by them.

Palaephatus was even more incredulous, and mentions that it was said, among his contemporaries, that the Amazons were really male barbarians of a savage tribe 'wearing tunics down to their feet like the women of Thrace, binding their hair and shaving their beards, and, therefore, called women by their enemies'.

In view of the scepticism expressed by both modern authorities and ancient historians, there is a particular significance in certain archaeological discoveries in the Caucasus some decades ago. Bayern was excavating sites near Terek when he came on a grave on the property of a Chevsur at New Djuta. This grave contained the 'skeleton of a woman with armour, arrowheads, a discus of slate and an iron knife'. And this discovery was followed by another in the same district at Aul Stepan Zminda (called Kasbek by the Russians). 'All that I have found here,' he writes, 'belonged to women and warriors . . . The horses' bits, the ornamental harness and the stirrup irons suggest equestrian nomads, and even the stirrups were adorned with bells suggesting female riders. I could not find anything that was likely to have been used by a man.'

Carus Sterne believes that the Amazonian legends of antiquity referred to gynocracies or matriarchal communities such as are now known still to exist. He connects this social structure with the cult of the Moon-goddess or Earth-Mother, and suggests that the struggle between the Achaians or the Nordic Siegfried and the warrior-women is the fight between this ancient worship and that of the Sun-god.

CHAPTER X

Endings

In the life of any organism we are able to distinguish three main divisions: the period of growth and development; the period of florescence; and the period of decay. One may designate these three periods also as the youth, maturity and old age of the individual. The old age of woman makes its beginning at the climacteric: when 'the change sets in', as women express it, then the years of her blossoming are past.

i. The Menopause

The time in a woman's life when menstruation comes to an end is called the menopause, or the climacteric, a culminating point characterized in particular by the involution of various glands of internal secretion, such as the ovaries, which are more or less eliminated in this declining period of life in which the building up of the bodily structure ceases. Just as in the period of puberty, when the real structure began, the glands which were decisive for childhood (thymus, etc.) were eliminated, so in both periods there is a greater predisposition to psychic disturbances, etc. Both points, the beginning and the culminating point, are causes and periods of discomfort.

Naturally, this is not the place to go into the full details of all the clinical symptoms of the climacteric. Those who are interested may be referred to the work of Wiesel, where they will also find an abundance of literature on the subject.

Comparatively little is certain as to the actual time of the climacteric. It has, however, been ascertained that among civilized nations this time is a very vacillating one. Whether the matter is analogous among primitive peoples, observations have so far not been able to decide. 'In our part of the globe,' says Scanzoni, 'menstruation ceases forever as a rule in the forty-fifth to forty-eighth year.' D. W. H. Busch gives forty-five to fifty, whilst the author of the books of 'Faithful Eckarth' speaks of the fiftieth to fifty-third year.

Turkish women, according to Oppenheim, lose their menses at thirty years of age.

Vasiliev found among the Kirghiz women, who generally marry in the seventeenth year, the average beginning of the climacteric in the forty-fourth year. Similarly, Minassian, on the ground of a great number of observations, states the beginning of the climacteric to be in the ages of forty to forty-five among Armenians.

Pilsudski supposes the climacteric with Ainu women in Sakhalin to be not before the age of fifty.

Most North American Indian women cease to menstruate in the fortieth year, according to Rusk; while according to Keating the Indian women in Michigan retain their courses till the fiftieth, and, indeed, even till their sixtieth, year.

Of the Eskimo women of Cumberland Sound, Schliephake says that they age very early; von Haven ascertained the fortieth year as that of the climacteric.

According to Mayer-Ahrens, menstruation ceases with the Indian women of Peru usually at forty years of age but often much earlier.

For the Wolof Negresses, A. T. de Rochebrune fixes the thirty-fifth to fortieth year as the time of the climacteric. Berchon states that with the Negresses of the Senegal this time does not come till the sixtieth year. (In the case of this assertion we must not, of course, underestimate the difficulties there are in such uncivilized peoples of finding out this time, on the one hand, and, on the other, of ascertaining with approximate accuracy the age of these persons.)

Among the Chinese women, according to Mondière, menstruation lasts at the latest till the fortieth year. In Java, it is due to the early marriage customary among the native women that they rarely become pregnant after thirty-five years of age.

Narbeshuber states of the women in south Tunisia that, when young, they are really 'very beautiful', but that at the beginning of their thirties, with their hard life, they fade quickly, and then they are the ugliest women he has ever seen. This fading, however, does not coincide with the climacteric, for the same informant says that the latter sets in only at about the fiftieth year. Moreover, he knows cases where menstruation still presented itself regularly after the fifty-fourth year.

With women in northern Germany, forty-five is regarded as the average age when the menopause sets in, and the confinement of a woman who has passed her fortieth year is, among the masses, considered a great exception. This latter view is, however, erroneous, as statistics indicate. In Berlin, for example, in the eight years from 1892–9, no fewer than 15,031 births took place where the mothers were from forty to forty-five years of age. Moreover there were 1,205 children born of mothers between forty-five and fifty years of age, and forty-five women were confined even at the age of over fifty.

ii. Withering

The time at which the decline begins in girls of our race is on the average about the twenty-seventh or twenty-eighth year, although the first traces of these states of transformation are sometimes to be found as early as the twenty-fifth year. Once begun, the process usually advances without ceasing to the condition described above.

We have already encountered the works of 'Faithful Eckarth'. Our present theme also received his attention and he described the fading woman in the following words:

> Just as in young women, so long as their blooming takes its orderly course, all is in full flower and motion, so with those women who have lost their bloom, all spirit and briskness decline. The colour which excites love changes to a faded paleness; the once tense muscles and flesh-covered fibres become slack, and wrinkles take the place of the former smoothness and beauty. Indeed, the whole form is altered so that when one compares the present figure with the earlier beauty, it is difficult to find any likeness . . . In fine, all that a lover once held beautiful is now repulsive to him and arouses in him a disgust and horror of un-comeliness.

Now it is in the highest degree worthy of notice, not only for the physician but also for the anthropologist, that there is an effective remedy not only for stopping this process of decline, but also for restoring the vanished bloom, if not quite in its former splendour, yet to a not inconsiderable degree. It is a great pity that our social conditions admit and make possible its use only in the very rarest cases. This remedy consists in regular and systematic sexual intercourse. One often sees in a girl already passée or not far from the beginning of decline that, if an opportunity for marriage offers, in a very short time after her marriage she becomes rounded in shape again, the roses return to her cheeks and the eyes recover their former fresh lustre. Thus love is the true source of youth for the female sex.

The changes in the years of life which concern us here make themselves perceptible in all parts of the female body. These are due not least to a considerable and sometimes even quite astonishing increase of adipose tissue on every part of the body. In such a woman the face often seems much bulkier and broader in the region of the cheeks, but also in the lower mental region, than formerly. The figure, too, has quite obviously increased in circumference, this being noticeable in the whole of the middle of the body, the hips and buttocks becoming much fatter and broader. Now it is, of course, the subcutaneous fat which, in the youthful female body, gives the peculiar charm to the lines, and the roundness, which has such a pleasing effect to the male eye. But how differently this abundant accumulation of fat acts in the case of the matron! The elastic firmness which the plump parts of the young girl show have gone; the bands of connective tissue which separate and, at the same time, support the individual fat lobules have become loose and easily extensible. This is the reason why the effect of weight, to which in youth the elasticity of the tissues offers sufficient resistance, makes itself felt so excessively.

As old age approaches, it causes the rounded contours of the female body to disappear, makes all the limbs dry and lean, and draws deep furrows in the once full face. Now, as in infancy, it is more difficult to distinguish the sexes but for the particular fashion of wearing the hair or the character of the clothes or the adornment of the body. Moreover, a sparse beard often sprouts on the face of old women, and, whilst in old men the voice almost always becomes higher and squeakier than before, in old women it grows rougher and deeper, more like that of the male.

iii. Death

If we visualize again how throughout life the female sex – in anatomical and physiological as well as pathological and psychological respects, and in its whole physical structure, thought and feeling – presents very considerable differences from the male sex, then we shall be able to understand and even be obliged to expect *a priori* that also the extinction of the functions of life and the entrance of death in woman must present important and interesting deviations from analogous phenomena in the male sex.

This, too, has not escaped the observations of scientific investigators in the sphere of the life of woman, and what D. W. H. Busch has written from his own and Vigaroux's observation on the subject which interests us here is instructive and worth knowing:

> In general, a woman's life is longer than that of a man, and therefore it is a natural phenomenon that she fears death less than he. Vigaroux tries to explain this from the peculiar constitution of woman . . . [he] compares woman to a delicate reed which, incapable of resistance, humbly bows its head before the approaching storm and gently raises it again when the storm has passed; but man is like the tall oak which is swept away only because it is strong enough to resist.
>
> Man often sacrifices his life for an idea and is indifferent at the death of others, setting great value on this contempt for death and regarding it as something splendid and manly; he is afraid [only] of the death which

might overcome him in illness. Woman, on the other hand, although deeply affected by the death of others, cannot understand how man can sacrifice his life for an idea, thinks lightly of her own life, and in illness is more careless of the outcome ... In woman, death takes place more gently and gradually, and represents more an extinction of life, or, in other words, a kind of uniform exhaustion.

The reader may be reminded again that, as a matter of course, the whole manner of living and the difference in the position which the two sexes have to occupy in nature must also involve quite different dangers to life for woman than for man. Thus we come across sexual distinctions also in death, the anthropological significance of which should in no way be underestimated.

UNNATURAL DEATH

With the differences in the manner of living of the two sexes is also involved the fact that an unnatural death overtakes men considerably oftener than women. They are killed in open battle or by the treacherous weapon of the rival or the head-hunter; they fall victims in their dangerous hunting or they perish in their occupation with machines or with the elements. It is quite different with the female sex; it also is not spared from unnatural ways of death, but the causes bringing about this unnatural death are of quite a different kind.

We have already learnt in earlier sections of two of these causes and of various examples of unnatural death in the female sex: one based on the rights appertaining to the husband of killing the adulteress, and the other on the killing of widows. But it is not always sufficient for the arrogance of man to have only his widow with him in death. In the life beyond, he and she would lack the necessary service if no maids stood by them. Hence, in addition to the widow, sometimes a number of other women suffer death as well. Avebury, for example, records that when a chief of the Fiji Islanders died, it was customary to 'send' a few of his wives and slaves with him. And Kund records from the Congo: 'It may be said that almost from the Pool to the Falls no free man of good standing dies without a few wives and slaves being killed. Sometimes, especially higher up, this madness when a man dies is said to draw over a hundred others with him into the grave.'

The dread of providing for old age may also cause the killing of women. Thus Cranz says of the Eskimo in Greenland:

Many widows who are old and ill and have no well-to-do relative who can provide for them without difficulty are also buried alive, and the children do not consider this cruelty, but kindness, because they spare them the pains of a long sick-bed from which they will not rise again, and themselves trouble, distress and pity.

We also find a very interesting contribution on this matter from Avebury. According to him, a missionary named Hunt once received from a young Fiji Islander an invitation to the funeral of his mother. Mr Hunt accepted the invitation. When the funeral procession started off, to his surprise he saw no corpse. When he asked about it, the young savage pointed to his mother, who was walking with him, and was just as gay and lively as all the other guests and seemed obviously to be enjoying herself. He added that he was treating his mother thus for love of her and because of this love he was now about to bury her, and that only her children, and nobody else, might perform such a sacred service. She was their mother and they, her children, and therefore it was their duty to kill her. Mr Hunt maintains, in spite of this, that they have a very cogent reason for abandoning this world before they are decrepit; that is to say, they not only believe in a future existence, but they are also convinced that as soon as they depart from this life they awaken again beyond.

SUICIDE

Among civilized peoples, we have a not inconsiderable number of examples which show that women, impelled by despair, are not afraid to take their own lives. Unrequited or lost love is by far the most common motive for this act. But also the heroic resolve to save their chastity from violation has, as is well known, driven not a few women to death by their own hand.

In the methods of committing suicide one can recognize on the whole certain sex differences. Death by shooting, cutting the throat, opening arteries, and by knife or sword are used chiefly by men; poisoning, drowning and hanging are preferred by the female sex. According to a summary given by R. Gaupp, there killed themselves in Prussia in the year 1898:

By hanging:	61.3% of the male,	44.5% of the female suicides
By drowning:	14.0% "	38.2% "
By shooting:	16.2% "	2.5% "
By poisoning:	3.2% "	7.1% "

In Japan, suicide among women is very common. The ratio, according to Gaupp, is much higher than in white races, being 1:1.8.

Katscher also speaks of Chinese women's great propensity for suicide. According to him, the polygamy in those Chinese families which embrace it produces 'envy, malice, uncharitableness and hate', and drives many jealous women to suicide. No wonder, then, if many Chinese women resist marriage. To escape it, many girls become nuns; others prefer to commit suicide. Once, during the reign of the Emperor Taukwang, no fewer than fifteen virgins decided to take their own lives because they had learnt that they had been betrothed by their parents. They threw themselves into a tributary of the Canton in the vicinity of the village where they lived and were buried in a common grave which people call the Virgins' Grave. A similar case occurred in the year 1873 in a village near Whampoa. Eight girls put on their best clothes, tied themselves together, and jumped into a tributary of the Canton.

Suicide among women is by no means to be regarded as a deplorable acquisition of civilization. It occurs as well among the so-called primitive peoples, although it appears to be less frequent, and in this matter also, there is another extensive field open to ethnological research.

We know of American Indians who, because unlucky in love, have thrown themselves from rocks. We have also learnt that many widows among the Tautin Indians in Oregon die voluntarily in order to escape the humiliation and torment which, in accordance with the custom of the country, were associated with their widowhood. Of the Wahpeton and Sisseton Indians, McChesney records: 'Twenty or more years ago it was quite a common occurrence when a woman's favourite child died for her to hang herself with her lariat on the branch of a tree. This seldom happens now.'

The Dyak women in Borneo, according to Ling Roth, are not infrequently driven to suicide by an unkind word. They try to poison themselves, but often the dose is too small, and an emetic, which they are forced to take, restores them to life.

The same thing happens in New Guinea. The missionary Keysser says that with the Kai, suicide occurs more frequently among women than men, and then it is an act of revenge rather than of despair. That is to say, the women, by their deed, which certainly costs them their lives, cause their husbands no little embarrassment, for the wife's relatives make him responsible for her death and demand compensation.

Of the Wakinga (East Africa), the missionary Hübner (in Fülleborn) records similar cases. Now and again it happens that a woman takes her own life merely from annoyance, to avenge herself on her husband for bad treatment, to be particularly spiteful to him, and to cause him sorrow for the loss of property entailed by her death.

Jacobs says of the women of Achin: 'Suicide among the Achinese occurs hardly at all: in any case, it is most exceptional. The few cases which they could tell me about concerned young women or girls who were betrayed by promises of marriage which were not fulfilled.'

BURIAL

The inferior position, in a social sense, which woman is accustomed to occupy in many nations makes its influence felt far beyond the grave.

The separate position which woman occupies we recognize also from the fact that in many places quite a special and separate place is assigned to her in the common burial ground. The world-famed cemetery at the Certosa of Bologna consists substantially of four connected square cloisters in which people of high rank are laid to rest. The square spaces enclosed by these cloisters, which are open to the sky, are the burial ground of the poorer population, and one square is for men only, another for women, the third for boys, and the fourth for girls. And it is the same in many other parts of Italy.

Among the Parsees in India also, it is a rule that female corpses be separated from male. Their burial places, which are called *dakhmas*, or 'towers of silence', are in very wide, low, round towers, situated on lonely heights covered with beautiful vegetation, and are quite open and uncovered at the top. The interior is divided into three concentric sections by quite low step-like walls, whilst the middle point is formed by a wide, round, walled hollow. Similar walls, arranged radially, divide the concentric rings into individual sub-sections, in which the corpses are placed. The central concentric circle belongs exclusively to women whilst the inmost is reserved for children's corpses; the outermost and, of course, the biggest, is for the corpses of men. The corpses are bare: 'Naked we come into the world, and naked must we leave it again,' say the Parsees. Flocks of vultures sit waiting on the edge of the enclosing wall and fall upon the new arrival immediately the bearers have departed from this place of horrors. In a few minutes (in one or two hours, according to Patell) the soft parts are devoured, and only the skeleton is left. Horrible as this kind of burial seems, yet it has its advantages; the smell of decomposition is, at any rate, prevented as far as possible.

Among the Ossetes in the Caucasus, according to Jankó, only the women are buried. The corpses of men are sewn into a buffalo skin and hung on a sacred tree.

Among many peoples is to be found also the custom of making women's graves distinguishable from those of men by certain external signs.

Concerning the graves of the Turks, we read in Sonntag that a flat gravestone is erected at the head and at the foot. The upper part of the head end forms a turban, a fez or a dervish hat. The gravestones for women have either no headstone or they run out into a leaf, a shell or some kind of arabesque.

M. Bartels received by letter from F. S. Krauss noteworthy information about the graves of the southern Slavs:

> Among the Bulgarian Serbian peasantry, only the man gets a real funeral. As a rule, too, a gravestone is put up for him, whilst for a woman, especially the deceased head of a joint household, they place a wooden cross on the grave. The graves of virgins are adorned with wreaths of beach grass and basilicum and now and again also with myrtle wreaths. Men keep away from the funeral ceremonies of women; only the fathers and brothers lead the procession of mourning women ... In Bosnia ... the period of mourning for a woman does not last longer than at most eight days. To shed tears for a woman is regarded as extremely disgraceful.

The custom of giving the deceased in death the objects used by him in life is ancient and widespread. For example, Dall writes of the graves of the Inuit in Alaska that 'a woman's coffin is easy to know by the kettles and women's gear hung on it'. The same is true of the Ingaliks (Kaiyuhkhotana) of Ulukuk; one such woman's grave is shown in Fig. 30. Similarly, men's and women's graves (according to de Jong in Schmeltz) in New Guinea are easy to distinguish externally by the fact that a water container made of coconut

Fig. 30   Ingalik female grave from Ulukuk (after Yarrow)

is put on a woman's grave and, on a man's, big lassoes made of *rotang*, arrows and spears.

iv. Thereafter

In her life thereafter, the fate of a woman (and of her children) is determined by the phase of life she occupied at the time of her death.

THE DEAD VIRGIN

According to the ideas of many peoples, a girl who has reached puberty and does not contract a marriage leads an unnatural life, a *vita praeter naturam*, and so, as she has been different from her companions in life, in death also she has to occupy an exceptional position. After her death, therefore, such a virgin goes to hell without hope of rescue. We learn from a statement by du Perron that the modern Parsees still have quite a similar view.

According to Christian ideas, on the contrary, heaven is opened above all to the immaculate and chaste virgin at her death. Even nowadays, in many places, her corpse as well as her coffin and grave are adorned with the bridal wreath to indicate that she has now become a bride of Jesus, united with her divine bridegroom. Naturally, the holy virgins of God who have been betrothed to the Saviour in their life have first claim to such a union. Hence we find that the last resting-places of nuns and female beings corresponding to them are always separated from the graves in which the children of this world are buried. But woe to the bride of heaven who was tempted by 'fleshly lusts' to break her vows. She was buried alive or walled up and left to die a lingering death from suffocation and hunger. 'The nun's hole at Mönchgut in Rügen,' says Sepp, 'is unfathomable. There fallen nuns from the town of Bergen were brought at night and thrown in; and, therefore, wailing forms still wander there.'

The ideas which prevail in Upper Italy are more poetic. In the districts of Treviso and Belluno, it is believed that young girls who die must gather roses in Paradise, so the country people do not omit to put an apron into the coffin with them (Bastanzi), while in the province of Bari in Apulia, the mourning of heaven over the death of a virgin is well expressed by the superstition which says that when it rains at the death of a young girl then it must go on raining for nine months.

Popular belief and wit, however, often describe quite otherwise the fate of the poor despised old maid. In England, it is said that old maids have to guide apes to hell. In east Prussia, at the beginning of the last century, people maintained (and perhaps still do) that they do not get to heaven but have assigned to them as their stopping-place the green meadow in front of it. In this, it is their destiny to gather up sheep's dirt through all eternity. In many other parts of Germany also, as Haberland records, the old maid, because her life was useless and a failure, is given an occupation after death which is just as useless and never fulfils its purpose. In Strasburg she has to help put a cover round the citadel, and in Basel it is the church tower; in Vienna she has to scour and clean St Stephen's Tower; in Frankfurt, 'to polish the Parthorn'; in Nuremberg, to sweep the white tower with the beards of old maids; in the Tyrol, to measure the Sterzinger Moos by spans with her fingers; and she is also said to have to offer tinder for sale in hell.

Haberland states that 'these ideas that human destiny is not fulfilled without the procreation of offspring are ingeniously expressed by the Munich custom of putting a wisp of straw before the doors of unmarried dead people because they have given no grain'.

An unmarried Mohammedan woman cannot get into heaven in any circumstances, for a woman gains admission only through her husband. It runs in the Koran: 'For a woman, paradise is under the soles of her husband's feet.' As to the fate of widows, old maids and young girls, the Koran is silent: they are creatures who can claim no notice at all.

In Siam, the souls of dead virgins hold their dances in the twilight and kill anybody who surprises them at it; they also kill little girls and women. These ghosts of virgins which kill children are also known to the Greek population in the Gello (see Haberland).

DEATH DURING MENSTRUATION

It is interesting to see how menstruation is regarded by many tribes as such a special condition that the exceptional position in which it places woman makes itself felt even after death.

Thus one reads in Crooke that in India the belief is widespread that a woman who dies during the prescribed period of her uncleanness later lives as a ghost. The Churel, as this ghost is known, is particularly harmful to its own family, but also to others. It appears in various forms. Usually it assumes the form of a beautiful young woman and leads young men astray at night, especially those who are good-looking. She takes them out of their realm into her own and keeps them there till they have lost their manly beauty. Then she sends them back into the world as grey-haired old men who find all their friends long dead. Sometimes the Churel appears beautiful from the front and black from the rear; she always has her feet turned the wrong way round with the heels in front and the toes behind.

To prevent a dead woman becoming a Churel the Majhwár of Mizapur do not burn her corpse but bury it. Then they fill the grave with thorns and pile heavy stones on it to keep back the ghost.

DEATH DURING PREGNANCY

Among the Basutos, pregnant women have to be buried in the fields far from the house, for it is believed that their dead bodies will keep the rain away from the land. But as it is horrible for the relatives to think of their dead thus in the wilderness, many use cunning and dig them up again when it is dark and rebury them in their native mountains. Another reason for the secret exhumation, however, comes into consideration, for the rain magician and chief are eager for such corpses. They dig them up and cut open the abdomen and the uterus. The liquor amnii is drained off with great care into vessels held ready, but the child is simply thrown away. At home, the chief has a house 'where oxen-horns look upwards'. The liquor amnii is poured into these horns and that brings rain.

Baumstark reports the opening of women who have died in pregnancy by the Warangi in the East-African Masai plateau. The embryo is then taken out and mother and child are buried separately.

Niebuhr reports similarly about the Hindus. There they are said to open the pregnant women who have died, take out and bury the child, but burn the corpse of the mother.

If a Guinea Negress dies during pregnancy, as the missionary Monrad reports, this brings great disgrace to her family, as people say she could not bear a child. Her corpse is not buried but thrown into the open fields. Similarly, with the Battak in Tobah Tinging in Sumatra, as Hagen records, the corpse of a woman who has died in pregnancy is burnt and the ashes strewn in the sea, while in Bali, according to Jacobs, if a woman dies during pregnancy her corpse may neither be burnt nor buried, but must, as a mark of the greatest contempt, either be thrown into a sewer or laid in an open grave or pit two feet deep. According to Balinese ideas, this is the greatest disgrace that can fall to anybody's lot, and holds good for all classes and castes, even for princesses.

In the Caroline Island of Mamoluk, people believe that 'the gods do not want to have with them the souls of women who have died in pregnancy or those who have had one child, because they have an unpleasant smell. They go instead to the land of Pikenekataula, the distant land which lies where heaven and earth meet' (Girschner).

Among the Menangkabau in the Padang highlands, on the other hand, it is supposed that a woman who dies during pregnancy gets into heaven at once (Jacobs).

Krauss has recorded a noteworthy idea of the southern Slavs, who have the belief that a woman who dies during pregnancy is able to give away the child which she was unable to carry to full time. He says: 'Many barren women betake themselves to a grave in which a pregnant woman has been buried, bite away grass from the grave, call the dead woman by name and beg her to give them her child. Then they take a little earth from the grave and carry this earth always with them under their girdle.'

In the south of Sweden, according to Eva Ugström, people are convinced that the dead pregnant woman is confined while her coffin is being carried across the churchyard. 'Hence the old custom of putting the coffin down for a moment', and of laying baby clothes and a pair of scissors inside.

Frankl records of the Jews in Beirut that when the corpse of a woman who has died in pregnancy has been washed and dressed in the shroud, the women who lay out corpses watch with eye and ear whether the young life in the dead woman stirs. If so, they rain blows on the abdomen of the corpse till all is still within. It would be a dishonour for the dead woman and her family if they ventured to open the corpse, and it would be a sin to bury the living child alive (Stern).

DEATH DURING LABOUR

If the death of a pregnant woman before the actual time of delivery is an affecting occurrence, one can easily understand how much deeper an impression it must make on the minds of primitive peoples when they see how an unfortunate woman in labour, wasting her strength in fruitless straining, is unable to bring her child into the world and how, instead of experiencing the joys of motherhood, she suffers a miserable death.

The Israelites regarded the death of a woman in labour as a punishment for her sins. Buxtorf records: 'We read in the Talmud also that women die in labour because of three kinds of sin: when they do not take challa dough; do not light the Sabbath candles; and do not pay attention to their monthly periods.'

Stern quotes a dictum of Mohammed: 'The mother who dies in labour is raised to the rank of martyr and goes immediately to Paradise.'

In Madagascar, the death of a woman in labour is regarded as proof that, at the beginning of labour, she did not confess honestly to her husband how often she had been unfaithful to him.

Very many tribes are unable to believe that a woman who has died in labour can find peace in the world beyond. The Ewe Negroes on the Slave Coast are of the opinion that such a woman is a person forsaken by the gods and that she will become a 'bloodthirsty being'. She does not have an honourable burial, but is buried in a special place prepared for the reception of such bloodthirsty beings (Zündel).

In Cambodia, the cause of a sudden acute illness is supposed to be that the spirit of a woman who has died in childbirth has come upon the person affected, as such spirits fly about seeking a dwelling-place.

In Java, if women die during labour, they go on fretting after death because of their lost maternal happiness. They cannot rest and, as they are evil by nature, they try to get at the expense of others the happiness they were not able to enjoy. When they fly lamenting through the air and notice a house where the wife awaits her hour, they race each other to the house and try to get into the woman in order to taste the joys of motherhood in her stead. The unfortunate woman, however, goes mad. Naturally in such cases the dwellings are very carefully guarded and protected.

In the Amboina group, the body of a woman who has died in childbirth is treated in a special way in order to prevent it going about later as a *Buntiana* to torment men and pregnant women. After the corpse has been washed, thorns of lagu or pins are stuck between the joints of the fingers and toes and into the knees, shoulders and elbows. Then, once it has been dressed, ducks' and hens' eggs are put under the chin and in the armpits. Instead of covering the corpse with a net, part of the hair is drawn out and the coffin lid nailed down securely at this place. The purpose of this proceeding is to keep the corpse in the grave. Because of the thorns and pins, she cannot, they believe, move her limbs well enough to be able to fly out of the coffin in the shape of a bird; this is prevented also by the tightly nailed hair. If she has assumed the nature of a bird, she is supposed also not to leave behind the eggs put in beside her (Riedel).

In the Kei or Ewaabu islands, if a woman dies in labour, and if the child cannot be brought into the world alive, it is stabbed to death inside the uterus so that the woman may not become a *Bumbunanah* or *Pontianaq* and pursue her husband in order to emasculate him (Riedel).

According to Haberland, the Malays believe that women who have died in childbirth stand like statues in the woods and entice men to them.

DEATH IN CHILDBED

Just as in the belief of many peoples the woman in childbed is regarded as unclean for a certain period and a purification ceremony is necessary to permit her to return to the society of her fellows again, so the deceased woman in childbed is still unclean in death and remains so, as, of course, she did not live to perform the ceremony of purification. As an unclean person, however, she has even, after her death, a contaminating and injurious effect on those who go near her. In Eckarth's *Die unvorsichtige Heb-Amme*, for example, it runs:

> Also virgins and wives when they have their courses should avoid those churchyards and churches in which lying-in women and soldiers who have lost their lives before the enemy have been buried, for if they walk over such a grave the discharge will increase and cause great alarm. For this reason, the foresight of a government is to be praised for having persons who have died in childbed buried apart in a safe place.

It is still quite possible to find traces of this view.

Moreover, not inconsiderable dangers may, according to the views of certain peoples, accrue to the survivors owing to women who have died in childbed. We have already learnt of isolated examples of this in the sections on the deceased pregnant woman and the deceased woman in labour, and this fear of danger is given expression in certain ways in which people try to get rid of the corpse and make it harmless.

In Styria, people believe that a woman who dies in childbed goes straight to heaven without passing through purgatory, but they are convinced that two more from the same parish will die soon after her. (Fossel justly points out that this superstition may well be due to the experience, unfortunately only too common, that with the infectious nature of puerperal fever, direct transmission of the fatal disease used to take place through the midwife to the next woman in labour. Indeed, the Loa proceed with the corpse of a woman in childbed exactly as with those who have died of epidemic diseases.)

The dead lying-in woman's heart clings to her child, and we frequently come across the belief that she leaves her grave at night to return to it.

Among the Negroes of the Loango coast, according to Pechuel-Loesche, there is prevalent the belief that the dead mother continues to watch over her children to protect them from evil beings as well as from spirits, while in several places in the Bavarian Upper Palatinate, her bed is prepared with all care every evening for six weeks and her slippers put under the bed, because, as they believe, she comes every night to look out for her child. Similarly, if a mother dies in childbirth in Bohemia, it is said that she comes to her child for six weeks and bathes it; indeed, when a woman in childbed dies, they put baby's napkins in her coffin so that she can put her child to bed dry.

There is a corresponding belief in Aargau that every lying-in woman who has died returns for six weeks more to suckle the baby left behind. A 'dummy' must be put ready for her with which she can quieten the surviving child at night, otherwise the child may get bad milk poisoned by witches. Nobody sees the mother but they hear the child sucking (Rochholz).

According to Bezzenberger, the Lithuanians also believe that the dead lying-in woman leaves her grave each night in order to give the breast to her child. She cannot be seen by anybody, but there is no doubt that when doing so she sits down by the cradle, for it all at once stays still and cannot be moved again as long as the mother is there.

In German sagas and tales, too, we often meet with the poetic feature of the mother returning from the realm of the dead or some other supernatural world, wanting to nurse and attend at night the helpless children she has left behind. Let us call to mind in particular Melusine, whose husband's perfidy, distrust and curiosity drove her to death, and who after her departure often came back at night to suckle her babes. The romance of her vicissitudes was a favourite book in the Middle Ages.

In White Russia (Smolensk), on the other hand, only a witch is supposed to visit and feed her child for six weeks after her death. This is prevented by having exorcisms done by the priest (Paul Bartels).

A superstition in Achin in Sumatra, which Jacobs records, may also be mentioned. It is generally believed there that a barren woman has to suckle a snake at her breast after her death, and in the fear of this fate is to be found not the least part of the reason why women use every possible and impossible means of bringing at least one child into the world.

We must finally call here to mind still another view which is unfortunately very widespread. This is the conviction that, because a child from whom the mother is torn away at such a tender age cannot itself live long, it is best for the little arrival not to be separated from the mother at all.

Thus Bancroft records that among the Dorachos, an Indian tribe of Central America, if a mother dies who is still nursing her child, then the child is placed on her breast alive and burnt with her so that she can go on suckling it with her milk in the future life.

In the same way, according to Avebury, among the Eskimo in Unalaska, a child which has had the misfortune of losing its mother is normally buried with her, and Cranz, too, reports the same thing.

A similar custom appears to have been prevalent in Brittany, for in the old Breton graves archaeologists often found the bones of a woman and of a little child together.

Among the Australian Aborigines, too, if a mother of a suckling dies, then, as Collins and Barrington record, the child is placed alive in its mother's arms and buried with her. But here a reservation is made, for it is added: 'if no foster-parents can be found for the poor creature'.

For fairly similar reasons, with the Baining in New Britain, the child is killed if the mother dies in childbirth 'because otherwise there is nobody who would take charge of it, feed it and bring it up' (Parkinson).

Of the Bushmen in the Kalahari, Passarge tells that when a woman dies in childbirth, they bury mother and child together.

Among the Ama-Xosa also, it is permitted to kill the surviving babe, although use is not always made of this permission. Kropf reports: 'If a woman dies in childbed, the child is not killed in every case. It is given milk in a nipple shield which is made of antelope skin.'

The idea has so far been that the surviving child would have to die miserably without the feeding and care of its mother, yet we come across other ideas which result in the death of the suckling. That is to say, people sometimes believe that a child which has met with such a misfortune will itself be a bringer of ill-luck to its fellow-tribesmen.

Thus, in Nias, they kill the child which has lost its mother in childbirth or childbed in the belief that it is destined to become a terrible and dangerous individual. For this reason, the child is put into a sack which is hung on a tree and so remains in this way in the woods, left to its cruel fate (Modigliani).

From a Chingpaw in Upper Burma, Anderson heard that a custom used to exist whereby, when a lying-in woman died within a month after delivery, the surviving child was burnt unless somebody offered to adopt it. The father was not permitted to claim the child for himself (Wehrli).

In other cases the child suffers death because it is regarded as the murderer of its mother. This view we find in Madagascar, where the poor little creature is buried alive together with the woman who has died in childbed (*Globus*, 44).

The Dyaks in Borneo likewise punish the new-born babe with death if the mother loses her life in the confinement. Roth has put together the following reports of Legatt and the Rev. Mr Holland concerning these facts. He states that with the Sea Dyaks custom required (till a civilized government prevented such horrible murder) that if the mother died after her confinement the child also had to die because it was the cause of the mother's death. It was put alive into the coffin with its mother and the two were buried together, not infrequently without asking the father, who had the power to prevent this custom from being carried out and to keep the child. No woman could be found willing to suckle such an orphan as it would bring misfortune to her own children.

Index

Page numbers in italics refer to an illustration.

MORE ABOUT PENGUINS, PELICANS, PEREGRINES AND PUFFINS

For further information about books available from Penguins please write to Dept EP, Penguin Books Ltd, Harmondsworth, Middlesex UB7 0DA.

In the U.S.A.: For a complete list of books available from Penguins in the United States write to Dept DG, Penguin Books, 299 Murray Hill Parkway, East Rutherford, New Jersey 07073.

In Canada: For a complete list of books available from Penguins in Canada write to Penguin Books Canada Ltd, 2801 John Street, Markham, Ontario L3R 1B4.

In Australia: For a complete list of books available from Penguins in Australia write to the Marketing Department, Penguin Books Australia Ltd, P.O. Box 257, Ringwood, Victoria 3134.

In New Zealand: For a complete list of books available from Penguins in New Zealand write to the Marketing Department, Penguin Books (N.Z.) Ltd, Private Bag, Takapuna, Auckland 9.

In India: For a complete list of books available from Penguins in India write to Penguin Overseas Ltd, 706 Eros Apartments, 56 Nehru Place, New Delhi 110019.

A CHOICE OF PENGUINS

☐ **The Complete Penguin Stereo Record and Cassette Guide**
Greenfield, Layton and March £7.95

A new edition, now including information on compact discs. 'One of the few indispensables on the record collector's bookshelf' – *Gramophone*

☐ **Selected Letters of Malcolm Lowry**
Edited by Harvey Breit and Margerie Bonner Lowry £5.95

'Lowry emerges from these letters not only as an extremely interesting man, but also a lovable one' – Philip Toynbee

☐ **The First Day on the Somme**
Martin Middlebrook £3.95

1 July 1916 was the blackest day of slaughter in the history of the British Army. 'The soldiers receive the best service a historian can provide: their story told in their own words' – *Guardian*

☐ **A Better Class of Person** **John Osborne** £2.50

The playwright's autobiography, 1929–56. 'Splendidly enjoyable' – John Mortimer. 'One of the best, richest and most bitterly truthful autobiographies that I have ever read' – Melvyn Bragg

☐ **The Winning Streak** **Goldsmith and Clutterbuck** £2.95

Marks & Spencer, Saatchi & Saatchi, United Biscuits, GEC . . . The UK's top companies reveal their formulas for success, in an important and stimulating book that no British manager can afford to ignore.

☐ **The First World War** **A. J. P. Taylor** £4.95

'He manages in some 200 illustrated pages to say almost everything that is important . . . A special text . . . a remarkable collection of photographs' – *Observer*

A CHOICE OF PENGUINS

☐ *Man and the Natural World* **Keith Thomas** £4.95

Changing attitudes in England, 1500–1800. 'An encyclopedic study of man's relationship to animals and plants . . . a book to read again and again' – Paul Theroux, *Sunday Times* Books of the Year

☐ *Jean Rhys: Letters 1931–66*
Edited by Francis Wyndham and Diana Melly £4.95

'Eloquent and invaluable . . . her life emerges, and with it a portrait of an unexpectedly indomitable figure' – Marina Warner in the *Sunday Times*

☐ *The French Revolution* **Christopher Hibbert** £4.95

'One of the best accounts of the Revolution that I know . . . Mr Hibbert is outstanding' – J. H. Plumb in the *Sunday Telegraph*

☐ *Isak Dinesen* **Judith Thurman** £4.95

The acclaimed life of Karen Blixen, 'beautiful bride, disappointed wife, radiant lover, bereft and widowed woman, writer, sibyl, Scheherazade, child of Lucifer, Baroness; always a unique human being . . . an assiduously researched and finely narrated biography' – *Books & Bookmen*

☐ *The Amateur Naturalist*
Gerald Durrell with Lee Durrell £4.95

'Delight . . . on every page . . . packed with authoritative writing, learning without pomposity . . . it represents a real bargain' – *The Times Educational Supplement*. 'What treats are in store for the average British household' – *Daily Express*

☐ *When the Wind Blows* **Raymond Briggs** £2.95

'A visual parable against nuclear war: all the more chilling for being in the form of a strip cartoon' – *Sunday Times*. 'The most eloquent anti-Bomb statement you are likely to read' – *Daily Mail*

PENGUIN TRAVEL BOOKS

☐ *Arabian Sands* **Wilfred Thesiger**   £3.50

'In the tradition of Burton, Doughty, Lawrence, Philby and Thomas, it is, very likely, the book about Arabia to end all books about Arabia' – *Daily Telegraph*

☐ *The Flight of Ikaros* **Kevin Andrews**   £3.50

'He also is in love with the country . . . but he sees the other side of that dazzling medal or moon . . . If you want some truth about Greece, here it is' – Louis MacNeice in the *Observer*

☐ *D. H. Lawrence and Italy*   £4.95

In *Twilight in Italy, Sea and Sardinia* and *Etruscan Places,* Lawrence recorded his impressions while living, writing and travelling in 'one of the most beautiful countries in the world'.

☐ *Maiden Voyage* **Denton Welch**   £3.50

Opening during his last term at public school, from which the author absconded, *Maiden Voyage* turns into a brilliantly idiosyncratic account of China in the 1930s.

☐ *The Grand Irish Tour* **Peter Somerville-Large**   £4.95

The account of a year's journey round Ireland. 'Marvellous . . . describes to me afresh a landscape I thought I knew' – Edna O'Brien in the *Observer*

☐ *Slow Boats to China* **Gavin Young**   £3.95

On an ancient steamer, a cargo dhow, a Filipino kumpit and twenty more agreeably cranky boats, Gavin Young sailed from Piraeus to Canton in seven crowded and colourful months. 'A pleasure to read' – Paul Theroux

PENGUIN TRAVEL BOOKS

☐ *The Kingdom by the Sea* **Paul Theroux**   £2.50

1982, the year of the Falklands War and the Royal Baby, was the ideal time, Theroux found, to travel round the coast of Britain and surprise the British into talking about themselves. 'He describes it all brilliantly and honestly' – Anthony Burgess

☐ *One's Company* **Peter Fleming**   £3.50

His journey to China as special correspondent to *The Times* in 1933. 'One reads him for literary delight . . . But, he is also an observer of penetrating intellect' – Vita Sackville West

☐ *The Traveller's Tree* **Patrick Leigh Fermor**   £3.95

'A picture of the Indies more penetrating and original than any that has been presented before' – *Observer*

☐ *The Path to Rome* **Hilaire Belloc**   £3.95

'The only book I ever wrote for love,' is how Belloc described the wonderful blend of anecdote, humour and reflection that makes up the story of his pilgrimage to Rome.

☐ *The Light Garden of the Angel King* **Peter Levi**   £2.95

Afghanistan has been a wild rocky highway for nomads and merchants, Alexander the Great, Buddhist monks, great Moghul conquerors and the armies of the Raj. Here, quite brilliantly, Levi writes about their journeys and his own.

☐ *Among the Russians* **Colin Thubron**   £3.95

'The Thubron approach to travelling has an integrity that belongs to another age' – Dervla Murphy in the *Irish Times*. 'A magnificent achievement' – Nikolai Tolstoy

A CHOICE OF PENGUINS

☐ **Small World** David Lodge £2.50

A jet-propelled academic romance, sequel to *Changing Places*. 'A new comic débâcle on every page' – *The Times*. 'Here is everything one expects from Lodge but three times as entertaining as anything he has written before' – *Sunday Telegraph*

☐ **The Neverending Story** Michael Ende £3.50

The international bestseller, now a major film: 'A tale of magical adventure, pursuit and delay, danger, suspense, triumph' – *The Times Literary Supplement*

☐ **The Sword of Honour Trilogy** Evelyn Waugh £3.95

Containing *Men at Arms, Officers and Gentlemen* and *Unconditional Surrender*, the trilogy described by Cyril Connolly as 'unquestionably the finest novels to have come out of the war'.

☐ **The Honorary Consul** Graham Greene £1.95

In a provincial Argentinian town, a group of revolutionaries kidnap the wrong man . . . 'The tension never relaxes and one reads hungrily from page to page, dreading the moment it will all end' – Auberon Waugh in the *Evening Standard*

☐ **The First Rumpole Omnibus** John Mortimer £4.95

Containing *Rumpole of the Bailey*, *The Trials of Rumpole* and *Rumpole's Return*. 'A fruity, foxy masterpiece, defender of our wilting faith in mankind' – *Sunday Times*

☐ **Scandal** A. N. Wilson £2.25

Sexual peccadillos, treason and blackmail are all ingredients on the boil in A. N. Wilson's new, *cordon noir* comedy. 'Drily witty, deliciously nasty' – *Sunday Telegraph*

A CHOICE OF PENGUINS

☐ *Stanley and the Women* **Kingsley Amis**   £2.50

'Very good, very powerful ... beautifully written ... This is Amis
père at his best' – Anthony Burgess in the *Observer*. 'Everybody
should read it' – *Daily Mail*

☐ *The Mysterious Mr Ripley* **Patricia Highsmith**   £4.95

Containing *The Talented Mr Ripley, Ripley Underground* and
Ripley's Game. 'Patricia Highsmith is the poet of apprehension' –
Graham Greene. 'The Ripley books are marvellously, insanely read-
able' – *The Times*

☐ *Earthly Powers* **Anthony Burgess**   £4.95

'Crowded, crammed, bursting with manic erudition, garlicky puns,
omnilingual jokes ... (a novel) which meshes the real and personal-
ized history of the twentieth century' – Martin Amis

☐ *Life & Times of Michael K* **J. M. Coetzee**   £2.95

The Booker Prize-winning novel: 'It is hard to convey ... just what
Coetzee's special quality is. His writing gives off whiffs of Conrad, of
Nabokov, of Golding, of the Paul Theroux of *The Mosquito Coast*.
But he is none of these, he is a harsh, compelling new voice' –
Victoria Glendinning

☐ *The Stories of William Trevor*   £5.95

'Trevor packs into each separate five or six thousand words more
richness, more laughter, more ache, more multifarious human-ness
than many good writers manage to get into a whole novel' – *Punch*

☐ *The Book of Laughter and Forgetting*
    Milan Kundera   £3.95

'A whirling dance of a book ... a masterpiece full of angels, terror,
ostriches and love ... No question about it. The most important
novel published in Britain this year' – Salman Rushdie

A CHOICE OF
PELICANS AND PEREGRINES

☐ *The Knight, the Lady and the Priest*
Georges Duby   £6.95

The acclaimed study of the making of modern marriage in medieval France. 'He has traced this story – sometimes amusing, often horrifying, always startling – in a series of brilliant vignettes' – *Observer*

☐ *The Limits of Soviet Power* **Jonathan Steele**   £3.95

The Kremlin's foreign policy – Brezhnev to Chernenko, is discussed in this informed, informative 'wholly invaluable and extraordinarily timely study' – *Guardian*

☐ *Understanding Organizations* **Charles B. Handy**   £4.95

Third Edition. Designed as a practical source-book for managers, this Pelican looks at the concepts, key issues and current fashions in tackling organizational problems.

☐ *The Pelican Freud Library: Volume 12*   £5.95

Containing the major essays: *Civilization, Society and Religion, Group Psychology* and *Civilization and Its Discontents*, plus other works.

☐ *Windows on the Mind* **Erich Harth**   £4.95

Is there a physical explanation for the various phenomena that we call 'mind'? Professor Harth takes in age-old philosophers as well as the latest neuroscientific theories in his masterly study of memory, perception, free will, selfhood, sensation and other richly controversial fields.

☐ *The Pelican History of the World*
J. M. Roberts   £5.95

'A stupendous achievement . . . This is the unrivalled World History for our day' – A. J. P. Taylor

A CHOICE OF
PELICANS AND PEREGRINES

☐ *A Question of Economics* **Peter Donaldson**   £4.95

Twenty key issues – from the City and big business to trades unions – clarified and discussed by Peter Donaldson, author of *10 × Economics* and one of our greatest popularizers of economics.

☐ *Inside the Inner City* **Paul Harrison**   £4.95

A report on urban poverty and conflict by the author of *Inside the Third World*. 'A major piece of evidence' – *Sunday Times*. 'A classic: it tells us what it is really like to be poor, and why' – *Time Out*

☐ *What Philosophy Is* **Anthony O'Hear**   £4.95

What are human beings? How should people act? How do our thoughts and words relate to reality? Contemporary attitudes to these age-old questions are discussed in this new study, an eloquent and brilliant introduction to philosophy today.

☐ *The Arabs* **Peter Mansfield**   £4.95

New Edition. 'Should be studied by anyone who wants to know about the Arab world and how the Arabs have become what they are today' – *Sunday Times*

☐ *Religion and the Rise of Capitalism*
R. H. Tawney   £3.95

The classic study of religious thought of social and economic issues from the later middle ages to the early eighteenth century.

☐ *The Mathematical Experience*
Philip J. Davis and Reuben Hersh   £7.95

Not since *Gödel, Escher, Bach* has such an entertaining book been written on the relationship of mathematics to the arts and sciences. 'It deserves to be read by everyone ... an instant classic' – *New Scientist*

A CHOICE OF
PELICANS AND PEREGRINES

☐ *Crowds and Power* **Elias Canetti**   £4.95

'Marvellous . . . an immensely interesting, often profound reflection
about the nature of society, in particular the nature of violence' –
Susan Sontag in *The New York Review of Books*

☐ *The Death and Life of Great American Cities*
   Jane Jacobs   £5.95

One of the most exciting and wittily written attacks on contemporary
city planning to have appeared in recent years – thought-provoking
reading and, as one critic noted, 'extremely apposite to conditions in
the UK'.

☐ *Computer Power and Human Reason*
   Joseph Weizenbaum   £3.95

Internationally acclaimed by scientists and humanists alike: 'This is
the best book I have read on the impact of computers on society, and
on technology and on man's image of himself' – *Psychology Today*

These books should be available at all good bookshops or news-
agents, but if you live in the UK or the Republic of Ireland and have
difficulty in getting to a bookshop, they can be ordered by post.
Please indicate the titles required and fill in the form below.

NAME_____ BLOCK CAPITALS

ADDRESS_____

_____

_____

Enclose a cheque or postal order payable to The Penguin Bookshop
to cover the total price of books ordered, plus 50p for postage.
Readers in the Republic of Ireland should send £1R equivalent to the
sterling prices, plus 67p for postage. Send to: The Penguin Bookshop, 54/56 Bridlesmith Gate, Nottingham, NG1 2GP.

You can also order by phoning (0602) 599295, and quoting your
Barclaycard or Access number.

Every effort is made to ensure the accuracy of the price and availability of
books at the time of going to press, but it is sometimes necessary to increase
prices and in these circumstances retail prices may be shown on the covers of
books which may differ from the prices shown in this list or elsewhere. This list
is not an offer to supply any book.

**This order service is only available to residents in the UK and the Republic of
Ireland.**